MEN LIE

MEN LIE

David Maxwell

INSOMNIAC PRESS

Edited by Lee Shedden
Copy edited by Richard Almonte and Christine Schuler
Designed by Mike O'Connor

Canadian Cataloguing in Publication Data

Maxwell, David, 1954-
　　Men lie: a mystery

ISBN 1-895837-88-X

I. Title.

PS8576.A85998M46 2000　　C813'.6　　C00-932257-4
PR9199.3.M416M46 2000

The publisher gratefully acknowledges the support of the Canada Council, the Ontario Arts Council and Department of Canadian Heritage through the Book Publishing Industry Development Program.

Printed and bound in Canada

Insomniac Press, 192 Spadina Avenue, Suite 403,
Toronto, Ontario, Canada, M5T 2C2
www.insomniacpress.com

THE CANADA COUNCIL | LE CONSEIL DES ARTS
FOR THE ARTS | DU CANADA
SINCE 1957 | DEPUIS 1957

This book is dedicated to my lovely wife, Debbie,
for all her support and encouragement.

I am most grateful to: Paul Fraser Q.C. for believing in the book and directing me to people who helped me improve my writing and storytelling skills, Robin Fraser for undertaking the daunting task of the book's initial edit, Barbara Lambert for her expert advice on story development and her great enthusiasm, Wendy Twining for her assistance in developing the book's characters, Michael Hicks for his advice on criminal law and Lee Shedden for his meticulous editing of the book.

PROLOGUE

Kim's voice, high-pitched and agitated, drew Mrs. Rattenbury away from her evening cup of tea to the window overlooking the courtyard entrance to her apartment building.

As the manager of the Barclay, a three storey walk-up in Vancouver's West End, Mrs. Rattenbury made a point of knowing what was happening around her premises. The West End was a jungle of apartment buildings alive with people whose ethnic, religious and sexual persuasions made Mrs. Rattenbury's skin crawl. And she well knew that the concrete towers which cast the Barclay in constant shadow also provided good cover for drug dealers and burglars.

"You don't understand," Kim screamed at Mark Henderson, a sometimes tenant, who at the moment was pinned against the glass entrance like an escaped convict caught in the beam of a searchlight. He was fiddling with the door handle while enduring Kim's onslaught. "This can't happen! I won't allow it!" she cried.

Kim and Mr. Henderson were alone in the courtyard, which was nestled between the two wings of the building. Kim wasn't her real name, just the name that Mrs. Rattenbury had given her to clothe her in a certain identity and character. In this way, Mrs. Rattenbury could imagine Kim's background, what drove her to her affair with the reprobate Henderson, and the heartache she must feel now that the inevitable had happened and she was being replaced. Recently, Mrs. Rattenbury had seen Henderson around the building with a new lover, a mystery woman whom she had christened Carmen.

Kim and Carmen were as different as day and night. Kim was really only a girl. She stood five-foot-nine or -ten on long willowy legs. Her thick, straight, sun-blonde hair, cut to shoulder-length, swept across her forehead and curled in under her chin. She was absolutely beautiful. Carmen, on the other hand, was a mature woman, obscure in her ever-present dark glasses, long charcoal overcoat and scarf. She always acted furtively when visiting Mr. Henderson, usually arriving in a separate car, occasionally meeting him at the entrance, but most often making her way to the apartment alone.

But Kim was not about to let Henderson abandon her. And so this confrontation was inevitable.

The entrance door swung open and Henderson stumbled backwards into the empty lobby; Kim followed, scolding and bullying him. Mrs. Rattenbury couldn't make out what was being said anymore, she could only hear muffled yelling, but she could see into the lobby through the large glass wall at the front of the building. Kim lurched towards Henderson with animated gestures. He finally stopped backpedaling at the base of the staircase which ascended from right to left at the rear of the lobby. Then, to Mrs. Rattenbury's surprise, he smiled at Kim. Like a red flag to a bull, this suggestion of his contempt sent Kim into a rage and she struck out at him, throwing haymakers angrily if not skillfully at his head and chest.

Mrs. Rattenbury sensed that tragedy was going to overtake this drama if she didn't do something quickly. But what? Her husband would have marched into the lobby and ordered peace in his building with the authority of a military commander. But he had died five years ago, and she didn't have the gumption. Besides, with her rotund five- foot-two frame presently covered in an old baby blue robe, zipped from her slippered toes to her neck, her hair in curlers under a scarf and her face retired for the evening, she didn't feel very authoritative. Instead, she fretted her way over to the telephone in the front hallway and called 911.

It seemed forever before an operator answered with, "Police, fire, or EHS?" Meanwhile, the ruckus in the lobby grew steadily louder. But when Mrs. Rattenbury finally began to explain to the operator that she needed police assistance to calm a couple who were fighting in her lobby, the commotion suddenly stopped.

In an instant came the loud crack of a gun. Mrs. Rattenbury jumped.

A tingling quiet followed, except for the accelerated pounding of her heart. She struggled to answer the barrage of questions over the phone line without crumpling to the floor in a quivering mass of fear. Only when the police arrived and rang her intercom did she venture out from the safety and anonymity of her apartment. In the surrounding excitement, she saw glimpses of the calamity. Henderson lay awkwardly on his back in the corner of the lobby, while Kim's crumpled figure rested by the foot of the stairs. Neither body moved. Along one side of the lobby was a spattered arc of blood fanning out across the mirrored wall like the feathers of a wing.

Four officers huddled around the scene. "Report a homicide," one officer instructed another. "We'll need Detective Campbell and forensics here, right away." The other officer started for his police cruiser. "And a couple of ambulances," yelled the first officer as he bent over Kim. "Tell them one's dead—single gun shot wound to the heart. The other's unconscious. Not sure why yet."

A third officer turned and stared quizzically at Mrs. Rattenbury. "Are you the manager, ma'am?" he asked.

She was staring at the bodies. Feeling stunned and a little queasy, she didn't realize at first that he was speaking to her.

"Ma'am," he tried again. "Are you the manager? Did you call in this incident?"

She looked up at him and nodded vaguely.

"What's your name, ma'am?"

"Helen—ah, Helen Rattenbury."

"Mrs. Rattenbury. I'd like you to return to your apartment now." He gently took her elbow and walked her back to suite 101 where she had left the door open. "Please sit down and relax. Detective Campbell will be along shortly to ask you a few questions." She sat on a little chair by the telephone stand in her front hallway. "Leave the door open, if you don't mind," he said before he returned to work in the lobby.

In a daze, she watched out her apartment door as more and more serious looking people arrived. Eventually, a tall man, well dressed in a suit and tie under an open khaki trench coat, approached her.

"Mrs. Rattenbury. I'm Detective Campbell," he said with a subtle Scottish lilt. A badge appeared in his right hand and she automatically glanced at it. "May I ask you a few questions?"

She tried to answer the detective's questions as best she could, but the scene in the lobby and the swirl of activity in front of her made it hard to concentrate. Even so, she was able to tell Detective Campbell that, yes, she knew the gentleman who had been shot. His name was Mark Henderson. Yes, he was a tenant. No, she didn't know the girl's name, although she liked to call her Kim. They were fighting. No, she didn't see it happen.

"Mrs. Rattenbury, would you mind if we had a look at Mr. Henderson's suite?" Detective Campbell asked.

"I suppose not." She pulled open the drawer of the telephone stand beside her and extracted a ring of keys. "Henderson," she mumbled to herself as she flipped over the keys. "Now which is his apartment?" Looking up at Detective Campbell, she said, "He isn't always here, you know. Maybe only two or three days a week." She pursed her lips in disapproval. "Little love nest, that's what it is. Has different women coming and going. I should have evicted him. Something like this was bound to happen."

"Why do you say that?"

"'Cause she was in desperate love with him. I could tell. She was always hanging around, watching for him, waiting. Sometimes she'd hide in the shadows, spying on his new lover; sometimes, she'd stand at the entrance ringing the intercom." Mrs. Rattenbury paused. "203—that's it." She took the key off the ring and handed it to Detective Campbell.

"Thank you. Tell me, who is this new lover?"

"I don't know her real name." Mrs. Rattenbury looked slightly sheepish and added, "I like to call her Carmen."

"Why is that, Mrs. Rattenbury?"

"Oh. I don't know. It seems to suit her. She is very secretive. I'm sure she has her own key because she comes and goes. Quietly. Quickly. Always covered up."

Detective Campbell seemed to ponder this for a moment, then he said, "I'm going to take a little look around Mr. Henderson's apartment now. But I'd like to talk to you further when I'm finished, if I may?"

"Alright." She was actually relieved to know that he was going to be around the building for awhile.

"You know, a cup of tea would be marvelous. Would it be an imposition?"

She smiled faintly, then stood and brushed the wrinkles from the lap of her robe. "I'll put the pot to boil."

He turned and walked through the lobby toward the staircase.

CHAPTER 1

THREE WEEKS EARLIER

Another dreary and dank January settled on Vancouver. From horizon to horizon, gray, spongy clouds squeezed out a steady, icy drizzle over the city. As in an old black and white photo, the buildings distinguished themselves only in their differing shades of dull.

Doug Branston parked the car in his driveway, then ran, slightly hunched—as if that would save him from the force of the rain—to the shelter at his back door. His house, referred to as an 'old-timer' in the real estate trade, rested on a small lot at the fringe of Shaughnessy, an elderly and prestigious neighbourhood. When Doug and his wife Diane had first moved in, the building was desperate for a face-lift. Long hours spent plastering, painting and burying nails helped rejuvenate the place; but it was far from finished. The shiplap floorboards awaited a suitable covering. The exterior walls still displayed their tar-paper lining. And the yard, which by the middle of winter became little more than a mud slick in Vancouver's ceaseless rains, cried out for landscaping.

Doug and Diane had purchased the house with significant financial help from his mother soon after Doug had secured an articling position with the law firm of Larson Wren & Co. Doug's father had died a few years before, leaving a substantial life insurance policy as his only legacy. Although it named Doug's mother as sole beneficiary, the old man had requested in his will that funds be doled out to Doug and his younger brother, Paul, for a house once each had married.

Doug groaned as he hurdled the mud puddles on his way to the back door. Too much time had passed since the days when he had played varsity rugby. His six-foot frame, once trim and fit, now pushed the scales up near 200 pounds and his muscles had settled into mid-life complacency, confident they would no longer be called upon to undertake this sort of exertion.

When he reached the shelter of the canopy, he paused, as he always did before opening the door, to gaze back into the unfinished lily pond in the middle of the yard. The reflection of the house in its murky depths gave the illusion that the renovations were complete, and provided Doug with a moment of satisfaction and relief.

On the mat just inside the back door, he stomped his feet to clear the water and mud off his shoes. The rain had matted his silver-blonde hair, accentuating the widow's peak between his receding temples. As he reached for a towel to wipe the moisture from his head, he yelled "Hello? Anyone home?"

"Hey dad," was Matthew's response.

"Hi," shouted Adrian.

The boys' calls came from the family room, one wall away from where Doug was currently wrestling to remove his shoes. The otherworldly, fluorescent grey glow through the open door left little doubt of what was occupying their attention. As usual, reruns of *The Simpsons* provided perfect entertainment for his ten- and twelve-year- olds during the dead time between after-school play and supper. Homework, of course, was a *double* four-letter word never to be uttered before supper.

"Como estas, Conchita?" Doug greeted the boys' nanny as he walked through the door and into the kitchen-half of the family room.

Conchita, short and plump, whose laughing squinty eyes caused Doug to smile when she spoke—regardless of whether he understood her Spanish—was by the sink drying the dishes. "Senor Doug," she sang. "Esta muy mojado. Hay mucha lluvia, no?"

"Si," Doug said while kissing each of his boys on the cheek.

"Donde esta Diane?" Doug asked.

"Arriba, senor."

The bedrooms graced the second floor of the house. Doug darted up the stairs, loosening his tie as he went. Tonight, Larson Wren's best client, Frank Holden, was holding his annual party in celebration of yet another year of exceeding his company's profit projections and providing the firm with the revenues necessary to keep it in its luxurious digs. Doug planned to shower and quickly jump into his black tux in time to relax with a scotch and enjoy the view of Diane slipping into the black, lacy, abbreviated underwear she liked to wear under her best cocktail dress.

But when he bounded into the master bedroom he found Diane standing before the full-length mirror, concentrating hard as she sketched eyeliner around her jade-green eyes, the same eyes that had mesmerized Doug on their first meeting fifteen years before. Her auburn hair was tied back in a tight bun and her still-shapely five-foot- six figure was successfully hidden in a dark blue tweed pant suit.

"What's up?" Doug asked. "It's a party, not a convention. Aren't you dressed a little conservatively?"

Diane frowned at his reflection in the mirror. "I told you I couldn't make it tonight, Douglas. I've got a meeting I have to go to."

"What meeting? You never told me about a meeting. Jesus, Diane, this is the most important firm event of the year. You've got to be there."

"You know what your problem is?" Agitation crept into Diane's voice as she turned from the mirror. "You never listen when I tell you something. It's like whatever I have to say is meaningless."

"I would have remembered," he said. "It's just that it's important that you be there."

"I'm sorry. I can't be," she said and returned to her eyeliner.

Doug stared at her reflection for a moment, then shook his head in derision. "What's really going on here, Diane? You've always got a damn meeting at night. You're the only person I know that conducts all her business at night." He paused as if to plan for the overreaction that followed. "Except hookers!" Then, with spitting sarcasm he inquired, "Is that it? Is that what you do every night? Go and turn a couple of tricks? Got to be a pretty kinky john who gets off on the little-miss-executive outfit."

"No, Douglas," she replied with matching sarcasm, "I'm meeting my lover, haven't you figured that out by now?"

"Okay, look. Let's not do this again," he sighed. "I just get tired of you constantly out at night. And tonight particularly. Can't you postpone this meeting? It's a charity thing, isn't it?"

"You mean 'it's *just* a charity thing.' Not that important. Not as important as your firm party." She was now facing Doug with that familiar accusing look on her face.

"Well...no...What I mean is that the party cannot be rearranged. Surely your meeting can be."

Diane disappeared into the ensuite bathroom to pack up her makeup kit. "No. It can't," she called. "I'm meeting with three doctors, and they all have very busy schedules and can only meet together tonight."

Doug stared at his reflection in the mirror now abandoned by Diane. These arguments had become all too common. It was as if he and Diane were living separate lives, reuniting occasionally to decide their childrens' issues or satisfy each other sexually, but otherwise unaware of and disinterested in each other's activities. Somewhere, sometime ago—he couldn't pinpoint where or when—the devotion she had had for him had vanished. Now it seemed that all she wanted to do was get away from him. What had happened? Had their relationship simply run its course? Maybe she really did have a lover. He didn't know, but he wasn't sure he really cared. Except that he wanted to have her with him at Holden's party tonight. It was important to present the image to their host of a young, beautiful and ambitious couple.

As Diane exited the ensuite she reached for her purse on the bed, then stepped past Doug towards the door. Before she left the room she stopped and bowed her head. "I'm sorry, Doug," she said, as if offering an olive branch. With his back to her he failed to see the sadness in her eyes. "Please express my apologies to Mr. Holden."

"Diane—" Doug turned, but she was already halfway down the stairs.

On a clear day, Frank Holden's Tudor mansion, perched high on the hill above Spanish Banks, enjoyed a postcard view of the city. Sandy beaches at the base of the hill slid gently into the gray-green waters of English Bay. On the far side of the bay, Vancouver's jumble of office towers, reaching skyward like sailboat masts in a busy marina, sparkled under the heavy shoulders of the snowcapped mountain backdrop. But now, when January clouds engulfed the city, the mountains vanished, leaving the city's spires exposed to the wild white-capped waters of the bay. The wind and slashing rain swept in full force across the bay and slammed into the hill.

Inside Holden's home, however, there was no sign of the raging elements outside, other than a soft drum roll of rain on the picture windows. Doug lifted a champagne flute off the tray of a passing waiter while he stood at the edge of the foyer and scanned the grand sunken living-room before him. Figures in black and white stood together in small groups, or sniffed around the groups like dogs in the park on a Sunday afternoon. In one corner was a particularly large and animated gathering, drawn together primarily because of their vicinity to the bar. In the other corner a string quartet, also in black and white, gracefully coaxed music from their shapely instruments, while a handful of guests watched and listened with expressions of mixed curiosity and enjoyment.

"'Bout time you showed up," said Mark Henderson out of the corner of his mouth. He sidled up beside Doug, having come from the cross-hall dining room where the hors d'oeuvres were laid out in artistic abundance on the table. Henderson's left hand held a plate piled high with fried shrimp and calamari, while his right hand busily transferred the crispy morsels to his mouth.

"Better late than never, I suppose," Doug said as he continued to survey the living-room.

"Where's Diane? I didn't see her walk in."

"That would be because she didn't," Doug grumbled. "Yet another nocturnal meeting with her secret society." He looked at his friend and law partner, whose full cheeks were now even fuller from the seafood jammed into his mouth. Henderson stood about Doug's height, with a shock of salt and pepper hair over a permanently tanned face. Slim, impeccably dressed and exuding charm, wit and unbridled independence, he was an eternal fascination for women.

"And Marie? Did she make it?" Doug asked with a smirk. Marie— Henderson's live-in—though bright, beautiful and devoted to Henderson, seldom appeared at these functions. Henderson liked to explain that Marie, a lawyer at another firm in the city, felt awkward socializing with the lawyers of Larson Wren, especially at a party hosted by the firm's best client. Doug knew better, however. Marie's absence usually meant that Henderson was on the prowl, his proclivity being to live with one woman and secretly keep another.

"She couldn't make it," Henderson replied. "She's got a trial she's preparing for. Anyway, you know, she doesn't like to come to these events. Feels out of place a bit."

"I'm sorry Diane isn't here," he said, ignoring Doug's knowing smile. "She always livens things up." He lowered his voice and gave Doug a sideways glance. "Things okay at home, I hope."

Doug shrugged. "I don't know. I never see her. We…"

"There she is," Henderson announced, subtly pointing a fried shrimp towards the far side of the living-room.

Doug's eyes followed and immediately recognized the object of Henderson's attention. In a long black gown with slim spaghetti straps over her smooth white shoulders, a tall statuesque beauty stood talking with William Cuthbert, one of Doug's partners. Her blonde hair was drawn back off her sleek neck and gathered in a hair clip, and her flawless complexion glowed as though lit from within.

"My God," Doug gasped. "Who is she?"

"That, my friend, is the apple of our host's eye. His only daughter, the lovely Laura."

"Well, she's stunning," Doug said. "And look at those breasts! No restraints and they're still nice and firm."

"They should be. They're brand new—still under warranty."

Doug looked at Henderson quizzically. "Fake?"

"No," Henderson grinned and paused for full effect. "She's fifteen."

"You're kidding!" Doug shook his head in awe. "Jesus. They sure didn't make them like that when I was a teenager."

"Excuse me." Henderson stepped down onto the thick cream carpet of the sunken living-room and sauntered across the floor towards Laura.

Doug immediately followed, slightly shocked by Laura's age but mostly excited at the prospect of witnessing a master seducer charm the fifteen-year-old daughter of the firm's best client. Marriage to his true love while still in university had effectively taken Doug out of the game. Now, some innocent flirting around the office water-cooler was about all he could manage, whereas Henderson was still very much a player. His obsession with windsurfing and tennis kept him lean and fit and the colour of polished teak. Eighteen years of practicing law without the responsibility of a mortgage or the drain of children left him with the ready cash to indulge his epicurean desires: women, wine, cars, travel. Ironically, just like Doug, Henderson tended to live from pay cheque to pay cheque, his earnings being regularly squandered on investment disasters.

William Cuthbert wore a congenial smile while chatting with Laura, but it dropped slightly and his eyes narrowed when he saw Henderson approaching. As a fellow partner of Larson Wren, he was fully aware of Henderson's reputation. His expression, now, surely betrayed his concern about Henderson's intentions with Laura, because one thing was certain: Henderson was not coming over to talk to him.

"Bill," Henderson began, holding out his right hand to shake while patting Cuthbert's back with his left. "Haven't seen you in a few days. Been locked up in my office working on that huge oil spill matter I've got going."

Cuthbert shook Henderson's hand. "Oh. I thought you were playing tennis," he deadpanned.

"Wouldn't that be nice," Henderson chortled, then looked over at Laura and winked.

"Mark. Have you met Laura Holden?" Cuthbert inquired. "This is our host's daughter."

"Mark Henderson, at your service," Henderson said as he bowed his head slightly to Laura. He took her hand in his, gently, as if he were holding a frightened bird. "May I say, you look absolutely stunning tonight."

Laura's cheeks and neck flushed with colour as she smiled self-consciously. For a moment, she was lost in the piercing stare of Henderson's blue eyes.

"Thank you, Mr. Henderson," she managed eventually, shifting her eyes to the floor.

Still holding her hand, Henderson turned to Doug. "Laura, I'd like you to meet another lawyer from the firm, Doug Branston. He may look young and handsome, but he's just like me—much too old for you. Besides, he's married with children."

Laura laughed. Reluctantly removing her hand from Henderson's tender grip, she shook Doug's hand briskly. "Hello, Mr. Branston."

"It's so nice to meet you at last, Laura," Doug said.

Henderson nudged Cuthbert, and with a nod of sympathy towards Laura he said, "Mr. Holden must have something terrible on Laura to coerce her into sticking around for a party with a bunch of old farts like us, don't you think?"

Laura smiled. "Not at all. I wanted to be here."

"Hmmm." Henderson pondered this answer. "What do you think, Watson?" He leaned towards Doug while studying Laura, closely. "Do we believe her?"

Doug rubbed his chin thoughtfully, "Hard to say."

"It's true," Laura giggled. "How could I miss it? I made some of the hors d'oeuvres." She straightened her shoulders with pride. "Did you try them?"

"Which ones?" Cuthbert asked. "The sausage rolls were great."

"No. I made the breaded shrimp. Deep fried. Spicy. Didn't you try them?" She stuck out her pudgy, pink lower lip in an adorable pout.

"I'm sorry, I must have missed them," Henderson lied. "But they sound delicious." He held out his arm for her to take. "Please lead me to them."

She slipped her hand under his arm. Then, with a twinkle in her eye, she turned to Doug and Cuthbert and said, "Excuse us."

"Not at all." Cuthbert smiled. As Henderson and Laura walked away, arm in arm, he whispered to Doug, "There goes trouble."

Over the course of the evening, Doug studied Henderson's movements from across the room. Although Laura moved about the spectacular house seemingly alone, Henderson was always nearby overseeing her progress. When Reginald Wren, the firm's senior partner, and his snowy haired wife, Barbara, beckoned Laura to sit with them and tell them about her school, Henderson lingered in the background. After an appropriate delay, he casually joined the conversation—not for long—just until he had turned Laura's attention away from the Wrens. Then he drifted away a suitable distance before Laura moved on.

The control was subtle, but relentless. Like a puppeteer Henderson manipulated Laura's movements. But unlike the puppet, Laura was aware of Henderson's attention and obviously enjoyed it. Frequently, she checked to see if he was close by.

Late in the evening, Doug joined Henderson while he stood alone listening to the quartet. Laura was close by, impressing a small group of partners' wives and her father whose face beamed with pride.

"I've been watching you, man," Doug whispered out of the corner of his mouth. "Your single-minded pursuit of the young lady is quite remarkable."

"I'm not sure I know what you're talking about," Henderson replied while continuing to appraise the quartet.

"It was masterful," Doug said, ignoring Henderson's attempt at obtuseness. "You played her right into your horny little mitts."

"Oh. That." Henderson grinned slightly. "Yeah. I guess we danced a bit. You liked my steps, did you?"

"No doubt. But she's way too young for you. Not only that, she's Holden's daughter. Isn't that a little dangerous?"

Henderson scowled. "I know. The problem is, I'm already in a little too deep."

"Why?"

Now, he turned to look at Doug. "Well, I've had a little head start on tonight." A sheepish smile crossed his face. "I've been giving Laura a few tennis lessons." He quickly added, "At her dad's insistence."

"Yeah?"

Henderson looked Doug directly in the eye. "You mustn't tell anyone. Understand?" He glanced over at Laura and then back at Doug. "Things have already proceeded to the...uh...intimate stage."

Doug stared at Henderson, unable to hide his shock. "You're kidding me!" He paused, but Henderson said nothing. "Are you nuts?"

"You wouldn't believe the body, man. It's incredible. So new. No droop. No cellulite." He shook his head in amazement, then gave Doug a serious look. "Besides, I feel I'm, sort of, doing her a favour."

"How's that?"

"I'm teaching her to get in touch with her feelings and to lose her inhibitions. She's learning what it would take years for her to learn from the horny little shits she goes to school with."

Doug rolled his eyes. "Oh! I get it. Better to learn from a horny old shit, is it?" He laughed. "You don't truly believe that horseshit, do you?"

Henderson's eyes twinkled. "It doesn't really matter if I believe it or not, does it?" He turned to look over at Laura. When she caught his eye, she excused herself from her father and the other people she was with and started towards Henderson. Doug saw Frank Holden look past Laura to Henderson. The heavy shadow over his eyes and the stony set of his jaw revealed his suspicions.

"What are you two talking about?" Laura asked as she neared Henderson and Doug.

"You. Of course." Henderson said. "Doug thinks you're too young for me, don't you, Doug?"

Laura blushed slightly and looked at Doug as if he were an old prude. She was truly beautiful and Doug felt a wave of desire rush over him as he considered how to respond. "Well. Yeah. I guess I do. But who am I to judge?" He shrugged.

"You're just jealous," she said and playfully poked him in the stomach.

"That may well be so." Doug flushed like a schoolboy whose classmates have just spied him with an erection.

Henderson said, "No, Laura. You've got Doug all wrong. He's happily married with a couple of great kids. He doesn't look at other women."

"Really?" She looked around. "Is your wife here tonight? I haven't seen you with anyone."

"No," Doug shook his head. "She had a meeting she had to go to."

"That's too bad. I'd like to meet her. She must be quite something to keep a handsome guy like you out of trouble." She smiled at Doug. Her precociousness was making him feel particularly uncomfortable.

"Meet who?" Frank Holden stepped up beside Laura and placed a protective arm over her shoulder. From beneath his heavy gray brow, his eyes glowered down at Henderson and Doug. His great barrel chest seemed to swell up against the smooth silk of his black tuxedo.

Laura cringed perceptibly under the weight of her father's arm. "Oh. I was just asking Doug where his wife was tonight, daddy." She dropped her eyes to the floor, avoiding eye contact with Henderson or Doug.

"Indeed, Doug. Where is Diane tonight? Have something better to do, does she?"

Doug knew Holden expected a suitable amount of grovelling from his lawyers—and their spouses—for the millions of dollars he pumped into the firm each year. Only the most compelling excuse would assuage Holden's disappointment in Diane's absence. Unfortunately, there had not been a death in the family and Diane had not contracted a fatal disease.

"She sends her deepest apologies, Mr. Holden. She's volunteered her time to the Children's Hospital Charity drive. Tonight was the only time she could meet with some of the doctors on the board."

"That's a shame." He smiled. "Be careful, Doug. Wives that are always volunteering their time are bored at home. Today they're meeting the doctor to discuss the charity, tomorrow they're just meeting the doctor. If you get what I mean." He feigned a couple of nudges with his elbow.

An awkward silence passed as Doug digested Holden's remark. Henderson eventually came to Doug's rescue, "I have no doubt Diane would prefer to be here tonight. It's a terrific party."

Holden turned to Henderson and instinctively pulled Laura closer to him. "What about you, Mark? Where is your significant other tonight? Surely, you haven't left her at home so you can prowl an affair like this?"

Their eyes locked. "Where would you possibly get that idea?" Henderson jousted.

"Excuse me." Laura wriggled out from under her father's arm. "I think I'll get another Coke."

She escaped while Holden and Henderson continued to stare at each other. Finally, Holden said, "I'd like to speak with you privately, Mark, before you leave tonight. You too, Doug. Let me know when you're ready." He turned and followed Laura to the bar.

"Not good, man," Doug commented as he watched Holden catch up to Laura. "I think he suspects something."

"Oh, he more than suspects," Henderson replied, also staring after Holden.

Doug turned to Henderson with eyebrows raised in question.

"There are few things that Laura keeps from daddy. You know, they only have each other these days."

Doug wasn't sure he did know, so Henderson explained. "Holden's wife died in a car crash years ago. Then his son disowned the family. Joined a commune up in Bella Coolla, where—if you can believe it—he specializes in growing seedless marijuana. It's not bad stuff, actually. Anyway, it seems that in this atmosphere of father-daughter openness, Laura has mentioned a certain involvement with her tennis instructor."

"Hmmm. Not good for the tennis instructor, I wouldn't think."

"No. However, I have a card or two I can play to protect myself." Henderson looked at his watch. It was just past midnight. "When are you planning on leaving?"

"Soon."

"Can I get a ride? I came by cab tonight."

"Sure, but we've still got to meet with Holden." After a pause, Doug added, "Why does he want me there anyway?"

Henderson patted Doug on the shoulder. "You're the witness from the firm, pal. He's going to threaten to move his business if I don't leave his daughter alone. It's no good if he just makes the threat to me." He looked over to where Holden was standing by the bar. "Come on. Let's get this over with."

Holden ushered Henderson and Doug into his den at the back of the house, far away from the party. Low light from a lone polished brass reading lamp lingered on the dark mahogany panelling and bookshelves, and exposed the papers scattered across the antique desk in the middle of the room. Along one wall was a deep burgundy leather sofa, patterned with brass studding. Henderson and Doug dutifully took their seats on the sofa like two mischievous students summoned to the principal's office.

Holden closed the door behind them and stepped in front of the sofa. The light at his back cast his great chiselled face in constant shadow as he hovered over them. "I'll make this quick," he said to Henderson. "Stay the *fuck* away from my daughter"—*the fuck* being growled between gritted teeth. He continued to stare at Henderson for a long moment. "Otherwise," he added, "I'll lay charges."

Doug knew that this was no idle threat. It was a crime to have sexual contact with someone between the age of fourteen and eighteen if you were in a position of authority or trust—the tennis instructor, for example. The Criminal Code called it sexual exploitation and it could be punishable by a jail sentence.

There was silence.

"Get it?" Holden eventually barked.

Henderson nodded slowly.

Holden looked at Doug for the first time. "You tell your partners, Branston. If they don't rein in this perverted piece of shit"—he jerked his head towards Henderson—"they can kiss me and my business good *fucking* bye! Get it?" He barked again.

Holden didn't wait for Doug to answer. He stepped to the door and was about to rip it open when Henderson spoke, his voice as calm as a reflecting pool. "Mr. Holden, I know you don't like me, but you should, at least, respect my legal abilities. We have done some major deals together. Right now there are some matters that I'm working on for you of a sensitive nature. They involve large investments. You and the people you are doing business with would suffer greatly if the files had to be moved to another law firm because I was facing criminal charges." Henderson stood and started for the door. "Or—and, I would hate to see this happen—the circumstances of those deals became public as the result of a trial."

Holden strained to control his anger. Lines of shadow quivered in the yellow light along his cheek as he ground his teeth. He stared at Henderson before slowly, dramatically opening the door. As Henderson passed by him towards the open door, Holden leaned over to him, and in a low voice said, "Maybe I'll just kill you instead."

Henderson smiled. "There's a rational idea. Come on, Doug. This party's over." They left Holden standing at the entrance to the den, his face throbbing with rage.

CHAPTER 2

Doug burst through the revolving doors into the lobby of the office tower. He stomped his feet on the temporary rubber mats to shake off excess rainwater, then strode over to the bank of elevators on the far wall. When he stepped inside one, it silently rocketed to the top floors of the building. He leaned against the wall and stared at his reflection in the mirror across from him. "I hate Mondays," he said to the bleary-eyed image that stared back at him.

The elevator door soon opened at the thirty-second floor where he proceeded into the large, opulent lobby of Larson Wren & Co., Barristers and Solicitors. On either side of him the walls displayed original Northwest Coast Indian paintings in black and red, gifts from band leaders for the firm's expensive assistance on land claims. In the middle of the room, a circular mahogany receptionist's desk sat unattended like a pedestal waiting for a grand marble sculpture. Beyond the desk, as a backdrop to the entire lobby, floor-to-ceiling windows encased the inlet and mountains that made Vancouver one of the most beautiful cities in the world. On this day, however, the low cloud bank kept the spectacular view a secret.

He turned down the hallway that led to the office lunch room. A cup of coffee might make his Monday morning blues a little more tolerable.

"Morning, Doug," Henry Stemple's voice sprung from behind an open newspaper at the far side of the lunchroom. Stemple was ensconced in his usual chair reading the morning paper. Every morning when Doug arrived, Stemple's cheery greeting met him from behind sheets of newsprint. Doug supposed it could be anyone behind there, since the newspaper hid the speaker. No, it couldn't, he corrected himself. The shoes gave Stemple away. They were plain, black leather, lace-up shoes, old and scuffed—the sort of shoes found at a garage sale or on the odds-and-ends table at a church rummage sale, the same shoes that Doug had often spied in the cubicle next to him when he was on the throne.

"Morning," Doug replied as he reached into the cupboard for a coffee mug.

"I see your lovely wife has made the social page again."

Doug filled his cup with oily black coffee. "Oh?" He wandered over to where Stemple was sitting.

"Didn't you know?" Stemple dropped the paper on the table in front of Doug.

Doug shrugged. "I haven't had a chance to read the paper yet. I think I've been conscious for all of thirty minutes now, thirty-five of which has been spent driving here."

Stemple ignored Doug's witticism and pointed to the Malcolm Parry column on page three of the paper. Between paragraphs was a small photo of Diane, smiling, with her arm around a well-dressed man who was holding a poster-sized cheque for one million dollars. The paragraph above read:

> Dr. Randall Gentry and ubiquitous super-charity-spokesperson Diane Branston celebrate another successful fundraising drive for Vancouver's Children's Hospital, at the annual gala held in the Convention Centre last Friday.

Doug considered the paragraph and photo for a moment. "Huh. That must have been the volunteer stuff she was always going to."

Stemple looked at Doug. "You mean you didn't know she was working on this?"

"Oh, sure. I knew that she was doing some fundraising thing." Doug began to retreat to the door. "I wasn't clear on exactly what it was all about, though."

Stemple rolled his eyes and returned to reading the paper.

On his way to his office, Doug's mind drifted off to thoughts of Laura Holden. He knew Henderson would continue his relationship with Laura; Henderson had confirmed on the ride home from the party that he was unconcerned about her father's threats. Once again, Doug wrestled with the morality monster. She was too young! But she was absolutely beautiful—and, obviously, willing.

One thing Doug wasn't confused about was his envy of Henderson's lifestyle. It might have been his, had he not married while still penniless in university. The one apparent contradiction was Marie. Henderson had been living with Marie for over a year now. In many ways she was his antithesis. She loved to work around the apartment, care for the flower boxes and spend time in the kitchen. She was a marvellous cook. Dinner at Henderson's was always a culinary delight. On more than one occasion Doug had enjoyed a vast array of gourmet delicacies prepared lovingly by Marie. Everyone, even Henderson, agreed that Marie would be the perfect wife and mother. In fact, on occasion Henderson would announce to Doug his intention to marry Marie.

But Doug knew marriage was not in Henderson's plans. He also knew why Henderson maintained his relationship with Marie. It gave him an air of respectability when he needed it. If Henderson had to entertain a client, dinner at home always impressed. If he were in trouble with his partners, he'd have a few over for an evening with marvellous Marie to put things right. Everyone liked Marie. So, as long as Marie was with Henderson, there was something about him to like.

Even so, Doug was sure that there was a part of Henderson that actually enjoyed the home life Marie provided. He idolized Marie. And Doug suspected that in a way he felt guilty that he was not totally content in that relationship. He tried to protect her by closely guarding his infidelities. Although Doug knew of most of the women whom Henderson was involved with, he was sworn to secrecy. "The one golden rule," Henderson always reminded him, "is, guys don't tell on guys." Somehow, Henderson managed to get the other women to buy into this rule as well, each one convinced that there was a very important reason for their relationship to be kept quiet. Laura was an example. Not only had Henderson managed to seduce that lovely innocent, but he had become her mentor. Now, she was his, available to him whenever he wished, yet apparently content to meet covertly.

So, in fact, Marie was not a contradiction. Henderson's relationship with her made him the perfect example of why men are pigs: he had turned every man's fantasy into reality by balancing an enviable home life with a series of mistresses.

No sooner had Doug sat down at his desk than Henderson slipped into his office. "We need a road trip," he announced. "I figure we take a week and go to Toronto. Glad-hand a few clients. We can stay at my friend Mario's place. He's wild, man. His family owns a bunch of restaurants that Mario runs. He drives a Ferrari, lives in this fabulous penthouse. He's got these beautiful women all over him. It'll be great."

"Who are we going to see?" Doug asked.

"Well, actually, I've got to see this buddy of mine, Joey, too. We have a little business deal going." Henderson winked.

"No. I mean, what clients are we going to see?"

"Oh. Well." Henderson thought for a minute. "We could see some of the guys at the banks."

Doug liked the idea of going to Toronto with Henderson. He had been feeling a little irritable at work lately, and his home life continued to be non-existent. Time away would recharge his battery for the office and also give him a chance to consider what to do about his marriage. But he knew they needed a plausible itinerary for the partners to approve the trip at the firm's expense. Doug and Henderson had been on client development trips before. Their chits often triggered an inquisition by the partners. "Why did you fly first class? What's this car rental? A BMW? Who are these people you took to dinner? Are they clients?" In order to make this trip work, Doug and Henderson needed a plan to sell to the partners. Doug thought he might just have one.

"You and I do work for Certified Trust, right?" he pointed out. "They must have a bunch of run-off files now that they're out of the mortgage business. Maybe we could try to pick those up. I get along with the collections group. So do you."

"Sounds great," Henderson said halfway out the door of Doug's office. "You set it up. I've got a clear week next week. When you've made the arrangements, tell me and I'll call Mario." As usual, Henderson left the dirty work to Doug.

Reginald Wren, the senior partner of Larson Wren & Co., was tall and thin with wispy gray hair dragged to one side of his head. He always wore a dark blue three-piece suit regardless of the current trend in business attire. A single gold watch chain hung between his vest pockets, like a miniature suspension bridge across his non-existent belly. When anyone entered his office, Wren's practice was to reach into his right vest pocket, ostentatiously pull out his magnificent antique gold watch, and study the time.

"Mr. Wren, do you have a minute?" Doug asked as he gingerly pushed open the door to Reginald Wren's office. Wren was seated behind a fabulous oak desk reviewing a stack of papers. Without tilting his head, he raised his eyes to meet Doug's. His half-rims, perched on the end of his nose, reflected the document he had been reading. Doug was never sure whether he wore the glasses because he needed them, or whether it was to complete the image of a crusty old solicitor.

"Just, Mr. Branston, just," Wren answered, pulling out his watch.

"I'll get straight to the point," Doug offered. "I've been reviewing the file openings over the past six months and it's evident to me that our volume has slipped, particularly in our new civil litigation files."

A puzzled look came over Wren's face, not because of any surprise over the drop in file openings but because of Doug's apparent new-found interest in the business side of the practice. It was inconsistent with his usual carefree approach to law.

Ten years Doug had been with the firm, the last five as a partner. He had always been a good lawyer, bright, articulate, good common sense, excellent with clients. The partners had seen the potential in Doug during his first years with the firm and had asked him to join the partnership. He proved an adequate partner, balancing a general mix of civil and criminal litigation, but his weakness was business development. He failed to live and breathe the firm like some others. Although in many ways he was the best equipped to solicit new clients, he never showed any interest in doing so. Some of his partners were disappointed because he never seemed to reach his potential. As old Mr. Larson used to say, "There is nothing worse than apathy in a business constantly in need of more business."

To the partners' greater dismay, Doug had become a close friend of the firm's black sheep, Mark Henderson. Although Henderson usually agreed with what the firm wanted to do, he vehemently opposed how the partners planned to do it. In consequence, the partners tried to make decisions on firm problems without Henderson's input. This just initiated greater criticism from Henderson and greater animosity from his partners. Unfortunately for Doug, his friendship with Henderson caused his partners often to tar him with the same broad brush.

That's why the road trip had to be packaged just right. Luckily, Reginald Wren was not in the ignore-Henderson-and-Branston camp. He seemed more prepared than some to accept Doug for who he was.

Doug continued. "It's clear to me that if we can't tap into a regular source of files soon, we may have a crisis down the road."

Wren slowly removed his glasses, then held them up to the light for inspection. "You may be right," he said. "It may require a great effort from the litigation partners to avoid such a crisis." He began polishing the lenses with his white handkerchief.

"I'm keenly aware of that, Mr. Wren, and I think I may have a solution."

"What would that be, Mr. Branston?" Wren replaced his glasses on his nose and looked at Doug.

"Well, Certified Trust has been a client of this firm for some time. Even though they use other firms as well, I feel I have a very good relationship with their litigation manager. Now that they are closing down their mortgage department, I suspect they will have a number of run-off files. If I can time a visit to their head office when they're trying to decide where these files should go, perhaps I can make them an offer for the lot."

"What sort of offer would you propose?" Wren asked, curling his thumbs into the pockets of his suit vest. A frown of concentration squeezed his face into a star of wrinkles.

"I suspect most of the files would be foreclosures and collections on delinquent mortgages. Rather than billing on an hourly basis, we could handle these files on a contingency fee basis. We charge, say, thirty per cent of what we recover. Those collections are pretty straightforward. We may make better money than if we billed them at an hourly rate."

"And we may lose our shirts if we don't recover on the claims," Wren countered. "There's a risk to it."

"But that's why Certified Trust will like it. They're not taking the risk alone."

"I'm speaking of the personal risk to you, Mr. Branston." Wren's thumbs left the vest pockets. With both hands he removed his glasses again and held them at chest level. Looking directly at Doug he said, "If this doesn't work out, you could risk not making your billing target for the year. The firm can't afford that. Are you prepared to suffer the possible consequences?"

Doug knew what Wren was getting at. A desperate billing year might cause his percentage of firm profits to be reduced dramatically. Therefore, Wren's question identified the gamble: if Doug made the proposal to Certified Trust to obtain the files, they still may prove a cash drain for the firm, in which case Doug would be blamed. However, the files may just as likely become revenue producers, and Doug would be a hero. What gamble? Doug's billing year was already miserable; he needed a minor miracle to make his billing target, anyway.

"I think so," he replied. "But before you approve the trip, I have one more request."

"What's that?" Wren's eyebrows shot up.

Doug held his breath. "That Mark Henderson come with me."

"Why?" Wren asked. A flicker of a smile came to his face, perhaps in anticipation of Doug's justification for this request.

"Well, there's no doubt that Henderson is the lightning rod for the woes of this firm. Many of his partners are out to get him. And right now, like a lot of us, he's got little on his plate. If he could land this work along with me, his measure of worth with his partners would go up. That could only be good for the firm."

Wren shook his head slowly while he placed his glasses back on his nose. "But if you fail, the firm looks upon this trip as a costly boondoggle by you and Henderson. Why tie yourself to him, Douglas? Go on your own. If you fail to get the business by yourself, the firm will still respect your efforts. But go with Henderson, and your motives will be questioned."

"Henderson's my friend, Mr. Wren," Doug argued. "Sometimes I think he is my only friend in this firm. If I can help him, I will. Besides, you may not believe it, but he is excellent at entertaining clients. He will help a lot in landing this work."

"Well, it's your call, Mr. Branston," Wren said. His right hand slipped into his vest pocket and extracted the watch. "Good luck. I think you'll need it."

The conversation was over, but Doug had got what he wanted: the senior partner's consent to the trip.

"Thank you, Mr. Wren," he said, backing out of the office door. Wren had already returned to studying the documents on his desk.

Prior to leaving the office for the day, Doug dropped in on one of the firm's junior associates, Tom Woodley. Doug had originally hired Woodley as a student. The Law Society required that Woodley work with the firm as a student for a year, and then write the bar admission exams. Upon passing the exams, he became enrolled in the Law Society as a lawyer. The act of enrollment was commonly referred to as being 'called to the bar' (an appropriate phrase given that lawyers had the worst record of alcohol abuse of all professionals). After Tom's call to the bar, he had been invited to stay on with Larson Wren as a junior litigator.

Tom was a great addition to the firm. He had bags of energy and a quick wit. His olive complexion and curly black hair provided a backdrop for his bright, gentle smile. He spoke with a deep comfortable voice that seemed to rise up easily from the extra pounds around his waist. Perhaps it was due to his big swarthy appearance or the warm timbre of his voice, but to Doug the nickname Tom had acquired while a teenager on the prairies fit him like a white rhinestone jumpsuit.

"Elvis, how's it going?" Doug said as he turned into the young associate's office. Before Tom was able to answer, Doug continued, " I need a favour. I'm off to Toronto for a few days—a little business development. Could you keep an eye on my mail?"

"Not a problem," Tom replied. "Need anything done while you're away?"

Along with being fun around the office, Tom was keen and his work was good. "Not that I can think of," Doug replied. "I'll phone you every so often anyway, just to touch base. Thanks, man."

As Doug walked out of Tom's office and headed for the elevator, he heard the parting shot. "Burn the negatives!" Tom yelled.

Doug was still smiling when he got into his car to drive home.

It was seven o'clock and Diane was out for the evening. The boys had eaten already, so Doug sat down while Conchita served him the remains of the meal she had kept warm for him on the stove. He let the boys continue watching TV until he finished his dinner, then sent them up to their rooms to do homework and get ready for bed. Soon they were down for the night and Doug was stationed in front of the TV himself, fully armed with a scotch in one hand and the channel changer in the other. Another night of excitement. He surfed through the channels and let his mind ponder his situation. At what point had the groove he was in become a rut? Wasn't he where he wanted to be— good job, family, house? So why was he so bored?

The evening slipped by with Doug only moving off the couch periodically to replenish his glass. Eventually, he found his way to the bedroom and by midnight had descended into the twilight zone somewhere between wakefulness and sleep.

"You awake?" Diane asked in a whisper as she arrived under the bed sheets next to him.

He rolled onto his back and grunted in half-consciousness, "I was just drifting off".

"Were the boys okay?"

"Yeah."

Diane settled into her usual position, on her side facing away from him. "Good night, dear," she mumbled.

"Where were you tonight?" Doug asked.

She sighed with impatience. "The charity thing, Douglas. You know all about it."

Doug thought for a moment. "But I read in the paper today it was finished. You were in Malcolm Parry's column. Photo and everything."

"That's what Parry may think, but it's never *over*. One year ends, you start on the next."

"No rest for the wicked, eh?"

There was silence.

"Good night," Doug said finally. "Oh, by the way, I've got to go to Toronto with Henderson next week. You'll need to pare back your nocturnal charity activity to be with the kids. Okay?"

Some time passed before she turned over to face him. "You and Henderson? That's interesting."

Doug dodged this invitation to debate the reasons for the road trip.

He'd never fool Diane. She knew all about Henderson's reputation and she probably knew that Doug envied his friend's lifestyle. Instead, he turned to Diane; in the darkness he searched her lips and kissed them. "Just for a few days," he murmured, then kissed her again.

There was a familiar stirring in his boxer shorts. With growing inspiration, Doug slid his hand up Diane's bare thigh and under her nightshirt. She was not wearing panties. His fingers tiptoed between her legs, fingertips probing, encouraging her to respond. Diane seemed to relax for a moment, then she sighed and pushed Doug over onto his back. She briefly fondled his testicles through his boxer shorts before reaching under the elastic waistband. Doug spread his legs to allow Diane's hand full access. He was fully erect when she grasped him and began stroking steadily. She then slid his boxer shorts down to his ankles and took him completely into her mouth. He closed his eyes and sighed.

CHAPTER 3

The tie around Joey Marron's neck was tight and confining. He hated wearing it. In fact, he hated wearing the entire suit. Jeans and cowboy boots were much more comfortable. He had tried to tell Tony it would be better to dress as he liked, that he would feel less conspicuous. But Tony always had to call the shots, insisting that Joey wear the suit and tie, even though it was Joey's ass on the line. Now, Joey was standing in line, sweating like a stuck pig, his guts so full he didn't know if he was going to barf or shit.

"Next," the Customs officer said. He looked over at Joey and waved him forward to the booth.

"Citizenship?"

"Canadian." Joey slid his passport and declaration form onto the counter. He had an overwhelming desire to wipe the sweat from his brow. His face was a tomato.

"How long were you in Peru?" the officer asked, staring at him.

"Two weeks."

"Business or pleasure?"

"Bit of both."

"What do you do, Mr. Marron?" The officer's eyes finally moved from Joey's face to the passport on the counter.

"I'm an importer/exporter. I deal in food items mostly. Cooking utensils." Immediately, Joey regretted his unfortunate choice of words, which begged a follow-up question from the officer: *Anything else you "deal" in, Mr. Marron?*

"Are you bringing any perishables into the country, Mr. Marron, such as plants or fruits?"

"No, only some cookware described on the declaration form. I have some foodstuffs that I'll be bringing in by freight, but I'll advise Customs in advance of that shipment."

The Customs officer looked up from the passport. He studied Joey's face for a moment. "Do you feel alright? You look ill."

"Thank you, I'll be fine as soon as I get out of this suit. I feel like I've been wearing it for twenty-four hours straight," Joey grumbled.

"I feel the same way about this uniform sometimes," the officer chuckled. He scribbled a code in red on the declaration form, handed it back to Joey with his passport and looked past him. "Next."

Joey collected his passport and declaration form, then walked as casually as possible from the Customs booth to the luggage carousel. He was unsure what the code the Customs officer had put on the declaration form meant. It may instruct the next officer to conduct a thorough search of his luggage. Joey was not free yet. He stood staring at the opening where the suitcases arrived on the conveyor belt above the carousel, watching as the suitcases appeared one by one, then slid down the shiny steel plates to the bumper at the bottom of the carousel. The plates moved slowly counterclockwise around the carousel, exhibiting the suitcases of the passengers who had been on Joey's flight.

Watching the suitcases drop down from the conveyor belt, Joey was reminded of the secret luggage he was carrying in his own intestine, and how much he wanted to void it. The fullness of his insides was starting to become painful. He was hot, sweaty and uncomfortable. Tony had said that he had to get the stuff out of him within twelve hours or the latex would start to break down in his intestine. If the cocaine leached out of the safes, he was as good as dead. The flight had been eight hours, but had left an hour late. He had swallowed the condoms an hour before the flight was supposed to leave, and had landed at Toronto International almost an hour ago. This was cutting it a bit too close.

The fluorescent lights were too bright. Anxiety was rising to his head. He had to get out of there. Where's the bloody suitcase? If they wanted to search the goddamn thing, he'd keel over right in front of them.

Finally, his suitcase emerged from the opening above the carousel. As nonchalantly as possible, he hoisted it over the carousel bumper, landing it on its wheels. He grabbed the tow belt and started to pull the bag towards the exit. One more uniform to pass, the guy collecting the declaration forms. The line before the officer moved slowly forward. He appeared to be simply collecting the forms and letting everyone pass out of Customs. Joey's turn came and he handed over his form while moving, hoping to encourage the officer to let him pass.

"Hold it!" the officer barked without taking his eyes off the declaration form. Joey stopped. "You ill? You look awful."

"As a matter of fact I am," Joey replied with what he hoped was the right mixture of weariness and humour. "I think that bloody Peruvian airline poisoned me." The officer chuckled while waving Joey through.

Toronto's Terminal One was a zoo. People swarmed in every direction, greeting arriving friends or relatives, arranging transportation from the airport, checking in for flights, buying souvenirs, or just figuring out where the hell they were.

Joey fought his way through the crowd to the exit. As the doors opened automatically, he stepped out into the hustle for cabs and airport limousines. Immediately a wave of frigid air slapped him and the flecks of white swirled around him. Snow? Sleet? Hail? Definitely Toronto in winter.

Pools of light shone from Terminal One's superstructure through the darkness onto the asphalt and concrete, like the crossing through Checkpoint Charlie. "Easy now," he told himself. "You've already cleared Customs. Next stop, pay-off."

A taxi pulled up and Joey jumped in.

"Do you know a bar called Hangars?" he asked.

"Yeah," the cabbie yelled over his shoulder. He watched Joey in the rear-view mirror. "It's about five minutes down the road. That as far as you're going?"

As Joey nodded, the cabbie mumbled something under his breath and stepped on the gas.

Hangars was a ritzy strip bar catering to businessmen in transit or staying only briefly in Toronto. The raised stage, adorned with a series of lights and brass columns, dominated the room. The seating area around the stage consisted of large tables for four with upholstered chairs in dark wine hues. The carpet was deep pile. Low lighting made it difficult to determine its colour, maybe turquoise or a teal blue. Mirrors, extending from floor to ceiling in ten-inch-wide panels, covered all the walls. They created an effect akin to mirrors on a merry-go-round, the narrowness of each panel breaking up the reflections into disjointed, fractured images.

The waitresses all came from the same mould: tall, lean and sultry with long flowing hair, each squeezed into patterned black nylons and a tight, black body stocking. On black four-inch heels they balanced around the bar, always ready to perform a personal show for any patron willing to part with five dollars. In that event, the waitress would put down her tray and bring her small pedestal to her client's table. Then, as music played for the main act on stage, she would peel her body stocking off for his particular pleasure.

An investment of extra money made the table dance more intimate.

Although patrons were prohibited from touching, the women were free to do everything short of grab the patrons. A pseudo-bondage scene often resulted, the poor patron sitting back in his chair on his hands while the table dancer climbed naked onto the arms of the chair, letting her long hair fall over his face and neck and her breasts lightly brush against him. A slow torture. Not surprisingly, many of the waitresses ran their own business on the side. Their breaks from waiting tables were often spent turning quick tricks in one of the rooms above the bar.

The cab pulled into the parking lot of Hangars. A single light shone over the entrance to the nondescript building. On the wall beside the door, partly in shadow, was a small marquee. Below the name "Hangars" were the words "Featuring this week," and below that, five photos of women in various stages of undress, lying provocatively on different pieces of furniture. Each dancer's name appeared below her photo: "Bad Barbie," "Penelope Pussy," "Trixie Wilde," "Moanah," and "Randi."

Joey paid the cab driver, adding a hefty tip to make up for being such a short fare. As the cab left, Joey, bracing himself against the wind, walked his suitcase over to a parked car nearby. He opened the trunk, threw the suitcase in, then jogged back to the entrance to Hangars.

The music was loud inside the club; multi-coloured lights were flashing. Trixie Wilde was in mid-routine on stage, while scattered throughout the room various waitresses performed table dances. When he entered the room, Joey was greeted by Tony, the bouncer.

"Hey Joey, good to see ya." Tony held out his hand. When Joey shook it, he felt a slip of paper being passed between their palms. He continued to shake Tony's hand, then let go and slipped the note into his pocket without looking at it.

"Place is packed, Tony." Joey's hungry eyes devoured the room.

Tony assured him that there was always a spot close to the stage for a good customer. Then, indicating for Joey to follow him, he strode between tables.

Tony was an impressive figure: six-foot-three, 250 pounds. It was obvious he worked out, for his body was in top condition. He wore a black, double-breasted suit with a black silk shirt buttoned to the neck, no tie. His chest strained against the containment of the jacket lapels. On his feet were black snake skin cowboy boots polished to a high sheen, the large heels giving him an extra inch-and-a-half on his already imposing frame.

"Here you go." Tony pointed to an empty table. Then, as Joey sat down, Tony bent over so his mouth was at Joey's right ear. Joey smelled the gel in Tony's slicked-back black hair; he saw the tight band holding the short, straight pony-tail. "Order a drink, then go to the can," Tony whispered.

Joey gave a slight nod to indicate that he understood the instructions.

Tony straightened up and looked around for a waitress who was free. "Kristy." He waved over a statuesque beauty. "Take care of my friend," he instructed, patting Joey on the shoulder before returning to the bar entrance.

Joey ordered a Scotch and rocks from Kristy but his eyes remained on the stage. Trixie was now into the final song of her routine. She was naked, on her hands and knees, prowling the stage like a cat in heat. When she caught the eye of one of the more self-conscious patrons she smiled and slid her remarkable long tongue out of her mouth, slithering it around as if she were licking a huge ice-cream cone. The music was slow, suggestive. Bette Middler was crooning, "Do ya, do ya, do ya wanna dance?"

Slowly, she came around the stage until she was kneeling right in front of him. "Welcome back, Joey," she mouthed as she rolled on her back with her legs towards him. She spread them so he could see every detail of her coiffured pussy. "Meet me later," she said.

How could he refuse? He winked at her, then left his chair to go to the men's room.

There were three urinals against the far wall, and three cubicles beside them. Along the wall to Joey's right were three basins below a wall-sized mirror. Two men stood at urinals with their backs to him talking about the Leafs. Joey pulled the note that Tony had given him out of his pocket. "Stall 3," it read.

The door of each cubicle had a number on it. He stepped into cubicle number three and locked the door behind him. Beside the toilet was a wastepaper basket lined with a plastic bag to protect it from moisture, and to allow the cleaners to remove the trash easily. Joey pulled out the plastic bag, revealing a small glass vial on the bottom of the basket. He retrieved the vial, then pulled down his pants and sat on the toilet. Although it was unlabelled, Joey knew the vial's purpose. He unscrewed the top and drank the contents.

The liquid, with the consistency of oil, slowly crept down Joey's esophagus and into his stomach. Before he drank the potion, his stomach and intestine had been hopelessly knotted. Within minutes, the knots began loosening, then suddenly they let go. His whole insides seemed to give way as ten thumb-sized condoms stuffed with pure, uncut cocaine shot into the toilet bowl. He groaned and closed his eyes euphorically just before seven more fired out, followed by another six, and then four. In the end, twenty-seven small white packages bobbed in the bowl amongst shreds of feces, like giant maggots crawling over pieces of rotten meat.

After a moment's silence he cleaned himself off, stood up and rebuckled his pants. Gingerly, he pulled the condoms out of the toilet, then cleaned and dried each one with toilet paper. Twenty-three of the condoms and the empty vial he put on the bottom of the basket before return-ing the plastic liner. The four remaining condoms he wrapped in toilet paper and slipped into the inside breast pocket of his jacket.

He took a final look around to ensure that everything was in place, flushed the toilet and stepped out of the cubicle. A quick scrub of the hands and he'd be out of there.

At the basin, he washed and checked himself over in the mirror. His face was shiny with sweat; his hair was unkept. He leaned over and splashed cool, refreshing water on his face and hair. As he straightened up and looked for a paper towel to dry himself, he saw in the mirror the reflection of the club custodian slowly working his way down the line of cubicles with a cart containing a large trash can and assorted brushes and mops. The custodian disappeared into cubicle number two. After a few seconds, he re-emerged with the plastic liner from the paper basket in his hand and tossed it into the trash can.

Joey found the paper towel dispenser and pulled off a length of paper. While he dried his face, he spied on the custodian in the mirror. It seemed that he took slightly longer in cubicle three, but eventually he reap-peared, throwing the plastic liner into the trash can. He turned the cart around and pushed it towards the exit. For a split second before he left the washroom, his eyes met Joey's in the mirror.

Somewhat refreshed, feeling ten pounds lighter and a lot less agitated, Joey returned to his seat by the stage where his drink was waiting. He gulped it down while looking for Kristy to take his order for another.

When she caught his eye, she came over to his table. Instead of taking his order, however, she handed him the bill for his drink. "Trixie wants you to meet her at Mario's club," she purred. "She's already left."

Joey picked up the bill and felt a fat envelope underneath it. He knew it was the pay-off for his delivery. Tony apparently wanted him out of the club as soon as possible. No problem. He slid the envelope into his breast pocket with the intention of counting it later, then drew out his wallet and gave Kristy his credit card.

After signing the receipt, Joey started for the exit. "Hey, Joey, where you going in such a hurry?" Tony called after him.

"I'm going to grab a shower and a change of clothes. Then I'm going to meet Trixie at Mario's."

"Look, my shift just ended. Can I hitch a ride with you? I got to pop by the club myself."

Joey suspected that Tony wanted to get the coke out of Hangar's and into the boss's hands quickly. Although Tony was the one who organized the mule runs to South America, he liked to keep the strip joint as clean as possible. Besides, the more rapidly the stuff was moved and the more hands it touched, the tougher it was to trace the operation.

Joey agreed to give Tony a ride if he didn't mind stopping at the apartment. They jogged across the parking lot to Joey's car, a black Chrysler Talon that had been sitting in the parking lot since he made the trip to Peru five days before. A light dusting of snow covered its iced-over body. Once inside the car, Joey turned the engine over until it caught, then blasted on the heater/defroster and sat back to wait for the windows to clear.

Tony settled into the passenger seat next to Joey. "Have any problems on the trip?" he asked, as he pulled out a pack of Camels and placed a cigarette between his lips.

Joey hated people smoking in his car, but Tony was a little intimidating and Joey wasn't inclined to tell him to put the cigarette away. Instead, he advised that the trip went smoothly except he didn't like wearing the suit.

"Did you see Carlos?" Tony was now searching his pocket for a lighter. The cigarette bobbed up and down in his mouth as he spoke.

"Yeah. Briefly."

"How's he doing?" Tony was still searching and the cigarette was still bobbing.

"Fine," Joey answered, although he really had no idea how Carlos was.

"Did he actually give you the stuff?"

"Yeah. He delivered it to me at the trade show. We talked over the counter for a few minutes, then I split." Joey reached up to the rear-view mirror. He caught a glimpse of his eyes—wide open and alert—as he adjusted it.

"Only twenty-three condoms, eh?" Tony asked. He was now searching the dashboard for the car cigarette lighter.

Joey was prepared for this. "No, twenty-seven."

"Well, how come I've only got twenty-three, then?" Tony asked, abruptly turning to stare at Joey with the unlit cigarette still in his mouth. He had abandoned his search for the lighter.

Joey looked at Tony as casually as he was able. "I could only keep down twenty-three," he replied.

The engine of the car was now warm and the windows had cleared somewhat. Joey turned on the wipers to clear the streaks of melting ice, put the car into gear and pulled out of the parking space.

"So where did you leave the other four?"

"I flushed them," Joey said nonchalantly. He stopped the car at the exit of the parking lot to check the traffic before entering the highway that led into Toronto.

"You what?"

"I flushed them down the toilet. Some Peruvian fish is so high right now he's probably half-way to Australia."

"Why didn't you give them back to Carlos?" There was a note of disbelief in Tony's voice.

"Because I was at the fucking airport and he was long gone. I wasn't about to start looking for him with twenty-three safes full of cocaine in my fucking guts." Joey saw a break in the traffic and accelerated out of the parking lot.

Tony fell silent for a few minutes. They were now on the highway into Toronto, and Joey was trying to keep the spunky Talon within the speed limit in order to avoid the attention of the highway patrol.

Tony removed the cigarette from his lips and restowed it in the package. "I don't get it. I thought you loaded them at the trade show" he said.

"I did." Joey knew Tony wanted a more detailed explanation so he launched into his whole story. "I go to the trade show every day, just like you said. On the last day I meet Carlos at one of the counters. We talk for awhile about Peruvian food and shit, and then he slips me a bag with the safes in it. I make like I'm paying him for buying something at the counter and then I head to a back room that's shown on a map inside the bag. There's this little guy there that helps me get all the safes down—you know, he massages them through my stomach and into my guts as I'm swallowing them. After getting the twenty-three down, I think one more and I'm going to puke. But this little shit is insistent, so I choke down the last four. But they never make it past the back of my fucking throat. Meanwhile, I got a plane to catch. So I grab a cab for the airport. Well, by the time I get there, after weaving in and out of Lima traffic and breathing all the fucking diesel fumes, I know I'm going to spew. I barely get into the can at the airport before I toss the last four safes."

Tony frowned and scratched the stubble on his cheek.

Joey added, "I'm sorry, Tony. But just be thankful I didn't lose the whole fucking freight. I'm telling you, it took a shitload of concentration to hold onto the rest. So here I am, I'm in the fucking airport. Carlos ain't around and my plane is waiting. You told me the mule has got to make the ultimate call, so I flushed them. I had no choice."

Tony stared out the windshield, continuing to scratch his cheek absentmindedly. Finally, he commented, "There's something that just doesn't make sense, Joey."

"What's that?" Joey tried to stifle the tension in his voice.

"Well, Carlos tells me you never went to the can at the airport. You got there, you checked in and you went straight to the gate and boarded the plane."

"That's bullshit!"

"He was watching you, Joey. I asked him to," Tony stated evenly. "So what did you really do with the other four safes?"

"I told you, I flushed them down the can," Joey pleaded.

"You didn't, Joey." Anger and impatience were starting to creep into Tony's voice. "You went to the back room, you choked down the safes. You grabbed a cab to the airport, checked in and got on the plane. No racing to the can. And no flushing safes down the fucking toilet. Carlos was watching the whole time. It's his job. He reports to me all the mule's moves from the drop till he gets on the plane. Now where are the other safes, Joey?"

Casually, Tony reached into his jacket with his right hand. Without a word he pulled out a surprisingly large gun. He pointed it at Joey, allowing Joey time to recognize the magnitude of trouble he was in.

"What the fuck are you doing?" Joey cried, his eyes as big as saucers as they jumped from the gun to the road in front and back to the gun. "Jesus, Tony, put that away. I can't drive with it pointing at me."

"Joey, you don't seem to understand. It's my ass that's on the line now. So where are they?" Tony now held the gun right at Joey's temple.

Feeling the cold steel pressing against his skin, Joey realized this was serious. "Okay, shit, okay. Here, take them." He reached into his breast pocket, pulled out the four condoms wrapped in toilet paper and handed them to Tony.

"Thank you," Tony said. "Now, tell me, Joey, what the hell were you planning to do with this shit? You going to start your own business? Is that it?"

"No. No way, Tony," Joey argued defensively. "It was just some extra for me."

"You sure? It's a lot of blow for one guy." Tony paused. "Who else is in on this, Joey? Who the fuck are you doing this for?"

"No one, Tony. I swear. I wanted my own stash. That's all. I always work alone, you know that!"

"Yeah, right." Tony lay the gun on his lap and put the condoms in his breast pocket. "Pull over. I'm not going to your apartment," he explained. "I've got a car following that will take me straight to Mario's."

Joey pulled the car over to the shoulder of the highway. As he stopped, he noticed in his rear-view mirror the lights of a car pull in behind.

Tony got out of the car. He was about to close the door when he leaned back in and said, "I'm sorry, Joey, but you're such an asshole."

He lifted the gun to Joey's head and pulled the trigger. Then he threw the gun on the passenger seat, closed the door and ran back to the other car. Jumping into the front passenger seat, he yelled to Trixie. "Let's go!"

She waited for a break in the traffic and gunned the engine. The car shot onto the highway and was gone.

CHAPTER 4

Doug flew east on his own, Henderson having left a few days earlier to visit his mother, who lived just outside Toronto. While alone on the plane Doug wrestled with his future with Diane. Their relationship was hanging by the thread of decent sex—that is, they had been with each other long enough to know which buttons to push, but it was little more than a stress release; the romance was gone. Outside the bedroom they had become complete strangers, living separate lives under the same roof, and it had started to affect the children. Constant miscues from one parent or the other had replaced the 'all for one and one for all' sense of family. Now Doug avoided decisions on what the children should or should not do, or how they should behave, because Diane always undermined his authority. She misread his reticence as disinterest. Why had they not talked it out? Neither really wanted to work that hard. Doug was playing lawyer and Diane was playing martyr. It was too bad; they had married for love, but that was a long time ago.

As an attractive flight attendant leaned over him to retrieve a glass from the window-seat passenger, Doug admitted to himself that there was another side to the issue—his own unsettledness. He was approaching forty, still young enough and with some money. There were a lot of fine women out there who were available if only he were unattached. Doug found himself noticing, more than ever, how good the secretaries, students and young associates in the firm always looked.

Staff were off limits though, no matter what Doug's marital status. As Henderson put it, "You don't shit where you eat." But Doug had also been tantalized while on road trips with Henderson, although nothing had ever transpired. Fortunately, or unfortunately, Henderson always came to the rescue whenever Doug managed to corner some prospect, by slipping in in the lady's presence that Doug was married with children. Poof! Doug became invisible, allowing Henderson to step into the void.

By the time the plane landed in Toronto, Doug had decided that things were going to change on this road trip. He wanted to break through, find out what he was missing. So, when Henderson arrived at the hotel to pick him up, Doug told him to back off. "I want to see how far I can go," he announced. It wasn't going to hurt his marriage; that was already fatally wounded. In fact, this trip might actually convince him whether to pull it off the life supports.

Henderson reacted oddly to Doug's request. "Why do you want to jump some tart, Branston? How is that going to help you and Diane?"

"Maybe by confirming that it's time to move on."

"But you don't want to do that. You've got two kids."

"What's worse for them? Living separate lives under one roof, or acknowledging the relationship is over? Christ, they'd probably be better off—probably get more attention—if we were apart."

"I doubt it. Kids need both parents together," Henderson announced with that end-of-conversation tone and started for the door.

"Why do you care about my marriage, man? You're not the most faithful guy. How many times a week do you put your relationship with Marie on the line for a run at some young stuff?"

"I don't have kids." He paused, then with a pat on Doug's shoulder he said, "But I know, it's none of my business. Tonight, stud, you're on your own. Follow the old Henderson philosophy and go wherever the night takes you."

In the middle of Yorkville, one of Toronto's trendy downtown neighbourhoods, stood Mario's Restaurant and Night Club, two storeys high with an elaborate black-lacquered wood facade. Across the second storey in gold block lettering was emblazoned 'MARIO'S'. Flood lights illuminated the letters from underneath, creating a sinister shade over each like a black hood. Two fluted Corinthian columns guarded the entrance, and a frieze with sculpted relief figures intertwined in erotic repose sat over them. Above the frieze, a gable-like pediment was outlined by intricately detailed cornices in white marble. The whole conjured up images of a Roman temple.

Doug and Henderson entered the building and immediately joined a crush of people huddled in the foyer of the restaurant, all thankful to be sheltered from the biting chill outside and waiting patiently to be seated by one of the hostesses at the desk facing them. Strategically-placed halogen fixtures cast pools of light about the restaurant. At the far end, a raised stage cluttered with instruments, microphones and wires, anticipated the arrival of the band. There appeared to be a dance floor in between the stage and the dining tables, but it was hard to see from the entrance.

Henderson, with Doug in tow, pushed his way through the crowd to the desk where one of the hostesses was studying the reservation list. "Julie, hi," Henderson said as he slid up to the desk. The hostess was tall and beautiful with wavy blonde hair cascading over a long black dress, cut close to feature the elegant curves of her body.

"Hi, Mark," she greeted him with a particularly friendly smile. Then, looking past him to Doug, she asked, "Is this your friend Doug? I've heard so much about you, I feel I know you."

"I hope not all bad," Doug blurted out lamely. She smiled while she shook his hand.

"Mario is upstairs." She pointed to a serpentine staircase, in front of which stood a burly man dressed in black with hair slicked back into a pony-tail. Henderson kissed Julie's cheek in thanks before waving Doug forward like a cavalry commander leading the charge.

"Tony, remember me?" Henderson said, approaching the man in black and reaching out his right hand in greeting. "Mark Henderson."

"Of course, nice to see you, Mr. H." Tony's hand encircled Henderson's.

After Henderson had introduced Doug, Tony ushered the two of them upstairs to the Lair, an opulent den welcoming only Mario's special guests, complete with bar, leather couches and a full-size pool table. For added entertainment, those who enjoyed Mario's hospitality in the Lair could assess the comings and goings of the club's patrons in comfortable anonymity from a balcony overlooking the restaurant and dance floor.

Henderson's eyes, black bullets with silver casing, focused down the barrel of the pool cue to the cue ball, motionless and white on the green felt. He aimed through the cue ball toward the red ball and the pocket beyond, his field of vision skewed to encompass both balls and the pocket simultaneously. Slowly, silently, he eased the cue back, sliding it easily along the bridge of his left thumb. He struck the cue ball low. It kissed the red ball into the pocket, then backspun into position for the next shot. Henderson was an excellent player, always planning a few shots ahead.

Only the two of them remained in the Lair now. When first arriving, they had met Mario, an amiable man permanently surrounded by a gaggle of girls. He had a thin, athletic build, a baby face, and an engaging smile. Large, horn-rimmed glasses sat on the end of his imposing nose, creating a resemblance to Buddy Holly. They had eaten spaghetti, and drunk red wine and expensive liqueurs. But shortly after, Mario had retired to attend to the business of running the nightclub and the girls had gradually disappeared.

Doug casually watched Henderson stroke the cue ball. It cracked another ball slightly off centre, sending it cleanly into the pocket. Doug turned away again and surveyed the rising tide of people on the dance floor below him. With a pool cue in one hand and a tumbler of scotch in the other he leaned against the railing of the balcony and let the energy swirling up from below fill him with excitement. Although it was close to midnight Toronto time, he was still working on west coast time, three hours behind.

He was trying to watch Julie, but the hostess desk was out of eyeshot, allowing him only occasional glimpses of her manoeuvering between the tables to seat late arrivals. The band was now playing an old R&B favourite, the dance floor was bouncing and Doug's mercury was rising up from his toes. He sang along with the woman on stage:

> *If you feel like loving me,*
> *If you've got the notion,*
> *I second that emotion.*

He surveyed the dance floor once more like the mirrored ball that swirled patterns of light onto the dancers. The longer he scanned, the more his eyes returned to one figure slithering sensuously to the rhythm. A black patternless silk gown hung loosely from the spaghetti straps on her shoulders. She wore no necklace or bracelet. Her long, straight, black hair caressed the small of her back, its silky smoothness complementing the subtlety of her gown. She danced with her arms above her head, her wrists and hands intertwining now and then like a hula dancer's. When she turned towards Doug, he was able to confirm his suspicion that she was Asian, but from the distance of the balcony, her facial features remained a mystery. He needed a closer look.

"Scrap the pool, Henderson, the action's on the dance floor," Doug said, as he dropped the cue back in the rack and headed for the stairs. Henderson was concentrating on a shot. He realized he had been abandoned only when Doug was half-way down the stairs.

Doug found a spot close to the dance floor where he could scrutinize his slinky subject more closely. She was about ten feet away from him now. Her almond eyes were closed and her full lips pressed together in a satisfied smile. She was enjoying herself, oblivious to the spastic jerks of her dance partner. Doug watched in a trance while she smoothly shifted her weight from one sandalled foot to the other, her hips slanting seductively this way and that, revealing her supple shape momentarily in the sway of her gown.

As he watched her move, he imagined the contour of her slim body under the gown. He was leaning his head to study her every angle when she slowly opened her eyes to him. She held his stare while her smile increased slightly, knowingly. Doug found her soft, rose-painted lips so inviting. He returned her smile, then motioned to her that he wanted the next dance. She closed her eyes and bowed her head.

For a few seconds after the music ended, she continued to hold her arms over her head, her eyes closed again as if she needed a moment's reflection before she returned to reality. Then her eyes opened. She dropped her hands to her side, nodded a curt thank you to her dance partner and turned to face Doug. The band started again, an old, slow favourite. She reached both hands out to Doug and he stepped up to her, taking her in his arms. Having been married for eleven years, Doug found close contact with another woman slightly foreign, but he was a good dancer and generally comfortable on the dance floor. He began swaying to the soft tones of the music. She wrapped her arms tightly around his neck, lifted her hips to him and slid her right thigh between his legs so that he felt the pressure of her entire body against him.

Within seconds Doug's mind was swimming. He felt her cheek against his, the touch of her lips against his skin and her fingers in the hair at the back of his neck. Her thighs caressed his right leg, the relentless force of her hip against his groin awakening his erection. Doug's heart was pounding. He slid his hands slowly down her back. His fingertips glided over her buttocks, outlined the parting between them and cupped each one. In response, she arched her hips against him, rubbed herself against his thigh and moaned quietly into his ear. He turned his head to look at her and she returned his gaze with half-closed eyes; their lips touched, mouths apart. He was losing control, about to burst before the music even ended.

"Lets get out of here," he whispered into her ear.

"I'll get my coat," she said.

"Meet me at the front door. We'll get a cab."

Doug headed back to the Lair for his coat. At the top of the stairs he met Henderson who had been watching the seduction from the balcony. "Where are you going?" Henderson asked, hands on hips.

"I need my coat. I'm getting lucky tonight," Doug replied as he hurried passed Henderson.

"Ah man, don't do it." Henderson said disgustedly. "Who is she? Think you're the first guy she's picked up in this place? She's probably got a dose."

Doug ignored Henderson and grabbed his coat.

"What about Diane, your kids? You going to risk that?"

"Fuck off!" Doug said. He ran back down the stairs, pulling on his over-coat as he went.

"Don't forget your six-pack!" Henderson yelled after him. His way of reminding Doug to wear a condom.

They met at the door and were oddly shy with each other, given their passion on the dance floor just minutes before. "I'm Doug," he said, extending his hand awkwardly to shake hers.

"Jenna," she purred, shaking his hand and kissing him on the cheek.

"Wait here, I'll get a cab," he said, as he pushed his way out the door into the cold night air.

Within minutes they were speeding towards his hotel. Doug worked to keep his mind vacant of thought, refusing to consider Henderson's comments. Tonight, it wasn't his brain that was doing the thinking.

CHAPTER 5

Doug pushed his plate away. Finally, he broke the silence that had engulfed them like a fog around the breakfast table. "I've decided I'm leaving Diane when I get back from this trip," he announced.

Henderson was dousing the runny eggs on his plate with gobs of ketchup. "Why?" he asked. "Because you got your end wet last night?"

"It's not just last night, although last night was un-fucking-believable." Doug paused to honour the event with a moment's silence. "We don't have a relationship anymore, Diane and me. So why pretend we do?"

Henderson looked up from his plate, hesitated, then grabbed for his napkin and sneezed. "Damn," he mumbled, as he wiped his nose and put his napkin back in his lap. "What are you going to do about the kids?"

"Yeah, I know. We'd have to be careful that the kids are affected as little as possible, but I think we could sort that out pretty amicably. Diane's got to know that our marriage is on the rocks. She'll eventually realize that it's best to separate. Then we'll split the kids' time between us."

"Who gets the house?" Henderson was now swabbing the goo on his plate with a piece of toast.

"Diane, of course. She'll have the kids living with her. I'll take an apartment somewhere." Doug had thought this through at about four a.m. while lying in the afterglow of wild sex.

"It's going to cost megabucks, man. You'll be paying for the apartment, the mortgage on your house, the kids." Henderson sniffed and tried to ignore his running nose.

"I know." Doug frowned. "But we're stagnating, man. I think we both need a little freedom."

"Ah. You got a taste of freedom last night and now you want some more, eh? Well, take some advice from someone who knows. It ain't all it's cut out to be."

"Neither is marriage."

"I think you're making a big mistake. Diane is a wonderful woman. You've got great kids. It doesn't look so bad to me." Henderson put one last piece of toast, dripping with egg and ketchup, into his mouth. "Christ, I envy you," he garbled through a mouthful of food. He swallowed, wiped his lips with his napkin and then blew his nose. It honked. "I'm still hungry," he announced. "Want to share an omelette?"

"No. Have my hashbrowns." Doug handed his plate to Henderson, who immediately reached for the ketchup bottle.

"You know," Henderson said, "I'm seriously thinking of marrying Marie when I get back."

Doug rolled his eyes. "Where have I heard that before?"

Henderson ignored Doug's sarcasm. "She'd make the perfect wife. She never argues. She's always sweet. Great with kids. Athletic. Super cook."

"No doubt. But you'll never marry anyone, Henderson. You're having too much fun."

"Yeah." Henderson smiled, then forced a serious expression. "But, it's gonna end. Look at me." He pointed to himself with his knife as he shoveled hash browns into his mouth with his fork. "I'm forty-three. Starting to lose my hair. What's left is turning gray. I'm having a hell of a time keeping the weight off. Any minute now I'm going to turn the corner and it'll be over. No young chicks will be interested."

A tall, buxom young waitress stopped at their table. "How is everything here?" she asked.

"Fine, thank you," Doug replied. She moved on.

"You see." Henderson slammed his knife and fork down in mock disgust. "It's already happening. Not even a twinkle from her. Man, it's time to settle down. I'm losing my touch."

"What about Laura?" It was Doug's turn to lay the guilt trip on Henderson.

"That's over. I had to end it. She was getting way too serious. She was planning holidays together. She even wanted to go to her dad and explain that we were in love. She wanted to live together. Christ, she's still in high school."

Henderson picked up his napkin and wiped his nose again. Then, pushing his plate of breakfast scraps away, he leaned forward, elbows on the table. "Look. My point is, Doug, time is running out for you to be a playboy. You're at an age where playboys are thinking of settling down.

And the reason is that they're getting old. The young chicks aren't interested anymore. So you're better off sticking with what you've got than taking your chances on your own."

Doug contemplated this for a moment. Finally, he said, "It seems to me you're still doing alright, Henderson. And I'll believe your talk of settling down when I see it." He sat back and crossed his arms. "Anyway, it's not just a matter of wanting to get laid. Diane and I have become strangers. We don't do anything together. We don't plan together—hell, we barely talk. Things are civil enough. We just lead separate lives."

"Sounds to me like all the relationship needs is a little work."

They sat silent for awhile. "Why all the interest in me and Diane, anyway? What's it to you?" Doug asked finally.

Henderson sniffed as he considered how to answer. "You see, Doug, you're one of the good guys. You're married, raising a couple of fine boys. Got a good job, a house. You're responsible. I admire that." He touched his chest with the fingers of his right hand and bowed his head for emphasis. "I," he said, "on the other hand, am a shit. Marie is a fantastic woman. She adores me. And whenever I'm away from her, what am I doing? I'm looking for tail. Speaking of which, wait till you see the woman I met last night. Sandra. God, what a body." He shook his head. "Anyway, I don't own a house. I have no money saved. I have no kids. I take no responsibility for anything." He let out a heavy sigh. "Now I'm thinking I've got to change; maybe marry Marie, have some kids. Settle down before I'm too old and no one is interested in me. Be more like you. Then you tell me your life sucks and you want to be more like me. That's not what I want to hear. So, don't be an asshole; patch things up with Diane." He added as an afterthought, "For my sake."

Doug smiled at the idea of his marriage being a model for Henderson. "I don't know, man." He got up from the table. "Let's get out of here. I've got to call Elvis and check in." Henderson picked up the bill and followed Doug to the cashier.

While Doug confirmed with Tom that everything was fine back at the firm, Henderson returned to his own room to check for messages on his voice mail at the office. When he finally arrived at Doug's room to develop a strategy for their lunch meeting with Certified Trust, he was obviously perturbed by one of the messages he had received.

"Bad news?" Doug asked.

"Mm-hm," Henderson confirmed as he stepped over to the window. He peered out between the sheers, like a spy searching for his adversary. "Another bad investment decision," he sighed.

Doug had heard this all before. Always looking for the big winner, Henderson had often invested in the worst loser. "Oh well. Those stocks usually come back. Give it time."

Henderson turned back. "Maybe. But I wanted the dough now. Mario's got a deal he wants me to get into…" He didn't elaborate, just moved to the lounge chair and sat down. "Anyway," he said after a moment, "how do you want to approach lunch?"

They began planning how to convince Certified Trust to send its run-off mortgage work to the firm. When they put their minds to it, the two worked remarkably well together. They complemented each other— Henderson the brilliant eccentric and Branston the faithful pragmatist.

Doug and Henderson met the Vice-President of Mortgages for Certified Trust and the Manager of Claims at a steak house in the heart of downtown Toronto. Henderson had predicted that their guests would take full advantage of the free meal and drink a week's supply of booze. Events proved him right. A round of double vodka martinis—straight up, dry with olives—kick-started the party while the conversation sputtered along about work, the traffic in Toronto and the weather. But into the second round, the gist of the conversation began to change. The waitress's body underwent thorough analysis, rude stories surfaced about secretaries in the Certified Trust office and lewd jokes bounced around the table. Soon everyone was laughing and leering and loading up on another round of martinis.

Then came lunch. They all carved into thick, bloody steaks, lavished butter and sour cream on baked potatoes, and washed it all down with heavy red wine. Henderson and Doug were on a roll, chiding one another, each taking his turn as the straight man. "Branston strikes out so much, he can't lift his bat," Henderson started, followed by Doug's reply, "At least I need two hands to lift my bat, not two fingers." More laughter, great male bonding.

At just the right moment, with the finesse of a championship fighter, Doug eased the conversation around to the topic of the run-off mortgages. He and Henderson combined their charm, pragmatism and irreverence to convince their guests of the firm's expertise in commercial and real-estate litigation. Then, knowing their guests were eager to save on legal fees because it would make them look good in the eyes of their superiors, perhaps even help their cause at salary review time, they mapped out a billing scheme to benefit the client in return for the firm receiving a volume of files.

By the time the post-meal cognacs arrived at the table, Doug and Henderson had extracted a promise from their guests that a deal would be arranged. They toasted its success. Another round was considered, then rejected when they realized the time. They tumbled out of the restaurant into the mid-afternoon darkness that had descended on Toronto. The air was rapier sharp, but the alcohol in their veins offered a shield.

Doug had a meeting scheduled with an old client for the next day, Friday. After that, Henderson and Doug were going to party through the weekend in the excellent company of Mario and his staff before flying home on Sunday. Arrangements had already been made for Doug and Henderson to stay at Mario's apartment. Henderson had a key to the Yorkville apartment, close to Mario's Restaurant and Night Club.

No one was there when they arrived. They found a couple of bedrooms on the second floor, changed out of their suits and into jeans, then settled down in deep leather chairs before the gas fireplace with a couple of tall cool beers from Mario's well-stocked fridge. Henderson and Mario had planned dinner in. Mario was going to bring one of the chefs from the restaurant and a few of the women. After the feast they might move on to the night club—depending, of course, on developments at the apartment.

Doug was into his second beer and was starting to feel a snooze coming on when Mario, six stylish ladies and a corpulent, bearded companion burst through the door. Both men carried a bag of groceries, while the ladies toted a half-dozen bottles of champagne and wine. Introductions were made as Mario opened a bottle of champagne. Among the ladies was Julie, the hostess from the previous evening.

The chubby chef, Giorgio, set up in the kitchen, and soon had water boiling for the pasta and filets of delicate veal sizzling in a lemon and wine sauce. Chopping and dicing—a touch of spice here, a splash of wine there—he danced, surprisingly daintily, around his creations, singing along heartily with the Three Tenors blaring from the stereo: "I like-a to leev in Amereeka." While he fussed and twirled, the ladies set the dining-room table.

Meanwhile, Mario entertained Henderson and Doug in the living-room with anecdotes from the lives of the rich and infamous. He listed the notorious people who had frequented his club and their bizarre requests. He told of lavish parties, of women and men taking hours to appoint themselves in gorgeous tuxedos and gowns, only to rip them off in the back of limousines or the cubicles of washrooms. Then he turned their attention to the ladies in the dining room. He knew each one intimately. Their likes and dislikes, the compromising situations he had found himself in, and how he had managed to extricate himself, were all divulged to Doug and Henderson in excited whispers. He pointed out which ones still loved him, which ones didn't, who owed him and whom he owed. And he advised Doug and Henderson of the ones who were available and the ones who were a waste of time.

When Mario finally got to Julie, he placed his hand on his heart and sighed. "An absolute sweetheart, no, Mark?" he said. Henderson nodded in agreement. Doug wanted to hear more, but he received few details other than the fact that she had dated both men at different times and they found her extraordinary in every way.

Throughout Mario's revelations Doug laughed, cast expectant glances at the ladies in the dining-room and, each time, grinned at his infatuated expression in the mirror on the far side of the dining-room table. All the while, Henderson nodded and smiled dutifully, but he seemed less enthralled than Doug in Mario's confessions. Perhaps he had heard it all before.

"Hey, Mario." Henderson eventually interrupted yet another anecdote. "Where's Joey? I haven't seen him around at all. He travelling again?"

Mario stopped cold. He stared at Henderson while the smile slowly left his face. "Joey Marron," he said and shook his head slowly. "I guess you didn't hear. Shot dead in his car on the expressway." After a moment, he added, "Just the other day."

Mario's and Henderson's eyes locked. "Jesus," Henderson exhaled.

"Drug deal gone wrong," Mario whispered. "That's what they figure."

Henderson's eyes finally broke away from Mario's and found the floor. "Jesus."

"Yeah. What a fucking shame."

For a time a respectful silence hovered over Mario, Henderson and Doug. But eventually it was snapped by a clap of Mario's hands. "Well. When are we going to eat?" He strolled into the kitchen. "How long till dinner, Giorgio?"

The chef held up his hand, indicating five minutes.

"Enough time for an appetizer," Mario announced, returning to the living-room.

He opened the silver cigarette box that sat on the coffee-table. Doug had last seen marijuana in his university days, but he quickly recognized the green and brown clippings which spilled onto the table. Mario dug into the stash, pulled out a package of rolling papers and expertly rolled a pinch of marijuana into a paper. He licked the joint, then lit it with his gold lighter. A pungent fume filled the air, and like an aromatic Pied Piper, drew the ladies into the living room. The joint was passed around the group; even Doug took a drag, his throat writhing in rejection as the hot, acrid smoke burned down into his lungs. He coughed and sputtered and exhaled most of it, then grabbed his champagne glass for a huge swallow to douse the fire. The others were laughing and coughing, trying to talk without letting the air out of their lungs. Doug sat back in his chair while a subtle buzz wrapped its fleece around him. He refused the second pass of the joint. In his university days he had learned the fine line between getting high and becoming paranoid.

Soon Giorgio appeared from the kitchen with a great platter bearing curls of pasta in tomato sauce. He called everyone to the table. Mad with hunger, they scrambled for chairs. Doug remembered the abbreviated background Mario had provided about Julie and managed to grab a chair beside her. She looked radiant. The platter circulated; wine was poured and everyone talked and laughed at once. Bits and pieces of conversations orbited the table: Giorgio's weight, Mario's ex-wife, the nightclub, last night, the party after closing, when people got to bed, with whom, when they got up, how they felt, how they spent the day.

The din swept over Doug like a swirling breeze. He smiled and laughed and looked around the table at the flushed faces, the huge toothy smiles and the eyes watery and wide. More pasta, a plate of veal, more wine, talk and laughter. He gobbled the food, relishing it; he slurped the wine. Almost in a dream, he noticed Julie turn to him.

"You left early last night," she said.

Doug laughed and nodded. He put more food in his mouth, but did not answer.

"I missed you. Where did you go?" She gave him a playful tap.

He sensed that Julie was flirting with him. Knowing he was a little out of control, he tried to concentrate in order to make a positive impression on her. "I went to my hotel," he said, a guilty smirk creeping over his lips.

"Oh, that's right! I saw you dancing with Jenna." She shook her index finger at him and frowned. "I thought you were a married man."

A distant beacon of reason was attempting to pierce the fog in Doug's brain. He had hoped that his antics the night before had been more anonymous. The idea that Julie and maybe the others at the dinner table knew what he had been up to made him uncomfortable. But, just as he was about to explain, Henderson—who, to this point, had been uncharacteristically quiet and pensive—spoke up.

"Doug saw God last night, didn't you big guy?" The crowd at the table instantly turned their attention to Doug. "Tell us mortals your path to enlightenment, how marriage cannot stand in the way of destiny," he continued to general laughter.

"Do I know the temptress?" Mario asked.

"The famous Jenna," answered Julie, shooting a knowing glance towards Mario.

"Ah! A fine choice, Signor Branston." He raised his glass to Doug. "A toast," he said to everyone in the room. "To Doug and his incipient walk on the wild side!"

Everyone at the table raised their glasses in Doug's direction. "To Doug!" they chimed and took long gulps of their wine.

A shadow of guilt worked its way into Doug's conscience. Perhaps he could justify to himself, and even to Henderson, why he slept with Jenna, but the others around the table did not know Diane, or how his relationship with her was dying. All they knew was that he, a married guy, had slept with Jenna, a nightclub regular, within twenty-four hours of leaving his wife and kids on the other side of the country. That was a sordid spin on the event, but how was he going to explain himself to this group?

Luckily, Mario interrupted the focus on Doug by accidentally spilling red wine on the white linen blouse of Henderson's conquest from the previous night, Sandra. She graciously refused Mario's offer to suck the wine out of the fabric. Instead, she ran to the kitchen and soaked the front of her blouse with soda water. When she returned to the table, Henderson suggested she remove the blouse to let it dry while Giorgio, standing, slightly stooped forward, with a neatly-folded napkin limply lying over his outstretched forearms—like a manservant recommending a suit to his lord—formally offered to dry Sandra's blouse. She ignored them all and sat back down; the wet blouse clung to her like spandex, leaving Doug and the good samaritans to enjoy the view of her, obviously naked underneath.

The doorbell rang—four peals from harmonic chimes. Without hesitation, Giorgio sprung from the table to open the door for Tony, in black from the top of his slicked-back hair to the tip of his cowboy boots.

Mario belched a greeting, and pushed his chair away from the table. He dragged his napkin across his rosy lips, slid it under his glasses in a strenuous effort to wipe his eyelids and, finally, asked with a sly smile, "Anyone for dessert?" While his eyes, now slightly squinted in inquiry, surveyed the guests at the table, he released another belch and called out, "Tony, what do you have on your dessert tray tonight?"

"This is my exit cue," Julie whispered to Doug from the corner of her mouth while she coyly smiled for Mario's passing glance.

"Why?" Doug asked, sober concern creeping into his brain. Julie leaving just when he detected a glimmer of attraction between them was distressing.

She slowly turned to face him, the smile still pinned to her cheeks. "Wait till you see what's for dessert," she breathed, without moving her lips.

Giorgio was already on his feet piling up the plates at his end of the table. Julie reached in front of Doug, grabbed his plate and passed it down to Giorgio. While the others passed their plates down, Sandra and

Henderson stood to remove the utensils from the table. She jostled him playfully, then stepped ahead of him before they passed through the kitchen door, and stuck out her right leg to prevent him from getting by her. Henderson sneaked his left arm around her waist, at the same time subtly brushing his crotch against her buttocks. She looked at him over her shoulder, smiled and tilted her hips back against him.

Within minutes the glass tabletop was bare. Tony now moved to the head of the table and, as some guests reseated themselves, removed a vial from his breast pocket, opened it with a flourish and neatly poured out a palmful of pristine white powder. It sat on the glass, stark and alluring, like a lone iceberg in an expanse of shimmering black arctic sea. The crowd oohed in unison as if Tony had just produced an exquisite Tiramisu with lots of dancing cream and chocolate.

"Dessert!" Tony announced.

Although Doug had never actually seen cocaine before, he tried to hide his surprise, tried to retain a worldly look like the others around the table, but from the corner of his eye he saw Henderson watching him, a grin of anticipation on his face, a challenge. *What do you think, Branston?* Henderson's eyes asked. *What are you going to do now? Are you really ready to play with the big boys?* Doug searched his sluggish brain for an answer while he continued to stare at the pile of white powder.

"Mario, it was a wonderful dinner," Julie said. She got up from her chair. "I'll pass on dessert. I should be at the club, anyway."

"Julie, you don't have to run off," Mario said. "There's lots of champagne I can offer you." But it was a half-hearted attempt to have Julie stay. Mario obviously knew her, and knew that she would leave.

"Thanks anyway," she replied. "Are you all coming to the club after?"

"Absolutely."

Doug leapt to his feet. "I think I'll go with Julie. Thanks, Mario. Great dinner. See you at the club."

No one bothered to argue that Doug should stay. In fact, after a moment, Henderson suggested, "Maybe I'll go with you. Wouldn't want to leave you alone after your performance last night." As the others around the table chuckled, Henderson rose from his seat.

"Are you kidding," Mario laughed. "You can't pass on dessert." His smile faded. "Besides, we've got some business to discuss."

With a self-conscious shrug, Henderson sat back down.

Outside, heavy snow was falling, creating an unusual calm on the street. Ghostly, silent traffic approached from the distance, gradually appearing from the gloom as the tight crunching sound of tires compacting snow stole the odd quiet of the night. Cars passed slowly, tentatively feeling their way along like hearses in a funeral procession. Their windshield wipers slid silently back and forth, laboriously clearing away the slush for the shadowy figures inside.

Doug and Julie stood under the canopy over the entrance to Mario's apartment block, their collars turned up against the cold. One of the phantom-like vehicles crawling down the street towards them had an extra white glow on its roof. Doug flagged the taxi down and they climbed into the back seat. As Doug instructed the driver to head for the nightclub, he was conscious that Julie had moved close to him, perhaps trying to keep warm. He turned to her, put his arm over her shoulder and asked, "You okay?"

"Yeah." She thought for a moment. "I guess I have mixed feelings about leaving." Turning her head away from Doug, she stared out the side window.

"How so?"

She continued to gaze out the window, even though the view was rapidly becoming obscured by the collecting snow. "Oh, I suppose I miss the party."

"So why leave? I'm a little new to all this, but it just seems to be a group of people having a good time." Doug had heard enough to know that cocaine was a prominent part of the party scene among the affluent. He was unsure if it was for him, but he failed to see why Julie needed to leave just because it appeared.

"I've done the coke thing," she said. "It was hell kicking the habit so I don't need the temptation. Besides, it's not just the coke. The coke's the teaser. I just find the whole thing makes me feel uncomfortable."

"Hmm. I think I'm missing something here."

"Well then, it's best you left with me."

The side windows were completely obscured by a layer of snow now. Julie turned back to face Doug. In the darkness of the cab he could make out only the side of her cheek, but it was intensely illuminated by the street lights through the front windshield. The pores of her skin were distinct, as were the transparent, microscopic hairs that stood on end, frozen by the cold. With his eyes, Doug traced the outline of her face, over her high cheekbones and along her jaw. The dark, the closeness, the cold—all contributed to a sense of intimacy. He moved his hand to touch her face as he bent to kiss her.

"Don't," she said.

Doug still let his hand brush the hair away from Julie's cheek, but the moment was gone. She shifted her position, straightened up, and moved slightly away from him. Facing forward, she searched out the front windshield to see where they were.

"What did I do?" Doug asked.

"Forget it. There's Mario's up ahead." She sat up on the edge of her seat and reached around for her purse. "I've got to make sure everything is working smoothly on the floor. I'll see you later. Do you mind covering the cab?"

The taxi came to a stop in front of the nightclub and she hopped out. By the time Doug had pulled out his wallet, she had disappeared through the front entrance.

When he entered the club, he saw Julie already deep in conversation with the hostess at the front desk. They were looking at the reservation list; Julie seemed to be engrossed in directing operations, for she hardly noticed Doug walk by her on his way to the Lair. He greeted the bouncer at the foot of the staircase like a long lost pal, then climbed the stairs to the second floor, ordered a tumbler of scotch over ice from the Lair's bartender, and leaned against the balcony to watch Julie at work on the floor below.

Reluctantly, his eyes left Julie and flitted over the crowd on the dance floor. A black silk dress suddenly caught his attention, causing him to perk up. Ah yes, Doug was down but not out; Jenna to the rescue. He sloshed back the scotch and made sure his shirt was tucked in before sauntering back down the stairs.

An hour passed before some of the crowd from Mario's apartment appeared at the nightclub. Doug and Jenna had been dancing close on the dance floor, their bodies remembering the night before. Now, they stood on the balcony and watched Mario enter the club, one arm around Henderson and the other around Sandra. Henderson looked slightly uncomfortable, perhaps at the prospect of Mario stealing Sandra away. Behind the late arrivals lurked Tony, but Giorgio and the other women were nowhere to be seen. "Left in the dust," chuckled Doug to himself.

Mario was the first up the stairs. He gave Jenna and Doug an enthusiastic greeting, then conducted animated introductions of Jenna to Henderson and Sandra. In a sideways comment that only Doug and Henderson were able hear, Mario complimented Doug on his choice.

"Much less trouble than Julie, don't you think, Mark?" Mario gave Henderson a wink.

Henderson smiled and nodded.

At Mario's invitation, the group went into his office just off the Lair. Tony, always in the shadows, followed them in and shut the door. Again he produced the vial, pouring the white powder onto the table in the centre of the room. This time, Doug was ready. He watched closely as each of the others inhaled the cocaine, Jenna's expertise being particularly impressive. When his turn came, he copied her, inhaling just like a pro the two lines Tony had made for him, one into each nostril, through a rolled-up five dollar bill.

Suddenly, he took off. No longer a voyeur, he was a voyager going a thousand miles an hour, touching down now and then, planting pearls of wisdom, then blasting off. Flying, bursting with power like a marathoner, like a boxer, not needing rest, going the distance. Dragging the crowd with him, under his wing. Jenna joined him on the odyssey. They swirled on the dance floor, flashed with the lights, sang to the music at the top of their lungs. Mario was there too, laughing and pointing, with Sandra, dancing like Fred Astaire and Ginger Rogers: taps and twirls and jive. Time flew alongside, a navigator, urging them on, directing them past obstacles without losing velocity, sweeping the night by like a swirling Milky Way. And in a second, Doug was back at Mario's apartment, with Jenna, charting the universe in the bedroom upstairs.

CHAPTER 6

His reflection loomed like an apparition in the window of the airplane, though the details of his face were lost to the view of the sky. It was just as well, considering the way he felt. Henderson dozed beside him with headphones on. At least they were in business class.

He blew his nose, lay back in the seat and tried to think of nothing, but his mind kept coming back to the conversation he had had with Henderson when they first got on the plane. Once again, Henderson had suggested to Doug that he consider the events in Toronto as a brief walk on the wild side, an aberration, a unique experience to be filed away with his other secrets. Now, with it out of his system, he should dedicate himself to rekindling his romance with Diane. But Doug didn't see it that way. On the contrary, the excitement in Toronto had convinced him more than ever that he had to leave Diane. There was too much happening out there, too many thrills that he had missed. People were living, while he was just existing. Certainly, he was being selfish, avoiding responsibilities; he knew that. But the seed was firmly planted now and all he wanted to do was give it room to grow.

Henderson was right in one sense: Doug was getting old. All the more reason to make the break now while he still had time to live unencumbered by anything but his own needs and desires. Who was going to suffer? Diane had her own life which excluded him. The kids he would see on weekends and he would talk to them regularly on the phone. Hell, he would probably have more conversations with them once he was away from home than he had now. Contrary to what Henderson thought, Doug was sure that his reasons for leaving Diane were more profound than simply wanting to spend more time in the candy store. He wanted to get a clear shot at really experiencing life. Who could begrudge him that? Certainly not Mark Henderson. What Doug wanted was close to what Henderson had. Sure, Henderson had Marie at home, but that was just a front. At least Doug's intentions showed some integrity. He planned to make a clean break with Diane, be forthright, rather than deceitful as Henderson was with Marie.

Doug decided that he would speak to Diane as soon as he got home, then take his still-packed suitcase and check into a hotel.

By the time the airplane landed and they had retrieved their luggage, it was nearly eight at night. They shared a limousine to Doug's house where Henderson actually wished him luck. He asked that Doug wait until the following day before telling him the details of the confrontation with Diane. Henderson explained that he was not going immediately home; he "had a stop to make." And if Marie ever asked, Doug was to confirm that they had been together for the evening. "Guys don't tell on guys," he reminded Doug.

With some trepidation, Doug climbed the stairs to the front door of his house. He had thought it over many times and was sure of his decision, but he knew the discussion with Diane was going to be rough. He turned the key in the door and stepped into the house. It was quiet inside, except for the distant sound of electronic music. As usual, the only light was the other-worldly phosphorescence of the television set filtering through from the adjoining family room. Doug strode through the front hall and into the kitchen. He heard music: the hypnotic, repetitive melody to some video game. On the edge of the coffee table, too close to the television, their faces lit up like x-rays, sat Doug's boys furiously fingering the game controllers they held in their hands, totally unaware that he had just walked in.

"Hi guys," he said. "How're you doing?"

His younger son immediately dropped his controller and leapt into Doug's arms. "Hey, dad. How was the trip?"

"Adrian!" Matthew screamed. "That's not fair. You can't just quit like that. I was beating you." Without turning his attention from the television, he added. "Welcome home, dad."

Adrian laughed. "No, you weren't. You never do."

"Come on, Adrian. One more. Come on, you chicken. You know I'll beat you this time."

The younger brother could not ignore the challenge. He slid from Doug's grasp and retrieved his controller from the floor. "I'll beat you one more time, then that's it, you loser."

Doug smiled while he leaned over to kiss each boy's cheek.

"You bring us anything?" Adrian asked, his full concentration now directed to the television screen.

"Sorry. Not this time. Where's Mom?"

"Upstairs," Matthew said before groaning painfully.

"Gotcha!"

"Shut up you little puke, or I'll beat the crap out of you!"

Doug took a deep breath and headed up the stairs to look for Diane. He found her in the computer room, sitting on the ergonomically correct chair, typing as madly on the keyboard as his boys were on their controllers down stairs. Her gaze reluctantly left the screen and focused on Doug.

"Hi, dear," she said, a slight suggestion in her voice that she was happy—or at least relieved—to see him back. "Good to see you home." She turned back to the screen. "Just let me finish this e-mail and then you can tell me about your trip."

Doug stood in the doorway watching her and wondering how he was going to start the conversation that he had rehearsed all the way home from Toronto.

"I hope you don't mind," Diane said while continuing to work on the e-mail. "Now that you're home, I thought I might go for a late work-out at the club."

"No, not at all." Doug scolded himself for the twinge of relief he felt at the thought that Diane was planning to go out. "But..." He hesitated. "There is something I need to talk to you about. And it really can't wait."

Diane finished the e-mail and pressed the send button. "O.K." She turned and looked at him quizzically. The expression on his face was full of concern. "What? What is it?"

"I think maybe we should talk in the bedroom," he said, while motioning her out of the computer room.

Diane immediately followed Doug to the bedroom. "Did something happen in Toronto, Douglas—with you and Mark?" She asked with incipient agitation.

"Well, it's difficult..."

"Oh! My god," she mumbled.

In the bedroom, she sat on the bed. Struggling for composure she crossed her legs and rested her hands in her lap, waiting for Doug to speak. It appeared as if she wanted to blurt something out, but was biting her tongue.

Doug put his hands in his pockets, and looked up at the ceiling, a habit he had developed when addressing a judge in court. It helped him focus on what he was about to say. "Look, Diane. I've been thinking a lot recently. You know. About us. About our relationship." He looked down from the ceiling at Diane. Her face had lost that quizzical look. It was blank now, emotionless, still watching him. He looked back up to the ceiling. "I think we've grown apart. I don't get the feeling that we're a couple. Do you know what I mean? We hardly see each other anymore. We seem to be passing all the time—one coming in, the other going out. We don't know what the other is doing. And we don't seem to really care. Am I wrong?"

He looked down again at Diane, ridiculously hoping she might give him some help in trying to explain his feelings. Her head was now bowed. Falling to one knee, he placed his hands on hers and peered up into her eyes. They were closed, her eyelashes wet with silent tears.

"Diane?" He waited for her response, ready for her to fly at him, to blame him for the failures in their marriage: he was never at home, he never cared about what she was doing, he never did anything to help around the house, he took her for granted, he never gave her any credit, he showed no affection towards her—God knows women need affection; or he was ready for her to dissolve into uncontrollable tears and beg him to try again. They could work it out, take a holiday, just the two of them, sort out their relationship, talk about their problems, rekindle the old flame.

She opened her eyes to look at him. "No," she said softly.

"Sorry?"

"No." She paused to take a deep breath. "You're not wrong. I've felt it too. I kept thinking that I should talk to you, but I didn't know how to start."

Doug was speechless. Her response was totally unexpected. They both sat silently, hands and heads together.

Finally, Diane asked in barely a whisper, "What are we going to do?"

Feeling less sure of himself than when he had entered the room, he still knew that he must persevere. "I think we need to separate for a while," he proposed. "Get our bearings. Decide what we want."

Diane offered no resistance.

Doug continued. "I was going to go to a hotel tonight. But I can stay if you want. I can move out in the morning. That might give us a chance to decide what we're going to tell the kids."

Diane nodded and sniffled. "Yes." Sighing deeply, she added. "You know, I really need to get out of here for awhile. Get some exercise. Work this all out." She shook her head, then jumped up, went back to the mirror and made a valiant attempt to clear away the tears from her face. Kissing Doug on the cheek as she passed, she headed towards the door. "Please stay tonight," she called over her shoulder. "We can work this out later. I just need a little time right now."

Doug stood motionless in the bedroom listening to Diane's footsteps as she descended the stairs. He heard her muffled instructions to the children. Only the sound of the door closing as she left the house broke the spell. He realized, then, that he had been staring at himself in the mirror. The deed was done and it was relatively painless. So why did he look so forlorn and alone?

He went down to the kitchen and sorted among the bottles in the liquor cabinet. With a full tumbler of scotch and ice in his hand he marshalled the kids into bed, then sat in front of the TV and watched mindlessly. His thoughts were elsewhere, going over the discussion with Diane, analyzing her response, planning what would happen next. Finally, overcome with fatigue from the excitement of the past few days, the magnitude of the decision he had made, and the scotch, he stumbled upstairs and climbed into bed. He was asleep within minutes.

Julie was calling Doug from just over the hill. He heard her voice very clearly but could not see her. Henderson was with him. But as soon as Henderson heard Julie's voice, he turned his back on Doug and walked away. Doug yelled at him to stop, but he seemed not to hear. He kept walking into the distance where Doug could see a young girl waiting for him. Doug ran to the top of the hill to find Julie. When he got there, though, he saw only Jenna. She was dancing for him, slowly, provocatively. He wanted to go to her, but he could still hear Julie's voice and it held him back. He was standing at the top of the hill watching Jenna dance when suddenly a noise rang out from the direction in which Henderson had gone. There was a loud ring and then another.

Doug's eyelids parted just slightly. He gazed around the charcoal darkness of the bedroom before he recognized the glow of the digital clock on the night table. It read 12:15 a.m. The telephone rang again. He picked up the receiver and croaked "Hello," into the mouthpiece.

An agitated voice responded, but it was muffled and hard to make out. "Doug? Is that you? Were you asleep?" There was a pause, then, "Oh, I'm sorry. It's Marie."

Doug sat up in his bed and turned the phone the right way around. "What is it? What's happened?"

"That's what I'd like to know. Where's Mark? Didn't he fly back with you?"

With consciousness came caution. Doug hesitated while he thought about how best to respond.

After a moment, Marie repeated, "Well. Where the hell is he?" Her words were laden with suspicion.

The image of Henderson walking away from Doug was still vivid. He reached to turn on the bedside light but it was hidden in the darkness. "I...uh...I just left him, Marie."

"Sure, Doug. Well he hasn't come home yet. Did he stop off at his little love nest?" She yelled into the receiver. "Do you think I don't know about it? What am I, an idiot?"

While Doug slowly surveyed the woolly, dark, motionless room, he ad libbed. "No, no, Marie, that's not it. The...uh...the flight was delayed. We just got in. Mark just dropped me off."

"Is that so?" Marie asked sarcastically. "Then the airline must have got it wrong when I phoned to find out when the plane landed."

"Marie. Look—"

"Don't say anything else, Doug. I get the picture." She hung up the phone.

He continued to stare into space with bewilderment. What was that all about? And, more importantly, why was Henderson's detour on the way home taking so long? It was unlike Henderson to allow so much room for speculation.

Eventually, the dead telephone line began to buzz. After three or four attempts he found the invisible cradle for the receiver and hung up the phone, then felt for Diane beside him. Where was she? Still groggy, he made his way downstairs to see if her car was in the driveway. As he got to the foot of the stairs he saw the eerie light from the television screen flickering against the darkness of the kitchen. He walked towards the light and found Diane on the couch in the family room staring at the TV screen, her face soaked with tears.

"Diane," he whispered as he sat on the edge of the couch. She made no attempt to acknowledge him.

"Diane. Don't worry. You know it's the best for both of us."

She turned her stare to him, but said nothing.

"You'll see. Everything will be just fine."

After a moment she heaved a heavy sigh. "I can't imagine how," she whispered with defeat.

"Come on, let's go to bed. We can take a fresh look at things in the morning."

They stood up together and started for the stairs.

CHAPTER 7

The clouds lay lugubriously over the city from horizon to horizon, a thousand feet thick, like an ocean in the sky. The heavy darkness was brightening ever so slightly in the east, but it was only a lighter shade of gray. On this typical winter morning there would be no peek at the sun, no islands of blue. The buildings of downtown appeared slowly, timidly, from the shadow of the gloom; their lights tiny and pathetic, their ramparts sulking drearily against the brooding sky, stark, defeated, devoid of any majesty.

Doug was always amazed at how immense the sky appeared when it was totally overcast. Maybe it was because there was no real contrast between the sky and the cityscape—just one large canvas of gray hues. It was raining, that steady, endless, mind-numbing patter on the windshield of the taxi, as he stared at nothing through the droplets that slid across the glass. On the seat beside him sat his suitbag, still packed with the clothes he had taken to Toronto.

In the dreary, damp darkness before any light revealed the disappointing morning, Doug and Diane had lain in bed discussing how to approach the children. Doug found the entire conversation disconcerting. Side by side, staring at the ceiling, they had conferred in a terse, pragmatic way on what the children should be told. Throughout, Diane had remained edgy and distant. Even so, they had managed to agree that they would tell the children at the breakfast table that Dad was going to move out of the house for awhile. He and Mom saw little of each other these days; Dad was working hard and Mom was busy with her volunteer work. They would tell the children that Dad and Mom continued to be good friends, and were just unsure if they still loved each other. The only way to find out was if they lived apart for awhile. They would assure the children that it had nothing to do with them, that Dad and Mom still loved them very much, and that Dad would still be around the house at times.

But Reginald Wren had spoiled the plan. He had phoned while Doug was showering off the discomfort of his discussion with Diane. Why she had let the answering machine take the message was a mystery, although the timing of the call was certainly poor. No doubt overcome by the stress of events, she had chosen to tune out the world. "The phone rang," she had mumbled from beneath the pillow when he left the bathroom. "Better see if there's a message." Doug had trundled down the stairs to the kitchen where the answering machine was located. He had listened to the crackling voice of Reginald Wren advising that the firm was having an extremely important partners' meeting at eight-thirty a.m. and Doug had to be there.

That seemed odd. Larson Wren hardly ever had a morning meeting, and when it did, it was announced well in advance, not at seven-thirty a.m. when half the partners were still in bed. He had phoned Wren back but the line was busy, so he had dialed Henderson's and Marie's number, but there was no answer. Maybe the meeting had been called while he was in Toronto and Wren had only been able to reach him this morning. That might explain the early phone call. But why was it imperative that he be there? Typically one or two partners missed meetings, especially if they had just returned from a business trip. What topic was so earth-shattering that attendance at a partners' meeting was mandatory?

So Doug left for the office before talking to the kids. He and Diane had agreed that he take some clothes, and sometime during the day check into a hotel. He would come home for dinner, at which time they would explain their situation to the children.

The cab pulled up to the front of the office tower. Doug paid the driver, and with his suitbag in hand, gingerly jumped out of the cab to avoid the torrent of water running along the edge of the curb. Without an overcoat or an umbrella—true to his belief that real locals spurn them—he dashed through the doors of the building, crossed the lobby and stepped into the first elevator available. Right behind him strode one of his partners, Peter Francis, deep in thought and oblivious to Doug's presence as usual.

"Peter. G'morning. This meeting been set for awhile?" Doug asked with inexplicable dread brewing in the pit of his stomach.

Peter was a tall, well-built man with a slightly awkward presence that suggested shyness or perhaps insecurity. Accentuating this awkwardness was what appeared to be absent-mindedness. In fact, Peter had a good mind, but it tended to be occupied analyzing esoteric legal issues to the exclusion of happenings around him.

Now, he filed away his inner thoughts, turned his focus to the source of the question and finally recognized Doug. "No," he said after a moment's reflection. "I got the call early this morning. It's just unbelievable. I am in shock."

As the elevator doors began to close, Doug felt the bubbling dread rise to his throat. He was about to ask what Peter was talking about when another lawyer from a different firm blocked the closing doors and stepped into the elevator.

"Gentlemen," he said. "I am truly sorry. He was a good lawyer. It's very sad. We will all miss him."

Doug knew now that something was terribly wrong. "What are you talking about?" he blurted out.

The two other lawyers looked at him with surprise. "Don't you know?" Peter gasped. "Mark Henderson was killed last night. Somewhere in the West End."

There it was, the explanation for Henderson's tardiness in arriving home the previous night. The mounting anxiety Doug had felt moments before dissipated, leaving a sinking emptiness. Henderson, his confidant, his mentor, his good friend, was dead. "What happened?" he asked.

Both lawyers shook their heads. "I have no idea," Peter said. "I guess we'll find out now."

The doors of the elevator opened at the thirty-second floor. Like a zombie, Doug followed Peter out into the lobby. The other lawyer continued to extend condolences from the elevator as its doors closed. Meanwhile, Peter and Doug headed to the main boardroom in silence. Most of the partners were already seated when the two arrived. They all turned expectantly when Doug walked in, but he acknowledged no one. Staring into nothingness, he walked to the far end of the boardroom table and sat down.

After a moment's silence, Alan Wadsworth, one of the senior partners, a brilliant lawyer, logical and objective, but lacking any real sympathy, spoke. "Do you know what happened last night, Doug?"

The room remained silent while everyone waited for the answer. Doug stared at his hands folded on the table in front of him. "No," he said turning his palms up in a shrugging gesture.

Alan patted the little tuft of hair on his forehead that guarded against the bald spot advancing from the rear. Age was finally catching up with him, which in the legal profession was considered a good thing. Lawyers always believed that some gray hair helped convince a judge of the correctness of their position. If this was true, then Alan's deteriorating appearance, now balding and chunky, was, at last, giving him the stature before the courts that he deserved.

"Were you with him?" Alan asked.

Doug shook his head slowly and continued to stare at his hands. "No."

"When did you last see him?"

For some reason that Doug failed to understand, he was feeling guilty, as if somehow he was to blame for Henderson's death. "We took a limousine from the airport together and he dropped me off at home."

"Did he tell you where he was going?" Jerry Nelson asked, interrupting the flow of Alan's questions, unable to let Alan conduct the interrogation alone. Jerry was junior to Doug in the firm, but had an ego the size of all the partners put together. Although he had seldom appeared in court, he was convinced of his superior ability to wrestle the truth from a witness. He looked at Doug now, his eyebrows raised and eyelids almost closed, with that air of pretension that Doug loathed.

While considering Nelson's question, Doug pictured Henderson's deep gray eyes boring in on him, demanding his acceptance of the law that men must live by: "Guys don't tell on guys." But it was too late to protect Henderson now.

"Well, he said he was stopping somewhere before he went home," Doug replied.

"Where?" Jerry asked quickly, moving in for the kill. He tilted his over-sized head forward like Boris Karloff, causing a shadow to cover his eyes.

"I don't know," Doug responded, while suspecting it was the little apartment in the West End.

"Why did he want to stop on the way home?" Alan asked in an attempt to regain the cross-examination from Jerry.

"He didn't say."

Alan and Jerry were warming to their role as inquisitors. They sat forward in their chairs now with their elbows on the table. Alan stayed motionless, his eyes watching Doug intently as he systematically pursued the facts. Jerry shifted about in his chair and frequently ran his hands through the tight curls of his short brown hair. When he posed his questions, the words shot from his mouth in excited rapid-fire phrases while his eyes darted amongst his partners, searching for approval. After each question he waited for the answer, nervously stroking his scraggly moustache with his index finger.

Everyone else in the room was quiet, listening intently to the exchange, genuinely interested in learning the circumstances of Henderson's death, even if some of the information was gained through the pomposity of Jerry Nelson.

Suddenly, the boardroom door swung open and Reginald Wren entered with a file of loose papers in his hand. He uttered an abrupt greeting as he took his usual seat at the head of the boardroom table. Alan easily turned his attention away from Doug and towards Wren. Jerry managed to remain silent, although visibly disappointed that his opportunity to exhibit his art of cross-examination had been cut short.

Wren opened the file on the table in front of him while waiting to make sure he had everyone's attention. Although he was a tall man, his habit of slouching forward in his chair with his elbows far apart and hands flat on the table, which allowed him to read his papers without putting his glasses on, made him look small and old.

Unlike many of his partners, Wren had truly liked Henderson, admiring Henderson's legal ability and quick mind. He had despaired over Henderson's chaotic personal life and had never tired of trying to direct him to what Wren thought was the appropriate path in life and within the firm. His partners were less patient. Doug suspected that there were those around the table who were glad to lose Henderson as a partner, even though the circumstances were unfortunate. But Wren was certainly not one of them. Today he appeared more hunched than normal, his chin almost resting on his hands as he scanned the faces around him.

He took a slow breath. Once satisfied that he had everyone's attention, he began. "This is a very sad day. We have lost one of our partners. A man of exceptional intellect. An excellent lawyer. A character who, no doubt, created turmoil at times within the firm, caused some friction within the partnership, but always had the best interests of the firm in mind. He challenged us, made us look at things from all sides and not narrowly. He promoted the firm with clients and other lawyers. He helped to mould the good reputation that this firm has in the legal community. We were lucky to have had an opportunity to practise law with him and to know him. I, for one, will miss him."

Rumblings of "hear, hear" and "Amen" came from around the table. At the same time a wave of sadness swept over Doug. His throat tightened into a large knot. He was going to miss Henderson deeply. They had understood each other, enjoyed the same things, felt the same way about people. Every day they had talked and schemed and laughed and teased each other, respected each other and admired how the other chose to live his life. Together they had provided both sides of the equation. Henderson had tried to make Doug a better person and Doug liked to think that maybe he had done the same for Henderson. Without Henderson, Doug's world was going to be a lot emptier.

Wren continued. "I spoke to Frank Holden early this morning. It appears that his daughter, Laura, was with Mark when he was killed last night."

"Oh. Isn't that just fucking great," said Vince Brodski, Doug's most cantankerous partner and the one who did much of Holden's work.

"Please let me finish what I have to say without interruption," Wren said sharply. "There are some complications that I need to get on the table, and then we can have a general discussion." He waited for a moment then began reading from notes he had in the file. "Laura Holden was found unconscious near Mark's body in the lobby of an apartment building in the West End. She had received a blow to the right side of the head. Mark had a single bullet hole in his chest that apparently was fatal." Wren lifted his eyes briefly then peered back down at the pages in front of him. "She had a gun in her hand. I understand it has been identified as the one that shot Mark."

A collective gasp was heard around the table. In order to stop the incipient murmurs, Wren said in a slightly raised voice, "The police are still investigating, but it is quite possible that she will be charged with Mark's murder. They think there may have been some kind of lovers' quarrel."

He raised his eyes from his notes once more. In order to add emphasis to what he was about to say, he looked from partner to partner around the table, demanding their full attention. Finally, he announced, "Holden wants us to investigate this matter on his daughter's behalf and defend her in the event that she is charged."

The ensuing shock of silence was finally broken by Jerry. "Well, how can we possibly do that?" he spouted. "It's an obvious conflict of interest."

"How so, Jerry?" Wren asked with a note of exasperation.

"Henderson was a partner of this firm. Now we are to defend his murderer? How are we to provide the best defence for her if her victim was our business colleague?" Jerry folded his arms across his chest.

"You're assuming she's guilty. She's not. The law considers her innocent until proven guilty. Obviously we want anyone who commits a heinous crime convicted—whether the victim is our partner or not—but if a man is charged with the crime and comes to us to defend him, what is our obligation? We provide him with the best defence we can in the circumstances."

"But the conflict is that we are at risk of allowing our emotions to get in the way of the best defence that Laura Holden is entitled to."

"Perhaps. But every lawyer defending someone charged with a heinous crime has that same conflict. His obligation is to remove himself from the case once he believes that he is no longer able to provide the best defence possible. And maybe that will occur at some point with this defence. But right now, I think everyone in this room would like to be sure that the person who really murdered Mark be caught. What better way to ensure that happens than to force the prosecution to prove its case beyond a reasonable doubt?"

Wren waited for further argument, but Jerry was digesting what had just been said.

"Besides," Wren continued, "a conflict may be overcome by the client accepting that it exists. Holden certainly knows that Mark was a partner of this firm, and he knows that we as much as anyone want the murderer caught. Yet he still wants us to defend his daughter. I might add that he is the largest client of this firm, and we want to keep his business. This may be incentive enough for us to provide Laura with the best defence possible. So, unless anyone has a more compelling argument why we cannot agree to act for Laura Holden, we will."

"I understand what you're saying, Reg," said Alan. "But it still makes me feel uncomfortable. I just don't think I can act for her. But I won't stand in the way of someone else here."

Wren looked at the blank faces around the table. No one appeared desperate to take on the task of being Laura Holden's counsel. It had the makings of a thankless job requiring a huge amount of time, and once the matter went to court the publicity would be overwhelming. Her counsel would have to field all sorts of questions relating to her relationship with Henderson, as well as questions relating to the firm's awkward position of defending the person accused of murdering a partner. And, if she was ultimately convicted, the firm would likely lose Holden's business anyway.

Jerry broke the silence that had settled on the room. "I'm with Alan. The conflict remains apparent to me, Reg, even if it is not actual. In all good conscience I could not act for Laura Holden. It just wouldn't feel right."

"Thank you, Mr. Nelson," Wren said. "Frankly, I would not have proposed that you handle the defence. The circumstances are just too complicated and high-profile for someone as junior as you." He looked to Alan. "I am disappointed, Alan, that you do not feel up to it. I had hoped that you would be prepared to take this on."

Alan was stubborn, an attribute that made him a good lawyer. If he was sure he was right about a position, he pressed it until a judge accepted it. His decision against acting for Laura Holden was immutable.

"Well, this is just fucking great," Vince grunted. "I bill more than any other lawyer in this goddamn firm. And it's primarily on the back of Holden's business. If we lose him as a client, I don't bill so much and you assholes don't make so much."

He reached into the pocket of his sports jacket and pulled out a pipe.

Although the office tower had been declared a non-smoking building years before, no one dared enforce the rule with Vince. He was a big, burly, black-bearded Bulgarian who had grown up on the streets. His expertise was contract negotiations, and his success resulted as much from his physical presence as his legal talents.

He took a handful of pipe tobacco from a pouch in his breast pocket, rubbed it between his hands and let the shreds fall out onto the boardroom table. Then he swept the tobacco into the barrel of the pipe, compressing it gently with his finger. As he lit the pipe and puffed big clouds of smoke into the sterile boardroom air, he growled, "Henderson was a fucking problem for this firm when he was alive, and now he's screwing us from the grave."

Every partners' meeting included at least one rant from Vince. It was always tolerated, however, because he was the highest-billing partner. Wren was usually able to rein him in when necessary and he tried to now.

"Calm down, Vincent," he said. "You're out of line." Before Vince argued the point with him, Wren said to everyone, "There is a solution here, we just need to find it." He turned to Richard Stern, one of the partners thought by some to be up-and-coming. "How about you, Richard? Would you be able to take this on?"

Richard was thin, effeminate, and a tireless student of firm politics, causing him to make a decision only after full consideration of what Doug liked to call the "P" word: Perception. That is, how would the firm and the legal community receive his decision? He would do nothing that might adversely affect his reputation. In fact, Doug was sure that he had sat silently through the discussion assessing whether there was any benefit to him if he took on Laura Holden's defence. On the one hand, the firm's senior partner wanted him to. Therefore, agreeing to do it might secure his position in the firm, at least for the short term. And if he handled it successfully, the firm would owe him. On the other hand, this case was a hot potato. If he blew it, his reputation in the legal community and his long-term position within the firm might be compromised

Doug had been listening to the disiscussion in a daze. He was barely able to accept that Henderson had been killed; now it was being suggested that Laura Holden was the one who had killed him. This was too much. He had met Laura, and Henderson had often talked to him about her. Certainly, she had a crush on Henderson, but she was sweet and shy and very much under Henderson's spell. Killing him would have been impossible for her.

Now Wren was proposing that Stern defend her. That made some sense since Stern had always hated Henderson (and vice versa, for that matter).

There would be no conflict, but there would be little effort to get to the truth of what happened either: Richard would be inclined to do everything necessary to defend Laura only. Henderson was owed more than that. At a minimum, he deserved that every effort be made to find his killer. Doug was beginning to recognize that there was only one way to ensure that that was done. He must defend Laura himself and, in the process, investigate the circumstances of the case thoroughly.

Just when Stern was about to answer, Doug interrupted.

"I would like to investigate this matter on behalf of Laura Holden, at least at the outset. In the event she is charged and I believe she has a good defence, I would like to defend her," Doug said.

"Fuck off, Branston," Vince Brodski bellowed. "Do you want to make sure we never get another goddamn file from Holden? As Henderson's *friend*"—he said this last word with enormous disdain—"you are the last one who should be defending Laura Holden."

Wren said, "I'm inclined to agree with Vincent, Douglas. Even though I maintain that there is no conflict in law here, you were Mark's best friend in the firm. Do you think you could honestly provide Laura with the best defence possible?"

"I think I can, because I don't believe that she killed him. I've met Laura. I've seen her and Henderson together. She and Henderson have tried to explain their relationship to me. I always felt that Laura idolized Henderson. But as a mentor, not a lover. Henderson was sort of like her teacher."

"And you bought that shit?" Vince groaned in total exasperation.

"It doesn't matter if I did. The fact is I'm sure *she* did. And if she still did last night, then I don't buy the lover's quarrel motive."

Wren responded before Vince started to bluster. "Well, it's still very early in the investigation," he said. "Who knows what the police will come up with as an explanation for the murder?"

"Fair enough," Doug replied. "As I said, it may be that at some point I have to withdraw. But Henderson is—was—my good friend. I want to know what happened to him. I owe him that. I know how he felt about Laura. I think I know how she felt about him. I don't believe she did it and I think Henderson would want me to prove that."

Stern seized on this opportunity. "I've given the matter a lot of thought," he said, "and, although I recognize the concerns raised by Alan, I would be honoured to act for Laura. However, I think Doug has made an excellent point. Who knew Mark better than him? Who is in a better position than he to assess the Crown's evidence against Laura? I think that, at least at the investigation stage, Doug is best suited to act, both for Laura's sake and for Mark's memory. Therefore, I am prepared to defer to

Doug and I propose that we throw the firm's full support behind him. If at some point in the future he cannot continue for any reason, then another partner will have to step in."

Stern was a champion at dodging anything that might get messy, while still making it sound like he was willing. Doug found it unbelievable that his partners were blind to the game Stern was playing. But there they sat—Wren, Wadsworth and even Brodski—with a look of admiration on their faces while they listened to Stern. They actually considered his comments to be genuine and heartfelt. It made Doug sick. Nevertheless, he was not going to complain this time, because regardless of the motive, Stern's position supported what Doug wanted. And the more he thought about it the more he realized that he had to act for Laura because he was the only litigator in the room who was prepared to take a real interest in finding Henderson's killer.

Wren considered Stern's comments for a moment, then turned to Doug. "Well, I'm not entirely convinced that you should handle this matter, Douglas. But maybe you are the best suited. What I propose is that you act for Laura during the initial investigation stage and report back regularly to the partnership. If you or the partnership decide at some point that you should not continue to act, then we will have to consider your replacement. In the meantime, I agree with Richard. The firm will provide you with full support. Anything you need, just ask. Does anyone disagree with this approach?"

The room was silent. Doug waited a moment, then addressed Wren. "I would like to have a junior help me on this. Tom Woodley would be best."

"Fine," Wren replied. "I suggest you speak to him as soon as this meeting is over. Holden wants to come in to see you this afternoon. Laura is in the hospital recovering from a concussion. You should arrange to go and see her, too." Wren looked around the table slowly. "Unless there is something else, this meeting is adjourned."

On his way to see Woodley, Doug detoured into Henderson's office for a quick look around. He was surveying the scene with no real goal in mind when Henderson's secretary, Edna, worried herself into the office behind him.

"Oh, Mr. Branston," she trembled, "It's such a tragedy. An absolute tragedy." She touched Doug's arm to connect their shared sorrow, while her eyes, moist and red, stared up at him through thick-lensed glasses.

Doug put his arm over her hunched shoulders and gave a hug to the only woman who had been a constant in Henderson's life over the years. "It is indeed, Edna," he said.

A spinster, Edna had dedicated her life to her job. So, after a moment of reflection and sniffling against Doug's lapel, she straightened up and returned to the business at hand. "I'm sorry, Mr. Branston. The police have asked me to make sure that nothing is touched until they have an opportunity to examine the office."

"Not to worry, Edna," Doug said while moving to the desk. "I only want to look around."

There were papers scattered about over piles of documents, but nothing that seemed particularly important or out of place. On the side of the desk sat the computer, left on as was Henderson's practice. Doug shook the mouse to clear the screen saver.

"Oh, Mr. Branston, I really don't think you should..."

"It's okay, Edna, I won't erase anything. I just want to check his e-mail." But, it turned out that there was nothing of interest, only the latest jokes that were the main staple of office e-mail. Doug returned the screen to the program menu. As he moved away from the computer Edna started for the door, hoping to draw him along behind her.

"Just a sec, Edna." He reached over to the telephone and hit the button for reviewing voice mail messages. Immediately, the voice of a fellow lawyer came over the speaker asking when he could come to the office to review some documents. That was followed by a beep and a computer voice indicating the day and time of the message. Marie's voice was next, telling Mark she wouldn't be able to talk to him before he left for Toronto. "Stay out of trouble!" she ordered jokingly. As Doug reflected on the pain Marie must now be experiencing, the third message began. He didn't recognize the voice, nor did its owner identify himself. "Henderson," it began. "Sorry I missed you. To answer your question: now is a terrible time to sell. The contract hasn't come through yet so the public announcement's been postponed. I'm afraid the stock's dropped, man. Sorry. It may be a good time to average down, though. Give me a shout when you get back from Hogtown and we'll see what we can do."

"Who's that? Doug asked Edna.

She took his arm in her hand and began to lead him to the door. "Oh, I think it's that broker friend of Mr. Henderson's," she replied. "I can't remember his name."

CHAPTER 8

Tom Woodley, a.k.a. Elvis, had been born and raised in a small farming community on the Prairies. He grew up living the stereotypical prairie boy's life, trudging three miles to school every day during winter through four-foot snow drifts, in temperatures well below zero, bound from head to toe in layers of clothing, bundled in a parka, scarf and toque. He also trudged home every day to the isolation of a farmhouse in the middle of 20,000 acres of flat prairie. He had one brother who was much younger than he, and consequently, never a real companion. Radio and television brought the world to his door. They also made him recognize, during the long winters, how very alone he was.

In the summers, as a teenager, he worked with other youngsters on the neighbouring farms. Slowly, he built a close group of friends who became inseparable—until the first snows of fall arrived. He crammed a year's worth of socializing into those few summer months.

At sixteen he got his driver's license and an old '64 Econoline van. For a month following his birthday he worked at camperizing the van. First, he constructed a wooden sub-floor over the metal floor of the storage area. Gathering remnants of different-coloured shag carpet from the dumpster and the home improvement store in town, he placed them on the floor, walls and ceiling, giving the space a kind of psychedelic, cave-like effect. Along the wall behind the driver's seat he constructed a storage box large enough to hold clothes, groceries and sports equipment, including his favourite water ski. A foam mattress and backrest sat on top of the box, transforming it into a comfortable bench.

Tom was particularly proud of his design of the lid of the box. It comprised three sections that folded out to cover the entire back of the van. He tailored the mattress and backrest so that they fit alongside each other on the lid sections when folded out, turning the entire back area into a bed. Curtains were strung from all the windows. He dubbed the van the "Shaggin' Wagon" and on the back door he painted the words which spawned his nickname: "The Hunk of Burnin' Love."

Tom and the van became infamous amongst young and old in the community. And when he announced, at eighteen, that he was going away to university, many local parents breathed a huge sigh of relief.

All his efforts while growing up had been directed to overcoming constant feelings of isolation. Now, in Vancouver, he was a city boy without any interest in returning to rural life. There was so much to do in the city, so many people to see and meet. He loved living in a high-rise in the densely-populated West End, loved to spend his free time walking the crowded streets, checking out the stores and restaurants, bars and nightclubs.

One casualty of urban existence was Tom's midriff. He no longer had access to the hard physical work of the farm to balance his large appetite for food and drink. To his constant embarrassment he had developed a belly over the washboard stomach of his youth, and he was unable to lose it regardless of how hard he tried. He had joined the fitness club in the firm's office tower. Three times a week he exercised for an hour after work. He worked hard on his cardio and on his abdominals, but whatever he did he was only able to maintain his rather chunky physique.

The one consolation of his larger girth, however, was that he filled out a double-breasted jacket quite opulently. He took as much advantage of this as possible, devoting considerable effort to the enhancement of his appearance as a young professional. He shopped at the trendier and more expensive men's stores in town; he kept track of the latest offerings from Hugo Boss and Giorgio Armani. Suits in charcoal or navy, and even the odd wine-coloured suit—never brown—were offset by an immaculate white shirt and understated silk tie. His breast pocket always remained empty; a handkerchief was gauche. And the jacket seldom came off, because when it did, the image suffered: the suave sophisticate became disheveled, his paunch spilling over his belt buckle and his shirt-tail trailing over his butt.

Doug Branston was Tom's mentor at the firm. He had hired Tom out of law school and had been the lawyer assigned to guide him through his articling year. During that time Tom had worked almost exclusively for Doug, learning from him how to run a file efficiently, how to deal responsibly and ethically with issues that arise in litigation, and how to communicate. He met Doug's clients, gained their confidence and, in time, began receiving files directly from them.

Since becoming an associate of the firm, Tom's practice had expanded beyond Doug's clients. He worked less for Doug now, but because he felt he owed Doug for giving him his start, he tried to make himself available to help Doug whenever he asked. Besides, he liked Doug and he recognized that there were always things to learn when working on files with him. This was especially true of Doug's latest request: assisting in the defence of Laura Holden on a possible charge of murder.

Tom had been daydreaming out his window while in the process of composing a dreary letter, when Doug stepped into his office and closed the door behind him. Doug looked particularly grim on this visit. Like Tom, he had his suit jacket on, but his tie was loosened at the collar and slightly askew. His shirt was wrinkled, his hair unkempt, and there was a slight shadow under his nose, a telltale sign of an aborted morning shave. He appeared to have rushed to the office and now was unhappy with the day he faced. Upon entering Tom's office, he avoided looking directly at Tom; instead, he walked over to the window and stared out at the gray sky. Tom waited patiently and silently for enlightenment on the purpose of the visit.

"Elvis, how's your work load these days?" Doug asked finally.

"How do you want it to be?"

"I'll tell you why I ask," Doug said, then proceeded to explain the shocking news about Henderson and Laura Holden.

Tom had already heard something about what had happened to Henderson through the rumour mill. But he had heard nothing about Laura's involvement until now.

"No. I don't believe it," he gasped. "Laura Holden? No way. I met her at Holden's parties, talked with her." He shook his head emphatically. "That kind of anger isn't in her. No way."

"Good. I'm glad you feel that way, 'cause we may have to defend her."

"Huh?"

"Frank Holden wants the firm to investigate Henderson's death on Laura's behalf and defend her if she's charged. I volunteered, and I need you to help."

The litigation Tom was doing for Larson Wren was all about moving money around between huge institutions, corporations and insurance companies who fought each other in the courts. What Doug was offering was an opportunity to leave that ivory tower and help someone who really needed it. Without hesitation, he responded, "I'm in. Absolutely." He began closing the files on the desk in front of him. "Where do we start?"

The first matter to address had nothing to do with the death of

Henderson. Doug confessed to Tom that he needed to get a hotel room because he had just left Diane. Before he realized what he was doing, Tom insisted that Doug move in with him, at least while they worked on the file together and while Doug sorted out his home life. Before Tom knew it, he was taking Doug and Doug's suitbag to his apartment in the West End.

Fortunately, the apartment was large enough to house both of them quite comfortably. Tom had originally rented it with a girlfriend he thought he was serious about. They had chosen it because it was sufficiently large to provide each of them with their own space—perhaps a sign of prescience—and because it had an extra bedroom for guests. Within a month it was clear to him that the relationship was unworkable. She moved out and he kept the apartment. The guest room was perfect for Doug, at least for the time being.

Tom and Doug arrived at the apartment at eleven forty-five in the morning. They had little time to review the apartment's ground rules because Doug wanted to go to a local restaurant for a quick lunch while they discussed how they were going to tackle the case. A meeting with Frank Holden was set for three o'clock back at the firm, before which Doug also wanted to have at least a preliminary talk with the prosecutor's office. Time was of the essence.

But before rushing out of the apartment for lunch, Doug knew he needed to call Diane and explain to her what was happening. He dialed the number and immediately realized that the chances of finding Diane at home were almost nil. What was he going to say if Conchita answered? While the phone rang he desperately tried to construct a sentence in Spanish to the effect that he would call Diane later.

The answering machine saved him. "Hi. It's me. Listen, I've got some very bad news about Mark Henderson. And…uh…things are a little crazy at the office right now. Anyway, you'll have to tell the kids that I'm going to be home late…later. Maybe I'll call. Maybe I'll try to call around dinner. I'm real sorry."

Doug paused for a moment while he thought about what else to add, then hung up. "Let's get out of here," he said to Tom.

The restaurant was a new one that Tom wanted to try—a funky, trendy spot in the West End. The menu blackboard behind the bar, written in pastel-coloured chalk, offered unusual sandwiches on bagels or multi-grain bread. The cold drinks were called "swoozles" and were made from puréed fruits with yogurt and tofu.

Doug and Tom found a table close to the window, sat down on the wooden chairs and scanned the blackboard. They both settled on chili con carne, the only dish that contained any meat. A skinny, pale waitress with long, limp, blonde hair, wearing baggy jeans and a heavy knit sweater, offered to take their order after putting two glasses of water on the table.

When she left to give their order to the kitchen, Doug and Tom pulled out their scratch pads to make notes. "First things first," Doug said. "Do you know anything about criminal law?"

"No." That was one answer Tom was able to give without equivocation.

"Good. I wouldn't want you to start out with any built-in biases." Doug smiled. "What makes this case a little different than most of the cases I've done is that Laura is a minor, so any charges she faces should be under the Young Offenders Act, which has got to be better than under the Criminal Code."

"But so far the Crown hasn't laid any charges, right?" Tom asked.

Their waitress returned with two mugs and a pot of coffee. Tom lifted his notepad and sat back in his chair to give her room to position the mugs and pour the coffee.

"Right." Doug replied. "Which means they're not satisfied yet that Laura actually killed Henderson. They're still investigating."

He checked the bowl containing the packaged cream and sugar, then asked the waitress to bring more.

"What I'm not sure of," he said to Tom, "is the effect the Young Offenders Act has on their investigation rights. For example, can they interview her without laying charges? Can they search her house? What kind of evidence do they need to lay charges under the Young Offenders Act? Are there any special things they have to do? And what do they have to disclose to us? That's going to be your first job, to find out this stuff. Okay?"

"Okay," Tom replied, scribbling down notes.

"And we're going to need answers to at least some of those questions before we meet with Holden this afternoon. Particularly, we have to know right away what rights they have to interview Laura and to search the house. I'm sure that's what the cops want to do as soon as possible."

Their waitress returned bearing two bowls of steaming chili with thick slices of dark brown bread on the side. Doug and Tom made more room on the table and the waitress placed the bowls down in front of them. Then she found a number of cream and sugar packages which she casually tossed onto the table.

Tom returned to scribbling down notes on the pad which now rested on his lap. "Will Laura be at the meeting this afternoon?" He put his pen down and picked up a spoon.

Tom and Doug each scooped up a spoonful of steaming chili. A moment passed before Doug gingerly swallowed.

"Holy shit!" he gasped. "That's hot chili!"

Tom was speechless. He grabbed the water glass in front of him and gulped. After draining half the glass, he put it down and smiled. His face was red; beads of sweat were visible on his forehead. "Yeah," he replied. "It's great, eh?"

Doug stared at Tom in disbelief, then at his bowl of chili, finally pushing it to the side. "I doubt Laura will be at the meeting with Holden," he said, grabbing two creamers and pouring the contents into his coffee. "She spent last night in hospital with a concussion. I expect we'll have to go there to talk to her. When we see Holden we'll ask him how she is and see if, maybe, we can talk to her later today or tonight."

Tom studied the notes he made on his notepad. At the same time he cautiously spooned up the chili. "I'll take a look through the Young Offenders Act and the texts on criminal procedure. Any ideas of where else I should look?"

"No. I expect you'll find most of the answers there."

Tom savoured the last of his chili, mopping it up with pieces of bread. Meanwhile, Doug looked around for the waitress. When he caught her eye he made a gesture in the air as though writing on a pad of paper. She nodded and delivered the bill to the table.

As they packed up their notepads, Doug summarized their tasks before the meeting with Holden. "So you find the answers we need and I'll try to talk with the Crown. Let's rendezvous at the office at about quarter to three so we're clear on what we want to tell Holden."

Reginald Wren planned to greet Holden when he arrived at the office, then sit in on the first part of the meeting to help explain, if it became necessary, why Doug was chosen to represent Laura.

At three o'clock precisely, while Doug and Tom were reviewing the information they had gathered since their lunch meeting, Doug's inter-office phone rang. It was Wren.

"He's here," Wren announced. "I'll meet you in the main boardroom."

Doug nodded a *let's go* to Tom as he hung up the phone. They picked up their scribbled notes and an annotated copy of the Canadian Criminal Code and headed to the main boardroom.

The usually dapper Frank Holden sat, in total disarray, at the end of the boardroom table. He wore an old, faded suede jacket over a heavy knit sweater. His hair hung over his ears and forehead in dishevelled clumps.

Bluish half-moons of flesh bulged under his eyes and the lower half of his face was a sickly gray hue from his unshaven beard. Under a heavy brow he watched Doug and Tom walk into the room. The contrast between Holden's defeated appearance and the alert focus of his eyes reminded Doug of a cornered animal, cowering and ready to spring at the same time.

Wren spoke first. "Frank, I believe you know Doug Branston. And this is Tom Woodley."

Holden nodded in the direction of Doug and Tom as they sat down at the table.

Doug gazed steadily at Holden. "Mr. Holden, we last spoke at your party a few weeks ago."

"Yes. I remember," Holden replied in an expressionless voice, returning Doug's gaze through tight eyes.

"This is a hell of an unfortunate situation, sir. I am truly sorry." Doug was surprised by a sudden stinging in his own eyes and a flush of emotion. He paused for a moment to get a grip on himself, then forged on. "You know Mark Henderson was a friend of mine. I will miss him." He swallowed hard. "I want to know who killed him. I can't believe it was Laura. From everything I know about both of them, it just doesn't make any sense to me. So, I think I can help Laura and, by helping her, maybe I can help find Henderson's murderer."

Holden digested this for a moment. When he eventually spoke he was slow and deliberate. "Mr. Branston. This firm, Reg, Vince Brodski, you, and me, and even Mark Henderson, we have all been through a hell of a lot over the years. The work of this firm has certainly helped me to be as successful as I am. And my business has paid for a lot of what I see around me here. We have always worked together and relied on each other. We know each other. There is no doubt in my goddamn mind that this is the right firm to act for my daughter."

He took a slow deep breath while the lawyers at the table nodded their agreement. Then he added forcefully, "Three weeks ago I warned Henderson to stay away from my daughter. I'm thinking that if he had honoured my request Laura wouldn't be in the position she is now." He raised his right hand from where it lay palm down on the table. Pointing his index finger directly at Doug he commanded, "This firm owes Laura and it owes me. I want you to represent Laura. You knew Henderson and you knew better than anyone about him and Laura. *You know goddamn well,*"—he emphasized the words through clenched teeth—"*that Laura did not shoot Mark Henderson.* And I expect you and this firm to do everything necessary to prove that."

Doug swallowed hard again, this time from the force of Holden's words.

"You have our commitment to do just that, Frank," Wren said with conviction. Then, having satisfied himself that his presence was no longer needed, he stood up and shook hands with Holden. "I understand that Douglas and Tom have some important things to discuss with you, so I'll leave now. I'm here if you need to speak to me."

Holden nodded slowly but said nothing.

The boardroom was quiet, almost oppressive, while Wren made his exit. But once he was gone and Doug was left to advise Holden alone, the room seemed to take on massive, sublime dimensions. Doug waited a moment to gather his thoughts, then he turned to his notepad and began to apprise Holden of the information he and Tom had gleaned from their initial investigation.

"I contacted the Crown Counsel's office," he said, "and spoke to one of the lawyers there in the homicide department. They are aware of the case, but they don't have any details because it's still being investigated by the police. Once the police finish their investigation, they'll report their findings to the Crown and maybe make some recommendations. The Crown will then decide whether to lay charges."

"How long will that take?" Holden asked.

"Anyone's guess. A day, a month, a year. It all depends on what the police are able to come up with. Anyway, the lawyer gave me the name of the detective in charge of the investigation." Doug studied his notes more closely. "It's Detective Russell Campbell."

"Yeah. I spoke to him on the phone this morning." Holden said. "He wanted to talk to Laura and conduct a search of the house."

"What did you tell him?" Doug asked.

"I said I wasn't going to let him do anything until I spoke to my lawyer."

"Right," Doug nodded his approval.. "Well, I was able to contact him a short while ago and speak to him briefly. He tells me that he now has a warrant to search your home and he wants to do it this afternoon."

"Can he do that?"

Tom had already found the answer to this question. "Yes, now that he has a court order. All he needed to do to get the order was provide a judge with some evidence indicating that he has—the exact words are—'reasonable and probable grounds' to believe that he may find something in the house relevant to the investigation. The fact that Laura was found at the scene with a gun in her hand was probably enough."

Doug continued. "Campbell told me that he's prepared to be as cooperative as he can. He says it's too early to tell whether Laura is a suspect. He wants to search the house, but because Laura's still in hospital, he's not in a big hurry. I guess he figures that if there is any evidence in the house, it'll remain intact as long as she's in her hospital bed. Anyway, he wants to go to the house with his search team at about five today. I think the best we can do is be there when the search takes place."

Doug allowed Holden time to contemplate the significance of a police search of his home. Holden lived in one of the most affluent areas of the city. No doubt he was an upstanding neighbour and a credit to his community. Now he was going to have a bunch of police cars on his front lawn and men in ill-fitting suits and long trench coats trudging in and out of his house.

"Any questions on that?" Doug asked eventually.

"I guess not."

"Now, as you know, there's a police officer at the hospital staying with Laura and just waiting for the green light to talk to her." Doug nodded in the direction of Tom. "Tom here has considered what rights they have in that regard."

"Yeah." Tom took a quick look at his notes. "Essentially, they have no rights. We can stonewall them completely if we want. So, for the time being anyway, I suggest we do just that—tell them that we're representing Laura and haven't had an opportunity to speak to her. Then, depending on her story, we can decide whether we want her saying anything to the police."

Holden's furrowed brow relaxed slightly. "That makes sense to me. Christ, I've hardly even spoken to her myself."

"We'd obviously like to interview Laura as soon as possible," Doug noted. "How is she doing?"

"Oh, I think she's coming along. Her head hurts and she's pretty upset about what has happened," Holden replied.

"Do you think we could see her after the police search, maybe at seven or eight tonight?"

"We can certainly try."

"Good." Doug turned again to Tom. "Now, there's one more thing we need to tell you."

Tom took the cue. "Because Laura is a minor," he began, "she falls under the Young Offenders Act. That Act provides certain protections for minors who are charged with Criminal Code offences. For example, their names cannot be publicized, they are entitled to a parent present during any interviews, etc., etc. But, most importantly, if convicted of a charge, sentencing is under the Act rather than the Code. A sentence under the Act is significantly lighter than under the Code; and it's normally served in a youth detention centre which is minimum security."

Holden became defiant. "Well, she isn't going to be charged and she isn't going to be convicted, because you guys are going to do your damn job," he roared, pointing at Tom and stabbing the air for greater emphasis.

Doug came to Tom's aid. "There is a reason why we're telling you this, Mr. Holden. You see, there's a provision in the Young Offenders Act that allows the Crown to ask for the proceedings to be elevated to adult court in circumstances where it believes that the youth system cannot adequately deal with sentencing and rehabilitation, and the public is at risk. The Crown lawyer I spoke to advised me that there is a policy within the department now that requires them to apply for elevation in all cases involving a homicide. That means that if Laura is charged with Henderson's death, she'll face a Crown application to be tried in adult court."

"And?" Holden asked.

"And that means that if the application is successful, she will no longer be protected by the Young Offenders Act. Her name will be publicized. And if she is convicted, she'll be sentenced to a longer jail term in a federal penitentiary."

Holden stared at Doug for a long moment, then began rubbing his eyes violently with the thumb and forefinger of his right hand. His fingers moved to his temples; he squeezed them hard in a pincer grip as if to keep the flood of information he was receiving from bursting out of his brain. His eyes remained tightly shut.

"Let me see if I get what you're telling me," he said. "If they decide to charge Laura with killing Henderson, they will want her tried as an adult."

"Right," Doug nodded.

"And if she is tried as an adult, then she is treated for all intents and purposes as if she is an adult. Even though she's still a little girl, fifteen goddamn years old. The press gets to spread her name all over the front page of the papers. And her face appears on the six o'clock fucking news." His voice became more incredulous as the gravity of what he was saying sank in. "She's only a kid, for Chrissake!"

"That's right." Doug confirmed. "And, perhaps worst of all, if she is convicted—and I can't believe that could happen, but if it did—she will be sentenced as an adult. Maybe twenty years in a prison rather than five in a youth centre."

Holden thought about this for a moment, continuing to massage his temples, then he slapped both hands down on the table and opened his eyes wide. "Well, as I said, it isn't going to happen because she didn't do it. And you guys are going to make sure the Crown understands that."

Doug and Tom both nodded their agreement. "Okay," Doug said. "Why don't Tom and I plan to be at your house around four-thirty or quarter to five so we're there when the search is done. Then we can go over to the hospital to see Laura afterwards."

"Good," Holden replied. "Now, there is one other matter I need to talk to you about." His demeanor suddenly changed from that of the tormented father to that of the shrewd business executive. "Henderson was handling one of my companies. It's completely separate from the business that Vince has been doing for me. I didn't want it mixed up with my other business; that's why Vince hasn't been handling it. And I don't want him taking it over now. I want you to take it on."

Doug was stunned. Holden had hated Henderson for his relationship with Laura. How could he have had Henderson continue to represent one of his companies?

"I can't say I'm not surprised," Doug replied.

"I expect you are," Holden agreed. "But, you know what they say: business sometimes makes for strange bedfellows."

Doug was still dismayed, but he looked at Tom and they both shrugged. "Well," he said, "there should be no problem with us looking after the company for you. Give us its name."

"Blackwater Holdings," Holden dictated to Tom, who jotted the name down on his notepad.

Holden then stood up and shook hands with both lawyers. "Thank you," he said. "I know we're in good hands. I'll see you at my house later this afternoon. And you'll report to me when you've had an opportunity to read the file on that company." This last comment was a statement, not a request.

Tom and Doug accompanied Holden to the elevator bay, then strolled back to their offices. Something in the back of Doug's mind kept nagging at him about Henderson acting for a Holden company, but he was unable to put his finger on what it was.

CHAPTER 9

Doug, Tom and Frank Holden arrived at the hospital about eight p.m. Doug was without a car due to his recent separation and Holden preferred not to drive given the circumstances, so Tom drove them all in his '76 Buick Montego—a great car in its day, but that day had ended long ago.

He parked in the open parking lot across from the hospital. Unrelenting rain illuminated in the street lights strafed the ground like tracer fire. A film of water covered the pavement, as shiny as black patent leather. They ran across the street from the parking lot to the hospital, raincoats pulled up over their heads. In their haste to get under cover they almost bowled over two male orderlies huddled in the hospital entrance sucking intensely on cigarettes. Those desperate figures reminded Doug of winos with brown-bagged bottles of bay rum.

Doug, Tom and Holden proceeded through the glass doors into the main reception area of the hospital. A uniformed policeman in the waiting area watched them check in with the receptionist and followed them to Laura's room. Before they could enter, he stopped them and asked to see identification. When he learned who Holden was, he mumbled an apology, stepped away from the entrance and allowed the three men to go in. They closed the door behind them.

The room was like that of any hospital: rectangular, with high bare walls painted a light minty green. A large square window in the centre of one wall was obscured by striped, almond drapes pulled shut so as to spare those in the room the sight of the dripping darkness outside. The floor, linoleum tile, gray with a brushstroke of green, shone opaquely through a yellow wax tint. Against one wall sat a bed and a night table.

A small lamp on the night table illuminated the book that Laura read while curled up in a jumble of blankets. Her hair was much shorter than Doug remembered and her face much paler, but she looked surprisingly content, lost in the fantasy of the story. Only after Holden knocked on the wall did she realize the three men were there. When she looked up at them, the magic drained from her face. She closed her book.

"Hi, sweetheart," Holden said tenderly, bending down to kiss Laura on her cheek.

She closed her eyes lightly as she lifted her cheek to him. "Hi, Daddy," she whispered.

Opening her eyes as he straightened up, she looked past him at Doug and Tom who were standing awkwardly in the shadows.

Holden turned in the direction of Laura's gaze. "Sweetie, these are two lawyers from Larson Wren. Do you remember Doug Branston?"

She gazed at Doug, her eyes aching with painful memories. "Yes. How are you, Doug?" she managed. She looked over at Tom and tried to smile. "Elvis. It's good to see you."

Doug and Tom both mumbled a reply, the paradox they faced making them feel very uncomfortable: here was Laura so small lying in the bed, so timid and vulnerable; she might have been hugging a teddy bear, feeling anxious about a nightmare she'd just had. Instead, she was recovering from a blow to the head that had occurred at the time her lover was killed. On top of that, she was being investigated for the murder, and perhaps it had been she who had killed him. It all seemed impossible.

Holden had told Doug and Tom before they arrived at the hospital that Laura was unaware of the gravity of her situation. She knew that Henderson was dead and that she had been knocked out, but she knew little else. This meeting would have to be handled delicately.

Doug sat down on the side of the bed. He leaned forward so his face was quite close to Laura's. "Laura," he started in a low voice, "it seems you were the last one to see Mark before he died. The police want to talk to you about what you remember."

Her eyes welled up and the slight composure she had mustered quickly dissipated. "But I don't remember anything," she cried, shaking her head.

Doug rubbed her shoulder and murmured, "It's okay. It's okay." He waited a few moments until Laura appeared calmer, then he began again. "What is the last thing you do remember?" he asked.

She dragged a corner of the bed sheet across her eyes to dry away the tears, took a couple of deep breaths and sniffled.

"Take your time," Holden encouraged as he and Tom leaned toward the bed in anticipation of what she might say.

"I remember we were having a terrible argument." She suddenly stopped, balancing on the edge of inconsolable grief. Seconds passed as she fought to control herself.

She began again. "I was so angry with him. I was screaming. Hitting him. And then, the next thing I remember is being in the ambulance coming here and they said that he was…" She convulsed into waves of tears. Doug knew that she was peering straight into the abyss now. He had to say something quickly or he would lose her.

"How did you get to the apartment building?" he blurted out.

"By taxi," Laura stuttered through sobs.

"Why did you go there?"

She took a deep staccato breath. "Because that's where we always used to go," she shuddered. "He has a place there. I knew I would find him there."

"Had you two planned to meet there?"

"Not that time. I went there because I knew I would find him there." She seemed to be regaining some control.

"Why did you want to see him last night?"

"I don't know. I was scared. He wanted to stop seeing me. He had sent me a letter saying it was over between us. That couldn't happen. It just couldn't happen. I had to tell him that. That he was wrong. We were meant for each other. We would be together forever. We couldn't live without each other."

Laura's eyes widened as she spoke; her voice gained strength. She was talking as if Henderson were in the room, as if she were trying to convince him not to break off their relationship. Then a shadow fell over her face. "He didn't believe me," she whispered. "He told me I had to leave. He was meeting someone else. He called me a little girl."

"Then what happened?" Doug encouraged.

"I got real mad at him."

"What did he do?"

"He kept backing away. And then…" She paused to gain strength for what she was about to say. " And then…he…he started laughing. He laughed at me," she cried in a voice full of incredulity.

"What did you do?"

"I started hitting and scratching him. I really lost it. But after that…I don't remember. Next thing I knew I was in the ambulance."

She gazed at Doug, then at the other two men standing by the bed. She seemed slowly to gain some recognition of the seriousness of her present situation. Her eyes searched theirs for answers. Finally, she looked at her father.

"Daddy, did I kill Mark?" she asked.

The three men looked at each other in awkward silence before Holden bent down and gave her a hug. "No, sweetheart. We're just trying to find out who did." Then, still holding Laura in his arms, he turned to Doug. "Anything else you want to ask, Doug?"

Doug thought for a moment. Yes, there was another question, but this was the wrong moment. Laura was very emotional. The last thing he wanted was for her to conclude that she had killed Henderson. He needed to do some independent investigation before asking her whether she or Henderson had a gun when they argued last night.

"No, I've got nothing further to ask right now," he said. "Thank you, Laura. I'm so sorry this happened." He patted her on the shoulder. Then a thought occurred to him. "Laura, would you have the letter that Mark sent you?"

"It's in my purse," she replied. "It should be in the closet with my clothes." She pointed to a door in the corner of the room.

"May I have a look?" Doug asked as he got up from the bed and crossed the room to the closet.

Laura nodded her assent.

The closet door was in shadow, away from the light of the bedside lamp. Doug opened it and peered into the darkness. A quick look at the clothes hanging in the closet revealed nothing odd, but no purse was to be seen.

"I don't see a purse here, Laura." He turned back to the others. "You sure it was in here?"

Laura looked slightly startled. "No. I'm not sure. I just assumed it would be with the rest of my stuff."

Holden and Tom both walked over to the closet, looked in and confirmed that the purse was not there.

"Are sure you had it with you last night?" Doug asked.

"Of course. I always have it with me."

"Well, it's gone now." Doug thought for a moment. "I think we need to talk to Detective Campbell." He gestured to Tom that it was time to leave. "Thanks, Laura. I'd like to come and see you tomorrow if I can."

Laura nodded but she was only half listening. She was now staring at her father who had returned to her bedside. Holden told Doug that he wanted to be alone for a minute with his daughter. As Doug and Tom left the room, they heard Laura's plaintive voice asking her father "Why would they take my purse, Daddy?"

Outside Laura's room they found Detective Campbell sitting on a chair. He jumped up to greet them as they closed the door behind them. Campbell was tall, perhaps six-foot-three or -four. He stood ramrod straight, which accentuated his height. His complexion was slightly tanned and his face was fleshy, especially around his full lips. He had black hair with a breath of gray, and blue eyes obscured by wire rim glasses. On closer inspection, it was evident that Campbell liked to wear fine things. His white shirt was monogrammed, his navy blazer appeared to be silk and his wire rim glasses had "Giorgio Armani" inscribed on each arm. He looked more like a British gentleman than a homicide detective. The impression was reinforced by his delicate Scottish accent.

"Good evening, gentlemen," he said with a genuine smile. "Corporal Peters advised me that you were here. As we have finished the search of the house, I thought I might pop over here to see if there was a chance you would allow me to speak to the young lady?"

"Not now, I'm afraid," Doug replied. "She has barely told us anything. She's still upset and a little confused."

"I understand. But I hope you will allow me an opportunity to speak to Ms. Holden sometime soon," Campbell pressed.

Doug was against making any promises at this stage, but he didn't want Campbell to think Laura had something to hide. "Should do," he replied vaguely. Then quickly changing topics, he asked, "How did your search go? Find anything that I should know about?"

"Ah." Campbell reached into his breast pocket and pulled out a photocopied sheet with handwriting on it. "Here's a copy of the list of items we have taken from the house for further review and inspection," He handed the list to Doug. "I can tell you that we have not found a 'smoking gun,' so to speak."

Doug reviewed the notes on the paper, choosing to ignore Campbell's pun. All the items listed, with the exception of one, were those removed from the house while Doug was present. They included Laura's school books and magazines, a portable stereo and tapes, various personal letters, a scrapbook, and a diary. The one exception, which Doug knew had not been taken from the house, was the purse.

"Interesting assortment of things," he said. "Is there something in particular that you're looking for?"

"Not really," Campbell replied. "Just anything that might give us a clue about what went on last night between Ms. Holden and the deceased."

"What about the purse? That didn't come from the house."

"No. You are quite right and I did intend to tell you about that." Campbell adjusted his glasses, as if that would assist him in explaining how the purse got onto the list. "As you know, Ms. Holden was taken to the hospital by ambulance from the scene. She regained consciousness only after she was placed in the ambulance. Upon arrival at the hospital, her clothes were removed and she was given a hospital gown. One of my team inspected the clothes and the purse before the items were delivered to the closet of her hospital room."

"And?" Doug asked. He motioned with his hand to encourage Campbell to continue his explanation.

"And the purse was of some interest to us, so we thought it best to have it undergo some examinations." Campbell looked at Doug. He adjusted his glasses once more, apparently signifying that he had completed his explanation.

"What was so interesting about the purse?"

"Maybe nothing. It's too early to tell."

"Can you give me a hint?"

"No. I'm sorry. Not at this time."

"Well, detective," Doug huffed, "it seems to me that you wouldn't have taken the purse without a reason."

Campbell smiled in response.

"Tell me this, though. I assume the purse was not empty when you grabbed it. What was in it?"

Campbell became slightly flustered. "Yes, of course. That information should have been on the list. My recollection is that the only item of interest to us was the letter from the deceased to Ms. Holden. But I may be wrong. And, in any event, I shall get you a list of all the items in the purse as soon as possible. May I deliver that over to your office first thing in the morning?"

Doug was annoyed. The police had had the purse from the time Laura arrived at the hospital and were only informing Doug now. And Doug sensed that if he had failed to ask for the list of items in the purse, Campbell would have made little effort to get that information to him expeditiously.

"No. I'd like it now. I think I'm entitled to know everything of Laura's that you have in your possession and I want to know that now." Doug said determinedly.

Campbell studied Doug, assessing whether he was going to be able to push Doug around as much as he had hoped. After a few moments he decided that it was best to be accommodating, at least at this stage. He turned to Corporal Peters who had been standing with his hands clasped behind his back staring out the window.

"Corporal Peters," Campbell stated authoritatively. "Please contact the exhibit man, McGrath. He's catalogued all the personal items that we've held. Have him fax to me here at the hospital a list of the contents of the purse."

Peters gave a single nod of his head, like a salute. He turned and strode down the hall towards the administration office to make the call.

Doug wanted to know what was written in Henderson's letter as well.

He called after Peters, "Have him fax a copy of the letter that was in the purse, too."

Without turning, Peters waved his hand to acknowledge Doug's request and continued down the hall.

Campbell, Doug and Tom were waiting awkwardly in the hallway for Peters to return when Holden left Laura's room. He strode directly up to Campbell. "She didn't do it," he bellowed. "When are you going to start looking for the real murderer?"

Campbell, unruffled, spoke without emotion. "Mr. Holden. Let me assure you that we are following all the leads we have, and in due course we shall know who is the real murderer."

"Christ," Holden muttered as he turned away, "it's not as if the bastard didn't deserve it."

"Excuse me—" Campbell began.

Doug broke in. "That's enough, Mr. Holden. We'll be leaving in a minute. In the meantime, I'd appreciate it if you would keep your comments to yourself." He turned to Tom. "Why don't you two wait in the car. I'll be there as soon as I get these faxes from the detective here."

Tom walked over to Holden and led him down the hallway towards the exit.

Campbell stood beside Doug while they watched Tom and Holden walk away. "Please don't stop him on my account," he chuckled. "If the gentleman has something he wants to get off of his chest, I am certainly here to oblige."

"I'm sure you are," Doug said absentmindedly. It continued to trouble him that even though Holden felt the way he did about Henderson, he still had him handle legal work for a Holden company. Doug made a mental note to have Tom take a look at the company files first thing in the morning.

As Holden and Tom disappeared out the front doors of the hospital, Doug's thoughts returned to Campbell. "Tell me, detective," he said while still gazing down the hallway, "do you really think that little girl in there killed Mark Henderson?"

Campbell stepped in front of Doug to break his gaze and to gain his full attention. "So far all the evidence points to her, Mr. Branston. All the evidence." He paused for effect. "But I do not draw any conclusions until we have analyzed everything."

"When am I going to see this evidence?" Doug asked.

"When, and if, charges are laid."

Doug's eyes strayed away from Campbell's and back down the hall. Peters was returning from the administration office. When he reached

Doug and Campbell he handed two sheets of paper to the detective which Campbell studied in turn, then handed to Doug.

"Here's some evidence for you to consider," he said.

Doug took the faxes from Campbell. The first contained a list of the items found in the purse: wallet, lipstick, makeup case, hairbrush, keys, address book, loose change, gum, Kleenex, an envelope and five condoms.

"Jesus," Doug said, "all this was in a purse?"

Campbell replied, "We've been referring to it as a purse, but it is really more like a leather carry bag."

Doug looked at the second fax. It was the letter Henderson had written to Laura, dated the day Henderson had left for Toronto. In Henderson's familiar scrawl was written:

Dear Laura,

The time has come for us to part. You are ready now to fly on your own and I cannot stand in your way. I wish you every happiness.

Love Mark

A large line was scratched across Henderson's words and at the bottom right hand corner of the letter was a sketch of a heart with the initials "M.H." and "L.H." in the middle and "FOREVER" written underneath.

Campbell peered over Doug's shoulder. Pointing to the sketch, he said, "Needless to say, the line across the letter and the notes at the bottom are in ink and handwriting that is different from that of the rest of the letter. We expect to match the handwriting with that in Ms. Holden's school books."

Doug folded the papers, put them into his breast pocket and contemplated where he could go for a stiff drink. "Well. I've got to go. Thank you, detective. I look forward to our next discussion," he said as he started down the hall.

Campbell called after Doug. "Be sure to let me know when I may speak to Ms. Holden."

Doug did not respond. Like Peters, he simply waved his hand and continued towards the exit.

CHAPTER 10

The beer was ice cold. Doug drained half the pint in one guzzle, waited a moment, and then stifled a tremendous belch. He glanced around. From his table in the corner he had a view of the whole room. He could also watch the racquetball players through the glass walls on the far side of the bar. A couple of sweaty, chubby old jocks pounded around one court, but in the other were two young and shapely women, one of whom was particularly eye-catching. She wore a tight fuchsia exercise suit over black leotards. When she bent over in anticipation of her opponent's serve, a collective sigh was heard from the men sitting in the bar.

Tom eventually emerged from the men's changing room with his hair still wet from the shower and his complexion rosy from exercising. Doug motioned the waitress to bring two more pints of beer. He thought about getting himself back into shape while he quaffed the remainder of his pint and watched Tom approach the table.

"Giving your eyes a little workout?" Tom chuckled, as he flopped into the chair across from Doug.

"Yeah. Unbelievable. She should charge admission," Doug replied. Then, changing the topic slightly, "I was just thinking how desperate my body is for some exercise. What's your routine?"

"I'm here about three times a week. Push weights for about an hour." Tom slapped his pot belly. "Can't you tell? It's like a rock."

"Do you use a trainer?"

"Nope. They set me up on a routine when I joined and I just follow it. Add a little weight when it gets too easy."

Doug smiled. Memories of lifting weights in the basement of his parents' home popped into his mind. "Ever heard of Joe Weider?"

Tom shook his head.

"You must be too young. You're part of the Arnie generation. Joe Weider was my hero growing up. He was on the cover of every weight-lifting magazine. Everybody had Joe Weider barbells in their basement." Doug took a slow sip of beer while he enjoyed the memory. "In those days you didn't do repetitions to develop muscles; it was simply how much you could lift. I always thought I was pretty strong," he pretended to flex a bicep while he lifted his beer glass. "But I remember this one nerdy guy in my high school class who regularly outlifted me." He laughed. "Here I was, working so hard to be cool, and there was this Bill Gates look-a-like constantly proving how much stronger he was." After another sip of beer he concluded, "Life is full of humbling experiences."

Doug's reminiscences came to a grinding halt when the glass door of the racquetball court swung open and the two female adversaries entered the bar. He didn't want to miss his first opportunity to get a good look at them. But as was so often the case, the full frontal view of the one who had first grabbed his attention failed to live up to earlier billing. True, her hair was impressive: long, sandy-coloured, and wildly curly. Her body was good as well, her breasts flattered her snug-fitting outfit. Her tummy was flat, her legs were a decent length and nicely toned. The disappointment was in her face. Her eyes were wan, her lips were narrow and pale and her chin was weak. Too bad. More proof that nothing in this world is perfect.

Tom interrupted Doug's analysis. "Her name is Cynthia," he said. "She goes out with the bald guy playing on the other court."

"Doesn't matter," Doug replied. "I'm not interested. The face is a bit of a mitt. But she does have a marvelous body."

"She does indeed. The best money can buy." Tom lifted his beer in a silent toast to Cynthia.

"What do you mean? They're fake?"

"Tits *and* ass, buddy." Tom took a slow drink of his beer, satisfied that he had shocked Doug.

"Jesus Christ. You're kidding?" Doug shook his head. "Tits *and* ass?" He thought about that for a moment. "How do you do the ass?"

"They can do anything now. Look at Michael Jackson," Tom laughed. "They made him into Diana Ross."

With a look of astonishment, Doug watched Cynthia disappear down the corridor to the women's change room.

"Does it bother you?" Tom asked.

Doug had never considered it before, but upon reflection, he answered, "Yeah, I guess it kinda does. There's something fraudulent about a woman having a chest and butt stuffed with silicone. Don't you think? The body's not hers. It's bought to make her look sexier. But it's not like a padded bra or high heels, which you can put on and take off. It's permanent. It's changing the body. Like taking steroids."

Tom chuckled. "You're such a fucking hypocrite. You're so holier-than-thou about how Cynthia gets her perfect body, but you're disappointed that her face can't match it."

"Such is life," Doug shrugged. "Aren't we all striving for what doesn't really exist?"

"I'm not," Tom replied. "I'm just striving to get laid tonight."

"And you're telling me that exists?" Doug laughed.

"It better. In fact, I thought I might have a couple of friends of mine join us for some dinner at the sushi bar around the corner. But I'm not sure where you're at right now. How are you feeling? It's been a hell of a last twenty-four hours for you."

That was true, but Doug wanted to avoid thinking or talking about it. He wanted to drink another beer instead; he wanted to ogle the women in the club; he wanted to go out to dinner with Tom and his friends and then fall dead asleep until morning, when there were plenty of other things to occupy his mind. He took another great gulp of beer and gave Tom the thumbs up.

"There's nothing I want more right now than to eat some raw fish," he said with conviction before downing the remainder of his beer. "Actually, that's not true. I want another beer first." He held up his hand to draw the waitress's attention once more.

"Why did you leave Diane anyway?"

"Long story," Doug answered, without any indication that he was about to relate it. He looked around to see if the waitress was getting the beer he had ordered.

Tom understood. Now was not the time. But there was going to be a time soon when Doug would have to face the fact that his life had just undergone some fundamental changes: the loss of his close friend, business partner and colleague, and the break-up of his family life. There wasn't enough beer in the world to keep those events from surfacing eventually. Tom dropped the topic for the present. Besides, the waitress was placing two more pints on the table. He took a quarter from his pocket and excused himself to call their dinner companions. Doug winked at him, then swallowed another mouthful of beer.

Within a few minutes Tom returned to announce that dinner was all arranged. His friends were going to meet them at the restaurant in thirty minutes, leaving them enough time to finish their beer leisurely. He settled back down in his chair and asked, "So what happens tomorrow?"

Doug stared into his beer glass while he thought about it. "I want to talk to Marie. And I think I'll wander over to the apartment building to take a look around. Actually, while I think about it, I'll tell you what I'd like you to do first thing tomorrow morning." He put his glass down and focused on Tom. "Take a look at the files on that Holden company Henderson was working on. I'm fascinated to know what the hell Henderson was doing for Holden other than screwing his pubescent daughter."

Doug suddenly stopped talking. A thought was working its way into his consciousness. He took another sip of beer, stared off into space and blinked hard a couple of times. Eventually it came to him. It was something Henderson had said to Holden when they had met in the den that night, something about the work he was doing for Holden not going to another lawyer or not being made public. It had obviously made an impact on Holden. What had his reaction been? What had he said? He had threatened to kill Henderson. Doug looked back at Tom. "Find out everything you can about what Henderson was doing for Holden's company," he said.

They finished their beer, paid the bar bill and strolled out of the club into the night and the interminable rain. Tom opened an umbrella over Doug and himself as they walked in the direction of the Japanese restaurant.

"So who are we meeting for dinner?" Doug asked.

The darkness hid Tom's devious smile as he advised Doug that they were about to meet Stern's secretary, Trudy, and her sister, Cathy. Immediately, Doug saw the humour. Stern's role in the partnership included hiring the firm secretaries. He always hired the cutest one for himself and, although he was married, flirted mercilessly with her in the office. Nothing ever happened, except in Stern's own fantasies. But it would drive him insane to know that his secretary was out socializing with a fellow partner and a lowly associate.

"You dating Trudy?" Doug asked.

"Yeah," Tom confessed. "I've been sort of seeing her for the last month or so. But it's a secret. You know, if Stern found out one of us would probably lose their job. Most likely me."

Doug thought about that. Tom might be right. The partners shared the general view that lawyers must avoid dating staff. The theory, as far as Doug was able to tell, was that a secretary who dates a lawyer is viewed by the other staff members as receiving special privileges. This creates petty jealousies that can lead to greater problems within the firm. There was logic to that theory, Doug knew, so he understood Tom's desire to keep his fledgling relationship private.

"Your secret is safe with me," Doug said, motioning with his fingers across his lips as if he was zipping his mouth closed. "Now, tell me about the sister."

Tom gave a glowing report of Cathy which Doug was able to confirm when they arrived at the restaurant. The four nestled in at the bar and ordered plates of sushi and sashimi from the chef facing them. Doug ate sushi with lots of soya sauce and wasabi, but he limited his choice of fish to salmon, tuna, shrimp and scallops. Cathy was more adventurous, trying all sorts of exotic seafood, including octopus, goeduck, eel and salmon roe with raw pheasant eggs on top.

Doug found something sensual about her. Her taste for new and different things. Or the way she opened her mouth, tilted her head back to exhibit the long curve of her neck, and placed the whole slice of raw fish at the back of her tongue. Doug could almost feel the meat sliding down her throat when she swallowed.

They chased the sushi down with lots of warm saki served in tiny ceramic cups. The burn from the saki and the spicy wasabi was the only sting Doug encountered during dinner. The topics of Henderson's death and Doug's separation were studiously avoided. Instead, everyone expressed their disgust with the weather and fantasized about where they would rather be.

"There's this place," Cathy told them, "on the border of Peru and Ecuador called Punta Sal. At the very end of a long dirt road. Totally untouched. They have these little huts by an endless sand beach. And the water's alive with every kind of tropical fish. They jump in the surf. And at night the day's catch is barbecued. There's nothing to do there but walk, swim, eat and sleep." She blushed perceptibly as she corrected herself, "Well, there is one other thing."

Doug pictured Punta Sal in his mind's eye, a gentle breeze fluttering through the palms hanging out over the beach, waves all the way from the Orient lapping weakly onto the flat sand as if exhausted from the long journey, and in the distance, silhouetted against the setting sun, the woman of his dreams strolling towards him through the ankle-deep sea. He sighed. The others at the bar laughed.

By the time they all left the restaurant, Doug felt mellow. Enough liquor, exotic food and talk of faraway places can take the mind off anything. Even the continuing rain failed to bother him.

When they stepped outside, Tom turned with Trudy and headed in the direction of the office. "My car's still in the parking lot," he indicated. "Come on."

"You know what?" Doug said. "I feel like walking back to your place. It's not that far. You guys go ahead and I'll see you there."

"I'll keep you company," Cathy offered quickly. "My apartment is only a couple of blocks from Tom's."

The couples parted and as Doug strolled down the sidewalk, Cathy put her arm in his.

They walked in silence for a long time. When they were within a block of Cathy's apartment she spoke shyly, "I really enjoyed tonight, Doug." He said nothing in response. A moment passed before she took a deep breath and said, "I hope this isn't too forward of me. But I know you and your wife just separated, and I expect you don't know if it's over or just on hold, but do you think you might be interested in seeing me again?"

Doug's mind was a million miles away. He only realized that something was astir when she finally stopped walking, turned to him and planted a firm, moist kiss on his lips.

"This is my building," she said. "Want to come up for a drink or coffee or something?"

He suddenly realized that he had completely lost his focus. This woman was cute, witty and interested in him, and he had failed to pursue his initial attraction to her. He had been in an alcohol-induced dream world, floating in the cosmos, shiny white in black nothingness, but her kiss had brought him back to the matters at hand.

Now that she had his attention, she issued the invitation again. He looked down at her eyes wide open and expectant, and heard himself say, "No. I'm sorry."

"I understand." She slowly unhooked her hand from his arm. "Call me if you want to get together sometime."

He nodded, kissed her lightly on the mouth, then watched her leave him and enter the apartment building.

After she disappeared, Doug turned towards Tom's apartment, cringing against the voice screaming in his head: *Are you nuts? Have you lost your mind? You idiot, she wanted you! Why did you let her go? What happened to 'go wherever the night takes you?' What happened to Mr. I-got-to-be-free? She was offering you exactly what you've been looking for. Why did you turn her down?*

He had no real answer, although the events of the last twenty-four hours probably had something to do with it. Maybe his subconscious felt a night of celibacy was a fitting remembrance for his dead friend who had experienced so few such nights himself. Whatever it was, it just felt wrong.

He walked on to Tom's apartment, hands in pockets, head down. Henderson would have laughed. "What a loser you are, Branston," he would have said. "You refused to listen to me. You wanted so badly to walk on the wild side. Well now you're there, buddy. Can you hack it? Maybe it's not so good, eh? Maybe it's kind of lonely?"

In the middle of this rumination Doug realized that he hadn't called Diane all evening. He looked at his watch. Midnight. Maybe she was still up. He quickened his pace, determined to phone her as soon as he got back to Tom's apartment.

Only the hall light was on when he arrived. Muffled conversation came from the other side of the closed door to Tom's bedroom as Doug tip-toed into the living room and turned on a lamp. He picked up the phone beside the lamp, dialed the familiar number and sat on the sofa, waiting. There were three long rings before Diane's sleepy voice answered.

"Hi. It's me," Doug said in a low, tentative voice. "Listen. I meant to call earlier but we've been working on this case, trying to get an idea of what happened, what the cops are doing. You know." Only silence at the other end of the line. "Oh god. I'm sorry. Did you know Mark Henderson was killed last night?"

There was a deep sigh. "Yes. It's just awful." They both waited for the other to say something. Finally Diane asked, "What do you mean 'we've been working on the case'?"

Doug explained the strange circumstances that had resulted in his appointment as the leading suspect's counsel.

"Do you really want to do that?" Diane asked with incredulity. "Do you really want to be investigating the death of your best friend? You know it's going to become a media zoo—especially, with that girl there when he was killed—even if she isn't charged." She paused before adding with greater agitation. "And what about our problems? How are you going to deal with them while this is going on? What are we going to tell the children?"

Doug explained. "No, Diane. I think this will be good for everybody. We can tell the kids that I have to move out of the house in order to han-dle an important case. That will give them time to get used to me being away from home. It will also give you and me a chance to understand our feelings about each other."

"I don't like it, Douglas. I'd really like you to rethink this."

"I'm afraid it's too late, I'm already too deeply involved to pull out."

"Well, at least, I wish you had called when the kids were awake," she scolded. "It would have helped if you had been able to explain why you're not at home. I could have used a little support when lying to them."

Doug was truly sorry, not only because he had forgotten to phone ear-lier but because he hated the idea of lying to the kids, especially when he and Diane insisted that the kids tell the truth. Parents are such hyp-ocrites. They expect their children to do things that they fail miserably to do themselves. Well, it was probably just as well. Diane was a much better liar than he was. If he had spoken to the kids, he would have screwed up his whole story.

"What did you tell them?" he asked.

"Oh, just that you've got a bunch of work that piled up while you were in Toronto and you had to stay late." There was rustling noise over the phone. Doug pictured Diane sitting up in bed and adjusting the receiver. "I think they bought it," she said finally, "but they'll want to know where you are tomorrow morning."

"Well, tell them I have to stay downtown for a big case. I promise I'll call tomorrow at dinnertime," Doug said with total conviction. Then, before he assessed whether it was appropriate, he asked, "How are you doing?"

The silence on the other end of the phone made him immediately regret the question. Eventually, he heard a faint shudder. "Not a good time," was Diane's stifled response.

He detected muffled sobs. "Diane, I—"

"I'll talk to you tomorrow," she mumbled, and hung up the phone.

Continuing to hold the phone to his ear, he stared off into space, confused. Diane's upset was so out of character. She was always strong and rational. Just that morning they had discussed their separation quite pragmatically without emotion. But now, with the deed actually done, she was distressed. He felt the lump rising involuntarily in his throat. He hated to hear Diane cry. It upset him. He still had feelings for her. Hell, they had been married for thirteen years and had two kids. Now a crack was appearing in Diane's facade of calm and it was exposing emotions that Doug had thought were long gone.

A beeping in his ear indicating that the telephone receiver remained unhooked interrupted his musing. He hung up the phone, turned off the light and shuffled to his bedroom.

For some time he lay in bed staring at the ceiling, unable to sleep. There was a constant buzz in his ears from the noise of the traffic on the street below and the patter of rain on the window. Light from the street lamps, the stores and the traffic flashed distortions on the curtains and ceiling like an old horror movie. There was no tranquillity in the West End and there was no peace in Doug's mind.

Things had made much more sense to him when he was in Toronto. He had known then what he wanted and what he had to do to get it. He had been able to explain to Henderson in clear terms why he had to leave Diane. Although Henderson had never agreed, in the end he seemed to understand. But now things were too complicated. Henderson was dead, and his death seemed to have taken the logic from Doug's decision. All

Doug knew now was that his kids were at home wondering why their father wanted to live away from them, his wife was at home weeping, wondering, like him, what had happened to their life, and he was lying in a bed in a West End apartment, alone, having just refused the type of offer that was the reason he had left his family in the first place.

What would Henderson have said about all this? Doug chuckled to himself. Henderson was great at I-told-you-so. In fact, what always annoyed Doug about their disagreements was how, in the end, Henderson usually turned out to be right. "You heard it here first," was Henderson's favourite introduction to a prediction. And, sure enough, his prophecies usually came true. Henderson had made no prediction when Doug had discussed leaving Diane but, given his view of Doug's decision, he might well have said, "You heard it here first. Doug Branston will realize, probably too late, that he made a terrible mistake in leaving his family."

Although it had yet to go that far, at the moment Doug felt less comfortable with his decision than when he had been in Toronto. "All in good time," Henderson would have responded with that supercilious smile on his face.

Doug continued to watch the flickering lights on the ceiling. Images of the good times with Henderson danced before his eyes: their road trips, their jibes, their partying, their arguments, the bars and nightclubs. They had had a lot of fun together. What Doug had and what he wanted seemed a lot clearer when Henderson was around berating him, always with that twinkle in his eye, with that omniscient smirk on his face that said, *You don't know what you're missing.* Too bad Henderson wasn't around. They'd have a hell of a laugh over how they both had messed up their lives.

He rolled over and closed his eyes. Only then did he realize that they were wet and he was immediately angry. Why was he feeling sorry for himself? He was in this bed alone because of decisions he had made. And Henderson was dead, no doubt, as a result of the life he chose to lead. Everyone must take responsibility for himself. But rationalization gave him no solace. He squeezed his eyes tight and pulled the covers over his head in a futile effort to block out the demons of doubt.

CHAPTER 11

Marie sat across from Doug at the kitchen table. Her eyes, normally a beautiful ice blue, were red and swollen from crying. Her blonde hair lay in a tumbleweed jumble on her shoulders. She wore only a plain white bathrobe loosely tied around her waist. She just looked tired and worn out, like a fighter who had gone too many rounds.

She had made coffee for them and now she stirred the black liquid in her cup aimlessly. Few words had been said since he had arrived. The apartment did not look messy, just neglected, with the curtains closed, plates and cups lying haphazardly around, and the plants, Marie's pride and joy, limp and lifeless. The whole setting was incredibly depressing and Doug had a great urge to turn and run. But he sat there witnessing Marie's open pain as if in penance for Henderson's sins, none of which was greater than his dying so unexpectedly.

"I'm so unhappy, Doug," she said finally. "I can't stop crying." She put her hand to her forehead and sobbed. "He doesn't deserve this much grieving."

She was right. Given the way she had been treated by Henderson, she should be relieved that he was finally out of her life. However, that would be the wrong thing to say, so Doug said nothing. He drank his coffee in silence wishing he were anywhere else.

As if reading his mind, she said, "I knew about his other apartment." She continued to stare into her coffee cup. "I knew he had other women. Women? Shit, some of them were only girls." She looked up at Doug. "You never approved of me being with Mark, did you, Doug? You thought I must have been blind or stupid or something?"

Doug wanted to avoid this discussion now. He remained silent, turning his gaze away from Marie and out the window.

"I know how you felt, Doug. But I don't think you understood everything."

Turning back to her, he said, "It doesn't matter what I thought, Marie. Hell, a lot of people criticized me for being his friend. What do they know? And what's more, what do I know?"

He hoped to end the discussion there, but Marie seemed intent on explaining herself. "There was one thing Mark never wanted anyone to know. I guess it doesn't matter anymore. You'll probably laugh," she said without humour in her voice, then took a sip of her coffee. "We had been seeing a psychiatrist, Mark and I. He had some kind of sexual disorder that made him addicted to sex."

She looked up at Doug expecting him to be amused by this revelation. Instead, he was surprised, not because his good friend was actually being treated for some obscure psychiatric disorder, but because Marie had accepted yet another of Henderson's deceits.

"I know you don't believe it, Doug," she said, again reading his mind. "But the way he treated me upset him terribly. He kept trying to stop chasing other women." She saw the doubt in Doug's eyes. "Anyway, I believe he really tried. And now, Doug, I don't want to be told otherwise." She looked at him hard for a few seconds, willing him to keep any secrets about Henderson to himself.

"I left him a million times," she continued after another sip of coffee, "only to have him beg me to come back. The last time I told him I would only come back if he was prepared to see a doctor. He agreed immediately, almost as if he was waiting for someone to tell him to get help."

Doug was having a difficult time listening to this. He liked Marie, admired and respected her, but he could not accept that Henderson's exploits were really a symptom of a psychiatric problem. This was her rationalization in order to justify staying with Henderson when she knew that he continued to be unfaithful. It was damaging Doug's memory of Henderson to hear that he had tricked Marie in this way.

"Marie, I'm sorry. Maybe I should go," he said, starting to rise from his chair.

"No, Doug," she said forcefully, placing her hand on his arm to restrain him. "Not yet. It's important for me to tell you this. I need you to know that I wasn't just blinded by Mark's charm. Our relationship was deeper, had more meaning."

Doug reluctantly resumed his seat, knowing that he was going to have to sit through Marie's explanation. "Is there any more coffee?" he asked.

She eased herself up from the table, retrieved the coffee pot from the stove and filled Doug's cup. "Look, Doug, I've wanted to tell you my side of the story for a long time. You may not accept it, but at least you'll know what was going through my mind. And I think from our professional deal-ings you know I'm not a total idiot."

That was true. Doug had great regard for Marie's intellect, which is why he was so astonished by her relationship with Henderson. How could someone as bright as Marie believe Henderson's lies?

She sat down and continued. "Mark went to a top psychiatrist who interviewed him extensively and conducted all sorts of tests. He conclud-ed that Mark had this addiction." She shrugged with resignation. "Apparently, people who suffer from sexual addiction often have had a very lonely childhood. You know, either they've been abandoned by their parents or neglected in some way. If that happens, they can grow up not knowing how to feel or express love for another person."

Doug sipped his coffee while he tried to maintain an understanding coun-tenance. However, of all Henderson's problems, he doubted that one of them was an inability to express love for another person. If anything, his problem was the opposite: he was too willing to express his love with anyone.

Marie sensed Doug's resistance. "That's why they're always wanting sex with different people. It temporarily fulfills their need to feel love and to express love." She sighed. Slowly the corners of her mouth turned down and her chin quivered. "That's all they're getting," she sobbed, "some physical satisfaction, nothing emotional, or spiritual, or lasting, no feeling of companionship."

Doug knew he must show his support for Marie now, because she had to be experiencing her own doubts. The last thing she needed was to feel his skepticism. "I don't know much about Mark's childhood," he said. "He never seemed to talk about it with me. I know his parents are divorced. Did he have the type of background that would create this kind of problem?"

Marie looked at Doug with relief. "Oh yes," she replied. "His father was a diplomat. They moved to a different part of the world every few years or so. I think by the time Mark was twelve he had been in half-a-dozen different schools."

"Tough for a kid to make any friends that way," Doug offered.

Marie nodded. "Then they sent him to a boarding school somewhere in the Laurentians. He didn't know anyone, didn't speak French. I think, at the time, his family was living in India or someplace like that."

Doug thought for a moment. "I don't even know if he had any brothers or sisters."

"Two younger sisters. They stayed with the parents while Mark was in boarding school." Marie looked out the window as she added, "A half a world away."

Doug's eyes followed Marie's gaze. Rain water ran in rivulets down the window pane. "So the psychiatrist figures that Mark developed a sexual addiction because of a feeling that he had been abandoned by his parents," he summarized, while rubbing his chin with the palm of his hand.

"He never saw his mom and dad together again," Marie argued. "They divorced before he graduated. He never really got to know his sisters." She looked back at Doug and shrugged again. "The doctor said it was a classic case."

Doug maintained a serious, contemplative expression, as if he were convinced by Marie's explanation. And maybe there was some logic to it. He had to concede that he knew nothing about psychiatric disorders, although he did know Henderson, and if Henderson truly had an addiction, he certainly never appeared to be suffering.

Marie watched Doug in silence, waiting for him to protest. When he said nothing, she continued. "We started going to weekly sessions together." She leaned forward and spoke to Doug softly, conspiratorially. "Doug, he would cry. He would curl up in a ball on the couch with his head on my lap and cry. He begged me not to leave him, to help him. What was I going to do? He needed me."

Marie searched Doug's face for some reaction. He was at a loss. Crying was going a little far, even for Henderson. He gave her an embarrassed smile. "How long had you been going to the psychiatrist?" he asked.

Marie stared at Doug, her eyes becoming glassy as she struggled to maintain her composure. She sat back in her chair, blinked hard a couple of times and quickly started talking in order to fend off further tears. "Six months, I guess," she said. "I really thought we were getting somewhere. He told me he wanted to get married, buy a house, start a family."

That was the same tale he had told Doug in Toronto. But his actions had been inconsistent with these good intentions: Sandra in Toronto, and then the fateful meeting at his hideaway upon his return.

Doug was mulling this over when a thought suddenly occurred to him. Wait a minute! What had Henderson said in the taxi? It was something about not going straight home, that Doug was going to be his alibi. Obviously, he had planned to go to the apartment. But why? Presumably to meet someone. Laura's story was that she had gone there because she knew that's where she would find him. They had not planned to meet. Had Laura lied about this? If so, why? If not, maybe he was going to meet someone else. But who? And if there was someone else, where was that person when Henderson was killed?

Marie was still talking. "Mark had some investments that he said were going to make him a lot of money. As soon as he cashed them in, he wanted to buy a house and get married."

Doug continued to wonder why Henderson had gone to the apartment. "Marie, can I ask you a question? I hope it's not too painful for you."

She gave Doug a weak smile. "Go ahead. I can't be hurt any more than I already am."

He took her hand and looked into her eyes. "Do you know why Mark went to the apartment the other night?" he asked.

Marie pulled her hand away. "Of course. To see that little Holden bitch," she cried. "The one who killed him. They're not releasing her name, but I know it was her."

"How do you know that?"

"The police said he was found with a girl, a juvenile. Holden is the only teenager I know that he was screwing. Please don't tell me there were others," she said disgustedly.

"Do you think he could have been there for another reason and just happened to run into the Holden girl?" Doug inquired.

"What other reason, Doug? To meet another one of his sluts? Shit, I don't know. I guess anything is possible." Then she said dejectedly, "I just can't accept that he was still going there after all we had been through."

Doug shook his head to show that he agreed with Marie's disbelief. She fell silent for a moment, lost in her own thoughts. Eventually, she sat back in her chair, lifted her head and fixed Doug with a probing stare. "Why are you asking that question anyway, Doug? What's on your mind?"

A sense of guilt made him flush as he realized he must tell Marie that he had been retained to protect Laura's interests.

Marie noticed his sudden discomfort. "What is it, Doug?" she asked with more concern.

"Marie, there's something I need to tell you. And I want you to hear me out before you say anything." He paused to let this sink in. Marie kept a steady gaze on him while she crossed her arms.

"To begin with," Doug said, "I want you to know that I am committed to do everything in my power to have Mark's killer brought to justice." He paused again, this time to emphasize the sincerity of his commitment. "But I must tell you that I don't believe Laura Holden killed Mark."

Marie's face hardened but Doug forged on. "Now, I have determined that the best way for me to help find Mark's murderer is to represent Laura."

Marie gasped.

Doug immediately raised his hand to stop her from speaking. "Please believe me, Marie. I know what I'm doing. Right now there are two things I am certain of: one is that Mark was killed, and two is that Laura didn't do it. So if she is charged and convicted, then someone out there will be getting away with murder. And no one wants that."

He sat back, steeling himself for Marie's reaction. She stared at him for a long time without moving. Finally, she uncrossed her arms and sat forward. When she spoke her voice shook from barely controlled emotions.

"I cannot believe it," she exhaled. "Did you know that Mark viewed you as one of his dearest friends. Did you know that, Doug? Did you know that he admired you, your integrity, the life you led, your family? Doug, he envied you. And this is how you treat his memory? You represent the prime suspect in his murder? And don't give me this shit that she didn't do it. The police have already told me that she was the only one at the scene and the gun was in her hand. What do you need? A confession?"

Marie stood up, pulled the collar of her bathrobe tightly around her neck and crossed her arms again. "I know what's happening here. And I can't believe you would be a part of it."

"What are you talking about?"

"You know damn well what I'm talking about. Larson Wren is quite happy to sacrifice the memory of Mark Henderson to hang onto its best client." With both hands she leaned on the table so that her face was inches away from Doug's. "The firm has sucked you into defending the murderer of your good friend in order to keep its best client. That stinks!"

The force of Marie's accusation threw Doug back in his chair. They stayed staring at each other for a few moments before Marie broke down in tears. Collapsing into her chair, she cried, "Jesus, Doug. How could you?"

"Marie, trust me on this. I'm doing the right thing—for Mark, not for the firm." He slowly rose from his chair. "I better go," he said. "You'll see, Marie. You'll see."

He started slowly towards the door but Marie remained in her seat, her head in her hands as she wept quietly. When he reached the door, he stopped and looked back at her. "Please, Marie. Let me know if I can do anything at all."

As he opened the door to leave, Marie called to him. He turned to face her. "The police phoned before you arrived," she said in a flat emotionless voice. "They've released the body. So I've arranged the funeral for tomorrow at two at St. Augustine's."

Doug nodded. "I'll be there." He stepped into the hallway and closed the door behind him.

It was raining when Doug left Marie's apartment building—like every day of his life, it seemed. But he was relieved to get away from Marie. He shook his head in disbelief at the thought of Henderson going to a psychiatrist because he was addicted to sex. That was just too much. Maybe he had a problem with commitment, but addicted to sex? That was like Babe Ruth asking for help because he was hitting too many home runs.

Doug got into Tom's Montego, parked by the curb. It had been a long time since he had driven such a tank. The heavy clutch and the standard three-speed gear shift on the steering column—the "three-on-the-tree"—were awkward, causing him either to stall the car or to screech its tires. However, the good old Yankee eight-cylinder engine had lots of life.

The interior of the "roguesmobile," as Tom fondly called the Montego, was suffering. The cream imitation leather upholstery looked gray; in some places the seams had torn, letting the foam innards spill out. The charcoal carpet was badly frayed. Unidentifiable white particles had gathered in all the folds and corners. Their origin was a mystery, but they liked to live in the places that were impossible to clean. The rubber weather stripping around the windshield had lost some of its adhesion, allowing rain water to run under the glass and drip unmercifully into the driver's lap.

With Doug at the wheel, the roguesmobile screeched away from the curb and rumbled down the street. Although the Gore-Tex coat jammed in his lap was uncomfortable, he had to agree with Tom that it was better than having a big wet stain on his crotch. He was headed for the scene of the crime with a new idea: maybe someone else had been present when Henderson was killed. He planned to interview the manager of the apartment building, and perhaps some of the tenants, about their recollection of that night. Likely the police had already done this, but he had better find out whatever the police already knew.

The roguesmobile's AM-only radio was tuned to an oldies station. A Harry Chapin song came crackling across the airwaves. The words suited Doug's mood, so he turned up the volume and sang along:

> It was raining hard in 'Frisco
> I needed one more fare to make my night.
> A lady up ahead turned to flag me down.
> She got in at the light.

In the solitude of the Montego, Doug belted out every lyric he could remember. He identified with what Harry was talking about. Sometimes it seems that a Wild Man Wizard was hiding in him, too.

Pulling up in front of the Barclay apartment building, he berthed the roguesmobile alongside the curb, then surveyed the typical West End street. Large, old maple trees lined both sides, their leafless branches intertwined like fishnets. Light standards zigzagged along the boulevards, their dormant lamps overhanging the wet pavement like swans' heads over black water. The main entrance to the building was, by Doug's guess, about forty feet back from the street. Wings of the building reached to the sidewalk, guarding a walkway through a landscaped garden.

Doug got out of the car and tramped through the rain up the walkway to the entrance door, counting his steps as he went to confirm his guess of the distance. As he paced, he thought he noticed out of the corner of his eye someone watching him from a ground floor window to his left.

The entrance door was solid glass within a wall of glass that stretched between the two wings. An intercom for the apartments hung in the glass facade to the right of the door. There were eight buttons on the intercom, one of which was for the manager. Doug perused the tenant list. All of the tenant buttons had a name beside them except apartment 201. None of the names was Henderson.

Peering through the glass into the lobby, he spied a large open area with a staircase against the back wall climbing from right to left. Since there was no sign of an elevator, he concluded that the building must be a walk-up. On the left side of the lobby was a door with the number 101. Underneath was a name card on which he deciphered the word "Manager." The right wall of the lobby was all mirror, broken only by the entrance to a hallway leading to the wing on Doug's right.

The mirrored wall made the lobby seem much larger than it was. As Doug tried to assess the lobby's actual size, his eyes met those of a stranger reflected in the mirror. A workman stood at the back of the lobby, cleaning the mirror glass. Just as Doug was about to signal the worker to let him in, an older woman stepped out of the manager's suite and walked to the entrance door.

"May I help you?" she asked nervously as she opened the door.

The woman was short and stout, and squinted at Doug through thick glasses. She wore a long baby blue housecoat, zipped up at the front, that hung off her like a tent. The wrinkles around her mouth twitched faintly but steadily. She seemed agitated. Who could blame her? Two days ago someone had been shot in this very lobby.

"I hope so," Doug replied. "My name is Doug Branston. Are you the manager by any chance?" He reached into the breast pocket of his suit jacket to pull out his wallet where he hoped he might find a business card.

"Yes," she answered. "I am Mrs. Rattenbury. I believe we do have one vacancy. It's a one bedroom on the second floor. But unfortunately, it isn't convenient right now to see the suite. Would you be able to come back later? Perhaps next Friday?"

Doug smiled as he searched through his wallet in vain for a business card. "I'm sorry, Mrs. Rattenbury, I had hoped I had a business card I could give you." He abandoned his search and put his wallet back in his pocket. "I'm not looking for an apartment—at least, not at the present. I'm a lawyer and I am involved in the investigation of the death of a Mr. Mark Henderson. I understand that he was killed in this lobby the night before last. I also believe that he was a tenant of yours."

The twitching of Mrs. Rattenbury's mouth accelerated. She flushed and nervously adjusted her glasses. "Uh...uh..." she stammered. "I...I've already spoken to the police. Goodbye, Mr...uh..." She stepped back from the door while trying to close it. But, like a good investigator, Doug had already placed his foot across the threshold.

"Mrs. Rattenbury, please. I know this is difficult for you. If I could have just a minute of your time," Doug said in his most courteous voice.

"Oh," Mrs. Rattenbury moaned. "I don't like this. The police. The reporters. I can't take it. Why did this have to happen in my building?" She looked at Doug. "Do I have to talk to you?" she pleaded.

Doug hated it when witnesses asked this question, because the simple answer was "no." One option, he supposed, was to lie like some of his colleagues did and to say that, yes, she was obliged to talk to him. But that was simply wrong, and a lawyer needed to be honest and have integrity. As well, that tactic would eventually come back to haunt him. Sooner or later Mrs. Rattenbury would be told that she was not obliged to talk to anyone. Then, not only would Doug look bad, but if she reported him to the Law Society, he would be reprimanded as well. Honesty, he knew, was always the best approach.

"No, Mrs. Rattenbury," he said. "You are not obliged to talk to anyone before a trial. However, if you are subpoenaed, you will have to tell a judge and jury everything you know that may be relevant. Now, if I am one of the lawyers on this case, it may be necessary for me to subpoena you just to find out what you do know." Well, that might be slightly inaccurate. It was unlikely he was going to subpoena her if he was unsure of what she was going to say. But Doug needed to keep the explanation simple. "However, if you answer a few questions now, it may be that I will not require you to attend a trial."

Mrs. Rattenbury was flustered. She made a whining sound as she thought of what to do. She looked anxiously over her shoulder at the workman in the lobby and then back at Doug. It amazed him how often he experienced this kind of reaction from people when he told them he was a lawyer. They acted as though they had encountered a junkyard dog.

"What kind of a lawyer are you, Mr...uh...?" Mrs. Rattenbury's shaky voice trailed off.

"Doug Branston. Please call me Doug, ma'am. I am a defence lawyer. I represent a suspect in Mr. Henderson's murder."

Mrs. Rattenbury's countenance relaxed slightly as she attempted a melancholy smile. "Oh, not that poor child? I'm sorry, I don't know her name. I always referred to her as Kim." She glanced up at Doug. "I never thought that she would actually kill him. But it was clear that she adored him and it seemed that he had lost interest in her. Love does strange things, I guess." Her gaze floated down to the ground. "I wouldn't know anymore," she said under her breath. "It's such a shame. I really liked her."

So, Mrs. Rattenbury knew who Doug's client was. He hoped her sympathy for Laura would get him through this door. "Mrs. Rattenbury," he said, "I'm not at liberty to tell you my client's name, but let's call her Kim. I want to help her as much as I can. It seems to me that you would like to help her too."

Mrs. Rattenbury nodded. "Yes, if I can. She seemed like such a sweet girl."

"May I come in then, ma'am? I think if you can answer a few questions for me, it may help." Doug moved forward to pressure Mrs. Rattenbury into allowing him to enter the building.

She hesitated momentarily, then moved aside and let him pass into the lobby. "Shall we go into my suite?" she suggested.

"That would be perfect," Doug agreed. Once he stepped into the lobby, though, he noticed that the area around the workman was carpetless. In fact, an entire section at the base of the staircase was missing. A new roll of carpet lay beside the workman, presumably the replacement for the section that had been removed.

Instead of following Mrs. Rattenbury to her apartment door, Doug strolled over toward the workman. "Is this where it happened, Mrs. Rattenbury?" he called over his shoulder.

She reluctantly walked over to stand beside Doug at the spot where the carpet had been removed. "Yes," she replied. "The police outlined on the carpet where they found Mr. Henderson's body and where Kim was lying unconscious. They took up that whole section. For evidence, I guess." Then almost as an afterthought she said in a low voice, "Besides, there was a lot of blood on the carpet. It was going to have to be replaced anyway."

Gesturing toward the workman, she said, "This fellow is cleaning the mirror. There was blood splattered all over this end of the glass and the back wall almost to the door to the storage room." She spread both arms to indicate the area covered by the blood spatter.

Mrs. Rattenbury was warming slowly to her role as Doug's ghoulish tour guide. She walked across the uncarpeted section of floor to the corner of the lobby where the back wall met the mirror. "See here," she said, pointing to a small hole in the corner, level with her eyes. "This is where they found the bullet that killed Mr. Henderson. They say it went right through his heart." She turned to face Doug and shook her head. "Isn't that symbolic?"

Doug surveyed the scene for a few moments. It appeared as if the shooting had happened almost at the foot of the staircase. The position of the bullet in the corner of the wall suggested that the killer had his (or her) back to the staircase. Also, the bullet must have travelled on a slight upward trajectory to have passed through Henderson's chest and penetrated the wall where it did.

Doug walked over to the door of the storage room. It was located at the foot of the stairs and camouflaged by the gaudy wallpaper on the back wall. When he tried the doorknob, the door opened. As he peered into the darkness of the storage area, he said, "I take it this isn't kept locked, Mrs. Rattenbury?"

"No need to," she said a little defensively. "Only tenants and their guests can get into the building. Anyway, all the storage compartments are individually locked."

"Is there another entrance to the storage area?"

"No. Only an emergency exit at the rear of the building. One of those one-way doors, you know. Crash doors. It opens onto the alley."

Doug closed the door and turned to face Mrs. Rattenbury who stood directly behind him. "Shall we go to your suite then?"

She ushered Doug into the living room of her apartment. The room was very large, comprising the entire ground floor of that wing of the building. Scatter rugs were spread haphazardly over sections of the hardwood floor, and small sofa tables were placed randomly, each laden with nick-nacks and little framed photos. Paintings and photographs blanketed the walls while a fake fireplace, with a sitting area facing it, occupied the centre of one wall.

There were only two windows in the living room. One faced the street and the other faced the front courtyard and entrance. An old, well-worn armchair sat by the window to the courtyard. It intrigued Doug that the chair faced back toward the building entrance rather than out to the street.

"Please sit anywhere, Mr. Branston," said Mrs. Rattenbury. "Why don't I make us some tea?"

Doug took a seat on the sofa beside the fireplace. "A cup of tea would be just what the doctor ordered right now, thank you."

Mrs. Rattenbury smiled before disappearing into the kitchen. "Make yourself at home," she called. "I'll just be a jiff."

He glanced at the various photos which were displayed around the room. They had all been taken years before. One was of a much younger Mrs. Rattenbury standing beside a tall man with slicked-back hair and a closely-clipped moustache. A black and white photo of the same man, youthful and in uniform, dominated the mantelpiece over the fake fireplace. Another photo portrayed the couple beside an old Buick four-holer that looked brand new in the picture. Several faded photos showed the couple, or one of them, with a little girl. Beside the black and white photo on the mantelpiece was a colour graduation photo of a young woman who had the little girl's eyes.

Doug tried to piece a family history together from what he saw around him. Judging by the lack of recent photos, he concluded that the tall man must be dead. The girl was likely a daughter who had graduated from university, moved away and left Mrs. Rattenbury to manage the apartment building on her own.

"Here we are," chirped Mrs. Rattenbury, carrying a tray into the living room. She was quite bubbly now. Doug suspected that she rarely had visitors. She sat on the sofa across from him and put the tray on the low table between them. "How do you take your tea, then, Mr. Branston?"

"Just a little milk, thank you," he replied. "Are the photos of your family?"

Mrs. Rattenbury busied herself with the tea service in front of her. There were two pots: one containing tea leaves and the other hot water. She poured the water into the pot with the tea leaves, mixed it around with a silver spoon and then placed a silver strainer on top of a cup and saucer. While she waited a moment for the tea to steep, she looked up at the photos on the mantelpiece.

"Yes. That's my late husband. He died five years ago. Heart attack. And the other is his daughter. She's an accountant. She's married and lives in Toronto." Mrs. Rattenbury poured the tea through the strainer.

"You run this apartment building all on your own, then?" Doug asked, trying to confirm what he already suspected.

"That's right," she said with some pathos and pride. She handed him a cup of tea. "Tell me if it's too strong, won't you."

He reached over the coffee table and took the cup from her. "I like it strong."

"So do I. Otherwise, its just warm pee," she giggled.

Doug wanted to bring the conversation around to Mrs. Rattenbury's recollection of the events from the other night. He asked if she had known Mr. Henderson well, to which she responded that he had been a tenant for about a year but they had seldom talked. "He liked to come and go." After some prodding from Doug, she confirmed that Henderson seemed to use the apartment only periodically. Doug asked her why she thought that was the case. She answered in a low, conspiratorial voice, that maybe he was doing things he shouldn't be. Then she winked.

Doug suspected that Mrs. Rattenbury knew a great deal about her tenants' private lives; life on her own had probably turned her into a snoop. He asked, "Are you suggesting that Mr. Henderson brought women to the apartment?"

She nodded in response, with an odd twinkle in her eye and a grin. Doug began to fear that she might be trying to flirt with him.

"More than one?" he asked.

She nodded again, enthusiastically. This time she raised her eyebrows a couple of times as if to say, *What a cad, eh?*

Doug stretched to place his tea cup on the table as a way of breaking eye contact with Mrs. Rattenbury. He asked if she knew how many women there were, if she knew their names or if she was able to describe them. She explained that there had been a few women over the past year, but that she only really remembered the most recent two: Kim, the young girl who was there when Henderson was killed, and another one whom Mrs. Rattenbury called Carmen.

"How long had he been seeing Carmen?" Doug inquired.

"I think it started about two months ago. Since then she's been coming around more and more, though. If you ask me, she was Kim's replacement. Which would explain why Kim was so angry the other night."

"Do you know if Carmen was here that night?"

"I didn't see her. I don't think she was. If she was, she would have been in the apartment waiting for Mr. Henderson. And the police searched it after they arrived and they didn't find anyone."

Doug asked what Carmen looked like, but Mrs. Rattenbury had difficulty describing her other than in general terms—late twenties or early thirties, average height with dark hair—because she was always covered up.

"She was very secretive," Mrs. Rattenbury said. Then she leaned forward and confided, "I don't think she wanted people to know she was coming here." Doug thought he detected a momentary puckering of Mrs. Rattenbury's lips after she said this.

Wanting to find out how Mrs. Rattenbury obtained all her information, without suggesting that she was a meddler in other people's affairs, he commented, "You are a very observant manager. No doubt you have to be vigilant in this area of town if you're going to avoid bad tenants."

"That's very true, Mr. Branston," she replied proudly. "The West End is filled with all sorts, as you probably know. I don't need them in my building." Doug tried not to roll his eyes.

"And how are you able to keep such a close eye on your tenants, Mrs. Rattenbury?" he asked, feigning interest in her dedication to the smooth operation of the apartment building.

She was dying to tell him. "I spend a great part of the day watching the front entrance through that window." She pointed to the window to the courtyard. "It's amazing what comings and goings I see from there."

"Did you see anything the night of Mr. Henderson's death?"

"I certainly did." She touched his knee with her hand for emphasis. Then she launched into a long discourse on the events that she had witnessed. Doug let her go on without interruption.

She recalled that she was first drawn to the window when she heard a loud voice outside the front entrance. She saw Henderson standing with his back to the entrance and Kim facing him. Mrs. Rattenbury couldn't recall all the words that were said, but Kim was yelling at Henderson. He then stepped into the lobby, and Kim followed, shouting at him "like a little terrier barking at the postman's heels." Once the entrance door closed the voices were muffled, but Mrs. Rattenbury was still able to see the couple arguing. Kim was definitely the aggressor. Henderson kept backing up towards the stairs. He shrugged his shoulders a few times, then he appeared to smile at Kim. That just angered her more, and she started to swing her fists at his chest and his face.

"I was afraid someone was going to get hurt," Mrs. Rattenbury said, "so I went to the phone to call the police."

"Where is your telephone located, Mrs. Rattenbury?" Doug asked, looking around the living room for it.

"Oh, it's in the front hallway by the entrance."

He stood up to look back through the living room towards the area of the front hallway. She rose from the sofa as well. Explaining that the telephone was out of view from where they were standing, she walked from the living room to the front hallway. Doug followed. There, she pointed out the small table across from the entrance door where the telephone was located.

"This is where you came to call the police," he said.

Mrs. Rattenbury confirmed this with a nod.

"Then what happened?"

"Well, I dialed 911 and eventually got the operator. She asked if I wanted police, fire or the E—uh—HS, whatever it is. I didn't know what to say so I told her there was a family squabble happening in the lobby and I was concerned someone was going to get hurt. A second later I heard a shot from the lobby. The operator must have heard it too. She began asking me all sorts of questions. Oh, Mr. Branston, I've never been so scared."

Mrs. Rattenbury was getting agitated as she recounted her story, so

Doug asked a few questions to keep her focused. "What time was this approximately?"

"I don't know, maybe nine, nine-thirty. The police told me the time, but I can't remember," she said, flustered.

"And do you recall how long you were away from the window before you heard the shot?"

She thought for a moment. "I don't know. A few minutes," she said, almost as a question.

"What kind of questions did the operator ask you?"

"Oh." Mrs. Rattenbury was able to answer this question more accurately. "She asked all sorts of questions. What had I seen? What could I see now? Of course, I couldn't see anything standing in the hallway. But the operator wanted me to stay on the line so I didn't go back to the window. I tried to spy through the peep hole in the front door." She pretended she had the receiver to her ear as she demonstrated how she had looked out the peep hole. "But you can't see very well all the way across the lobby. Take a look." She stepped away from the door.

Doug put his right eye up to the peep hole. All he saw was a distorted view of the lobby, as if he were looking through the wrong end of old binoculars. He could barely distinguish the workman still busy on the mirror at the far side of the room.

"Pretty hard to make anything out, isn't it?" Mrs. Rattenbury commented. She leaned on Doug while she pretended to look through the peep hole with him. "All I could tell—and I told the operator this—was that Mr. Henderson and Kim were no longer standing in the corner of the lobby. The operator asked if I could get a better look, but there was no way I was opening that door."

She stepped back and folded her arms across her chest to emphasize that she did nothing that she did not want to do. "So she told me to stay on the line because the police were on their way."

"Did you do that?"

"Of course," she nodded. "And within a couple of minutes they were ringing my intercom." She pointed to the receiver on the wall by the door. "I let them in. And only then did I go out into the lobby."

"What did you see?"

Mrs. Rattenbury adjusted her glasses to help her recollection. "Well, there were so many policemen in the lobby it was hard to see anything. And they immediately roped off the area at the foot of the stairs. But I was able to see Mr. Henderson lying on the floor in the corner. That whole area I showed you was splattered with blood."

"What about Kim?"

"As far as I could tell, she was lying at the foot of the stairs. Here, I'll show you."

Like the lady of the manor, Mrs. Rattenbury strode out the front door of her apartment and across the lobby to the staircase. Doug followed in her wake. She shooed the workman aside and pointed to the area on the floor where she had seen Henderson and Kim. She explained that both were lying on their backs. Henderson's head was toward the mirror and Kim's was toward the staircase.

"I didn't see anything else, really," she said. "The police got me away from the scene pretty quickly for an interview."

"So you didn't actually see Kim shoot Mr. Henderson? Correct?" he asked in his best courtroom voice.

"That's right."

"And in this whole sequence of events, did you see anyone else in the lobby other than Mr. Henderson and Kim?"

She shook her head *no*.

Doug asked if any of the other tenants knew anything about what had happened. She told him that she doubted it, however she agreed to give him the tenant list so he could contact them himself. He also proposed that he inspect Henderson's apartment, but she reluctantly refused. The police had told her that she must not let anyone enter the apartment without a court order or the consent of a member of Henderson's family.

Doug had exhausted all his questions. He thanked Mrs. Rattenbury and offered her his hand to shake. She grabbed it with both her hands, squeezing it warmly. When he advised her that he might have a few more questions for her at a later date, she invited him to call her anytime. She said "anytime" with a provocative lilt that worried Doug she might have intended the invitation to be suggestive. A shudder passed through him as he bid her farewell and left the building.

Doug powered the Montego over to the hospital where Laura was convalescing. She was asleep when he arrived and the nurse on duty refused to allow him to disturb her. He arranged for the nurse to leave a note on Laura's bedside table saying that he had been there, he hoped she was feeling a little better and he would call on her again soon.

With Laura unavailable, Doug's only choice was to return to the office and see what horrors awaited him. First, though, his stomach demanded attention. He steered the Montego into the line-up at the closest fast food drive-through for the ultimate test of coordination: eating a greasy burger and fries, water gathering on the Gore-Tex coat jammed between his legs, while driving a standard three-on-the-three in downtown traffic, in the rain. Although he didn't pass the test flawlessly, he was pleased with the result, given his lack of practice: one mustard stain on his tie, a grease mark on his sleeve from an ill-aimed french fry and dry trousers. He docked the Montego in the parking lot of the firm's office building and headed to the elevators.

As he passed the switchboard on the thirty-second floor, the receptionist handed him two pink messages. A quick look at the mail on his desk revealed only junk; his secretary had gone for the day with one of those unique secretarial ailments that strike at mid-afternoon when the boss is out, so he was left to deal with his messages alone.

One was from Tom reminding him that Trudy and Cathy were coming to the apartment for dinner. Doug knew Trudy was Stern's secretary, but he had to think for a moment before remembering that Cathy was his blind date from the previous night. The note commanded him to bring wine.

The other message was from the prosecutor's office, ominously requesting that Doug call back as soon as possible. He immediately returned the call but the prosecutor was out. The Crown secretary advised that the prosecutor hoped Doug was available to meet with him and Detective Campbell the next day following the close of the courts at four o'clock. Even though Henderson's funeral was scheduled for two o'clock that day, Doug thought he could make a meeting by four-thirty. Therefore, he confirmed a meeting for that time in the prosecutor's office at the criminal courthouse. Before disconnecting, the secretary requested that only counsel for Ms. Holden attend.

Doug recorded the meeting in his calendar, although there was little chance he was going to forget a meeting with the prosecutor to which Laura and her father were not invited. This was a fair indication that a decision had been made about whether charges were going to be laid. Doug had a good idea what that decision was.

CHAPTER 12

Tom loved to cook. That night he planned to serve veal parmigiana with linguini, bocconcini salad, lots of Italian bread with olive oil and balsamic vinegar, and dark red wine. He had to leave the office early to search for just the right ingredients. A trip to Little Italy and a meander through the produce and grocery *mercati* were, for Tom, an essential part of the pleasure of cooking. Besides, he was happy to take a break from the work that had monopolized his day, reviewing the file Henderson had been handling for Holden.

It had started easily. Tom had looked up the company name, Blackwater Holdings, on the computer in the firm's accounts department. He had obtained the file number and then retrieved the file from central storage. It was bulky enough—filling two expandable folders—and it was kept as only Henderson kept a file, loose documents stashed away in random order. Tom had dragged the folders back to his office for a page by page review.

The file started about two years before when Holden incorporated Blackwater Holdings as a vehicle to provide financial advice to clients. This was surprising since Holden's businesses had traditionally involved real estate sales and construction of residential and commercial buildings.

Early in his business career, Holden had done very well buying properties and flipping them to foreign interests. In fact, Tom understood that Holden had become a master at contracting to sell properties to foreign buyers before he even owned them. In that way, he avoided being stuck with an unsaleable property. He then ran the risk of being unable to deliver properties he had contracted to sell, but that had never happened.

Eventually, Holden expanded into the construction business. Foreign investors usually bought properties in order to build apartment buildings or office towers, so Holden acquired a couple of construction companies. He was then able to offer a package to foreign investors: the property and the builder. He had gained a good reputation internationally from the sale of real estate, and as a result, foreign interests were happy to hire one of his companies to do the construction, especially if it meant a reduction in the property's purchase price.

Holden's business background had clearly taught him a great deal about investment, particularly in residential and commercial real estate. Evidently, people began to seek his advice on financial investments, allowing him to develop his business as a financial advisor.

The Blackwater Holdings file appeared to deal exclusively with advice to off-shore captive insurance companies. Tom had some knowledge of the purpose of captive insurers. These companies were usually located in the Bahamas or Barbados, although the shareholders tended to be large Canadian organizations. A captive insurance company was set up by an organization as a separate corporate entity in order to provide property and casualty insurance exclusively to that organization. The organization benefited in three ways: it paid insurance premiums to a company that it owned, the premiums were lower than those charged by a private insurer and the company enjoyed significant tax advantages in the foreign jurisdiction.

Provided the organization had few insurance claims, the captive insurance company would become flush with cash and, consequently, would be constantly on the lookout for solid investments. That was where Holden came in. He advised captive insurance companies on investments in commercial and residential real estate, both domestic and foreign. Henderson, with his great ability to understand the laws of foreign jurisdictions and to sort out conflicts in the laws of different countries, was perfectly suited to provide legal advice on the investments. This was particularly important, because the captive insurance companies had to conform to the laws of the jurisdiction in which they were registered in order to gain tax advantages. The properties they were buying were often in other jurisdictions with less favourable tax laws. The purchase agreements and the payment schemes had to be drafted specifically to take advantage of the better tax laws. It was all very complicated and Tom had to struggle to understand any of it, but it explained why the file was so huge.

As he reviewed the Blackwater Holdings file, Tom noted that Henderson had also prepared the documents conveying the properties to the captive insurance companies. The documents themselves, however, were stored away in their own separate files. In order to retrieve them later,

Tom recorded the references to the properties conveyed while he reviewed the Blackwater Holdings file. When he finished reviewing the file, he had a list of fifteen properties, purchased by captive insurance companies in different jurisdictions throughout the world. By then it was mid-afternoon and he was not about to start searching for the conveyance files. Instead, he left the list with his secretary along with instructions to have the files on his desk for the next morning. Then, because Doug had taken the roguesmobile, he grabbed a cab to Little Italy to do the grocery shopping.

Another cab brought Tom and his purchases back to his apartment building. He lugged the groceries up to suite 2012 where he found Doug pacing back and forth in the living room while talking on the telephone.

"No, pal, no. It's just that I have this big case I have to work on right now, so I've got to stay downtown for a little while." Doug saw Tom and gave him a sheepish smile as he concentrated on the words coming through the phone line. Before continuing to speak, he turned away from Tom. "No. There is nothing wrong with Mom and me." He paused again, then said, "That's right. Don't worry. Everything is just fine. Now tell me, when do you play hockey this weekend?" Pause. "Okay. I'll come and watch you. Can you put your mom on?" Another pause. "See you, buddy. I love you."

Doug threw himself down onto the sofa while he waited for Diane to come on the line. He took a couple of sips from the beer that had been sitting on the side table.

"Oh. Hola, Conchita. Donde esta la senora?" He held the phone to his ear in silence, listening to Conchita's reply. Eventually, he began to shift in his seat and rock his head from side to side. Waving to Tom, he made hand signs indicating that Conchita was talking nonstop and he understood nothing. Finally, he held the phone away from his ear so that Tom could hear the high-pitched metallic sounds coming from the other end of the line.

"Conchita..." he said, returning the receiver to his ear. "Conchita...Gracias...Si...Gracias...." Pause. "Ya. Adios."

He hung up the phone. "I have no fucking clue what she just said, but she sounded pissed off." He stood up and downed his beer. "I need another." In the kitchen, with his head fully inside the refrigerator in search of a cold beer, Doug whined, "So, how was your day, dear?"

"Wonderful," Tom answered. "I love taking cabs in the rain." Then, like a good junior lawyer, he began to recount his discoveries in the Holden file.

"Hold it," Doug withdrew his head from the refrigerator. "No business. It's time to rest and relax, my friend. You can tell me all that tomorrow."

"Fine with me. I've had enough of Holden's money-making adventures for one day, anyhow." He turned to organizing the groceries he had bought for dinner. "Did you get my message?"

Doug pulled two beer bottles out of the refrigerator, opened them and handed one to Tom. "I did indeed," he confirmed before taking a large gulp. "And I must say that I am looking forward to it. Cathy is her name? Well, I propose a toast to Cathy," and he turned the bottle up once more.

The dinner guests were to arrive in an hour. Doug and Tom took turns showering and changing before meeting back in the kitchen to prepare the meal. They worked well together. Tom knew his way around the kitchen like a gourmet chef and Doug knew how to stay out of the way. Doug was totally incapable of cooking anything correctly. It came out either burnt or raw.

"Did I ever tell you about the time when Diane was out of town and I was cooking breakfast for the kids?" He asked Tom. "I was boiling these eggs, but I didn't put them all in the water at the same time. So, when the timer goes off, I don't have a clue which eggs went in first and which ones went in last. Turns out Adrian gets the egg that's been cooked for all of about thirty seconds and it's still sort of this clear jelly inside." He winced in recollection. "Well, I try to get Adrian to eat it anyway, but there's no way. Finally, I grab the egg and eat it myself. It was like eating warm snot. Yuk. That's when I hung up my cooking apron." He thought for a moment and then added, "I guess I'm going to have to learn, now."

Doug opened the wine to let it breathe, while Tom chopped up the vegetables. When Tom had finished with a bowl or plate, Doug quickly washed it, dried it and put it away. It reminded him of his university days when he had worked part-time as a dishwasher, then a busboy, in a local Greek restaurant. That was a wild time. The restaurant had three upper levels that all looked down onto the ground floor. On Friday nights it filled up with college kids who gathered there because of the slightly exotic atmosphere—Greek taverna music pumping out at full volume—and the cheap wine. It was there that Doug, like most of the patrons, had acquired his taste for Retsina.

Those were the days before AIDS when the worst thing to fear from a date was a phone call the next morning with a declaration of her undying love. That became a problem for some of the young men working at the restaurant. Certain women failed to understand the unwritten rule that relationships with staff were, by definition, one night stands. It never became a problem for Doug, though: he fell for a waitress named Diane only two weeks after starting at the restaurant. Rather than being the one who dreaded phone calls the next morning, he was the one making them. At first she had been standoffish, but Doug had persevered, eventually conquering her with charm. Before either of them knew what had happened they were married. Doug was struggling through law school, and Diane was continuing to work as a waitress to pay Doug's tuition and put bread on the table. Suddenly, life had become serious.

Well, that was then. Now, Doug's life was going to be a little less serious, at least for tonight. He finished his chores around Tom and gravitated to the refrigerator to retrieve another beer.

"How about some tunes?" he said. Without waiting for an answer, he strolled into the living room to inspect Tom's collection of CDs on the shelf beside the stereo. He flipped through a few before settling on the Counting Crows. "I love this song," he said, selecting "Mr. Jones."

The song's introductory guitar chords sounded over the speakers. Doug turned up the volume and gyrated around the room, wailing the words he knew into his beer bottle microphone:

Mr. Jones and me tell each other fairy tales
We stare at the beautiful women
"She's looking at you.
Ah, no, no, she's looking at me."

Over the noise, the intercom buzzed.

Doug picked up the receiver. "Come in, ladies," he growled, and pushed the door release button. Then he stepped into the hallway to meet the elevator's delivery of the dinner guests. When the elevator door opened, Cathy and Trudy stepped out. Cathy greeted him with a soft nuzzle on his cheek and then held his arm while they walked back to the apartment. This time Doug was determined to maintain his focus.

Cathy also appeared determined to keep Doug's level of interest high. As soon as they entered the apartment she produced a bottle of tequila, then headed straight to the kitchen and pulled out a mixing glass from one of the cupboards. She filled the glass with ice and poured in a healthy gurgle of tequila. Meanwhile, Trudy retrieved shotglasses from another cupboard.

Doug watched with interest as Cathy poured chilled tequila into each of the shotglasses. When all were full, Trudy handed one to Tom and one to Doug. She and Cathy picked up the remaining glasses and held them up in front of them.

"Anyone have a toast?" Trudy asked.

"Yeah, I do," Doug replied, raising his glass. He caught the twinkle in Cathy's eye just as he proposed, "To wherever the night takes you." They all clinked glasses, then tossed back the tequila. "I think another may be in order," Doug gasped.

"Ooo. I need a little latin beat," Trudy cooed. She replaced the introspective Counting Crows with a brassy salsa CD. Crying "Ai, yi, yi," she shuffled and swayed to the conga beat. Cathy joined in, moving to the music and casting suggestive glances at Doug.

Dinner barely interrupted the show. They ate ravenously, drank lots of wine, laughed and sang mumbo-jumbo along with the Latin singers. The problems of the day evaporated from Doug's mind, replaced by an overwhelming desire to see Cathy's breasts.

It was close to ten o'clock by the time the plates were empty and the antics around the table began to wind down.

"More wine?" Tom asked, about to open the third bottle.

In a moment of clarity, Doug suggested, "Let's save it." Then, smacking his lips, he added, "My palate's calling for something a little sweeter. What do you have in the liqueur department, Elvis?"

Tom opened the cupboard behind him to reveal a generous selection of bottles. "Jesus," Doug gasped, "I think Larson Wren must be paying you too much."

"You forget the roguesmobile," Tom replied.

Doug laughed. "Very true. Apparently, you prefer to spend your whopping wage on consumables rather than transportation."

With snifters full, they retired to the living room. The sofa, covered with a dark green quilt, sat along one wall. Beside it was the end table with the telephone, while beyond it was a large matching lounge chair. A wall unit holding various books, the stereo system and the television was across the room. Between the sofa and the wall unit was a coffee table.

Tom moved to his usual spot on the lounge chair, stopping on his way to change the music. k.d.lang provided just the right touch of mellow to go along with the liqueurs. Trudy sat half on Tom's lap and half on the arm of the chair while Doug and Cathy sat close together on the sofa.

The change of ambiance and music served its purpose. Everyone sat quietly, staring off into space, lost in their own thoughts. For Doug, his thoughts focused on the body leaning up against him. During dinner he had found himself scrutinizing Cathy's figure.

As he listened to the crooning over the stereo, he reflected on how he seemed more critical of Cathy's body than he had been of Jenna's. Why was that? He shrugged in a reflex response to the silent question and, in doing so, rubbed his arm against Cathy's cheek. Apparently she took this as a sign of affection because she cuddled a little closer to him, raised her head up and gave him a soft kiss on the ear. He turned his head to look down at her. Out of the corner of his eye he saw Tom and Trudy smile at each other.

Tom drank the last of his liqueur, then stared into the snifter for a moment to satisfy himself that there were no more drops hiding at the bottom. "Well, I'm ready to call it a night. What do you think, darling?" he said to Trudy.

Without answering, she got up off the chair, took Tom's hand and led him off to the bedroom. She gave a friendly wave to Doug and Cathy as she passed while Tom winked and said good night.

After a moment, Cathy shifted her position on the sofa so that her entire body was pressed against Doug. She put both arms around his neck and pulled his head down to hers. They briefly looked into each other's eyes, their faces inches apart, then she sighed, closed her eyes and opened her mouth. They kissed. It was soft and tentative at first, but gradually their mouths became bolder, their lips pressed harder and their tongues began probing each other's mouths, like New World explorers.

Initially Doug experienced difficulty fully enjoying the moment. As he became aroused his penis got hopelessly tangled in his boxer shorts. Doug tried shifting his legs to free things up, but was unsuccessful. Just then, Cathy's hand slid over his crotch and, with some fancy finger work, freed all constraints. A sense of liberty overcame Doug and he stretched out on the sofa with Cathy. Now their bodies were flat against each other, their hands racing over each other's curves, protuberances and depressions, their lips and tongues working busily.

Doug had not made out fully-clothed on a sofa since his university days. He was excited and exhilarated, but he avoided becoming too carried away and peaking prematurely. He remembered from ancient experience that it was capable of sneaking up and striking before he had time to react. Henderson's old rule helped him keep his passion in check: make sure the woman is ahead of you on the ladder to orgasm. When it appeared that he was scrambling up the rungs and about to overtake Cathy, he slackened his embrace and whispered into her ear, "Let's go to bed." Nuzzling his earlobe, she murmured her agreement in a throaty voice.

They slowly sat up, continuing to fondle each other. Finally Doug moved to pull himself off the sofa, but Cathy held him back.

"Wait," she said, reaching for her purse. "I really like to have a joint before sex."

She pulled out a fat joint from inside her purse and displayed it to Doug reverently. Keeping her eyes locked on his, she licked the joint from end to end with long, moist, strokes. Then she lit it, sucking deeply to ensure that the weed was burning well. Doug reached out to take the joint from Cathy but, instead of handing it to him, she leaned forward offering her open mouth for him to kiss. As their lips met she slowly exhaled the smoke from her lungs. He breathed it in. The smoke slipped easily down his windpipe, Cathy's body having absorbed its harshness. On hitting his lungs, it sent an instant rush to his head. They repeated this pleasure a few more times until every nerve in Doug's body was alive and tingling, so aroused he feared he was going to explode.

Suddenly, he was unable to wait any longer. He butted out the joint, grabbed Cathy and carried her to the bedroom. They fell onto the bed, tearing off each other's clothes until they were naked, writhing together on top of the sheets, madly caressing each other with hands and lips and tongues, climbing over each other like wrestlers, wallowing in each other's sweat and saliva. They were animals, lusting wantonly, insatiably, until eventually, as their energy waned and their fascination with each other's bodies calmed, they settled into a slow, steady rhythm that seemed as eternal as waves lapping against a shore.

Doug stared at his naked reflection in the mirror. His eyes were red tomatoes, he had a fish's mouth that opened and shut steadily, and his body was covered with shiny scales. In the mirror Henderson's image loomed as if he were standing behind Doug, but when Doug turned to look, no one was there. He turned back to the mirror to see the apparition once more. This time Henderson tried to say something, but Doug was unable to make out the words. Henderson laughed then, and turned to greet another figure hidden in the shadows. Doug watched their reflections in the mirror as they embraced. Who was Henderson with? Her face was hidden. Doug strained harder to see, and when the couple released each other, he recognized Cathy. Again, he turned to look behind him, but no one was there. He shivered.

The coldness of the room brought Doug back to consciousness. He opened his eyes to find that he was lying on top of the bed, naked, while Cathy snored delicately beside him. She had climbed under the covers while he slept. His head was pounding, a dry smoky taste lined his mouth, and he had a sense that the room was turning to his left. "Water," he wheezed, then eased himself to a sitting position on the side of the bed. After a few deep breaths he hoisted himself up and tottered toward the bathroom. As he passed Cathy's side of the bed he stooped to gaze down at her, but her features were obscured by the darkness.

He turned on the light in the bathroom and stared at himself in the mirror. It reminded him of the dream he had just had. "Jesus, Branston," he said to the blotchy image that stared back at him, "are we having any fun yet?"

CHAPTER 13

The Church of St. Augustine enjoyed a wooded, park-like setting in an affluent area of the city. It was a modest A-framed Anglican Church with a large white cross dividing the panes of glass over the entrance. A small Memorial Garden, where the ashes of dead parishioners were interred, nestled against the back wall of the church under the peaceful gaze of a large, stained-glass Christ attending to his flock. It was a fitting site for Henderson's ashes to rest, especially since right next door were four public tennis courts where he had loved to play on balmy spring afternoons instead of attending to his clients. Although he never expected to die so young, this was the place where Henderson had always said he wanted to have his ashes interred: "overlooking those public courts so I can keep an eternal eye on the girls in their little tennis skirts."

He had never been a religious man, never considered for a moment joining the parish of a church. However, with a sort of prescience, he had made a point of befriending the young and athletic minister of St. Augustine's. They had played tennis once a week in the park, weather permitting, and in return for allowing the good reverend an opportunity to enlighten him on the Christian way, and for a regular donation to the church, Henderson had gained a reservation in the Memorial Garden when the time came.

Tom and Doug were late for the service when Tom manoeuvred the roguesmobile into the church parking lot. The closed church doors indicated that the ceremony had already begun. Doug had not planned it this way, but, he admitted to himself, he preferred it. Now, he was able to sneak into the back of the church unnoticed, allowing himself an early escape route if needed.

Something about churches made him uncomfortable. Whether it was a wedding, a funeral or just Sunday worship, he found that his emotions became unbridled and free-flowing when he sat in a pew. From one moment to the next he might change from total dispassion to overwhelming pathos, causing his throat to tighten as if held in a noose, his hands to sweat and tears to stream from his eyes like icicles melting in the warm sun. He suspected these uncontrollable feelings came from a deep, subconscious sense of guilt that he was failing to live his life the way The Big Guy wanted. Given Doug's antics of the previous night, and the fact that he had come to bury his good friend, he fully expected to be overwhelmed with emotion when entering the sanctuary.

He had gone to the office early with Tom in order to review the Blackwater Holdings file and the conveyance files for the properties purchased by the captive insurance companies. Upon arrival at the office, Tom had given Doug a concise summary of the Blackwater Holdings file, following which they began reviewing the conveyance files. The material had absorbed them, time had run away from them, and they had become late for Henderson's funeral.

Blackwater Holdings conveyed properties all over the world. In each case, Henderson had acted as the legal representative for the purchaser, the captive insurance company. As Doug began to review the conveyance files, he recognized that Henderson had consistently placed himself in a potential conflict of interest. On the one hand, he had been advising Blackwater Holdings, the financial advisor for the captive insurance companies, with respect to the tax implications of its clients buying certain properties. Blackwater Holdings used that advice to encourage its clients to invest. On the other hand, he had been the clients' solicitor when conveying the properties. In the former case, his role was to advance the interests of Blackwater Holdings, but in the latter case, it was to protect the interests of the captive insurance companies.

But Doug's concerns were soon placated. Squirreled away in the back of each file was a Certificate of Independent Legal Advice signed and sealed by the purchaser. It stated that the purchaser agreed to have Henderson act for it on the conveyance, with full knowledge that Henderson had provided previous advice to Blackwater Holdings, and after Henderson had advised the purchaser to obtain independent legal advice to protect its own interests. Whether the purchaser ever obtained independent legal advice was irrelevant. The fact that it was aware of Henderson's conflicting role and that Henderson had advised it to obtain the independent advice protected him against a claim for conflict of interest.

The vendors of the properties had all been private Canadian corporations—usually registered in Ontario—even though many of the properties were located outside the country. Doug noted that the same law firm had acted as the vendors' solicitor on all the conveyances from Ontario-based companies. Likely there was some connection between the vendor companies. He suspected, as well, that Holden had something to do with that connection because there was a Holden characteristic to the transactions: in all cases the properties had been acquired by the vendor companies only a short time before the sale to the purchasers, reminiscent of Holden's own practice when selling properties to offshore purchasers.

Every one of the conveyance files included a real estate appraisal report on the market value of the property. What was perplexing was that each report had appraised the particular property at a value higher than the price paid by the captive insurance company. This meant that the vendor companies had acquired the properties and then flipped them quickly for below market value.

Doug was surprised that Frank Holden had actually allowed Henderson to continue to do his legal work after the relationship Henderson had spawned with Laura. It was also curious how Henderson had subtly threatened to publicize the legal work when Holden suggested laying charges against him. Now that Doug had reviewed the files, he was certain there was something fishy about the business Henderson and Holden were involved in. Why else would Holden be prepared to put up with Henderson?

Doug understood, as well, why Holden had asked him to look after the files now that Henderson was dead. Holden knew that there was a good chance Doug would learn in the course of defending Laura about the kind of legal work Henderson was doing for him. He knew, as well, that Henderson and Doug had been friends, that their relationship with their partners was distant, and that therefore, once Doug had reviewed the files and had recognized the work was suspicious, he would be inclined to come to Holden for an explanation before reporting it to his partners.

Doug considered whether to meet with Holden immediately for an explanation of the work Henderson had been doing, but he felt he needed more background information before approaching him. Besides, a more critical matter was about to take up all of his time. The meeting with the Crown Prosecutor was scheduled for after the funeral and Doug fully expected to be advised at that time that charges were going to be laid against Laura. Unfortunately, any further inquiry into the mysterious relationship between Holden and Henderson was going to have to wait. Nevertheless, before leaving for the funeral, Doug instructed his secretary to do a complete background check on all the vendor companies, so that when the opportunity arose, he would be able to investigate their connection with Holden.

Remarkably, Reginald Wren had managed to get all the lawyers in the firm to attend the funeral. Having spent the last few days away from the office investigating Henderson's death, Doug had missed the strong-arming that Wren must have undertaken to get his partners to the church. Attending Henderson's funeral was the last thing most of them wanted to do. In fact, Doug was sure that many of them simply thought: *good riddance*. However, when he walked through the wooden doors into the sanctuary of the church, there they were, all in their dark gray and blue suits, sitting shoulder to shoulder in the second pew, flipping absent-mindedly through hymn books, whispering to neighbours now and then, glancing artfully around the room, looking suitably glum and pious at the same time. A bunch of hallowed hypocrites.

With Tom, he slipped into the pew at the very back of the church. Doug had avoided attending church on a regular basis since he was a child, but he did acknowledge to himself that he harboured some rudimentary religious belief. So, before he sat down, he knelt on the prayer stool before him and bowed his head in the way he had learned as a boy.

With his head in his hands, he wondered if Henderson could see from his place on high this gathering of all his partners praying for his salvation. What an opportunity! One good bolt of lightning and Henderson could take them all with him. *Just aim for the front of the church, buddy,* Doug silently implored.

While Doug was still on his knees, the music suddenly burst forth into the overture for the introductory hymn, drawing the congregation to its feet to mumble the lyrics. Moments later, over the confused rumble of sounds, came the louder, clearer, more convincing voice of the minister as he turned from the altar to face the congregation. His singing provided the needed direction and the refrain gained enthusiasm.

When the hymn ended, the minister asked the congregation to sit. "Today," he began once all were seated and the church was quiet, "we have gathered here, not to mourn the loss of our friend and colleague, Mark Henderson, but to celebrate his life."

While the minister rambled through the standard theme, Doug looked around the half-full church and conducted an inventory of attendees. The church was about half full. Lawyers, students and some staff from the firm sat close to the front. A few lawyers from the wider legal community, some of whom Doug knew personally and others whom he knew only by reputation, were scattered throughout the church. A number of women were present as well. Doug had met some of them before, although he had long forgotten their names. Almost every one of them sat alone while their eyes, in constant motion, scrutinized the other women. Marie sat at the front of the church. A man who looked to be about Henderson's age sat with her, although Doug was unable to identify him from where he was sitting.

Doug remained composed while the minister spoke, but when Wren got up to say a few words, his emotional fortifications started to crumble. Wren, long and lanky, in his three-piece navy blue suit with the gold watch chain hanging from the waistcoat, gathered himself awkwardly off the pew and shambled slowly to the podium. During Henderson's years at the firm, Wren had always struggled to keep Henderson and his partners from killing each other. Now, Wren looked old, tired and depressed, as if he had lost the one adversary that made his life interesting. His melancholy impressed Doug, causing his emotions to gain hold as he had feared they would. He turned away from Tom while his eyes welled with tears.

Wren surveyed the room before he spoke, commanding everyone's full attention, as usual. Eventually, he announced, almost in defiance, "Mark Henderson was my friend."

Doug's emotions blurred his attentiveness to the words that followed. As he sat in silent grief at the back of the church, his mind wandered through other miseries in search of company. He thought of his father's untimely death and he pondered for the millionth time all the things that were left unsaid between them. He thought of his great childhood friend that he had abandoned because the boy had become an impediment to Doug's plans for success. And in the midst of his reverie, he thought of Diane and the children, the family he had left so that he could live his life more like Henderson's. Was Cathy it? Was what happened last night the life he had achieved at the expense of his family?

Wren finished speaking and returned slowly to his seat, his head bowed pensively, shouldering the gravity of the moment with the demeanor of a pallbearer. His partners watched him under sincere, furrowed brows and nodded their concurrence with the words he had spoken. When Wren sat down at the end of the second pew, Richard Stern reached over and gave him a solemn pat on the shoulder, acknowledging a heavy task well done.

The organ cranked up again, the minister crooned the first few notes of the closing hymn and the congregation stood to join in with gusto, relieved that the grim ritual was ending. Then the minister, singing as he went, his hymn book lying open on the palms of his hands—needlessly, since he knew the words by heart—strode down the centre aisle and out the main doors of the church. When the hymn finished, there was a moment's confusion while some of the congregation kneeled to say one more prayer. Everyone started to file out.

Doug and Tom slipped out the doors before being overtaken by the crowd clogging the aisle. Once they were outside, Doug said to Tom, "Get the roguesmobile, man. I'm going to wait and speak to Marie."

The congregation spilled slowly out of the church, comfortable now in their piety. Marie, the last one out, drew everyone's attention. She dutifully received their expressions of sympathy, even while sparks flashed between her and the women who had obviously been Henderson's lovers.

Marie soon noticed Doug. Immediately, she excused herself from the group she was with and walked over to him. "You must come with me," she said taking his elbow. "The minister is going to inter the ashes in the garden now. He prefers that only family be present while he does it. That means you and me."

Before he had a chance to object, Doug was led around the side of the church to the Memorial Garden. They found the minister waiting patiently for them on the grass at the edge of the recently-turned soil, the hymn book still open in his hands like an offering. Near him was a small hole in the earth in which sat an open cardboard box of ashes. Henderson—what was left of him.

The minister said a prayer, then turned the box upside down, letting the ashes fall gently onto the soil. Murmuring a benediction, he stooped to mix the soil and the ashes with a trowel. He straightened up after a moment, smiled at Marie and said with a sweeping gesture of his arm like a matador's cape, "I think Mark will like it here."

Doug's eyes were drawn immediately to the nearby tennis courts while he wondered whether Marie had understood the hidden significance of this comment. She simply smiled. "Thank you," she said and shook his hand.

As they walked back to the parking lot she slipped her arm through the crook of Doug's elbow. "I owe you an apology," she confessed. "I was feeling sorry for myself yesterday and wasn't prepared to recognize that you had lost someone dear to you as well. I don't know who killed him, Doug. But I do know that you are doing what you believe is right for Mark. I trust you." She stretched up to give Doug a kiss on the cheek.

"Thanks, Marie," Doug replied. They walked in silence for a moment, Marie's head against his shoulder. In the nearby parking lot the roguesmobile came to life with a deep rumble. "Are you going to need a ride?" Doug asked.

"No, thanks. I came with an old friend of Mark's. Tony Capetti." She looked ahead; a figure was walking towards them dressed entirely in black, his shiny hair pulled back into a pony-tail. "Here he comes now. Do you know him, Doug? He's from the East."

Doug recognized Tony immediately, having just been with him in Toronto, although it seemed like a century ago. They nodded, greeting each other solemnly, clumsily, conscious of the circumstances.

"I am in total shock," Tony said. "Can you believe we were with him in Toronto just last week? It's incredible!"

Doug shook his head sadly. An awkward pause followed, broken finally by Doug asking, "When did you arrive?"

"Just yesterday. I got away as soon as I could. Mario really wanted to come, but he's totally tied up in a business deal."

"Are you here for long? We should get together for lunch or something if you've got the time." Doug had little interest in lunching with Tony, but he wanted to avoid talking about Henderson and he was unable to think of anything else to say.

Tony nodded. "Yeah. I'm here for a few days anyway. There's some business Mario wants me to look into for him while I'm here." He dropped his voice, gave Marie a sad sympathetic smile and added, "I sure don't feel like doing much business right now though."

Doug looked at his watch: four o'clock. "Shit. I've got to go." He thought about giving Tony his card but was sure he had none in his wallet. Anyway, talk of lunch was just that—talk. "Look. Marie has my number. Give me a call and we'll set something up." He gave Tony's hand another shake, kissed Marie on the cheek and ran off towards the roguesmobile.

Tom had pulled up to the near side of the parking lot; the Montego idled patiently. Hopping into the front passenger seat, Doug instructed Tom to head straight for the prosecutor's office.

"You know who wasn't at the service?" Doug asked Tom, suddenly breaking the silence in the roguesmobile. Before Tom had a chance to answer he said, "Diane. You didn't see her there, did you?"

Tom shook his head.

"She knew Henderson pretty well. We used to do things together: Diane, me, Henderson and whoever. She never approved of him but she always liked him. I'm surprised she didn't show up."

Tom drove on without speaking. He knew it was best that Doug have this conversation with himself.

"I should have called her before we went to the church," Doug mused. "Shit. I didn't think our problems would stop her from coming to the funeral." He thought for a moment. "I wonder if she even knew about it. Remind me to call her after the meeting, okay?"

Tom nodded. The rain had slowed to a drizzle while they had been at the service, but now it was quickly becoming a downpour. The windshield wipers, on high speed, struggled to keep up with the fallout from the bombs of water hitting the glass. Tom adjusted the Gore-Tex jacket between his legs.

"I love this old boat," he said more to himself than to Doug. "But maybe it's time to get something a little more practical."

The prosecutor's office and the criminal courts were housed in one building, an old monstrosity that sat at the corner of two sleazy streets in the heart of the most decrepit part of the inner city. A hundred years ago this corner had been the centre of commerce and the building had been a brand new edifice built in neo-classical style, the pride of a fast-growing community. Since then the business district had gradually moved away from the corner, abandoning it to the destitutes who now called it home. However, with the city's steady growth there was a continual need for more criminal courts. Wings and sections had been added to the building, haphazardly, inartistically and cheaply, and the bold, true lines of the original flawless granite structure, which had so aptly symbolized the promise and ideals of the system it was built to protect, gradually became worn, stained and incongruous.

The building was undergoing yet another renovation when Doug and Tom entered the main lobby. Naked concrete floors displayed patches of old black sealant and zigzag trails of dried glue once used to keep carpet down. Gone were the ceiling tiles, in order to provide access to the building's wiring. The aluminum grid that had once held the tiles in place now hung over the corridors like jail bars.

The corridors and hallways were filled with people, mostly young men, loitering aimlessly as they waited for their cases to be called. Their vacant, defeated look contrasted with the manic energy of the young, naive public defenders who scurried about in preparation for their defence.

Two Natives, their black hair long and stringy, their faces ravaged and red, shared an elevator with Doug and Tom. They wore only vests over their bare shoulders, exposing their homemade tattoos. Poorly-drawn crosses, skulls and curses, all etched in dirty green, defaced their bodies like graffiti.

When the elevator doors opened at the prosecutor's office, Doug and Tom stepped into an area with four metal desks, each occupied by a secretary working at a computer. The woman at the desk closest to the elevator looked up from her screen and asked if she could be of help. Doug explained, as he noticed the clock on the far wall read four-forty, that he and Tom had a meeting with the prosecutor at four-thirty. In his mind the timing was perfect. Lawyers always like to make their visiting adversaries wait; at least by arriving late, the wait would be shorter.

The secretary reviewed the day timer on her desk. "Yes," she said without taking her eyes off the book, "I see you have a meeting with Mr. Christopher." Then she looked up at Doug and smiled patronizingly. "I'm sorry, Mr. Christopher is still in the pit. He should be back shortly. Would you like to have a seat?" She motioned to the threadbare couch by the elevator.

"The pit?"

"Oh," she giggled, holding her hand self-consciously up to her mouth. "Sorry. The pit is what we call Courtroom 101. Remand Court."

"Of course," Doug agreed.

The secretary added, as if speaking to a first-year law student, "You know. That's the court where the accused makes his initial appearance. They read the charge and set dates for a bail hearing and a trial." She gave Doug a self-satisfied smile. As he retreated to the couch, she continued, "But the court closed at four, so Mr. Christopher should be back any moment."

Doug thanked her and sat down beside Tom, who was flipping through a back edition of *People* magazine he had found on the table by the couch.

Moments later the elevator door opened and two men stepped out. Doug recognized Detective Campbell; the other man, he determined, was Christopher. The prosecutor was a little shorter than Doug, stocky, with tightly-curled brown hair. His friendly, boyish face was uncluttered with glasses or facial hair, allowing a full unobstructed view of his engaging smile.

Campbell and Christopher strode over to where Doug and Tom were sitting. Christopher held out his hand as Doug stood up. "You must be Doug Branston," he said, taking Doug's hand in a firm handshake. "I'm Bob Christopher. Look, I'm terribly sorry I'm late. I don't believe in this bullshit of making the other guy wait. It's simply rude. Please accept my apologies."

"No problem," Doug replied. Against his better judgment, he had a feeling that this guy Christopher might be sincere. He introduced Tom to Christopher, then shook hands with Detective Campbell.

They exchanged pleasantries and Christopher directed them all to a small boardroom on the other side of the office. As he passed the secretary who had spoken to Doug, Christopher asked, "Mary, did you set up the Henderson file in the boardroom?"

"It's all there," she replied officiously. "May I get anyone coffee?"

Doug seldom drank coffee while working, but he couldn't resist asking the irritatingly perfect Mary to bring him a cup of decaffeinated coffee with cream, not milk, and low-calorie sweetener, not sugar. With a quick wink at her, he entered the boardroom.

The four of them sat around a small circular table stacked high with documents, folders and loose papers. Christopher's amiable countenance soon faded to a grim, pragmatic look. He began speaking softly and slowly in order that Doug and Tom understood the importance of what he was telling them.

"I know that Mark Henderson was a friend of yours, Doug," he said. "You should know that he was a friend of mine too. We went to law school together. I'm married with kids now, so we kind of drifted apart. In the last few years we only got together for lunch a couple of times. But I always considered him a good friend. I greatly admired his abilities." Christopher paused and shook his head in wonder. "Although I must admit he was incredibly self-destructive. Christ, what was he doing with that Holden girl, anyway? He could have been her father. You know, old man Holden was talking about laying a sexual exploitation charge. What a prick that guy is, eh, Russ?"

Detective Campbell smiled and nodded sagely as though recalling events involving Holden that were known only to him and Christopher.

"Anyway, I expect in many ways I'm like you," Christopher said returning his gaze to Doug. "We both want Henderson's murderer punished. The only difference between us is that I am convinced from what I have seen"—he placed his hand on the stack of papers on the table—"that Laura Holden did it." He held Doug's gaze in order to emphasize his conviction.

"Now," he continued, "what I really want to do is prove this to you so that we can cut a deal." He leaned forward in his chair and dropped his voice. "You know, the Holden girl pleads guilty to a lesser charge. In that way we avoid a trial and a lot of publicity. Taking this through court isn't going to help Henderson's memory. I'd be forced to introduce a bunch of evidence of Henderson's decadent lifestyle which the papers would love to splash across their front pages. As a friend of Henderson I don't want that, and I'm sure you don't want it either."

"But there are certain restrictions on publication of evidence from proceedings in Youth Court," Doug suggested.

Christopher shook his head. "Doug, don't kid yourself. If this goes to trial, it'll be elevated to adult court." With a note of disgust in his voice he explained. "The Attorney General's Office, in its infinite wisdom, has made it mandatory that I apply for elevation in cases of homicide. And my experience is that the courts are disposed to grant it." He waved his hand in the air as if to push the point aside. "Besides, the only restriction on publication in Youth Court is the name of the accused. The evidence is still available to the press. So a Youth Court trial isn't going to help Henderson's memory."

Doug and Christopher stared at each other for a few moments while Doug tried to judge whether Christopher was bluffing and really only interested in a quick resolution of the case, or whether he was truly convinced of Laura's guilt and wanted to avoid a messy trial and save some posthumous dignity for Henderson. Christopher sensed Doug's dilemma. He stood up and reached for the files on the table.

"Look," he said, "I could force you to go through Discovery Court to obtain all the evidence we have. But, in good faith, I'm going to show you the basis of the Crown's case right now so that you will recognize that what I am proposing makes sense for everyone."

This was fine with Doug. A rule he always followed was to never stop an opposing lawyer from blabbing about his case and why he thought it was strong. Doug found that once he knew the other side's theory and how the lawyer expected to prove it, his job of meeting that case became much easier. The only thing to be wary of was a bluff by the other lawyer, either in relating a theory of his case that was not the one he was really pursuing, or in withholding a crucial piece of evidence in the hope that Doug might be unprepared to rebut it at trial. But Doug sensed that Christopher was genuine. Anyway, there was no harm in listening. He raised his eyebrows towards Tom who, understanding the silent instruction, pulled a notepad from his attaché case.

Christopher searched through the stack of documents. Eventually, he pulled out a file folder labelled "Forensic Investigation Report." He flipped it open and sat down.

"I've gone through the reports," he said, "and I've highlighted the evidence that I think the Crown would use to prove a case against Laura Holden. I'll summarize it for you and you can decide if you find it as overwhelming as I do."

He studied the file for a moment. "Let's look at the physical evidence first," he began. "Henderson's body was found in the lobby of the Barclay apartment building. He was supine in the corner of the room with a single bullet hole in his chest. The coroner's office has found that the bullet wound was fatal. The blood spatter on the mirror and the wall of the lobby indicate that he was shot from in front while standing. A .38 caliber bullet that matched the gun found at the scene was extracted from the wall. The fact that the bullet passed through Henderson and lodged in the wall indicates that he was shot at close range."

Christopher flipped through a few pages of the file looking for further information. Finally he stopped. "Okay. What about Ms. Holden?" he said. "She was found unconscious on the lobby floor, also in a supine position. Her feet were a short distance from Henderson's. If you had stood them both up, they would have been facing each other at a normal talking distance. She had a .38 caliber gun in her right hand with five bullets left in the six-chamber revolver. This gun matches the bullet found in the wall. It is the gun that shot Henderson dead."

Christopher raised his voice when he said "dead," for added emphasis. Then he paused and took a couple of deep noisy breaths through his nose. Doug suspected that this was a tactic he used when addressing a jury in order to hold their attention.

"The gun has no serial number, no history," Christopher continued. "The only prints on it are Ms. Holden's. Now, if you consider the standing position of Henderson and Ms. Holden just before the shooting—facing each other, a few feet apart—and then retrace the bullet's line of trajectory from where it entered the wall back through Henderson's chest, that line crosses Ms. Holden's body on the right side about hip high." Christopher stood up and demonstrated this location, his right hand alongside his hip like a gunslinger in the old west cocking a six-shooter beside his holster. "Right about here," he said.

He sat down and began flipping through pages again, talking as he did. "When Ms. Holden was found unconscious at the scene, she had a large leather bag looped over her right wrist." He stopped at a particular page, skimmed through it and then looked up at Doug. "The bag has a small round hole in the leather. Forensic analysis has concluded that"—he read from the file page he had turned to—" 'the size of the hole and the powder burns found around it indicate that it was caused by the same bullet' that killed Henderson. Therefore, the gun that killed Henderson was shot from Ms. Holden's purse. This is consistent with the bullet trajectory if you assume that the purse was strapped over her right shoulder before she fell to the ground. Which I suggest is a fair assumption."

Christopher closed the file and placed it on the table. He looked at Detective Campbell for confirmation that nothing had been left out. "So there is the summary of the physical evidence," he said, as Campbell nodded his concurrence. "Pretty impressive, eh?"

Doug resisted the urge to comment either way. If he agreed, it would indicate that he had some doubts about Laura's innocence; if he disagreed, he would be inviting a debate about which parts of the evidence he found weak, giving the Crown an opportunity to reconsider the evidence and improve upon it. Instead, he simply raised his eyebrows at Christopher and gave a noncommittal "Hmmmm," while admitting to himself that the evidence he had just heard was quite convincing. However, there was one event that Christopher's summary did not explain.

Doug and the prosecutor watched each other for some time. Finally, Christopher capitulated. "Okay. I know. How does Ms. Holden shoot Henderson dead and then end up unconscious herself? That's the weakness in the Crown's case." He stood up and searched through the stack of documents again. "I've got a preliminary opinion on this somewhere," he said, continuing to sift through papers. "We've only had the forensic evidence for a day, so there hasn't been enough time for our medical expert to finalize his report."

Christopher was unable to find what he was looking for. Eventually, he gave up and sat down. "It's in there somewhere. Have you seen it, Russ?" he asked Detective Campbell who shook his head nonchalantly. "Well, anyway, it's the doctor's view that Ms. Holden was knocked unconscious by a blow to the right side of her head. Perhaps the blow to the head was simultaneous with the gunshot." He thought for a moment. "In fact, I may be prepared to discuss the possibility that the blow to the head caused Ms. Holden to pull the trigger." He hesitated, waiting for a reaction, but Doug remained stone-faced. Christopher continued, "The other possibility— and our expert confirms that this is physically possible—is that she was struck, and in the moment before she fell to the floor unconscious, she pulled the trigger."

It is a golden rule in litigation not to dwell on the weak aspects of one's case. Acknowledge them if necessary, then move on to stronger points. With any luck, after all the evidence is in, the weaknesses will be forgotten or, at least, afforded little significance by an adversary. Christopher immediately grabbed another file entitled "Witness Statements."

"We know of no eyewitnesses to the shooting," he said. "The only witness to events surrounding the shooting is Mrs. Rattenbury. I understand that you have spoken to her so I won't bore you with the details of her evidence. Suffice to say that she confirms that Henderson and Ms. Holden had carried on a romantic"—he raised his hands and flexed the middle and index finger of each to indicate quotation marks around the word romantic—"relationship at the apartment for some time, but recently Henderson was showing up at the apartment with another woman. And the night of the murder, Henderson and Ms. Holden were in the lobby, alone, embroiled in a heated discussion. Mrs. Rattenbury was calling 911 when she heard a gunshot."

Christopher placed the "Witness Statements" file on the table. He stood once again to search through the stack of documents, found a file entitled "Documentary Evidence" and sat back down.

"I don't think there's any doubt that Henderson and Ms. Holden were involved sexually," he said. "Hell, a couple of weeks ago old man Holden wanted to nail Henderson for sexual exploitation of his daughter. In any event, the letter from Henderson to Ms. Holden would appear to confirm this. You've seen this."

He removed a copy of Henderson's letter to Laura from the file and handed it to Doug. Doug inspected the copy. He noted that it had the same lines and handwriting on it as the one he had received from Detective Campbell.

Campbell then spoke for the first time since the meeting started. "The handwriting matches that of Ms. Holden," he confirmed.

Christopher continued. "Obviously it helps the Crown's case if I can establish motive. Well, I suggest this document does just that. Ms. Holden was madly in love with Henderson. He was everything to her; he was her Svengali. And he dumped her. She lost it and decided that if she couldn't have him, then no one could. They argued; she became physical. Finally, he struck her, and before she hit the floor, she shot him."

Christopher looked back down at the file. He glanced through some pages, stopping a moment later. "Now, here is something I don't believe you've seen." He removed a document comprising fifteen photocopied pages stapled together. "This is a copy of Ms. Holden's diary for the past year. Up to the last few entries it is full of adoration of Henderson, of how he made love to her, of the promises he made to her, of their plans for the future. You read this and it's clear, without any doubt, that she was totally, absolutely, utterly, heart and soul, devoted to the guy. Then you read the last couple of entries made after she got the letter. Shit. It's certain that she couldn't deal with the relationship ending."

Christopher flipped to the last pages of the document and began reading excerpts, "'Mark cannot do this…He cannot touch anyone else…I must stop him…I will stop him…He will understand…We are meant for each other…We must be together forever…' and so on."

Then he turned to the last page of the document. "But here's the real clincher," he said. " 'Better dead than with someone else.' 'Dead' is underlined about five times." Christopher closed the document slowly, almost religiously. "There you have it," he said. "The Crown's case in a nutshell."

They all sat silently for some time digesting the weight of the evidence Christopher had divulged. Tom had done his best to scribble down the highlights; now he had pages of notes curled at the top of his notepad like a rolled-up newspaper.

The question that Doug had debated asking Laura the other night in the hospital nagged at him. He contemplated the harm that might be caused to Laura's case if he put the question to Christopher, then decided that it could only help her defence to hear all of the Crown's theories.

"How did she get the gun?" he asked.

Campbell smiled. "A .38 millimeter revolver? The so-called 'Saturday Night Special'? They're very easy to get. Talk to anyone who lives on the street. He can deliver to you an unregistered weapon like this within twenty-four hours for under fifty dollars." Campbell saw the doubt in Doug's expression. "It's done every day," he shrugged.

"So it's the Crown's theory that Laura bought the gun on the street?" Doug asked with exaggerated incredulity.

"Most likely," Christopher said. "But, to anticipate your next question—no, we have no evidence to establish that."

Doug pondered this small victory: the Crown had Laura at the scene of the crime with the murder weapon in her hand, but was unable to prove where she got it. He was trying to determine how this might help her defence when Christopher spoke up.

"Of course," he said, "enough of her acquaintances at school are connected with street kids that we can put together a pretty good theory of how she got the gun if we need to. Besides, I guess the decision you'd have to make at trial is whether you wanted to put her on the witness stand to deny that she had the gun."

Doug understood fully Christopher's point. In a criminal matter the Crown has the onus of proving its case against the accused beyond a reasonable doubt. The accused may refuse to give evidence in her own defence, and the trier of fact, either a judge or a jury, is not entitled to infer from an accused's silence that she is guilty. Therefore, defence counsel is always reluctant to have the accused give evidence because, once she is on the witness stand, she must submit to the prosecutor's cross-examination, which can be devastating.

Doug pondered the likely result if he put Laura on the stand to deny that she ever had the murder weapon. Christopher would be able to cross-examine her on her relationship with Henderson, on how she felt hurt and betrayed when he wanted to end it, on how she was determined not to let that happen, on how she felt he would be better off dead. Christopher would ask her why she went to the apartment building that night. He would confirm that she quarreled with Henderson, and finally, that she did not remember how he was shot. By the end of the cross-examination, the judge or jury—and probably Laura—would be convinced that she had killed Henderson. The mystery of her acquisition of the gun, the only reason for Doug to put her on the stand to begin with, would become an inconsequential discrepancy in the evidence.

Doug changed the subject. "So what are the charges?" he asked.

Christopher feigned pensiveness, as if he was only now putting his mind to this question. Doug knew better. Christopher must have analyzed the evidence thoroughly before the meeting in order to be able to advance his position as forcefully as possible. He knew exactly what charge he wanted to lay against Laura and what lesser charge he would be prepared to accept in return for a guilty plea. To get to his bottom line would take a great deal of negotiation which Doug was unprepared to start until he had reviewed all the evidence for himself. However, he was still interested in hearing Christopher's opening position.

"Well, let's see," Christopher said rubbing his eyes. "In my view, the evidence could support a charge of first degree murder. She took a gun to her meeting with Henderson. Why? Because, as she said in her diary, Henderson was better off dead. Put those two facts together and you've got planning, deliberation, murder one." He looked at Campbell, who gave him a single, judicious nod of approval. "However, I'm practical enough to recognize that the more likely conviction would be for second degree murder. At the moment she pulled the trigger she intended to kill him, but she hadn't really planned it. Her intent in taking the gun to the scene was just to scare him and not to shoot him."

Christopher pointed his index finger at Doug professorially. "Remember, of course, that second degree murder is an included offence in first degree. Therefore, the Crown can take a run at a first degree charge and settle for a second degree conviction."

Doug understood. An included offence was one that was an integral part of another offence. The common example was the offence of sexual assault which was comprised of sexual intercourse and the included offence of assault. If the Crown proceeded with a sexual assault charge, proved assault, but failed to prove sexual intercourse, the accused would be convicted of assault.

Christopher looked Doug in the eye. "I told you when we started— between you and me, no bullshit—that for the sake of Henderson's memory, I don't want this thing to go to trial." He flattened the palms of his hands on the table top. "Therefore, I'm putting my cards on the table now." A deep, noisy breath to retain Doug's full attention. "Although I think I could get at least a second degree murder conviction, I'm prepared to discuss with you a plea of manslaughter." He waited for Doug's reaction, but there was none. Disappointed, he said, "Well?"

Doug returned Christopher's stare. "Well. I don't know." He ran his hand through his hair. "Look, Bob," he started, in a chummy way. "I can't agree to anything until I review the evidence thoroughly myself and take my client's instructions. Let's be honest. That's going to take some time."

Christopher nodded vigorously, "I understand. I understand." He stood up and shuffled through the files on the desk. "These are all copies, right Russ?"

"That's right," Detective Campbell said.

"Good. Well, Doug, why don't you take the Forensic Investigation Report and the Documentary Evidence files? I think you've got everything else. Review them. Talk to your client. And get back to me." He handed the files over to Doug with a smile, but his serious expression quickly returned. "I'll need to hear from you shortly, though," he said, "because I've got to proceed with charges when Ms. Holden is released from hospital. And that's got to be in the next couple of days, right Russ?"

With a frown, Detective Campbell inclined his head to confirm.

The meeting had come to an end. Doug and Tom stood up from the table and packed the documents Christopher had given them, along with Tom's notepad, into the attaché case.

"Great," Doug said. "I appreciate your candor, Bob. I'll get right on this." He patted the attaché case. "We'll be in touch."

Christopher and Detective Campbell ushered Tom and Doug to the elevator, shook hands and bid them a warm farewell. Tom and Doug stepped into the elevator.

Once the doors had closed behind them, Tom mumbled, "Sounds like they've got a pretty good case."

"Mmmm," Doug replied, and then, "You know, I never got my cup of coffee."

CHAPTER 14

It was about six-thirty at night by the time the roguesmobile throbbed out of the parking lot of the old courthouse, although from the darkness outside it might have been midnight. They were headed to the hospital where Doug had arranged to meet Laura and her father. He had called Holden from the lobby of the courthouse to organize the impromptu meeting.

"Well, Elvis, what do you think?" Doug asked as he fastened his seatbelt. "Did she do it?"

Tom rocked his head back and forth in time with the windshield wipers. "Jesus. They've got some pretty convincing evidence, don't they?"

"Yeah. But did she do it? Gut feeling. After you've heard the evidence against her—and you're right, it's a good case, although it's all circumstantial; no one actually saw her pull the trigger—so, gut feeling, knowing Laura, and knowing Henderson, are you convinced? Did she do it?"

Tom considered the question while navigating the roguesmobile. Finally, he said, "I just don't see it. There's got to be some other explanation."

"Okay," Doug nodded. "Let's assume she didn't do it. What's the other explanation? She's got the gun in her hand and a bullet hole in her purse. If she didn't do it, someone wanted to make it look like she did."

"You mean someone set her up."

"Yeah."

Tom frowned. "But how does that happen? If you're going to set her up you've got to know she's going to be there. But she said they hadn't planned to meet. She just decided to show up at the apartment."

"Good point." Doug thought about this for a moment. "Unless," he raised his index finger to his mouth. "Unless, you're planning to kill

Henderson and along comes Laura, at just the right second, so you knock her out and put the gun in her hand."

"Maybe," Tom conceded. "Maybe."

"So let's start again. Assuming Laura was set up, who wanted Henderson dead?"

Tom smiled despite the grim question. "Where do you start?"

"Well," Doug began. "He was planning to meet someone—not Laura—at the apartment. Who was it? Was it that other broad he was seeing? What had the landlady called her? Carmen? Could she have done this? Or maybe some other woman he had pissed off?" Doug thought for a moment. "What about Marie? Jesus. Maybe she had had enough?"

Tom was unconvinced. "I don't know. You think Marie or one of his lovers would be able to knock Laura out, shoot Henderson through her purse and put the gun in her hand—all without leaving a trace?"

"I don't know. She could have hired someone to do it for her." Changing directions, Doug suggested, "Or what about Holden himself? You know he threatened to kill Henderson because he was banging Laura?"

"And let Laura take the fall?" Tom shook his head. "No, I don't think so."

There was silence as both men searched their brains for other possibilities. Finally, Doug said, "Well, maybe it's something we don't even know about yet. Maybe Henderson got himself into something that was bad news. Who the fuck knows? But I'm with you," he confirmed. "Even with all the Crown's evidence, I still can't believe Laura did it."

A few seconds passed before Doug added glumly, "But, of course, our gut feeling means dick if we don't come up with something to undermine the Crown's theory." He shook his head in distaste, "And let's face it, without some evidence of Laura's innocence we're going to have to consider Christopher's offer of a plea bargain."

"I wonder if Laura has any idea of what's happening here," Tom pondered.

Doug began thinking of how best to raise with Holden and Laura what had been discussed at the meeting with Christopher. "I don't know," he replied. "Maybe we should tell Holden what's going on first, without Laura present. He should have some idea of what we should say to Laura."

He thought for a few moments. "But ultimately, there's no way we can sugar-coat this pill. She's got to be told that she's facing charges that could result in a prison term." Then he added after a short pause, "And if she knows anything that might help prove her innocence, she better tell us."

Doug and Tom sat in silence for some time while Tom directed the roguesmobile through the drenched downtown traffic. They passed a corner where a plugged storm sewer had created a great pool of water on the street. As Tom navigated the Montego through the water like a tug boat between freighters, walls of spray rose beside the car windows. Pedestrians scrambled back to escape the crashing wake of the car.

"You know, Elvis, we've got no choice," Doug said finally. "We don't have any leads on another explanation for Henderson's murder. And the Crown isn't going to wait while we search for something. Even if we wanted to make a deal with the Crown—which we don't—we can't until we've examined all the evidence for ourselves and drawn an informed conclusion about whether they have enough to actually prove Laura did it. The only way we can guarantee that we have all the evidence, both good and bad from the Crown's point of view, is to go through Disclosure Court."

Tom nodded.

"But do you see what that means?" Doug asked. Then he answered his own question. "You don't get to Disclosure Court without charges being laid. So it seems to me that we can't even consider dealing with the Crown until after they lay charges against Laura. That means she will have to face arrest, a court appearance, a bail hearing, and possibly a move by the Crown to raise the matter to adult court before we can even determine whether we should be negotiating a plea."

They were close to the hospital now. "We've got some time before Holden arrives," Doug noted looking at his watch. "Let's grab a coffee before we go in."

Tom found moorage for the roguesmobile and they headed into the coffee shop across from the hospital. It was just one of the new chain stores that had burgeoned across the city serving designer coffees. Yuppies and the hip, groups that normally avoided the same hangouts, appeared comfortable together here, tasting the essences of the week—the biscotti, the apple crumbles—and reading newspapers.

Once seated with a steaming cup of cafe latte, Doug came back to his point. "I expect Laura will be released in the next day or two. From what Christopher said, if a deal isn't in place by then, they'll arrest her. Frankly, I don't see how we can avoid that. So we can only plan for it."

Doug's primary concern was the psychological impact that criminal charges and an appearance in court might have on Laura straight out of hospital. He and Tom were going to have to prepare her for what she was about to face, and at the same time arrange with Christopher and Detective Campbell to make the ordeal as painless as possible.

Doug wanted to meet privately with Holden first to apprise him of what had taken place at the meeting with Christopher. He needed Holden to help him determine the best way to approach the subject with Laura. It was Doug's initial view that Laura must be counseled immediately on the basis of the Crown's case against her, the charges she was facing and the steps she was going to have to follow during the process of arrest and her first court appearance. At least then she would have an opportunity to prepare herself. In the event Holden agreed with this approach, Doug planned to contact Christopher and work out the details of the charge and arrest before actually meeting with Laura.

Meanwhile, Tom had to find out from the medical staff at the hospital when Laura was to be released so that they would know the timing of the arrest and be able to plan for it. Doug advised him to take the opportunity to order a copy of the medical records relating to Laura's stay in hospital as well. Although the hospital would likely refuse to give Tom a copy without Holden's consent, at least someone would get the documents ready while Doug talked to Holden. The records were critical for an independent expert to analyze the causes and the effects of the blow to Laura's head.

With their duties sorted out, Tom and Doug finished their lattes leisurely. They were about to leave, when a thought occurred to Tom. "You wanted me to remind you to call Diane."

Doug hit the side of his forehead with the palm of his hand. "Oh shit," he said. "I better call her right now."

He started to get up from the table when Tom added another thought. "By the way, Trudy tells me that Cathy wants to see you again. They want to come over to the apartment, maybe tonight or tomorrow night."

The immediate, involuntary, sinking feeling in his stomach surprised Doug. What was this? Didn't he want to see Cathy tonight? His reaction made little sense. Cathy was exactly what he wanted, wild sex without a lot of responsibility. He stayed in his seat and tried to collect his thoughts.

Tom watched as Doug sat silently at the table. "Anything wrong?" Tom asked finally.

"I don't know," Doug sighed. Then he mumbled more to himself than to Tom, "I just don't get it. It always looked so good when it was Henderson. Why doesn't it feel good now?"

"He was a hero, alright," Tom nodded. "God knows how he did it. Living with Marie and keeping a steady flow of women on the side." He pondered Henderson's feat for a moment. "I tried that game for a while," he volunteered. "But, you know, I just couldn't keep it up." He smiled at his unintentional pun. "It all became kind of the same after awhile. And not very satisfying. I must be getting old. Now I find I've got my hands full just with Trudy." Then, as an afterthought, he chuckled, "Maybe Henderson was on viagra or something."

Or maybe he had an addiction to sex, Doug thought. But he answered, "Yeah. Henderson was quite a guy." He got up from the table to tele-phone Diane.

"What do you want me to tell the ladies?" Tom asked as Doug walked away.

He looked back at Tom. "Let's make it tomorrow night, okay?"

After four rings Diane answered the phone, sounding out of breath. She had just arrived back from the boys' school where Adrian's class had put on a play about Christopher Columbus. Her voice was animated and she breathed noisily as she described to Doug how Adrian, a puny swashbuckler in his little tights and a voluminous shirt, had marched boldly onto the stage, climbed up a rope ladder that represented the rigging to the crow's nest of the *Santa Maria* to a small platform at the top, and stood, his toothpick legs firmly shoulder width apart, one hand jauntily on his hip and the other shielding his eyes while he looked out over the audience. Left and right he had scanned, then straight ahead. Eventually, he had pointed directly out over the audience and clearly enunciated his four words.

Diane snorted and convulsed into laughter as she explained, "Adrian was supposed to say, 'Captain! Captain! Land ho!' but the actual words that came out of the poor boy's mouth were 'Captain! Captain! Hand lo!' "

Her laughter was contagious and Doug automatically chuckled along with her. But the moment quickly faded as they simultaneously remembered the present status of their relationship. It seemed inappropriate now to share an amusing moment involving their son. Somehow this was an intimacy for couples to share; Doug and Diane were no longer entitled. An uncomfortable silence followed while they both retreated into their new roles. Eventually Diane asked why Doug had phoned.

He hesitated before answering. Why had he phoned? His mind had gone blank, confused by the awkwardness. Then it came to him. Henderson's funeral—she hadn't been there. He asked why, hoping that she would not excoriate him for failing to tell her about it.

Diane fell silent for a few moments. Doug heard a shifting, rumbling sound through the telephone receiver as if she had placed her hand over the speaker. He heard muffled voices. She was telling the children something he couldn't make out. Then he heard her clear her throat before she came back on the line.

"I talked to Marie," she said. "I told her I couldn't make it. I had this thing for Adrian. I had to get him ready and everything." Doug thought he noticed her voice crack a bit when she said "everything."

There was another pause. He felt very uncomfortable. He needed to talk to Diane. He needed to discuss with her what had happened to Henderson, what was happening to Laura, what was happening to him. It was impossible now, though. After all, it was her sympathy that he was really seeking, her advice that he wanted. But he felt too timid, too guilty.

What was he supposed to say? "Diane, I'm drinking and smoking dope and fucking women. Do you think I'm doing the right thing?" And what would she say? "Gee, Doug, as long as you're happy."

But he wasn't happy. He had to see her. "I understand that Matthew has a hockey game on Saturday. Do you know when and where?" he inquired.

"Yeah," Diane answered warily. "Five, at the University arena."

Doug knew that only the older teams played early in the morning, but he asked, "Morning or evening?" anyway, in order to buy a moment of time to select carefully the words he was about to say. When Diane confirmed it was evening, the tough part came. He took a deep breath, feeling like he was about to ask someone out on a first date. "I was hoping to come and see the game," he said. "Do you think…I'd like to take you out for a bite to eat after. If you don't have any plans."

Diane's voice faltered again as she asked "Why?"

Good question. Because he needed her to tell him that he was not missing anything at home, that the kids still loved him and were not upset with him for not being there. Because he wanted to make sure that she and the kids would be there waiting, just in case he decided that he had done the wrong thing. He knew that he had to sound convincing. "Well. We've had a few days to think about things. It may be wise to meet and discuss where this is all going."

There was another muffled delay before Diane spoke. "I suppose we're going to have to talk this out some time," she conceded. "Isn't this a little premature, though?"

Doug chuckled nervously. "I don't think you can do too much talking in these situations." Then in a lower, more serious voice he said, "You know, Diane, it's best to keep the lines of communication as open as possible."

"Well, I guess that makes some sense," she replied. "Sure. I'll see if I can get someone to watch the kids." Then she added, "You're not suggesting that they come along are you?"

Doug confirmed that he thought it best for just the two of them to meet this first time. Besides, the kids were still unaware of the problem, so why burden them with it until Diane and he had come to terms with it themselves? She agreed. They planned to meet at Matthew's hockey game, after which they would drop the kids off with a babysitter and head to a restaurant. Doug hung up the phone, pleased that he had arranged to meet with Diane, and at the same time, disappointed by the clear reluctance in her voice at the prospect of meeting with him.

Holden was waiting when Doug and Tom arrived at the hospital. While Doug and Holden found a secluded table in the hospital restaurant to converse in private, Tom went off to talk to the hospital staff. As they sat down Doug noticed Detective Campbell sitting alone at a table on the other side of the restaurant. He nodded to Doug, who had the distinct impression that Campbell knew exactly the purpose of his meeting with Holden. Actually, Doug was relieved in a way to see Campbell; contacting him to work out the details of Laura's arrest would be easy now.

Doug had brought Tom's notes with him to provide Holden with as much detail as possible of the evidence summarized by Christopher. He addressed the Crown's case point by point while Holden listened silently and intently. Holden gazed unwaveringly at Doug, but as each point was explained, his eyes widened slightly as if slowly filling with fear of the case the Crown had built against Laura. When Doug finished recounting the evidence, Holden remained silent. His eyes, now glassy and unblinking, slid slowly away from Doug while he assimilated and cogitated over the information he had just been given. Doug waited patiently. Finally, Holden's focus returned to Doug, he swallowed hard and asked, "So what do we do now?"

Doug described the charges that the Crown was contemplating. He explained the difference between each charge, answering Holden's questions as thoroughly as possible. When he felt that Holden had digested the information and begun to appreciate the magnitude of the problem facing Laura, he broached the Crown's desire to negotiate a plea bargain. He explained to Holden how he thought this might be achieved, the advantages and disadvantages to Laura, and he responded to Holden's questions.

Holden fell silent once more. This time he stared at the floor, his shoulders hunched over and his head in his hands. He stayed in that position for some time while Doug waited, watching emotion overcome Holden like a tidal wave. Events were beyond his control; he was at their mercy and they were breaking him, slowly but inevitably. Doug felt he was witnessing Frank Holden's slow deterioration from the powerful business executive who dictated Larson Wren's fate to this pathetic shell.

Holden rolled his head in his hands. "I don't know what to do," he moaned. "What am I supposed to do?" He raised his head and looked at Doug through pleading eyes. They were like a lost child's, begging Doug to lead him.

Doug took his time. He wanted to be objective and dispassionate, because he knew that Holden needed him to be an island of calm and rationality. "I'm still convinced that Laura didn't do it," he started. "But that doesn't mean much unless we've got some evidence to prove it, or at least to undermine the Crown's case. There are some things we have to do." He raised his right thumb. "Firstly, we need all the evidence from the police investigation to determine where the weaknesses are in their case. Secondly"—he raised his index finger—"we need to retain the best possible medical specialist to analyze the blow to Laura's head. We need a strong opinion that refutes the Crown's view that Laura was able to fire the gun at the same time, or after, Henderson hit her. Thirdly"—his middle finger joined the other two—"we need to determine who else might have killed Henderson. This means: who wanted Henderson dead and Laura to take the blame for it?"

Doug watched Holden to see if there was any hint of understanding, any flicker that he had some idea of what might have really happened. But Holden simply blinked away the tears in his eyes and returned Doug's stare. Just as Doug was about to remind Holden of how he had threatened Henderson, Tom arrived. He pulled a chair away from a nearby table, turned it around as he did, so that the backrest was closest to Holden and Doug, straddled it like a cowboy and rested his elbows on the backrest.

"Well, they tell me that Laura will be released Friday afternoon," he said, looking from Doug to Holden and back to Doug. Then he pulled a sheet of paper out of his attaché case and placed it in front of Holden. "And Mr. Holden, would you sign this release form so that we can obtain all the hospital records relating to Laura's injury and treatment?"

Holden took the pen that Tom offered and scribbled his signature on the line at the bottom of the page without reading the form. After Holden handed it back, Doug suggested to Tom that he try to get the records right away. With a nod of agreement Tom dismounted from the chair and walked out of the restaurant, giving a wave in the direction of Detective Campbell on his way.

Doug returned his gaze to Holden. "She'll be released on Friday," he repeated.

Holden raised his eyebrows: *So?*

Doug inhaled deeply in order to keep himself controlled and objective. He explained to Holden that in his opinion, only if they themselves were satisfied that the Crown was able to prove Laura had pulled the trigger, should they even consider negotiating a plea bargain. And they could only reach a proper view on the strength of the Crown's case after they had reviewed all the police files, obtained their own expert's opinion and investigated Henderson's past to see if there was an explanation for the killing other than the obsessive love of a fifteen-year-old. Meanwhile, the Crown had to proceed against Laura with whatever charges it saw fit unless and until it was advised that Laura wanted to make a deal.

The only way to be sure that they had received all the evidence gathered by the police was through Disclosure Court which, Doug explained, was a pre-trial appearance before a judge used by the accused to ensure that the Crown had disclosed all its evidence. However, entitlement to a Disclosure Court appearance only arose after charges had been laid. As for the blow to Laura's head, a medical expert was going to need some time to determine its effect. And they were going to need some time, as well, to delve into Henderson's past. All this meant that they could not possibly be in a position to decide whether to negotiate a plea bargain with the Crown by Friday afternoon when Laura was to be released from hospital. This was Christopher's deadline. If no deal was cut by then, he was going to proceed with charges.

"Unfortunately, Mr. Holden," Doug concluded, "we can do nothing to ease the pain for Laura. She will have to go through the process of arrest."

Holden's head was back in his hands. "Oh God," he groaned, as he rubbed his eyes vigorously to erase the image in his mind of his little girl being taken away by the police. "What a fucking mess!"

Doug soldiered on. He needed to get to his point before he lost Holden totally. "What we need to concentrate on right now," he said, "is how we can minimize the length of Laura's stay in prison before she obtains bail. The immediate problem I see is that the police will be poised to arrest her when she's released from hospital. And by the time she's taken in, charged and fingerprinted, I expect the courts will be closed for the weekend, in which case we would be unable to bring her before a judge for a bail hearing until Monday. That means she would have to spend the weekend in jail."

Holden continued to rub his eyes slowly, hypnotically. Doug stopped talking and watched him to make sure that he was following what was being said. "Are you with me, Mr. Holden? It's very important that you understand what I'm saying." He waited.

Holden removed his hands from his eyes and looked at Doug. "Yes, Branston. I'm with you," he said with a shadow of fortitude.

"Good. I want your authority to arrange for Laura's smooth and quiet arrest and for a quick bail hearing. Maybe we can get the police to hold off on the arrest until Monday morning when we can get Laura immediately before a judge and out on bail. With any luck we could get it all done in the morning."

Holden sat back in his chair. He shook his head violently a couple of times as if to clear his mind, placed his hands palms down on the table and nodded slowly. "All right," he said. His actions appeared to have helped him gain some control over his emotions.

"I also want your authority to retain a medical expert."

"You've got it," Holden said resolutely while he stared at an invisible spot somewhere in the middle of the table.

"And Mr. Holden," Doug said more forcefully as he leaned forward, willing Holden's eyes to meet his, "I want you to think hard about whether you know of any other explanation for Henderson being killed."

Holden raised his eyes to Doug for a long moment. Finally, he blinked and looked away. "What are you suggesting, Branston?" he asked in a halting voice.

"You know damn well what I'm suggesting. I was there. Remember?"

Holden's eyes slowly returned to Doug's stare. "He seduced my daughter," he stated evenly. "So I threatened him—goddamn right I did—like any father would do. But I didn't kill him." He sneered. "That would make a lot of sense wouldn't it? Kill Henderson for seducing my daughter, and let her take the blame."

Tom returned. As he again straddled his chair he announced, "The hospital records will be ready at the end of the business day tomorrow."

"Good work," Doug said. "Now, first thing tomorrow I want you to contact Dr. Wall, the neurologist, and get him on a retainer to look at this matter for us. Then, when we get the records, we'll do a letter to him explaining the situation and enclosing all the information." He was about to continue his conversation with Holden when a voice from behind interrupted.

"Any indication yet of when Ms. Holden is to be released?" asked Detective Campbell.

"Sometime Friday afternoon, I understand," Doug replied. He had dismissed any thought of keeping the timing of Laura's release to himself. Detective Campbell had an officer stationed outside her room who would know the moment she was going to be released. Anyway, it was time to discuss the circumstances of Laura's arrest with Campbell.

"Why don't you sit down for a few moments, Detective," Doug said. "There's something we need to discuss." He motioned to Holden's chair. "Mr. Holden is just leaving to see Laura." Doug gave Holden a nod encouraging him to offer his seat to Detective Campbell. Reluctantly, Holden stood up.

"Tom and I will be up to meet with Laura in a moment," Doug said as Holden started for the exit. He had rejected the idea of developing a strategy with Holden for discussing the charges and the arrest with Laura. Holden was on too great an emotional roller-coaster right now to help Doug explain what was happening. It was up to Doug to take charge and advise Holden and Laura what had to be done.

Once Detective Campbell sat down, Doug initiated the discussion of how to make Laura's inevitable arrest as efficient and painless as possible. He noted that, although he had yet to consider what evidence he would need to obtain release on bail, he was sure—and Detective Campbell freely agreed—that a fifteen-year-old girl, charged with a crime of passion, with no history of criminal activity and a father who could afford a substantial surety bond, would obtain bail. Therefore, she would be out of jail following her appearance before a judge. However, if she were arrested upon her release from hospital on Friday afternoon, it was likely that she would have to wait in prison until Monday before a judge was available to hear a bail application. Doug proposed that, for compassionate reasons, Campbell wait until Monday to arrest her, in which case she could have her bail hearing the same day and avoid being stuck in prison over the weekend.

Detective Campbell was prepared to leave the arrest until Monday on two conditions. First, he needed Doug's and Holden's personal guarantees that Laura would remain in the Holden home from the time of her release from hospital until the time of her arrest. Second, he needed Christopher's approval.

Doug expected conditions along these lines. He advised Campbell that he was prepared to give his personal guarantee as soon as he'd had an opportunity to speak to Laura and Holden, following which he was sure Holden would give his own guarantee. Doug suggested that Campbell try to track down Christopher immediately to obtain his concurrence while he and Tom spoke to Laura and Holden. Happy to oblige, Campbell left the table to make some phone calls. Meanwhile, Doug and Tom headed off to Laura's hospital room.

They drove in silence, both turning over in their minds the meeting they had just had with Laura. Doug had done most of the talking, explaining to Laura that the police had conducted an investigation into the death of Henderson and had concluded from the information they were able to obtain that she had fired the fatal bullet. He added quickly that there were big gaps in the proof the police relied upon and that he, Tom, and her father did not believe for a moment that she had actually done the shooting. Their support provided little solace, however, for when Laura heard that the police suspected her, she sat in her bed stunned and motionless, staring into empty space like a zombie. Her father moved to comfort her, and she started to cry on his shoulder.

"I don't know, Daddy. I can't remember," she sobbed.

Doug went on to explain the arrangements made for her arrest on the following Monday. He told her that he was going to be at her side throughout, that he was sure the ordeal would be over by noon, after which she could return home. He did not mention the guarantee that he and her father had been required to give the police in order to postpone her arrest. It was clear from Laura's emotional state that once she got home, she was unlikely to leave her bedroom, let alone the house.

Doug was disappointed with Holden. He had hoped Holden would provide some support and enthusiasm, some rah-rah stuff to give Laura encouragement—"Don't worry, baby, we're going to fight this thing...Nobody hurts my little girl,"—but he said nothing during the meeting with his daughter. The best he did was provide a shoulder for her to cry on; Doug wondered who was really comforting whom.

Just before he and Tom left the hospital room, Doug sat down beside her, gently took her head in his hands and looked deeply into her eyes. Even bloodshot and puffy, they were beautiful: bright and open, inviting the onlooker into her soul. His heart ached in confirmation that these were not the eyes of a murderer.

While gazing at Laura, he said softly, "Laura, I think someone wanted Henderson killed and wants you to take the blame for it. Take your time this weekend. Think as hard as you can. Was Mark in any trouble? If you can think of anything that he said or did that seemed strange, let me or Elvis know."

Doug waited for a flicker of understanding, but she simply stared at him, her luminous blue eyes full of sadness and trust, the same eyes that had attracted Henderson like a shark to blood. And as Doug stood to leave, he shamefully chased from his mind his own involuntary rush of desire.

Tom was attempting to parallel park the Montego in a particularly tight space outside his apartment when Doug finally spoke. "Man, I wish I knew if I were doing the right thing. Maybe we should just be making a little plea bargain. We'd probably be able to keep her away from adult court. She'd get maybe eighteen months in some juvenile centre and be out after six." He sighed. "Now, the way things are, she's got to go through the whole system without knowing where it leads. And at some point Christopher is going to feel the pressure to apply to raise her to adult court."

Tom managed to get the roguesmobile parked, but in the process the rear tire had climbed the curb. The car was squeezed in too tightly to get the tire off. "A perfect fit," he said, stepping on the pedal of the emergency brake.

Only when they were riding the elevator up to the apartment did Tom respond to Doug's comments. "I don't know," he said. "It seems to me that we don't have a lot of choice. If we truly believe she didn't do it, then how can we agree to any plea bargain?"

Doug was stunned by the clarity of Tom's view. What he said made all the sense in the world. This was different from a civil case where all the parties give up a little in order to find a compromise settlement everyone can live with. Laura's liberty and reputation were at stake. There was no compromise to that. If she had not killed Henderson, and Doug believed that she had not, then a plea bargain was not an option.

CHAPTER 15

Alot of time had passed since Doug had done a murder trial. Therefore, he spent most of Thursday in the firm's library researching the charges that Laura might face, and confirming for himself the accuracy of Christopher's synopsis of first and second degree murder: the former requiring proof of an element of planning and deliberation, the latter, proof only of intent to kill at the time the gun went off. Manslaughter, Doug noted, requires no proof of intent to kill at all, only proof of an intentional act that resulted in death. He was also able to confirm Christopher's statement that second degree murder was an included offence of first degree murder; manslaughter was as well. Therefore, it was possible for the Crown to proceed with a first degree murder charge but obtain a conviction for second degree murder or even manslaughter.

Shortly before noon, Doug's secretary retrieved him from the library to take what she understood to be an urgent telephone call. When Doug answered the line, he was greeted by the booming, slightly ominous voice of Tony.

"Doug, sorry it's such short notice. Yesterday you mentioned getting together for lunch sometime. How about it?"

"Today?"

"Yeah. I can pick you up. I'm just five minutes away."

"Okay," slipped out of Doug's mouth before he was able to swallow it. He really did not have the time or interest to socialize with Mario's muscle. "Can't be long," he cautioned with defeat. "I've got a ton of work."

Over pasta in a below-street-level Italian restaurant only a shady character like Tony could sniff out, they talked about Henderson and how unbelievable it was that, only a week before, they had all been together in Toronto, partying wildly. Finally, Tony shook his head and smiled sadly. "He just couldn't stay away from the skirts, could he? The horny bastard."

"Nope," Doug agreed, trying to keep his responses short in order to move the lunch along.

Tony sensed Doug's impatience. He scooped up the last of the pasta on his plate, then put down his fork and spoon. "Look, I know you got a lot of things to do, what with defending the little broad that shot him—oops!" He rolled his eyes sheepishly. "I'm sorry. Marie tells me you think she's innocent."

"I know she is."

"How do you figure? I mean there's no one else there and she's got the fucking gun in her hand—at least, that's what Marie says."

"I just know." Doug avoided elaboration, especially since the only basis for his conviction was a feeling he had deep in his guts.

Tony brightened as an idea came to him. "Hey, maybe it was that other broad he was banging." He snapped his fingers and pointed at Doug. "You may want to follow up on this. Mario told me that Henderson was doing someone else at the same time as the teen queen. Do you know about her?"

"If it's who I think you mean, not much." Then Doug brightened, "Does Mario know who she is?"

Tony shook his head slowly. "So you don't even have a name?"

"Nope."

"What does she look like?"

"Apparently, she likes to hide under a scarf and sunglasses." Doug thought for a moment. "How does Mario know about her, anyway?"

Tony shrugged. "I guess Henderson told him." Then he gave a sympathetic grin. "Shit, man. Looks like you got your work cut out for you."

Doug nodded. "I think you're right. So, I've got to get back to work," he said as he signaled the waitress to bring the bill.

On his way back to the library, Doug puzzled over why Tony had suddenly wanted to meet him for lunch. To commiserate over a lost buddy? To suggest that the killer might be Carmen? To introduce him to a new Italian bistro? It seemed a little strange since Doug had only met Tony the previous week, and in totally different circumstances. But then, Tony was a little strange. So, without any clear explanation, Doug returned to reviewing the law.

Around three o'clock he was adrift in the mid-afternoon doldrums, gazing at the words while they gently shifted and rolled on the page. The room was warm and the air still. His eyelids were sagging like windless sails when Reginald Wren popped his head into the library. His "how's it going?" jolted Doug out of his semi-conscious state.

After a deep refreshing breath of air, Doug launched into a summary of events to date, quickly satisfying Wren that he was directing the appropriate care and attention to the difficulties being experienced by the daughter of the firm's best client. Nevertheless, before leaving Doug to his research, Wren instructed him to be prepared to report all developments to the partners at the next partnership meeting.

By evening, Doug was ready for a break from the books. He and Tom swung by the hospital to pick up a copy of Laura's records, then headed back to Tom's apartment to meet Trudy and Cathy for another intimate dinner party. When they opened the door, an overpowering waft of garlic and marijuana warned them that Trudy and Cathy had started without them. Doug was prepared for the challenge of catching up, however. He had a drink and a toke and ate some pan-fried veal. Within a couple of hours he was naked in bed with Cathy, cruising on automatic pilot.

Friday morning came and Doug had an enormous headache. The blood throbbed slowly and steadily through his veins like molasses pulsing through a hose. He was able to handle it while he lay spread-eagled on the bed, but as soon as he tried to raise himself, the exertion caused his heart to pump madly and his head to pound harder.

The bathroom called. As gently as possible he brought himself to a sitting position on the side of the bed. He waited a few moments for the violent vibration in his temples to pass, then pushed himself onto his feet.

In the bathroom, he tried to focus on his reflection in the mirror. "Good morning, Happy," he grumbled through a throat full of mucus, then turned to the toilet and relieved himself.

Now that he was standing he knew he had to avoid returning to bed; a second attempt to rise onto his feet might be fatal. They would find his head blown to pieces from too much pressure in the brain. The coroner would conclude that the victim's head had exploded when he sat up in bed while experiencing a massive hangover. Doug chuckled to himself, but that hurt, too.

What had he done last night? He tried to fit the fragments together. There was some dope, maybe a lot of dope. Some scotch. And wine, definitely a lot of wine. And? Doug turned to look back into the bedroom through the bathroom door. Oh, shit, he thought, as he spied the clear bottle sitting on the bedside table with a few ounces of colourless liquid still inside. Pisco, Peruvian fire-water. He looked back to the mirror and silently scolded the image staring at him.

For a few minutes the steaming shower provided some relief, massaging his veins and hammering back his blood pressure. Afterwards, he managed to get himself shaved and dressed. On his way out of the bedroom he gazed at Cathy's naked, motionless body tangled in the sheets of the bed, her open mouth leaving a wet drool mark on the pillow slip. It was a scene from a detective novel: the hooker's body found nude in the ravaged bed of a cheap motel room. Doug wondered for a moment if she was breathing. He thought about giving her a shake, then decided he couldn't bear a conversation.

Tom was in the kitchen downing coffee. He looked up when Doug entered and forced a smile. When he asked how late Doug and Cathy had stayed up the previous night Doug remembered that Tom and Trudy had slipped off to bed right after dinner, missing most of the festivities. He mumbled that he didn't remember, then suggested that they get going.

Back in the roguesmobile Doug was able to focus a little better on what he wanted to accomplish this day. He reminded Tom to draft a letter to the doctor enclosing the hospital records, summarizing the Crown's case against Laura, including a description of the preliminary opinion of the Crown's expert, and posing the questions on which they needed his opinion.

There was something else Doug had wanted Tom to do. Finally, it came to him. The list of tenants' names. Christopher had assured him that the tenants had all been interviewed and none of them knew anything. Nevertheless, Doug wanted Tom to interview each of them as well. Although he was sure Christopher was being honest with him, there might be something the police had missed. It would not be the first time.

Doug also wanted to find out more about the women in Henderson's life. He told Tom to speak to Mrs. Rattenbury to get as much detail as possible on the woman she called Carmen, and on any others that Henderson had brought to the apartment. Then all the women had to be tracked down and interviewed.

Doug planned to spend the morning considering what evidence he needed to present to the judge at the bail hearing, and what terms of bail were reasonable in Laura's case. He hoped to be in a position by noon to discuss with Christopher the charges to be laid against Laura, and to seek Christopher's concurrence to certain terms for bail. If he could get the Crown's agreement on bail, they could present a common recommendation to the judge, in which case Laura's arrest and court appearance would proceed smoothly and some of her worry would be eased. Before her release from hospital in the afternoon, he wanted to be able to advise her that all the arrangements had been made.

When Doug walked into his office he found a stack of documents on his desk. He hesitated before stepping up to take a closer look. Only when his secretary spoke did he realize that she had followed him into the room and was looking over his shoulder.

"The documents on the companies that sold the properties to the captives," Betty announced. "They came in by fax late yesterday afternoon. Remember, you wanted complete company searches."

He looked at the top page, then flipped casually through some of the other pages. The documents were stapled together in various bundles. Apparently, Betty had gathered the documents up as they came in over the fax and organized them into groups for each company.

As if reading his mind she said, "You'll see I've stapled together the documents for each company."

Doug had no time to look at the documents at the moment. He instructed her to put them into the corresponding conveyance files, but to keep them accessible.

"No problem." She leaned over to pick up the documents, turned and was about to walk out of the room when she added, "You know, I just don't get it. How could Mr. Henderson be acting for the purchaser of the property when he was the shareholder of the company that was selling the property? Isn't that a conflict or something?"

The significance of his secretary's comment failed to register immediately because Doug was sitting weakly at his desk feeling protective of his bruised brain. He was about to say that Henderson had covered his ass with Certificates of Independent Legal Advice, when her words penetrated the fog. "What did you say? Henderson was a shareholder?"

"Not for all the companies, but for a few of them. I noticed it when I was organizing this stuff. Isn't that a conflict?"

"Maybe I better take a look at this stuff now." Then, as she returned the documents to the desk, he added, "Do me a favour, Betty. Find out what time the hospital plans to release Laura Holden today."

Doug concentrated on reviewing the documents before him. In each bundle was a list of officers and directors for a vendor company, along with their addresses, and a list of the company shareholders. Soon Doug was able to confirm what his secretary had told him. There were fifteen companies in all, and Henderson was a shareholder in four of them. Doug shook his head in disbelief as he counted the different hats Henderson had been wearing: lawyer for the purchasers' financial adviser, lawyer for the purchasers on the conveyances, and, in some cases, a shareholder of the vendor companies.

The names of some of the other shareholders of the vendor companies were also interesting: Giorgio Reni, Julie Chandler, Tony Capetti, Joey Marron. Mario Bartelli was either a director or an officer of many of the companies. Some of the names were familiar to Doug; he had spent a great deal of time the previous week partying with people named Giorgio, Julie, and Mario. And he had had lunch with Tony just the previous day. He knew none of their last names, though. Or did he? Marie had mentioned Tony's last name when they met at the church a couple of days ago. It was something Italian. Could have been Capetti. And Joey Marron? Wasn't that the name of the guy Henderson wanted to see while he was in Toronto? The guy who Mario said had been killed in a drug deal? What was more, all these familiar names had addresses in greater Toronto. It looked like the vendor companies were the creations of Henderson's good buddy Mario and his associates. Were these the 'investments' that Henderson had spoken about? The ones that Mario had wanted Henderson to get involved in?

Reviewing the documents a second time, Doug noticed that Terra Holdings appeared as a shareholder of some of the companies. He made a mental note to have his secretary do a search of that company as well.

All this information churned in the vacuous recesses of Doug's brain for some time before a suspicion came to him. He searched his office for the conveyance files then concluded that his secretary must have removed them.

"You looking for the conveyance files?" she asked when he shuffled out to her desk. She picked up a stack of files and offered them to him. "I had them here to file the incorporation documents when you finished looking at them."

Doug took the files and headed back to his office. "Three o'clock," Betty called after him. He turned with a quizzical look. "That's when Ms. Holden will be released," she explained. "Three o'clock."

Back in his office, he compared the information in the conveyance files to that in the incorporation files. Before long, he was able to confirm his suspicion: the contract to sell each property was entered before the vendor company was incorporated and the property was acquired. It appeared to be a system for flipping properties, but it seemed a little unwieldy to be using new companies for each transaction. The only reason for doing it this way, he suspected, would be to conceal the fact that certain people were involved in all the transactions.

From the documents he reviewed, Doug concluded that there was nothing illegal about what they were doing, except perhaps for Henderson's involvement. Certainly, he was in breach of the Law Society rules regarding conflicts of interest, and probably he was in breach of the fiduciary duty he owed to the purchasers. This was particularly baffling. Henderson was a good lawyer. He would have known that he was in a hopeless conflict and that the Certificates of Independent Legal Advice were inapplicable to his ownership of shares in vendor companies. So why was he so deeply involved, risking suspension or even disbarment from the Law Society, and perhaps civil action as well?

Something was very fishy. Despite his hangover, Doug was sufficiently lucid to realize that Henderson's death might somehow be connected. He needed some quick answers and determined that the time had come to talk to Holden. Picking up the phone, he dialed the number for Holden's office. It took some time to get through but finally Holden came on the line.

"Yes, Branston," he sighed.

Too much had taken place in the last week for Doug and Holden to share small talk. He thought about arranging a meeting with Holden to review his findings and elicit an explanation, but there was no time. He still needed to complete his research, make some arrangements with Christopher and be at the hospital before Laura was released at three.

"Mr. Holden. I've been going through these files that Henderson was handling for you. I'm wondering if you could explain a few things to me."

"Go ahead."

"From what I can gather, the principals and shareholders of all the vendor companies are connected. And it appears that each of the companies was incorporated for one real estate transaction only. Were you aware of that?"

Holden was silent for a moment, then answered. "Yes. This was a group of investors that Henderson actually introduced me to. It was headed up by a friend of his named—now let me think for a moment—Mario Bartelli." He paused. "You're right. They liked to run each property transaction through a different company. I never understood why exactly, but then it was really none of my business. I was just the financial advisor for the purchasers. As long as I thought the price was right, I didn't give a shit who the seller was."

"Henderson was advising you and doing the conveyance for the purchasers."

"Yes. That was part of the service I offered the purchasers. I'd arrange for the conveyance, although they'd have to pay the legal fees." Then he added quickly, "Henderson had each purchaser execute a Certificate of Independent Legal Advice. He told me that was sufficient to avoid any conflict issues." And, almost defensively, "He should have known. He was the lawyer."

"Did you know that Henderson was a shareholder in some of the vendor companies?"

Again there was silence. Then, in a great exhaling of air Holden said

"Noooo. Are you kidding me? Jesus, that's a real conflict, isn't it?"

"I would think so," Doug said, affirming the obvious. "And you're saying that you knew nothing about that, Mr. Holden?"

"Absolutely nothing," Holden said emphatically. "Jesus, why would he get himself involved like that?" Then, he added with pointed disgust, "But that was the kind of guy he was. Thought he could do whatever the fuck he liked."

"You know, Mr. Holden, something doesn't look right to me with this whole thing. And I just wonder if it might have something to do with Henderson getting killed. Would you have any thoughts on that?"

The silence on the other end of the line seemed to last forever. Finally, Doug broke it. "Mr. Holden?"

"Yes. Yes. I'm thinking." Pause. "No. I'm afraid not. As far as I know everything was legitimate and above board. There was certainly nothing I was aware of that would suggest anything shady."

Neither Doug nor Holden spoke for some time, like a standoff. Each waited for the other to blink. Static crackled subtly over the phone line. Doug wasn't convinced by Holden's assertion of ignorance, but it was evident that even if Holden knew something, he was not going to volunteer any information. Doug would have to make inquiries elsewhere. "Thank you, Mr. Holden," he said, finally. "I understand that Laura is to be released from hospital at three. Do you plan on being there?"

"Certainly," Holden answered quickly. Doug thought he detected some relief in his voice.

"Good. Well, I'll see you then. Goodbye."

Doug sat staring out his window. Layers of gray cloud drifted low over the city like zeppelins, blocking any view of the mountains. It was hard to tell, but it seemed that the rain had stopped. At least it was no longer leaving slashing spatters of water against the window pane.

He mulled over why Holden seemed so unhelpful. If Holden was aware of anything to help substantiate a connection between the real estate transactions and Henderson's death, he should reveal it to help save his daughter from a criminal conviction. So, maybe the fact Holden had said nothing meant Doug's suspicions were wrong, or that Holden honestly knew nothing. On the other hand, maybe Holden was scared. After all, if there was anything to Doug's suspicions, it meant that the people Holden was dealing with were capable of murder.

Doug needed to talk to someone else who might know what was going on with Henderson and these real estate deals. Julie came to mind. When he was in Toronto, it seemed that she was trying to distance herself from Mario and his group. She had left the dinner at Mario's apartment when

Tony arrived with the cocaine; in the taxi she had told Doug that the drugs were only part of the problem. "The coke's the teaser," she had said. Doug had not understood her meaning at the time, and she did not elaborate, but there was something about Mario's group that she disliked. If Doug was able to track her down, maybe she would tell him what it was.

The document that showed Julie Chandler as a shareholder also listed her address in Toronto. Phoning the office switchboard, Doug gave Julie's name and address to the receptionist and asked her to track down the phone number. He had barely resumed his meditation out the window when the receptionist called him back with the information. His watch read nine a.m.—noon in Toronto. Julie was a night person, working at Mario's club until the early hours of the morning. If he phoned now he might still catch her at home, maybe still asleep. He dialed the number.

It rang five times before a groggy female voice answered.

"Julie. Is that you?" Doug asked.

There was a delay before "Who's this?"

"Doug…uh…Doug Branston. Remember? We met last week. I was Mark Henderson's friend."

There was a slow sigh of recognition. "Of course, Doug, I remember you. You're the one who tried so hard to be like Mark." Then, as sleep wore off and she recalled Henderson's fate, she lamented "Poor Mark."

Julie's comment stung Doug. He wasn't trying *hard* to be like Henderson. He simply admired Henderson's free, laissez-faire attitude and tried to bring some of that to his own life. But Julie didn't really know him, he told himself. And, given the circumstances in which they had met so briefly, it was understandable that she had assumed he was Henderson's protégé.

Anyway, Doug liked Julie. She seemed a little melancholy, so he asked, "Julie, how are you?"

"Oh. I'm fine, thank you," she said hesitatingly. "How are you doing?" Then, in order to emphasize that what she really meant was *How are you handling Henderson's death?* she added, "I am so sorry about Mark."

"Yes," Doug responded. He let a few seconds of silence go by in reverence for Henderson's memory, then addressed the point of the phone call.

He had determined to avoid telling Julie that he was acting for the person about to be charged with Henderson's murder, because he feared she might realize that his interest in calling her was really to investigate whether the real estate deals involving Mario and his group had any connection with Henderson's death. If they were connected then she, knowingly or unknowingly, was involved. In that case, Doug's representation of Laura might cause her to clam up, or even worse, run to Mario.

"Julie, I've been asked to assume conduct of some of Henderson's files," he began. "There are a few things that I don't understand in them and I thought you may be able to help me. But, first off, I must advise this is all subject to solicitor-client privilege, and so, I've got to ask you to keep confidential whatever we discuss." As he said this, he realized what an absurd request it was. He was talking to a woman whom he hardly knew, about to ask her questions concerning transactions in which she was involved, and hoping she might unwittingly volunteer some information which indicated the transactions were pernicious and possibly the cause of Henderson's death. Even if she agreed to keep their conversation quiet, why should he believe her?

Cautiously, she replied. "It's hard to promise that, Doug, without knowing what you want to discuss with me. Let's say this. I won't repeat anything you tell me and I'll decide whether I want to tell you anything."

That was good enough. Doug needed some quick answers so he was prepared to risk Julie's breaking her promise. Besides, he concluded that there was nothing to lose. If Julie was unable to tell him anything, then the conversation would have been about Henderson's actions only, which was a legitimate concern for the lawyer taking over the files. If she did tell him something then she would have her own reasons to keep the conversation confidential.

"The files I've been reviewing have to do with the real estate transactions involving Mario and some of his associates, including yourself and Henderson. It's apparent that Henderson was counseling the financial adviser for the purchasers; he was handling the legal aspects of the conveyance for the purchasers; and, in some cases at least, he was a shareholder of the vendor companies. All these different roles put him in a terrible conflict. Did you know anything about this?"

She groaned audibly, took a deep breath and held it for a moment. Doug thought that she was about to say something, but she just exhaled.

"How's Marie?" she asked eventually.

"She's doing okay I guess, all things considered," Doug answered. "I didn't know you knew her." He sensed that Julie wanted to tell him something, but he knew not to push her yet.

"Not well." Her voice drifted off. Then after a moment she added, "But she seems like a lovely person. I told Mark that once. I told him that he should hang on to her."

"Well, I think he knew how good she was for him," Doug said. "Mark was certainly no saint, but he adored Marie." He reflected on the conversation he had had with Henderson over breakfast that morning in Toronto. "Mark told me that he wanted to marry Marie, settle down, have some kids," he added.

"Yes. Yes. He told me that as well. But, true to form, he wanted to do it first class."

Doug thought he knew what Julie meant, but he decided to ask anyway. "I'm not sure I understand you."

"Oh, you know Mark. He wasn't going to become domesticated until he had the house, the two cars and the membership at the local club. That took money." She laughed sadly. "And all he ever earned was going to support his lifestyle and his crazy investments. Mark didn't have any savings."

His crazy investments. Doug smiled; that was certainly true. The quick score, the inside track to instant success: Henderson's eternal quest. Sometimes it worked, but more often he lost; and on occasion he lost big. That's what the voice mail message from Henderson's broker had indicated. Apparently, his final deal had tanked as well. "Well, it's too bad. I think he may have been ready to settle down."

"I think he was and I think that may be why..."

Doug waited. He sensed Julie was on the verge of giving him some insight into the real estate transactions, but she had stopped in mid sentence. This time, she made no attempt to change the subject, she just remained silent. Now was the time to apply a little pressure. "Julie?" he said. "Julie, what is it? 'That may be why'—what?"

"Doug, I really can't talk about this."

"I don't understand. We're talking about Henderson's reputation, Julie. That's all he's got left." He waited for her to continue, but there was nothing. "What were you going to say?" He prompted her: "'That may be why'...what? Why he was so deeply involved in these deals? So he could make some extra dough? So he could settle down with Marie?"

"Yes, I suppose that's what I was going to say. But—" and she lowered her voice to a conspiratorial whisper, "it's not just about Henderson, Doug. There are others involved, too." She paused, then said in a more emphatic voice. "Doug, I'm sorry, I can't talk about this. Not over the phone."

"Why is that, Julie?"

"I just can't, Doug. It's not something I should talk about at all. But certainly not over the phone." Then she mused, "Maybe if you were here..."

Doug understood. "Julie, I'd be prepared to get on a plane and fly to Toronto right now if I thought you could tell me something that would help me understand what the hell Mark was doing. You know—anything that might help me protect his reputation..."

Julie thought this over for awhile. "No one must know, Doug. I mean it."

"Is it that serious?"

"Yes."

Doug caught the red-eye at midnight, arriving in Toronto at around seven a.m. Toronto time on Saturday. Julie was going to pick him up at the airport.

Before he got on the plane he made sure that the tasks he had set aside for himself and Tom were accomplished. He completed his investigation on Laura's bail, determining that for someone Laura's age, without a prior record, the terms of bail would probably be a surety bond of a few thousand dollars and a promise that she remain at the family residence when she was not attending school. Then he contacted Christopher. They discussed whether a plea bargain was possible. Doug explained that he couldn't advise his client properly until after a Disclosure Court proceeding, which meant that the Crown had to proceed with laying charges. Christopher, grudgingly recognizing Doug's problem, confirmed that the Crown was going to proceed with a charge of second degree murder against Laura. He made it clear that he was prepared to abandon a run at first degree murder in the hope that a plea might eventually be negotiated. This was an offer of good faith; if the Crown wanted to play hardball it would proceed with a charge of first degree murder, even though its evidence supported, at best, a conviction for second degree murder, or perhaps only manslaughter.

Doug suspected that this also meant Christopher was prepared to accept a manslaughter plea, the next step down from second degree murder, because he had to be prepared to give up something in order to avoid a trial. It made Doug wonder whether there was an even lesser offence Christopher might ultimately settle for in return for a guilty plea. Maybe criminal negligence causing death. Before he left for Toronto he instructed Tom to look into this.

During their conversation, Christopher agreed to a joint application before the Youth Court judge on Monday morning to set Laura's bail. Doug advised Christopher that he was prepared to recommend to his client, as terms of bail, that a surety bond of $10,000 be posted and that Laura's father provide an affidavit to the court promising that Laura would remain at the family residence pending her trial, except to attend school. Christopher was prepared to support these terms on the condition that Holden appear at the hearing to provide the surety bond and make his promise personally to the judge.

In the afternoon, Doug went to the hospital to be there for Laura's release. At the time, he advised Holden of the arrangements for Laura's bail and obtained Holden's agreement to the conditions. The only thing left to arrange was the timing of Laura's arrest and court appearance. Christopher was looking into this, but did not expect to have it coordinated until Saturday, so Doug left Tom in charge of finalizing the time with Christopher over the weekend.

Doug smiled as he got on the plane. Tom was going to have a busy weekend. He was already working on the letter to the doctor, which Doug expected to see in draft form on Monday morning. In addition, although Tom had made some inquiries of the tenants at the Barclay, it was clear that he would have to hang around the building most of the weekend in order to meet and interview all of them. Now he had more tasks. Along with researching offences of a lesser degree than manslaughter, he had to prepare Holden's affidavit for the bail hearing and finalize arrangements for Laura's arrest and court appearance on Monday.

As Doug settled into his seat on the airplane, he reflected briefly on the vicissitudes of being a junior associate, then turned to flag down the flight attendant. Maybe he could get a drink before the plane took off.

By the time Doug arrived in Toronto, he was exhausted. Instead of sleeping on the plane, he had continually shifted back and forth in his seat like a restless child, in an eternal search for the perfect position. Now it was seven a.m. The day was just beginning, but all he could think about was how lousy he felt. Flying in an airplane was like being locked in a sensory deprivation chamber, confined for hours at a time, condemned to endure the steady, unrelenting white noise from the plane's engines and to pick at the tasteless, prepackaged food that was distributed at too-regular intervals.

Julie met him at the airport. Outside, it was seventeen below zero with the wind chill factor, and snow was blowing at an impossible angle. Doug pulled his overcoat tightly around him and raised the collar, leaving only his forehead exposed, then ran with Julie from the terminal across the street to the parking lot. By the time she found her car, Doug's body was shaking and his forehead ached numbly as if it had been struck by a baseball bat. He fell into the passenger seat, the fatigue and cold having drained all his energy.

"How about a tall steaming latte?" Julie proposed as she turned on the car's ignition.

"With extra caffeine. Sounds great." Doug crouched into a tight ball while he waited expectantly for the soothing effects of the car heater.

Soon, they were racing with the traffic on the Gardner Expressway towards Toronto. Just outside the airport they had passed a big billboard announcing "Executive Entertainment at the Show Lounge next to the Airport: Hangars." Doug smiled to himself. It had been several years since he and Henderson had hunkered down there for a few beers before catching the flight home. At one time it had been a compulsory stopover. Doug wondered if the dancers were still as tall, lean and totally uninhibited as they had been when he had frequented the place.

While staring out the window of the car, he reminisced about the last time he and Henderson had engaged a table dance. A stripper's perfect body had commanded their attention. Her face was fresh and innocent as a schoolgirl's. She seemed to have picked Doug and Henderson out of the crowd as well, because she kept watching them even while performing for another table. Once she even stuck her tongue out at them. That did it. Henderson had waved her over to their table like a producer selecting a starlet at an audition. And wanting to maintain the role, to appear cool and not just another lonely, horny guy searching for a fantasy, he had told her that, for the price of a table dance, he and his partner wanted to discuss her future. With an uncertain shrug she sat down on her dancing pedestal. Then, to Doug's everlasting mortification, Henderson had told her in his most officious and patronizing manner that he was very impressed by her figure and her dancing and that he knew people who might be prepared to introduce her into modelling. She had smirked at both of them, having heard every come-on a thousand times. Unperturbed, Henderson had continued to drop names while she surveyed the other tables. When the song ended, she took her five dollars for the table dance, picked up her dancing pedestal and moved on. She paid no further attention to Doug or Henderson.

That might have been the last time they were in Hangars. What a shame. They had had some good times there.

Julie pulled the car up to the curb outside a coffee house. They found a table by the frosted window and ordered two lattes. While waiting, Doug kneaded his frozen forehead roughly like a sculptor attempting to bring life to a cold hunk of clay.

"You look like shit," Julie announced.

"I don't know why," Doug said through chattering teeth. "I feel marvelous."

"You west coasters are such wimps. You should feel proud. This is the True North Strong and Free-zing." She paused for Doug's response but he just frowned. "When we've finished our lattes," she suggested more sympathetically, "I'll take you back to my place and you can sleep for awhile."

"Ooooh. Sounds intriguing."

Julie looked at him disgustedly. "Don't get any ideas, bucko. And now that I think of it, when are you leaving?"

"I don't know. I don't have a return flight but I've got to be home by late tomorrow. So whenever you and I are done, I guess." He winked, but Julie was expressionless. "Why don't we talk about this thing with Henderson and then I'll check the flight schedules."

The lattes arrived. Doug sighed as he wrapped his hands tightly around the large mug. "So what was going on with Henderson and all these companies, Julie?"

She glanced around the room to make sure their conversation would remain private. Then she turned back to Doug and regarded him silently before she spoke. Doug recognized in her eyes a sense of confusion and despondency.

"Doug, there was a time when I thought that I was in love with Mark," she began. "He would come to Toronto and stay a few days. We would have a great time. We partied..." She smiled and her eyes widened as if awed by the memories. "And to Mark's credit he never led me on, never gave me any reason to believe that our relationship was more than just two people having fun."

She paused before continuing with her story while Doug sipped his latte. "Anyway, in time I recognized that I was not really in love with Mark but more with the fun I had when he was around. And slowly we developed from lovers into friends." She grinned. "Sort of the opposite of most relationships, eh?"

Doug nodded sagely, waiting for Julie to get to the point.

"Mark helped me a lot. I had been in a relationship that was pretty abusive. I had been doing a fair amount of drugs. Mark supported me and taught me a little self respect."

The look of admiration in Julie's eyes told Doug that her thoughts were far away. He recognized that look. It had been in Laura's eyes as well.

"I had started working at Mario's as a hostess," she said. "Whenever Mark was in town we would meet there. Mario liked Mark from the moment he first met him. Mark would always arrive a little early to pick me up and Mario would call him up to the Lair to pass the time. When the restaurant closed for the night we'd all go up to the Lair and party. There was always lots of liquor and dope. It was pretty wild."

She paused again in reflection, then refocused on Doug. "But, you know, at the same time that Mark was helping me get control of myself, he was slipping deeper and deeper into that scene. He'd arrive at the restaurant earlier and earlier and then he wouldn't want to leave the Lair. He thought he could handle it. But I didn't. So we kind of drifted apart."

As if a sedative had been slipped into his latte, Doug's weariness started to interfere with his concentration. Almost involuntarily he closed his eyes and began rubbing his temples.

Perhaps Julie read this as an indication of impatience, for she said, "I'm sorry. This must be boring you." She reached out and touched his arm. "There is a point to all this. Mark was special to me and that's why I want you to know what he—I mean what we—were all doing. But I want you to know that this is a little difficult for me. And I'm sticking my neck out. Please don't let anyone know that I've told you all of this."

Doug stopped rubbing his temples. He opened his eyes and gazed at Julie, trying to regain his concentration. "I don't think you've really told me anything yet, Julie," he said, perhaps a little too bluntly.

She glanced around the room again, then leaned forward and said in a low voice, "Mario is a major cocaine dealer in Ontario. He markets the stuff from the Lair."

Julie had now won Doug's full attention. He sat up in his chair and put his hands flat on the table. "Okay," he said, "I'm listening."

She looked at him with genuine fear in her eyes. "Please, Doug," she pleaded, "you can never say that you heard any of this from me."

"You have my word," Doug said solemnly.

Her eyes searched his for an indication that he was trustworthy. Maybe she determined that he was, or maybe she just needed to unburden herself. Whatever the reason, she continued.

"Drug sales create a lot of money. Mario had stacks of cash that he had to find a way to invest. He and Mark cooked up this scheme and enlisted the help of all Mario's employees. Our wages were increased dramatically and in return, all we had to do was become shareholders of these companies that Mario created from time to time. He dumped a bunch of money into our bank accounts and then, when he instructed us, we'd sign it over to the companies as shareholders' loans."

This all fit with Doug's own research so he saw where it was going. "These companies," he offered, "used the money to buy real estate, then quickly flipped it, replacing the drug cash with clean cash on the sale of the property."

Julie nodded. "That's the idea, as I understand it."

Doug tried to conjure up a mental diagram of the movement of the money: from suitcases in the Lair to the shareholders' accounts, to the companies, to the property purchases, and then the return of the new money from the sale of the properties to the companies. Something was missing.

"But how does the clean money come out of the companies once the properties are sold?" he asked. "How does Mario get his hands on it?"

Julie shrugged. "I don't know." She thought for a moment. "Maybe it all gets tied up in Mario's holding company."

"What company is that?"

Julie stared at Doug without answering. Thinking. "What the hell is that company called?" she asked aloud, as she racked her brain for the answer. "I get some of the literature for it. You know, the companies that I'm a shareholder of are shareholders of Mario's company. So I get notices of meetings and stuff." She suddenly looked up at Doug with satisfaction. "Terra Holdings, that's it," she said, pointing her index finger at him as an exclamation mark.

"I've seen that name, Julie. It's a shareholder of some of the companies that buy and sell the real estate, isn't it?"

"It may be. I really don't follow much of what's going on."

"Well, assuming it is..." Doug hesitated while he thought this through, "then what you have is a sort of pyramid." He pulled out a pen from his breast pocket and drew a triangle on the napkin. "At the top," he said pointing to the peak of the pyramid, "is Terra Holdings. And I bet you that Mario and his close associates are the officers and directors of that company. In the middle are the shareholders of Terra." He drew a line through the middle of the pyramid. "These are the companies that buy and sell the real estate. The money from the property sales goes to Terra in the way of shareholders' loans. And at the bottom are the shareholders of those companies. But in some cases, these shareholders are Mario or his close associates, or even Terra Holdings which they control."

Doug drew an arrow from the top of the pyramid to the bottom. "It's all tied in, you see. The money starts at the bottom as drug money. It's cleaned at the middle by the sale of the real estate. Then it goes to the top, Terra Holdings, where it's invested in whatever legitimate projects Terra operates. Eventually, it comes out to the officers and directors."

Julie looked at the diagram and shrugged. "Makes sense to me," she acknowledged. She drained her latte and looked out the window, apparently unimpressed with Doug's Sherlockian deductions. He finished off his own latte while he pondered the diagram. Finally he said "Why would Henderson want to get involved in this?"

"That's easy," Julie replied returning her gaze to Doug. "As I told you on the phone, for the money. Mario was paying everyone very well for their role in this thing."

"And maybe Henderson wanted the money so that he could make a quick change of lifestyle, from playboy to suburbanite," Doug added. He considered this for awhile. "You were saying that Mario provides you with a bunch of money to pay into these companies as shareholders' loans. How much are we talking about?"

"Oh, I don't know. Whatever he could put into our accounts without causing an investigation. He used several accounts from different banks."

"So how much was an average shareholder's loan from these different accounts?"

Julie contemplated this for a moment. "Maybe fifty or sixty grand."

"So, what's to stop you from just taking the money out of the accounts yourself?"

She laughed. "Are you kidding? Take money from Mario? Why not just jump off a bridge?"

This answer came as no surprise to Doug. To operate a drug business successfully you needed the terror factor. There was just too much money and too many people involved to be anything less than ruthless with those who refused to play the game. Which brought him to the critical question, and he contemplated once more whether he should ask it. What was the risk? Maybe it was this: if there was a connection between Mario's operation and Henderson's death and if Julie knew about it, she might decide for some reason to tell Mario of Doug's prying. And then what? Mario would come after Doug? Not likely. It would create too many questions, ultimately exposing the whole operation. The more probable result would be a cover-up by Mario, perhaps even an elimination of some of the weak links in the operation. Julie might be expendable, especially if Mario learned that she had told Doug as much as she already had. Doug concluded that this risk was enough to keep Julie quiet, but just in case she failed to recognize it, he determined to point it out to her. With that in mind, he was about to pose the question when Julie spoke.

"Sometimes I think Mark's fate was inevitable," she said returning her gaze to the frozen street outside. "If a woman hadn't got him, then Mario would have."

Now they had arrived at the topic that had brought Doug to Toronto. "Are you saying that Mario wanted Henderson dead?" he asked.

"No. No. I don't think so. But you know how Mark was. He always thought he could do anything he wanted and get away with it. He was the Teflon Man. And sooner or later he would have done something that would have pissed Mario off." She shook her head sadly. "Look at what happened to Joey Marron."

"I've heard that name before. I think Henderson knew the guy. Wasn't he killed in some drug deal?"

Julie nodded her head vigorously. "Yeah. He tried to rip Mario off!" she said in wide-eyed horror.

"How?"

"All I know is Joey was one of Mario's mules and he tried to keep some of the coke he brought in for himself. I guess Mario found out."

Doug recalled something Henderson had said to him. "Henderson told me he had some business deal with Marron. Do you know what that would be about?"

Julie rolled her eyes. "The only 'business' Joey was in, that I know of, was the drug import business. If Mark and him had some deal going, I hate to think what it was."

Doug felt he was getting close to something and decided that it was time to advise Julie of his special interest. "Julie, I need to tell you something very important, but again, this whole conversation must be between us."

Julie drew slowly away from the window and looked back at Doug. Eventually, she nodded her head. "Of course, Doug. I've already told you enough to get myself killed. So it better be just between us."

"I'm acting for the girl who the police think shot Henderson," he said, then waited for the shock to leave Julie's face before he continued. "I'm convinced that she didn't do it." He returned Julie's stare to persuade her of his conviction. When he thought he had done so he added, "I want to find out who did do it."

"And you think that Mario did it?"

"I don't know. I'm just looking for any other explanation. But what I need to know is whether you are aware of anything that happened between Henderson and Mario that might have caused Mario to want Henderson dead."

Julie frowned in concentration, ran her hand through her hair as she thought about the question and, finally, answered, "No. As far as I know, there was nothing going on." She paused before adding, "But then I don't know a lot of what was going on."

"Henderson told me Mario wanted him to invest in something, but he couldn't come up with the money because one of his 'crazy investments' had backfired. Does any of that ring a bell for you?"

Julie thought for a moment. "No," she shook her head. "But I don't know why Mario was asking Mark to invest. Usually, he just told you, 'you're going to be a shareholder of this company and I'm putting so much into various bank accounts in your name'. That's it. You didn't have a say."

"And you don't know anything about some deal between Henderson and Joey Marron that might have got him shot?"

She shook her head.

Doug digested this for a while before getting up from his chair. He pulled his overcoat tightly around him, turned up the collar and shuddered involuntarily. "Shall we go?"

They left the coffee house and hurried across the frozen sidewalk to Julie's car. Once inside, before Julie turned on the ignition, Doug asked, "Julie, if you hear of anything that might suggest Mario had Mark eliminated, will you please tell me?"

"Absolutely," she replied as she started the engine.

It was nine o'clock when they arrived at Julie's neat, stylish and tiny studio apartment in Yorkville. They were both exhausted. For Doug it was six a.m. and he was still feeling the effects of a sleepless flight. For Julie it was the middle of the night; work ended around two or three a.m., so morning never started before eleven.

Doug was able to book a return flight for early that evening, giving him a good seven hours or so to get some rest. Julie offered him the sofa in the living-room/bedroom opposite her single bed/couch which was strewn with pillows and cushions shaped like hearts and animals. She offered him full use of the bathroom, as well, where he took great pleasure in an overdue shower and shave.

Refreshed and wrapped in a bath towel slung low like a Tahitian dancer's grass skirt, Doug exited the bathroom to find Julie curled up between the sheets of her bed. A neatly folded blanket waited for him on the sofa. He had an impulse to join Julie instead, but just as he was about to tiptoe over to her bed she spoke. "Don't even think about it, Doug." And like a chastened dog, he slunk to the sofa.

He was struggling with the blanket and trying to concertina his body within the confines of the sofa when Julie asked softly, "Why do you want to sleep with me, Doug?"

He resisted the immediate response that came to his mind—a variation on the famous answer of George Leigh Mallory when asked why he climbed mountains—"Because you're there." Instead he tried a more diplomatic approach. "I'm really attracted to you, Julie."

Unconvinced, she laughed. "Sure, like you're really attracted to Jenna." Then she asked with a note of sarcasm, "By the way, do you want to call her now that you're in town? I can get the number for you."

"No," he smiled. "I don't think I have time to see her. Next time, maybe."

Julie became serious. "Are you really enjoying yourself, Doug? Living on booze, drugs and casual sex?"

He was surprised by her glib description of his life over the past couple of weeks. He liked to think that his actions were a little more profound, but was too tired and too uncomfortable to protest.

She continued. "Don't you feel that you've sacrificed some of your integrity?"

He gave up his struggle and lay on his back, feet hanging over the arm of the sofa. "Truly, Julie," he sighed, "I don't know what I feel anymore. I thought I was missing something when Diane and I were together." With an exaggerated gesture, he threw his arms straight above him as if beseeching the heavens. "The rapture of life!" he announced. His arms dropped abruptly to his side. "But now that I'm on my own, I find I'm not enraptured. I'm just going through the motions. And I'm starting to feel that I'm missing something because I'm not with Diane." He exhaled in total exasperation, "I am such a fuck-up."

"The grass is always greener, eh?"

Doug continued with the old metaphor. "It sure seemed that way when I was watching Henderson from the other side of the fence. But now that I've hopped over, I realize it's just grass and it ain't my yard." He laughed at his own weak humour.

"Seems to me that Mark wasn't the only one caught up in a bunch of lies. What was it with you two guys? You both seemed to want what the other had. But it just doesn't fit, does it?"

Doug shook his head. "Not well, that's for sure." He lay back against the sofa and closed his eyes. His thoughts circled like an airplane closer and closer around his home. In his mind's eye he saw his house and Diane and the children busy with their various routines. He was wondering what plans they had for the weekend when it suddenly occurred to him that he had promised to go to his son's hockey game that afternoon and then to dinner with Diane. Shit. A quick calculation of flying time, taking into account various delays at both airports, made him realize that it was impossible to make it back in time.

He sat back up on the sofa. "I've got to call Diane."

CHAPTER 16

Tom spent most of the weekend sitting in the roguesmobile outside the Barclay watching the tenants come and go. It took him until mid-afternoon on Sunday to interview all of them, only to confirm Christopher's advice that no one witnessed anything.

The exercise had its entertaining moments, however. In particular, there was the tenant who Tom managed to interview on Saturday evening. When she first came clicking out of the entrance door on ice-pick heels, her tall, shapely figure grabbed his attention. He approached her and was instantly stunned by her sexy, slick and sophisticated style. A beautiful, long, chocolate brown overcoat hung off her shoulders, open to exhibit a flouncy, deep-cut, pink silk blouse and burgundy leather trousers, calf length and tight, fastened high on her waist by a wide black belt. A large multi-coloured silk scarf was wrapped haphazardly around her neck over a string of brilliant white pearls that stretched to her waist. Only when Tom sidled up beside her and introduced himself did his hackles shoot up. Her voice was deeper than his and a five o'clock shadow bristled through her makeup.

He drew her over to the splash of a street light, then asked her about Henderson and the events on the night of his death. She had a clear recollection of Henderson as the suave scoundrel who had kept a rotation of women passing through apartment 2B. A devil, she called him with a wink. But to her everlasting disappointment, he had not been interested in what she had to offer. Unfortunately, on the night of Henderson's death she had stayed over at a friend's apartment, so knew nothing. She was useless, as well, when asked to describe the women who had frequented Henderson's apartment. They were all tramps, unworthy of a second glance.

She was extremely sorry that she was unable to help Tom in his inves-tigation. Slipping her arm through the crook of his elbow, she offered to make it up to him by buying him a drink. When he awkwardly declined, she turned and minced down the sidewalk in a huff.

Tom also spoke to Mrs. Rattenbury, who initially complained that she had been asked the same questions by Mr. Branston, the police, other lawyers and even reporters—either in person or over the phone. Her story hadn't changed; she still had no useful information to offer. With the exception of Kim and Carmen, she described the women who Henderson had taken to the apartment in only the vaguest terms. And her descrip-tion of Carmen might have matched a thousand women living in the West End. At least Mrs. Rattenbury was able to confirm that, to her knowledge, only Kim and Carmen had been to visit Henderson for sever-al weeks prior to his death.

Tom asked about that night, informing her that Henderson had been expecting to meet someone other than Kim. Was there anyone else around the building that Ms. Rattenbury recognized—perhaps Carmen? The answer was no.

So Tom's weekend of private-eyeing turned up nothing. Back in the office on Sunday night he prepared the draft letter to Dr. Wall for Doug to review upon his return. In the course of doing so, Tom examined the records from Laura's stay in hospital. He noted that the diagnostic report prepared on Laura's admission the night of Henderson's death indicated a hematoma in the area of the right temple, with no rupture of the skin, resulting in loss of consciousness. X-rays had been taken, highlighting a fracture of the skull by the right temple. The rest of the records consisted mostly of nurses' notes recording the day-to-day treatment of Laura, but the handwriting was almost impossible to decipher.

On his return from Toronto on Sunday, Doug went straight to the Holden home where he met first with Frank Holden who told him that Laura had recovered some of her old spirit when she had first arrived home, railing against the accusation that she had killed Henderson. How could it be true? She loved him, adored him, idolized him. It was impos-sible for her to have killed him. She had spent considerable time staring out her bedroom window going over in her mind the events of that night, searching for the key to her innocence, but she kept reaching the same point in time where her recollection ceased. Consequently, as the weekend passed she had become more and more despondent, weeping inconsolably, as she began to understand her predicament. At one point, she had told her father that her life was meaningless without Mark and that she had thought of all sorts of ways to end it; but she was unable to do so and she hated herself for her cowardice.

Doug asked to see Laura, and with some gentle prodding, she repeated her story to him: she had known Henderson would be at the apartment so she had gone there to tell him that he must not end their relationship, they were meant for each other, they would be together forever. Besides, she knew there was someone else and she knew Henderson had to be stopped before he became too involved with that other woman. Something had gone wrong, though. They had argued. She had hit him and scratched him.

"I can see it all in my mind," she said, "the empty lobby, our fight." As she described it, she became more excited, more passionate. "But then the picture ends, suddenly." And the scene that kept replaying in her mind, time after time, frame by frame, stopped abruptly, always at the same point, before Henderson was killed.

Laura was simply unable to remember what had happened at the crucial moment, and without some explanation of events, she recognized that all the evidence seemed to point to her. The only submission she was able to make in her own defence was that it was impossible for her to have had a gun with her that night. She had no idea where to get a gun, and even if she had a gun, she was totally ignorant of how to use it. Doug and her father believed her, but they were not a judge or jury.

Laura's arrest came early on Monday morning. The police, sensitive to the situation, sent an unmarked vehicle with two plainclothes police officers to the Holden home. There were no handcuffs. Even so, it was a nightmare for Laura. As she left the house and walked to the waiting car, her skin appeared white with a faint bluish tinge. Her eyes were dark and puffy from crying, and her mouth was turned down at the corners, her lips pale and lifeless. She was a zombie walking between the officers, whispering one-word answers to their questions.

Doug tried to make sure everything went as quickly and smoothly as possible. He and Holden followed the police car to the station where the fingerprinting took place, after which Laura was taken to the Youth Courts to be held in custody pending her appearance in court later that morning.

The court appearance proceeded according to Doug's expectations. They managed to get on the list for the morning session, and the judge was amenable to the joint submission of Christopher and Doug on the terms of bail. Christopher advised the judge that the Crown would apply to elevate the case to adult court, and the judge agreed to schedule that hearing for the following week. As soon as the decision on elevation was made, a trial date would be set. The whole matter took less than half an hour of court time, and through it all Laura sat in the dock for the accused like a waif, stunned and emotionless, staring blankly into space.

On Monday afternoon Tom and Doug met to finalize the draft letter to the doctor. To begin with they discussed what they needed the doctor's evidence to establish in order to win the case. The Crown's theory of the sequence of events was that Henderson had struck Laura, then she had shot him, and finally she had fallen to the floor unconscious from the force of his punch. Doug and Tom agreed that there were two ways in which the doctor's evidence might help them attack this theory: first, if Dr. Wall concluded that Laura's injuries made it impossible for her to have been struck from in front by Henderson, and second, if the doctor concluded that it was physically impossible for Laura to have fired the gun in the instant after receiving a blow to her head and before falling to the floor unconscious. If the doctor was able to reach either conclusion, it suggested that another person was in the room at the time of the killing which raised a doubt, perhaps reasonable, that Laura had pulled the trigger.

Doug suggested a few changes to the background narrative in the body of Tom's draft letter. Then they concentrated on itemizing the specific issues they wanted the doctor to address in order to make his opinion as clear and strong as possible. Eventually, they settled on directing the doctor to provide an opinion on the following questions:

1. In your opinion, what caused Ms. Holden's loss of consciousness?

2. Assuming the answer to 1. is a blow to the right temple, are you able to say from what direction that blow came? Please explain your answer.

3. In your opinion, could Ms. Holden's loss of consciousness have been caused by a blow from a fist or open hand of someone standing in front of Ms. Holden?

4. In your opinion, how soon after receiving the blow to the head would Ms. Holden have lost consciousness?

5. In your opinion, could Ms. Holden have fired a .38 caliber hand gun from her purse after she had received the blow to the head? Please explain your answer.

The letter was delivered to the doctor in the late afternoon, just before Doug gave Tom a new set of instructions. He told Tom, in general terms, of Henderson's involvement with the money laundering operation, while at the same time trying to keep his promise of secrecy to Julie. Then, he directed Tom to consider what discreet investigations might be undertaken to determine whether this activity had any relation to Henderson's death, but cautioned Tom that no step was to be taken until approved by him.

In the days following Laura's court appearance, Doug devoted his time to preparing a court submission in support of keeping the matter at the Youth Court level. There were innumerable advantages to a Youth Court hearing, most notably that the name of the accused was withheld from the press and the sentence in the event of conviction would be about a quarter as long as in adult court. However, he soon realized that it was going to be an uphill battle.

From his research, he learned that the test the court liked to apply when considering elevation to adult court was actually a balance between the seriousness of the crime and the general danger of the accused to society. He was confident that he could meet the latter part of the test; the judge only needed to see Laura to be satisfied that she was no threat to anyone except, perhaps, herself. But it was evident that the law regarded the former part of the test to be critical in the case of a homicide.

Christopher had been right. The predilection of Youth Court judges was to raise to adult court matters that involved homicide where the accused was fifteen years or older. The policy seemed to be that a crime resulting in death was so serious that, regardless of whether the accused was a threat to society, the matter ought to be heard in adult court. This was a sign of the times. Violence in the city was growing and spreading like a cancer and the public was fed up with the protection the Youth Court system provided offenders who happened to be minors.

Doug arrived at the hearing armed with affidavits from upstanding members of the community, from Holden family members and from neighbours, all attesting to Laura's good character. Christopher, on the contrary, had no factual material supporting his position other than the indictment and the Information document describing the circumstances of the charge against her. However, he had brought a large binder labeled "Brief of Authorities" which Doug guessed contained all the cases he had reviewed that were in support of elevation—and probably a few that he had missed.

Although the courtroom was small, it was divided into three distinct areas. The public gallery, just inside the entrance door, consisted of two rows of seating. In the centre of the room, beyond the gallery and symbolically separated from it by a brass rail, was the counsel area. A long counsel table sat in the middle of this area opposite the witness stand and the counter for the court clerk and reporter. The chairs for the court clerk and reporter nestled in the shadow of the great elevated judge's desk, commonly referred to as "the bench," which dominated the entire courtroom like an altar. Behind the bench was the judge's exclusive domain with a separate door on the far wall connecting the courtroom to a mysterious private hold: the judges' chambers. The door allowed the judge access to the bench without encountering the public or counsel.

The prisoner's dock, halfway between the counsel table and the brass rail, in a no man's land between the law and the people, stood out in contrast to the efficient symmetry of the rest of the courtroom.

The walls of the courtroom were papered in subtle tan hues, which were calming against the blood red carpet. On the wall behind the bench the enormous national shield stood guard from its perch; flags rested at ease on gold-tipped poles on either side of the judge's large scarlet leather chair, the Canadian flag on the right and the British Columbian flag on the left. Sombre directional lights bathed the entire room except for piercing spotlights over the counsel table, the judge's bench and the witness box. The oppressive stillness of the room was cut by the constant whirring of ceiling fans.

Court was in recess when Doug and Christopher first walked in, but the court clerk was at her counter busily preparing a list of applications scheduled for the day, ordering them from most to least critical. A scattering of lawyers milled about, each waiting to have his or her application heard by the judge. Doug and Christopher strolled up to the counter to check in with the court clerk. After reviewing her list of applications, she advised them that their matter would be heard second.

They found a couple of seats in the public gallery because the chairs around the counsel table were all taken. Meanwhile, the court clerk called loudly "Are there any more matters for hearing today?" She waited a moment but there was no reply. "If not, I will go and get the judge." She waited another moment then stepped around the bench and out the back door to retrieve the judge from his chambers. Seconds later she returned and in an authoritarian voice announced, "Order in court."

Everyone rose as the judge stepped into the room. A young, intense-looking man in a black gown with scarlet trim strode up to the bench, took a quick look at the scrum of lawyers in the court, bowed and sat down. Everyone in the courtroom returned his bow, then sat down as well.

Doug daydreamed through the first application. When his case was called, he and Christopher marched to the counsel table and each, in turn, introduced himself to the judge.

Christopher had the floor first. He began by advising the judge of the nature of the application, then conceded that Laura Holden was an unusual accused to be considered for elevation to adult court because she had no history of problems with the law. She came from a well-to-do family, had done well at school, and by all accounts was a valued member of the community, he noted.

Doug recognized the old litigators' trick that Christopher was employing. By presenting the points helpful to Laura's position, Christopher was rebutting Doug's argument before he had a chance to advance it.

Next, Christopher presented his own position, commencing with the platitudes that he knew would influence the judge. "Your Honour, this is a case of murder—not shoplifting, or joy riding, or possession of drugs, or even trafficking in drugs. Murder." He paused to let the word hang in the air like a noose. "The most detestable of all crimes," he added, spreading his arms like Moses addressing the masses. "A crime that is repugnant to civilized people everywhere."

"Ms. Holden has been charged with second degree murder: the *intentional* killing of Mark Henderson. It is the Crown's contention that she shot Mr. Henderson with a .38 mm revolver that she had concealed in her purse. Now, if that is proven, then we are dealing with a young woman who carried a gun to the scene." Christopher shrugged his shoulders in an exaggerated fashion. "Why?" he asked. "No one just *happens* to have a gun in her purse. Why did Ms. Holden carry a gun? She must have had a reason."

After a moment's hesitation, Christopher answered his own question. "Perhaps she planned to shoot Mr. Henderson." He paused. "Or maybe she carried the gun just in case she felt she needed to use it. Either way, this fifteen-year-old girl made a conscious decision to carry a weapon with her when she went to see Mr. Henderson. That weapon could realistically be used for only one thing—to shoot another human being. And that is exactly what happened. She used it to shoot and kill Mr. Henderson.

"Maybe Ms. Holden's history is impeccable. Maybe she was the perfect student, the perfect member of the community. But, at least from the moment she went to see Mark Henderson, that changed. She chose to go armed and she ended up taking his life. That is an action that society must not tolerate."

Christopher paused while he picked up the three copies of the Brief of Authorities that were lying on the counsel table. He handed a copy to Doug. "Your Honour," he said, "I am passing up a volume of authorities that, in my submission, illustrates how the courts have dealt with this issue." The court clerk accepted a copy of the Brief from Christopher and handed it up to the judge.

Christopher forced a smile. "I don't propose to review all of these cases in detail,"—he flipped through the pages ostentatiously—"but I would like to direct you to some of the highlights which, in my submission, indicate what the court has done in cases similar to this one."

He proceeded to refer the judge to every case in the Brief, first summarizing the facts, then the court's reasoning, and finally, the decision. For Doug there were no surprises. Every case dealt with homicide allegedly committed by an accused fifteen years or older, and in each case, the court had decided to elevate the matter to adult court.

Christopher concluded, "I suggest, Your Honour, that the decisions I have referred to clearly state the test to be applied by the court. That is, the severity of the crime balanced against the threat of the accused to society. And in the case of murder, that balance is weighted heavily in favour of elevation. In fact, I have not seen one decision dealing with an accused of fifteen years or older where the court has found his or her character to be so agreeable, so devoid of danger to society, that it has refused the application to elevate. I suggest, Your Honour, that this is because the court has determined that the very nature of the crime proves that the accused is a threat to society, and therefore, the test is always met.

"I submit as well, Your Honour, that there is a strong public policy reason for the accused to be elevated to adult court: it is to expose the accused to the scrutiny of the press and the public so that others will get the clear message that society will not give an accused the benefit of the Youth Court system if the crime illustrates a rejection of the very basics for which society stands."

Christopher stood silently at the lectern as if in prayer, then packed up the papers he had in front of him and bowed to the judge. "Thank you, Your Honour," he said with great ceremony, and sat down.

The judge nodded to Christopher while scribbling notes in his court book. Doug had the sinking feeling that the judge had already made his decision and was writing the outline of his judgment before even hearing Doug's submission. Eventually, he looked up. With a sigh of impatience he grunted, "Yes, Mr. Branston."

Doug moved to the lectern, laid out the affidavits he had brought and advised the judge that he planned to refer to these documents in the course of his argument. He asked for permission to hand copies up to the bench so that the judge might follow along. When the judge reluctantly agreed, the court clerk took the copies from Doug and handed them up to the judge. As a courtesy Doug handed a second set of copies to Christopher. He was about to refer to the first affidavit when the judge spoke up.

"Mr. Branston," he said as he idly flipped through the affidavits, "is it really necessary for you to review all these affidavits?" He raised his eyebrows to emphasize the daunting task. "I suspect that they indicate what a good person the accused was. But your friend"—a euphemism used to describe opposing counsel—"has already conceded that point, hasn't he?" The judge looked down at Christopher who nodded in confirmation.

Doug felt a sense of discouragement. Before he had even started his submission, the judge seemed to be cutting him off. It was so typical. Christopher had played it well and now Doug's strongest argument was being taken from him. He was going to have to ad-lib. So what else was new?

"Well, My Lord..." he started.

The judge interrupted again. "Mr. Branston, have you forgotten that down here in the criminal trenches we are still referred to as 'Your Honour'? I'm afraid I haven't reached the lofty title of 'My Lord' yet." Some time had passed since Doug's last appearance in Provincial Court and he had forgotten that judges here were referred to as "Your Honour," unlike their superior court brethren who were referred to as "My Lord".

He gulped in a reflex response to his inauspicious beginning. "I apologize, Your Honour." He made a slight bow and forged on. "What I was about to say"—*before I was interrupted by Your Pompousness*, he added to himself—"was that I'm not sure that my friend has conceded the point I wish to make with these affidavits. However, if he has, then I certainly will not take up the court's time in reviewing them."

Doug looked briefly at Christopher. "The point I wish to make with these affidavits is that Ms. Holden *is* a cherished member of her family, her school and her community. The operative word being *is*, not *was*. I believe my friend has tried to make that distinction. He has suggested that the crime alleged against Ms. Holden has somehow made her a social pariah. That, I submit, is not the case at all. *If* Ms. Holden committed the crime alleged—and I say *if* because I firmly believe that the Crown will fail to prove its case against her—then it was a crime of passion. The victim, Mr. Henderson, was forty-three years old, only two years younger than Ms. Holden's father. Ms. Holden is fifteen years old. Mr. Henderson had seduced her. He had carried on a relationship with her for some time prior to his death, filling her mind with all sorts of fantasies about the future. She was infatuated with him, devoted to him. He had become…"—he used Christopher's word—"her Svengali."

Doug let a moment pass to allow the judge time to picture in his mind the total imbalance of the relationship between Laura and Henderson.

"And then," Doug said, raising his voice to ensure the judge's attention, "and then, he suddenly ends their relationship." He paused. "These affidavits"—he picked them up to illustrate his point—"do not only tell of Ms. Holden's character, they describe her total devastation and humiliation when she received the letter from Mr. Henderson advising that he was ending their relationship. Which brings me to the essence of my submission."

Doug looked directly at the judge. "Even if Laura Holden did kill Mark Henderson, that act was totally at odds with her general character. It resulted from a relationship in which she was, in many ways, the victim. So I take issue with my friend's submission that Ms. Holden's character changed when she went to meet Mr. Henderson that night. At worst it was overridden for the moment by very extenuating circumstances, circumstances that would test the basic nature of any young member of our society. Therefore, we should not be repulsed by Ms. Holden; on the contrary, we should be using the system to help her overcome this aberration in her character because she is *still* a valued member of society. The best way to do this, Your Honour, is by keeping her in the Youth Court system."

Doug put down the affidavits, picked up his copy of the Crown's Brief of Authorities and held it in the air. "My friend has reviewed all these cases and it is true that in each one the court has ordered elevation. But, I suggest, in none of these cases is the character of the accused as outstanding as that of Ms. Holden. And in my submission it is simply too glib to say, as my friend does, that the crime substantiates the character. In the case of Ms. Holden, that is just untrue. Every rule has its exception, and this is one."

Doug reached for the affidavits once more. "Your Honour, I am prepared to review these affidavits in order to illustrate my point."

Before the judge was able to comment Christopher stood up. "I don't think that will be necessary, Your Honour," he said. "I am certainly prepared to concede everything that my friend says about the accused's character and her devastation when Mr. Henderson ended their relationship. However, I do not accept that she was a victim. There is only one victim here. Mark Henderson. And in my submission, it doesn't matter if the accused *was* of fine character or *is* of fine character. The fact remains that she is alleged to have shot to death Mr. Henderson with a gun that she brought with her to her rendezvous with him. That fact alone is enough, I say, for this matter to be raised to adult court."

Christopher and Doug both sat down. Doug had made his point and Christopher had not really challenged it. The issue came down to whether a charge of murder was sufficient to raise the matter to adult court regardless of the accused's character.

The judge looked at Doug. "Given your friend's comments, I don't think it will be necessary to review all the affidavit material, do you, Mr. Branston?"

Doug stood and answered, "No, Your Honour."

They sat silently while the judge wrote more notes in his court book. Eventually he finished, glanced at the clock on the wall and put his pen in his breast pocket. It was time for the morning recess. He advised both counsel that he planned to consider the matter over the break and return with a decision when court reconvened.

The court clerk, having fought valiantly to remain awake through the submissions, jumped to her feet. "Order in court," she called. Everyone rose along with the judge who bowed and left through the back door.

If there was one thing Doug hated about being a trial lawyer it was the amount of time he spent loitering in corridors outside courtrooms waiting for things to happen. The wheels of justice moved painfully slowly. Perhaps the worst part of it was having to pass the down time with the lawyer on the other side of the case. Inevitably the conversation was about Doug's argument, about his opponent's argument, about what they thought the judge would do. It reminded Doug of university days and the suffocating moments before writing exams when the doors to the lecture hall were still closed and the students gathered in the corridor, waiting. Tension hung in the air like an oppressive fog. And always the nervous discussions among the crowd turned to issues Doug had failed to study, raising his level of panic.

Fortunately, Christopher was more interested in passing the recess time talking about his friendship with Henderson than the issue before the judge. Doug actually found the time passed agreeably as they reminisced about the exciting times they had spent with Henderson. After what seemed to be a very short break, the clerk unlocked the doors to the court-room and invited Doug and Christopher back in.

The judge chose to render his decision orally from the bench while Doug and Christopher sat at the counsel table. He began summarizing the circumstances of Henderson's death from the facts that appeared in the Information. Then he referred in some detail to Laura's character, causing Doug to conclude, with heightened respect, that he had read the affidavits during the recess. After noting that the Crown took no issue with the description of the accused's character that appeared in the affidavits, the judge came to his decision.

"The Crown submits that the law is clear: in the case of homicide where the accused is the age of Ms. Holden, it is appropriate to raise the trial to adult court. And, indeed, that is what all the cases to which I have been referred say. However, counsel for the accused submits that none of these cases deals with circumstances as unique as in the matter before me. Specifically, he points out that, in this case, the accused was, in his words, the 'victim' of the deceased because of the control he had over her. Therefore, if she did kill the deceased, it was a crime of passion and total-ly out of character. Counsel argues that for this reason, the case law referred to by the Crown is distinguishable and should not be followed in this instance."

The judge looked up at each counsel in order to verify that his sum-mary of the arguments was accurate. He then continued. "When consid-ering elevation, the court must take into account the crime and the char-acter of the accused. If the character of the accused suggests that the crime was an anomaly, then the accused may be entitled to the protection of the Youth Court system. But if the crime is consistent with a character that is at odds with society's mores, then the accused may face the full force of society's justice system.

"From my review of the law, it is apparent that this balance between the crime and the character of the accused shifts depending on the severity of the crime. In other words, if the crime is relatively trivial, then the charac-ter of the accused may be poor and yet the matter will remain in the Youth Court system. However, if the crime is significant, then the character of the accused must be impeccable for the matter not to be elevated.

"Where the case is one of murder, the court has, without exception, ele-vated the trial to adult court after considering the accused's character. And while I am sympathetic to Mr. Branston's position, I am not satisfied that he has given me sufficient reason not to follow the case law. Perhaps, as Mr. Branston says, the accused here meets an even higher standard of character than those other cases. That may be. But, in my view, it does not matter at the end of the day. I must agree with Mr. Christopher. The crime in this case is so severe that it dictates the outcome of this application.

"I am not prepared to say that all cases of homicide must be elevated no matter what the evidence is of the accused's character. But I have decided that in this case, the evidence of Ms. Holden's good character is not sufficient to counter successfully the heavy weight of the crime. Therefore, the matter will be elevated to adult court."

Doug was not surprised. Judges are disinclined to make decisions that are contrary to those of their brethren, even if the facts of the cases are distinguishable. He sat contemplating the consequences of this decision for Laura, and his approach to her defence.

The judge asked if there was anything else counsel wished him to decide. Christopher looked at Doug and then replied, "No, Your Honour. I will be discussing with my friend the scheduling of a Disclosure Court hearing and a preliminary hearing. Thank you, Your Honour." He and Doug stood to pack up their materials, then bowed to the judge and stepped away from the counsel table. Already the court clerk was on her feet calling the next matter.

In the corridor outside the courtroom Christopher and Doug discussed briefly where things would go from here. They agreed on a date a week thereafter for a Disclosure Court hearing after which they would discuss the timing of a preliminary hearing. Christopher raised the subject, once more, of the possibility of a plea bargain. Again Doug indicated that he was unable to seek instructions on this until after the Disclosure Court hearing.

As Doug left the courthouse he felt a black morass of dread bubbling up from deep in his guts and recognized its familiar, involuntary warning that he was fighting a losing case. He knew it was too early to reach that conclusion; he was still awaiting the opinion from Dr. Wall on the blow to Laura's head and he had yet to see all the Crown's evidence. Still, Tom had turned up nothing from his interview of the tenants or from Mrs. Rattenbury, and his assiduous investigations of the money laundering operation had, so far, been fruitless.

Doug knew that if they failed to come up with hard evidence in Laura's favour soon, their only option would be to seriously consider Christopher's offer of a plea bargain. He hated having that feeling in his guts because it was seldom wrong.

Deep in disturbed thought, Doug drifted towards the lawyers' lounge in the bowels of the courthouse. He had to call Holden who, he knew, was waiting for news of the judge's decision. Although he had prepared Holden for the loss, it was still going to be a shock. Doug imagined the newspaper headlines the next morning. This was the type of story that would command a front page spread, with lots of photos of Laura, Holden and Henderson.

He stepped into one of the telephone cubicles in the lawyers' lounge. As he picked up the receiver to call Holden's office, he thought of Diane. The awkward phone call he had made from Julie's apartment in Toronto to cancel their dinner date had upset Diane. It had proved to her—once again, as she had said—that he was totally self-absorbed, unprepared to allow room in his schedule for their relationship. Since his return they had managed to get together a few times, but their conversation had revolved around the children. Any attempts by Doug to talk about the future of their marriage was met with stony silence. Surprisingly, her reticence made Doug all that more determined. He had no idea where it was all headed, but he knew that he enjoyed seeing her even if she was cool toward him. At least it was saving him from continued debauchery with Cathy. He had put that relationship on hold while he tried to reacquaint himself with Diane.

Doug dialed his home number as he weighed the chances Diane would be there in the middle of the day.

"Hello," Diane answered.

His heart leapt. "Hi, Diane. It's Doug."

"Oh. Hello."

"Ah…are you free for dinner tonight?" he asked.

Diane sighed. "I am afraid it's too short notice, Douglas. I have other plans."

What about tomorrow?"

"No," she said emphatically. "Unlike you, I plan ahead." Then she added, "And I make a point of keeping the commitments I make."

Doug grimaced. "You're right," he mumbled. "I'm sorry." They were both silent for a time, which Doug chose to take as a sign that she had not given up on him entirely. At least she wasn't hanging up the phone. "Let me try again, Diane," he suggested. "There's a new restaurant in Yaletown that they say is fantastic. I'd love to take you to dinner there next Friday night." He paused before asking, "Are you available?"

"Just a moment." There was muffled silence before she came back on the phone. "It appears I am," she said wearily.

"Great. I'll call you during the week to confirm the arrangements."

"You'd better."

CHAPTER 17

On the following Thursday, Dr. Wall's report finally arrived on Doug's desk. He tore open the envelope and scanned the document, only to find that it was equivocal. Although there was some helpful information, the opinion was too weak to support Laura's defence.

The doctor had reviewed the medical records forwarded to him by Tom. He had also taken the time to visit Laura at her home, interview her, and conduct a brief medical exam. The bulk of the report described the information contained in the medical records and summarized the doctor's findings from his interview and examination of Laura. On the last page the doctor addressed the specific questions posed in Tom's letter.

First, he confirmed that Laura's loss of consciousness likely resulted from a blow to the right temple area of her head. This was established by the skull fracture in that location. "Skull fractures," he noted, "create concussions and loss of consciousness."

He answered the third question next by stating that the blow probably came from the fist of a man—"not a woman"—and had to have been particularly forceful. "It is improbable," he stated, "that a knock from an open hand had caused the skull to fracture."

Returning to the second question, he opined that the blow to the head came from Laura's right. He confirmed the possibility that the source of the blow was the left fist of a man standing in front of Laura at the time.

He was unable to give a conclusive answer to the fourth question, stating only that loss of consciousness usually follows a fracture of the skull, although there is no evidence to suggest that it is instantaneous. His best "guestimate" was that Laura's loss of consciousness occurred within a few seconds of the blow that caused the skull fracture.

Finally, he provided a particularly unhelpful answer to the crucial fifth question. If Laura's hand was on the gun at the time of the blow to her head, he suggested, her reaction to the blow may have caused the gun to go off; alternatively, it was possible that Laura fired the gun in the moments after the blow but before she lost consciousness.

As a consolation, Dr. Wall disclaimed any expertise in the use of firearms.

Doug went over the report a couple of times. The only positive thing he was able to find concerned the force of the blow. Had Henderson thrown it, he would have had to punch Laura violently with his left fist. Doug had never seen Henderson strike anyone regardless of how angry he was, and the idea of him taking a full swing at his fifteen-year-old ex-lover was utterly unimaginable. In any event, Henderson was right-handed. That, of course, did not prohibit him from throwing a punch with his left hand, but it made it even less likely. And if he didn't throw it, then someone else did.

Still, Doug cringed as he envisioned Dr. Wall testifying at the trial. The rules of criminal legal procedure required that if he was going to put the good doctor on the witness stand, Doug had to serve the prosecution, in advance, with a copy of the doctor's report. In that way Christopher would have an opportunity to identify all of the report's weaknesses beforehand. Once the doctor was on the stand, Doug would restrict his own questions to the doctor's opinion on the force of the blow. This would lay the foundation for evidence from Henderson's friends that Henderson had never hit anyone in his life. But before Doug could use this evidence to argue that Henderson was incapable of throwing a blow fierce enough to cause Laura to lose consciousness, Christopher's cross-examination of the doctor would dismantle Doug's carefully laid foundation, piece by shaky piece.

Doug considered the simplicity of the cross-examination, starting with the question: would the doctor agree that the fractured skull was consistent with a blow from a fist?

Clearly the answer would be yes.

Next question: Is it possible that a man the size of Henderson, right-handed and facing Laura, could have delivered a punch capable of fracturing her skull?

Again, the doctor would have to answer yes.

And, is it possible that, after receiving such a blow, Laura could have discharged a firearm before losing consciousness?

Yes.

Does the doctor proffer any opinion as to whether Mr. Henderson was psychologically capable of delivering a blow to the accused of the force described?

No—not his specialty.

Then the backbreaker: it is the Crown's theory that Mr. Henderson struck the accused during an argument, causing her to lose consciousness. But after being struck and before losing consciousness, the accused discharged a firearm killing Mr. Henderson. Is it fair to say that the doctor's evidence is consistent with that theory?

His answer would be yes.

Five questions and Christopher would be able to sit down, leaving the jury to wonder how the doctor had possibly helped the accused's case, and leaving Doug to persuade the jury that, although Henderson was capable of seducing, brainwashing and then dumping Laura, he was incapable of punching her, even after she had mauled him.

No. Doug shook his head; Dr. Wall's evidence was of little help to Laura. He had an urge to throw the report into the waste bin, but he knew that Holden and Laura had to see it. Instead, he sat back in his chair and contemplated where he was with Laura's defence. There were neither witnesses, nor any expert evidence to assist her. So far, no strong evidence supported a theory of how Henderson came to be shot that was helpful to Laura. Then there was the Crown's case. Prior to the Disclosure Court hearing, Christopher had provided Doug with all the documentation gathered by the police in their investigation. The only hole seemed to be the lack of an eyewitness to the shooting. And, without any evidence to suggest the Crown's theory was wrong, that hole was microscopic.

Doug sighed. The preliminary hearing was scheduled to start in a week. Although he still felt deep down that Laura had not killed Henderson, he had to face the fact that time was running out on finding some evidence to help her. And without some breakthrough, there was a strong possibility of Laura being convicted. He thought of the report Wren had asked him to prepare for the next partners' meeting and contemplated calling a special meeting to seek his partners' advice on how to proceed. But, first, he needed to have a serious discussion with Holden and Laura about where things stood. He leaned over, picked up the phone and dialed Holden's office to arrange a meeting for the following afternoon.

The next day Doug arrived at the firm early to review all the evidence. He wanted to be able to give Holden and Laura a complete rundown of the Crown's case and Laura's defence. When he was barely through the door of his office, Nancy, the temporary receptionist, tiptoed in with an envelope in her hand.

"Oh, Mr. Branston," she whispered, "I hope I'm not disturbing you. This was delivered just after I opened up this morning." When she leaned over Doug's desk to hand him the envelope, a waft of stale cigarette smoke engulfed him like tear gas.

Doug took the letter while holding his breath against the smell of the smoke. At the same time, he thanked Nancy who turned and started out of the room. As she reached the door she turned. "Just ring me if you need anything else, Mr. B," she offered.

Doug nodded, cleared his throat, and quickly looked down at the sealed envelope. Typed on one side was simply "Douglas Branston. Personal and Confidential." He slit it open and read the letter inside.

Dear Mr. Branston,
I have been reading in the newspapers about the criminal case arising from the death of Mark Henderson. I understand that you are the lawyer who is defending Ms. Laura Holden, the girl who is charged with killing Mr. Henderson. I am writing to advise you that I witnessed the shooting.

Doug sat up in his seat. Flipping over to the other page of the letter he looked for the author's name. None was given. He studied the typeface for a moment before he continued reading: standard computer font, from any one of a million computer printers. He went back to the body of the letter.

Mr. Henderson and I had arranged to meet at the apartment that night. Apparently he arrived before me, for as I came up the front walk, I saw through the glass that he was in the lobby with Ms. Holden. She had a leather bag over her right shoulder. They were arguing so I did not inter- rupt. Instead, I watched them from the shadows of the front courtyard. Ms. Holden was very upset. She attacked Mr. Henderson several times, pushing and hitting him. He kept fending her off.

They were facing each other—Ms. Holden with her back to the stairs— when suddenly a man with a gun in his right hand ran down the stairs. He grabbed Ms. Holden from behind, his left arm over her shoulder and his hand on her mouth. In that same motion he pushed the gun into her open leather bag and fired. The bullet struck Mr. Henderson and he was thrown backwards against the wall. The man must have dropped the gun into the purse because he then struck Ms. Holden with his fist causing her

*to fall to the ground where she remained still. I am sure that she was
unconscious. He removed the gun from her purse and placed it in her
right hand.*

Doug looked up from the letter in shock. He stared unseeing across the
office, his body tingling and his heart racing. Adrenaline beat in his ears
like drums. This might be it. This might be Laura's salvation. Closing his
eyes hard, he tried to keep the euphoria in check.

Wait a minute. He took a deep breath. Wait a minute. Was this letter
legitimate? Or was this some kind of hoax? He had to be wary. Now, with
the papers carrying the story, there were all sorts of people reading about
it. Maybe this letter was written by a weirdo full of hallucinations, wanting his or her own publicity.

He forced himself to calm down, then tried to picture in his mind the
scene that the anonymous author was describing. Was it consistent with
everything he already knew about Henderson's death? Methodically, he
reviewed all the evidence but was unable to find any discrepancy.
Moreover, he realized that there was some information in the letter that
was consistent with evidence that had been kept from the press, particularly the fact that the gun was shot from inside the purse. Only someone
who had access to the police investigation reports or had actually been
there could have known about that. As he turned this over in his mind
the giddiness started to return.

He read on.

*I am sure that it only took the man who shot Mr. Henderson a few sec-
onds to appear and disappear but I will never forget him as long as I live.
He was dressed entirely in black. His hair was slicked back and was held
in a short pony-tail.*

There was only one guy Doug knew that fit that description. And he
had been at Henderson's funeral. "In town for some business" or something like that. Bullshit. He was here to take out Mark. But why? Maybe
it had something to do with the drug operation. Maybe Mario had ordered
the hit.

He looked back at the letter.

*Before he died, Mr. Henderson looked over to the front door and saw me.
I think he tried to say my name. The man must have noticed because he
glanced up to the mirrored wall. I was wearing sunglasses, but had taken
them off to get a better look at him. Our eyes met in the reflection and he*

hesitated for an instant. He had to know that I had seen what he had done. I'm sure he was calculating whether he could get me before someone came who had heard the shot. Then, he turned and vanished through the door to the storage area.

I know it is weak of me not to come forward and give evidence of what I saw. But I cannot. I must admit that I am afraid that the man who killed Mr. Henderson is just waiting for an opportunity to kill me, and if I come forward, he will know who I am. Perhaps more importantly, though, I am a married woman. If I were to give evidence at the trial it would be in the newspapers and would ruin my personal life. However, I am unable to continue to sit back and do nothing while Ms. Holden goes to jail for something that she did not do. That is why I wrote this letter.

I pray that this information will help you and the police find the real murderer of Mr. Henderson.

Doug exhaled slowly. Wow. He reread the letter, thinking how best to use it in Laura's defence. Christopher had to see it, he determined, and reached for the phone. Hold it. What was Christopher going to say? "This is an anonymous letter. Who's to say it's legitimate?" Christopher will be unable to do anything unless he can actually speak to the author and satisfy himself that the evidence is valid. But who wrote it? Obviously, a woman. Maybe Carmen. Probably Carmen.

Doug turned the letter over in his hands looking for some clue to the identity of the author. He picked up the envelope and examined it as well. No return address. No address for the firm either, just his name and "Personal and Confidential" typed under it. There was no stamp. He grabbed the phone, suddenly realizing that the letter had to have been delivered by hand.

"Nancy," he said when the receptionist came on the line. "Nancy, please come to my office, immediately."

"Just a moment Mr. Branston. Can I put you on hold? I just have to take this message on the other line." Then, before cutting him off she added, "It's a madhouse out here."

Doug slammed down the receiver, grabbed the letter and envelope and ran out of his office towards the lobby. Nancy's giggles greeted him when he arrived. She was sitting alone at the switchboard desk, slightly hunched over so that her face was hidden from view. The band of the telephone headset crowned the top of her white-blonde hair like a cheap tiara.

"Oh aren't you sweet," she cooed into the telephone. "No. I really couldn't." Then, "Oh Mr. Peters..." she tittered.

When she looked up to see Doug striding towards her, the smile vanished and she announced authoritatively, "Oh, I'm sorry, Mr. Peters. I've got another call coming in. I have to go. I'll make sure he gets the message. Bye bye." She punched the disconnect button on the switchboard.

"That Mr. Peters. Such a talker," she said shaking her head. "I can never get him off the line."

Doug shoved the letter and envelope in front of Nancy's face. "This was delivered by hand, right?"

"Yeah," she replied somewhat indignantly, as if to say, "So what's your point?"

"Tell me who delivered it, Nancy." He shook the papers for emphasis.

"The security guy downstairs. Why?" She let her lower jaw hang slack displaying the plasticky blue mush of chewing gum on her tongue. The Nancys of the world seemed to be born with a mouthful of chewing gum. They walked, talked, smoked, ate and even drank while chewing gum.

"Did he say where he got it from?"

"Yeah. He said that some woman had given him ten bucks to bring it up to the office." She rolled her eyes upwards while adding, "She told him she was scared of elevators or something."

The switchboard started ringing. Doug ignored it and asked, "Where can I find this security guy?"

Nancy held up her hand like a traffic cop, ordering Doug to put on the brakes of his questioning. She punched the button to answer the incoming call. "Larson Wren and Company," she sang.

Doug waited impatiently while Nancy, with great officiousness, advised the caller that Mr. Brodski was not in the office at the moment and offered to take a message. Apparently the caller decided against leaving his name, because Nancy grunted a brisk goodbye. Ostentatiously, she pressed the disconnect button.

"I'm sorry, Mr. Branston," she sighed, "this job really gives me little time to talk."

Doug refrained from rolling his eyes. "Nancy, where do I find the security guy? This is very important."

The line rang again and Nancy moved to answer it, but before she was able to, Doug reached over the desk and hit the disconnect button. "Leave it, for Chrissake!" he shouted.

She looked up at him, startled. "Well, I just hope that wasn't the long distance call that Mr. Wren was waiting for."

"The security guy, Nancy. Where do I find him?"

"At the security desk in the main lobby of the building. Where else?"

She sat back on her chair, folding her arms across her chest to telegraph her resentment to his questioning her while she was trying to work.

"I want you to come with me now so you can point him out. Who replaces you on your coffee break?"

Nancy gave him the other receptionist's name and Doug sprinted off to find her. By the time Doug and Nancy were in the elevator descending to the main lobby, Nancy's demeanor had changed. She was feeling important, no longer the victim of her boss's interrogation. Now the boss needed her, and she was getting an unscheduled break from her job.

The elevator dropped them at the lobby where they strode over to the large security area against the far wall. Behind the grand walnut counter sat two uniformed security guards, each facing a set of three video monitors stacked on the counter. Black and white scenes of areas of the building flashed on the screens like slide shows.

As Doug and Nancy crossed the lobby he asked her to point out which guard had handed her the letter. She squinted her eyes as they drew nearer to the counter. Both the security guards were cut from the same mold. Clean shaven with brush cuts, they wore pressed khaki shirts, ties and pants. Name tags were pinned to their left breast pockets: one read "Larry," the other, "Ralph."

Nancy shook her head as she reached the counter. "No. Neither of these guys."

"Can you describe him?" Doug prompted.

She did, and immediately the guards knew whom Doug was looking for. Larry advised that the guard's name was Bahlbir Singh, his shift had ended at eight a.m. and presumably he had gone home. Ralph offered that they were unaware of Singh's home address; in any event, such information was classified. They were only allowed to volunteer that Mr. Singh's next shift started at eight that night.

Doug gave this some thought. He wanted to know immediately who the anonymous author was. Every minute wasted increased the chance of Singh's memory fading and the anonymous author disappearing. He knew that only the security manager would be able to release Singh's telephone number and address. The guards were happy to direct Doug to the manager's office in the basement of the office tower.

Harry, the security manager, was reading the newspaper when Doug and Nancy knocked on his door. Doug explained, while he slipped a twenty-dollar bill into the breast pocket of Harry's shirt, why he needed to talk to Mr. Singh. Harry was pleased to help. He found Singh's name on the employee list and tried the phone number, but there was no answer. Doug had half expected this since he had learned long ago that nothing, absolutely nothing in this world, is easy. Fortunately, a little cajoling of Harry, and a twenty-dollar bill, rewarded Doug with Mr. Singh's address.

On the elevator back to the firm Doug briefed Nancy on her assignment for the day. She was off switchboard duty in order to accompany Tom on a stakeout of Mr. Singh's house. The moment she spotted Mr. Singh, she was to help Tom interview him and obtain as clear a description as possible of the anonymous author.

When they exited the elevator at the thirty-second floor, Doug immediately advised the substitute receptionist that she had to stay on the switchboard until Nancy returned from a crucial assignment. Nancy apologized profusely to the other woman, all the time smiling and flashing her eyes with excitement like an older sister going on her first date, barely able to contain the thrill of adventure she felt in leaving the switchboard and spending the day roaring around in Tom's car.

And within minutes she was riding the elevator down to the lobby again, this time with Tom who was armed with a copy of the letter and envelope, the address of Mr. Singh and the keys to the roguesmobile.

Doug, meanwhile, returned to his office and phoned Christopher. He reached the receptionist at the Crown Counsel Office who told him that Christopher was on the phone. She offered to take a message. Doug declined, stating that he would prefer to hold, as the matter was urgent. While waiting he put the receiver on speaker and read the letter once more.

Eventually Christopher came on the line. Doug explained to him the circumstances of receiving the letter, then read the letter over the phone. When he had finished, there was a brief silence while Christopher digested the contents of the letter. After a moment, he asked Doug to read it again.

"Hmmm. Interesting," Christopher said when Doug had finished reading the letter a second time. "So who do you think wrote it?"

"I don't know," Doug answered, "although it is consistent with what Henderson told me that night when he dropped me off at my house. He said he wasn't going straight home. Presumably he was going to meet someone. And, strictly off the record, I'll let you in on a bit of evidence from the accused." He waited until Christopher confirmed this information would not be used against Laura. "She recalls that during their argument in the lobby, Henderson told her to leave because he was expecting to meet someone."

"Let me guess, the elusive Carmen."

"That's my bet. She's the only other woman that Mrs. Rattenbury remembers being around the apartment in the last few months."

"You may be right. But you know, Doug," Christopher started in a fatalistic voice. "Unless we can interview whoever wrote that letter and verify the accuracy of the story, I can't do anything about the charges against Ms. Holden. For all we know this letter is from some crackpot. Or—and I hate to say this—it could have been written by Frank Holden or the accused herself, for that matter. It wouldn't be the first time."

"I know, Bob. I know you need something more than an anonymous letter. But I think I know the guy who's being described."

"Oh?" Christopher replied. "Who?"

"A guy out of Toronto named Tony Capetti. He fits the description in the letter, and…" Doug knew he had to be careful with what he said about Mario's drug operation in order to protect Julie. "…And Henderson had some…uh…business deals with associates of Capetti."

Christopher waited for elaboration on these so-called business deals, but Doug remained silent. Eventually, Christopher prompted him. "What sort of business deals, Doug?" Then, before Doug answered he asked again in a more forceful voice. "What sort of business deal gets Henderson shot?"

Doug sought legal refuge. "Look, Bob, I can't say anything more. The deals involve a client of the firm, so they're subject to solicitor-client privilege. You know that."

Christopher's agitation was evident in his voice. "Let me get this straight, *Doug*…" He spat the name out with disgust. "You know, I have to be honest with you. It always pisses me off when defence counsel come up with some theory of the crime that exculpates their client, but when they're asked for information to support the theory, they hide behind solicitor-client privilege." He paused after this digression to take a deep breath. "So let me get this straight," he began again. "You're telling me that you think, based on an anonymous letter, that some business associate of Henderson killed him, but you won't tell me what the business was." He sighed. "What do you want me to do with this information?"

Doug had to agree that there was little evidence for Christopher to work with. He thought for a moment. If Holden agreed to release the solicitor-client privilege, the information in the files might provide a basis for Christopher to launch an investigation.

"Bob, what if I were to get the solicitor-client privilege lifted? Would you start an investigation?"

"Frankly," Christopher replied, "we're obliged to follow up on the anonymous letter. But I can't see much coming of it. We've already tried to find this Carmen. But we've come up with dick. Nobody can give us a decent description of her. We searched the apartment and the place Henderson had with Marie. There are no telephone numbers, no notes. I think we managed to get a few fingerprints. But she's obviously never been arrested before because we have nothing to compare them to."

"I'm trying to trace the delivery of the letter," Doug offered. "Maybe that'll turn up something."

"Well, look. As I told you at the start of this whole thing, Henderson was a friend of mine, too. And I'm only interested in putting away whoever did the crime. Why don't you fax me a copy of the letter and I'll pass it on to Detective Campbell. He can contact you and maybe the two of you can figure out a way to find the author. Maybe you can give him an idea about this Tony Capetti guy, as well, and he can do some snooping around." Christopher took a slow breath. "Now, to answer your question, if you were able to provide us with the privileged file material, that would obviously give us a better basis for conducting an investigation into these so-called business deals."

"Okay. That's great. I'll have my secretary fax this letter over to you now and I'll see what I can do about lifting the privilege." Doug had Christopher give him the Crown fax number. They agreed to keep in touch, then hung up.

The meeting with Holden and Laura went ahead as planned in the sunken living room of Holden's plush westside home. The grand picture window promised a spectacular view of the sea and the mountains if the curtain of cloud would ever lift. In the middle of the room, facing each other, sat two sumptuous cream sofas, while in the far corner a white baby grand piano, angled jauntily to the room, contrasted the elegant symmetry like the cap on a parade-dressed soldier.

They sat facing each other. Unconsciously, Holden placed his arm protectively around Laura who hunched into him, her drawn face, ashen like the view behind her, revealing the strain of the past few weeks.

Reaching into his briefcase, Doug extracted the letter, then slowly read it out loud. When he had finished, Holden let out a yelp of glee and pumped his fists in the air like a prize fighter upon winning the title. Hugging Laura, he cried "That's it, sweetheart. This nightmare is over."

Laura's demeanor remained unchanged. Except for a brief obliging smile for her father, she sat motionless, staring into space. "It doesn't bring Mark back, though," she whispered.

"No, Laura. That's true," Doug sympathized. "But it *may* keep you out of prison."

"May?" Holden roared. "What do you mean, 'may'?"

Doug explained that the letter was useless unless they knew who the author was. Then focusing on Laura, he asked if she had any idea who the other woman was that Henderson had been seeing.

In a low monotone Laura confessed that on more than one occasion she had hidden in the garden of the apartment building's front courtyard and watched for the other woman to arrive, but the few times that she had seen her, it was only a brief, partially-obscured glimpse. The woman usually came alone in a taxi and moved quickly through the lobby. She always wore a long overcoat, a scarf over her head and, even if it was late at night, dark glasses. "I could never get a good look," Laura sighed. "I guess she was average height, sort of old. But there was only the one other woman," she added defensively. "I'm sure she was the person Mark planned to meet that night. Maybe she was hiding in the garden watching me, just like I used to watch her. I don't know."

Doug asked, "Do you remember the type of cab she used?"

"They were yellow."

Doug took note of this. It was a long shot, but maybe someone at Yellow Cabs remembered dropping Carmen off that night and could give a better description of her. Or if he was very lucky, maybe she used a credit card to pay her fare. He decided to pass this information on to Tom for further investigation.

Once Laura had exhausted her recollection of the other woman, Doug asked her to give him a few minutes alone with her father. Then, as she was leaving the living-room, a thought came to him. "Is there anything in the letter that helps you recall the events of that night, Laura? Do you remember being grabbed from behind, a hand over your mouth, a gun going off, anything?"

As he regarded her pale, expressionless face, Doug knew that she had already tortured herself trying to remember other details from that terrible night, but there was nothing. She shook her head slowly in answer to his question.

Doug turned to Holden after Laura had left the room. "I think I know the man described in this letter," Doug said. "Ever hear of a guy named Tony Capetti?" No response. "Well, he happens to be a flunky for Mario Bartelli. You know, the guy you were doing the land deals with."

Holden cleared his throat before he spoke. "Yes, I know who Mario Bartelli is." He shook his head slowly. "But, Tony...whatever you said his last name was. I don't think so."

The time for playing games was over. Doug needed some answers. "Look, Mr. Holden, I have reason to believe that the land deals you were doing with Mario Bartelli and his many companies were part of a money-laundering scheme operated by Bartelli to move money from his drug operation. And it's just possible that Henderson spread himself too thin and became expendable."

"I don't know what you're talking about," Holden blustered. "A money-laundering scheme? Where could you have possibly got that idea? As far as I'm concerned, we were involved in legitimate land transfers. Anyway, I'm not interested in talking to you about those land deals. I'm interested in keeping my daughter out of jail." He picked up the letter from its resting place on the coffee table. "Now we've got a witness here that clears my little girl," he said, extending the letter to Doug. "Let's spend our energy trying to find her, for God's sake."

"But that's my point. I think the two are related. I think Tony Capetti killed Henderson because of problems with Bartelli's operation. I've already spoken to the police. They tell me they are obliged to look into the letter and they're going to do that. They also want to investigate these land deals to see if there was anything fishy going on. I want you to agree to lift the privilege on those files so the police can have a look at them."

Holden's eyes left Doug and scanned the room. "I don't know, Branston. That's why I left those files in your hands. You know, they involve some sensitive stuff regarding my relationship with Henderson that I don't really want people to know about."

"Listen. Everyone has tried to find this woman," Doug pointed at the document in Holden's hands, "and we've all come up with zip. The chances of finding her now are no better. The letter doesn't tell us who she is. But it does tell us what she knows. I think she's describing Capetti. Capetti is linked with Mario, and Mario is linked with Henderson on these land deals. We've got to look into it."

Holden sat silently, frowning, staring at the floor as if hoping it would open and swallow him whole. It was clear that he disliked the idea of handing these files over to the police. Doug expected he knew why: Holden had to be aware of the money laundering. If he turned the files over to the police, he would surely implicate himself.

"We're talking about your daughter's freedom here," Doug prompted.

Holden exploded. "I know what the fuck we're talking about. And it isn't just Laura." He dragged his hand through his hair, pulled at it, then rubbed his eyes. Suddenly he jumped out of his chair and strode over to the window, muttering to himself and pinching his chin. For some time he stalked back and forth in front of the window like a lion in a cage. Finally he stopped and turned to Doug.

"Okay. Okay. Here it is," he said, more to himself than to Doug. "You,"— he pointed at Doug like an Uncle Sam poster—"are my lawyer. So what I tell you is confidential. You can't divulge it unless I consent, right?"

"Of course. That's why I'm asking you to surrender your privilege on the files."

"Right. Well here's a little more privileged information. I knew about the money laundering." He looked at Doug as if expecting him to drop dead with shock.

"No kidding?" Doug said sarcastically.

Holden was clearly disappointed at Doug's lack of surprise, but he pressed on. "If I turn over those files and the police figure out the money-laundering angle, I could be in deep shit." Doug was about to comment but Holden held up his hand. "Not only that," he continued. "If you're right and Mario had Henderson killed, what do you think is going to happen to me when he finds out I've handed the files to the police?"

It was Doug's turn to explode. Jumping to his feet, he stepped up to Holden so that they were almost nose to nose. "You know what?" he yelled. "You're a fucking selfish asshole. Stop worrying about your own hide and start worrying about your daughter's."

Holden was rocked by the vehemence in Doug's voice. "If I thought it would help..." he equivocated.

"Man, it's the only chance she's got."

While Holden struggled between his own sense of self-preservation and the well-being of his daughter, Doug continued to push. "You once said to me that you should have prosecuted Henderson for seducing Laura. If you had you done that, you said, Laura probably wouldn't be in the mess she is now. But at that time you were more interested in saving your precious land deals from public exposure than you were in saving your daughter from Henderson. Are you going to do that again?"

Holden's face drained of colour as Doug's words sunk in. He jerked his head away from Doug's stare, strolled back to the window and gazed out for a long time.

"I owned this city," he eventually whispered proudly. He took a deep anguished breath, then asked in a hollow voice, "Do you think the police would cut me a deal if I talked? Maybe give me some protection?"

"There's only one way to find out. Why don't I call Christopher and set up a meeting?"

Doug started for the phone expecting Holden to stop him at any moment; but Holden had finished protesting. Doug lifted the receiver and dialed the number for the Crown Counsel's Office. As the phone rang, he looked at Holden and raised his eyebrows in question. Holden nodded.

Christopher soon came on the line. They arranged a meeting for later that afternoon. Christopher agreed to make sure Detective Campbell attended.

Doug was about to hang up when Christopher remembered that he had received a report from Campbell. It had something to do with tracking down Tony Capetti. Doug heard papers being shuffled on the other end of the line.

"Ah. Here it is," Christopher said. "Yeah. They ran a CPIC on Capetti. You know, the police computer check. He's got a few prior convictions in Ontario—all for violent offences. The Toronto police are presently investigating him for the murder of a drug dealer named Joey Marron. I've told Campbell to follow up on this guy."

CHAPTER 18

The meeting with Holden and Christopher took place in the same boardroom where Doug had first heard the summary of the Crown's case against Laura. Doug brought the Blackwater Holdings file, the conveyance files and the information that had been gathered about the various companies. At Christopher's insistence, Detective Campbell had broken away from his other duties to join them. His reluctance to attend attested to his skepticism that Capetti had actually killed Henderson. "The evidence against the Holden girl is overwhelming," he had insisted when Christopher told him about the meeting. "What is there to implicate Capetti? Some anonymous letter that materializes mysteriously at the eleventh hour? You remember Holden, Bob. I wouldn't put it past him to have prepared that letter. Bloody hell, he knows about the phantom Carmen woman."

Campbell remained silent at the end of the boardroom table as Doug and Holden reviewed, step by step, the process of each deal: the initial identification of the land to be sold; the formation of the companies; the appraisal of the properties; and ultimately the sales. The pattern was clear. The properties had been moved quickly for less than market value, the vendor companies having then invested the return on the property sales in Terra Holdings by way of shareholders' loans.

Once everyone recognized that the deals made little business sense, Holden provided the explanation. Selling for under market value guaranteed a quick flip of property and the exchange of clean money for dirty. The laundered money was then invested in Terra Holdings which was, to Holden's knowledge, involved only in legitimate enterprises.

Based on the documentary information and Holden's evidence, Christopher instructed Detective Campbell to initiate an investigation. He insisted on Holden's cooperation, in return for which he was prepared to provide him with protection and to consider forgoing any charges against him.

The meeting was about to conclude when Detective Campbell finally spoke up. "Mr. Holden, one of the names that appears in these documents is Tony Capetti. I understand that he is an associate of Mario Bartelli. Do you know him?"

Holden looked at Campbell. "Doug has asked me that question already. Obviously I've seen the name in the documents, but it means nothing to me. I'm sure I've never met the man."

Campbell's eyes held Holden's for a long moment as if judging whether Holden was telling the truth. Finally, Campbell looked down at his watch. "Eight-thirty," he said. "I must be going."

Doug had arranged to have dinner with Diane following the meeting. He was already late for his date, but he needed to know, first, whether Tom had had any luck tracking down Bahlbir Singh. He called Tom's apartment from the phone in Christopher's office. After the third ring Tom answered.

"Elvis, it's Branston. How did it go?"

"Hey, Doug. I've been trying to get a hold of you. Where have you been?"

Doug had no time for chat. Tonight he wanted to start applying some pressure on Diane regarding their future. His cause would be jeopardized if he were late. "I'm sorry, man, I'm really rushed," he said. "I'll tell you about my day later. What did you find out about Bahlbir Singh?"

Tom chuckled. "Well, what do you want: the good news or the bad news?"

"Elvis!" Doug snapped. "Just tell me what happened."

"Okay. Okay. We managed to catch up with Singh, but the guy was no real help. He says that the woman who gave him the letter was all bundled up and wearing dark glasses. Besides, he says, all white women look the same. Can you believe that?"

Doug thought about this for a moment. "Where did she approach him? At the front desk?"

"No. She caught up with him while he was doing his rounds through the underground parking lot. Told him that she was scared of elevators and gave him ten bucks to deliver the letter." Tom paused, but before Doug asked the obvious question he added, "No, she wasn't in a car."

"Has he ever seen her in the building before?"

"Nope. But that doesn't mean much 'cause he's only been working there for the last couple of weeks."

Doug exhaled noisily. "Shit," he grumbled. "Okay. Look. I've got to go and meet Diane. Think about how we can track this woman down and we'll talk later."

"You staying here tonight?" Tom inquired.

"Most likely. Unless something amazing happens. But don't worry, I'll be as quiet as a mouse." He hung up.

Outside the courthouse he flagged a cab to take him to his former home. While sitting in the back seat he thought of Diane. He recognized that he was enjoying her company. Now, every so often, he found himself thinking of them back together again as a family. He had certainly not suggested this to Diane; the relationship he was trying to renovate had a long way to go before it was habitable. But he sensed the chance was there. More importantly, he was starting to feel it was a chance he wanted to pursue.

Inevitably the lawyer in him analyzed the changes he had experienced since Henderson's death and searched for their meaning. Perhaps the lustre of the wild, single life had tarnished because what wears well on one is uncomfortable on another. Certainly, the way Henderson lived had always fascinated Doug. Henderson's life had been exciting, always extreme and on the edge. And every time Doug had been with Henderson he had felt a thrill, as if somehow his life was more exciting, freer, more irreverent, just by being in close proximity to him. Once he had crossed over, though, once he had succumbed to his own envy and fascination and become a disciple of the decadent Henderson lifestyle, the magic had vanished. It did not work for Doug. It did not fit him. He was not Mark Henderson.

Or perhaps it was because Doug had come to understand Mark Henderson only after his death, recognizing then that Henderson was not a mythical hero, not a brilliant eccentric with a great passion for women and life. Like every man's, Henderson's character was much more complex, loaded with contradictions and imperfections. Henderson's relationship with Laura, Doug now suspected, was not that of a mentor as Henderson had liked to maintain, but simply a rerun of the old Lolita theme: age's eternal attraction to youth. Henderson had taken advantage of Laura's naiveté in order to blind himself, however momentarily, to the inescapable advancement of years. In doing so, he provided one more hint of the weakness in his character.

Doug now came to realize, finally, that Marie's belief that Henderson was suffering from sexual addiction was not one of the deceits. It was the one thing about Henderson that was real. And it proved the truth of what Henderson had always maintained: Doug's life was the one to be envied.

The sad thing was that as much as Henderson envied Doug's life, he was unable to live it. And the irony for Doug was that he may have sacrificed that life for the illusion of Henderson's life. Now his only hope was that he still had time to correct the mistake.

He thought of the children as well. Although Diane and he had maintained that the only reason he lived away was because of a big case, the boys had to be wondering why Dad never stayed at home. The charade had almost run its course. Either he and Diane put things back together soon or they must tell the children the truth.

The cab pulled up at the front of the house. He had avoided even passing by since the morning after Henderson's death. Now he paused in the back seat of the cab, watching the property like a spy. It looked the same and he immediately felt a wave of nostalgia wash over him, the countless hours he had spent remodelling, revamping, adding, removing. He had kneaded and massaged the property for years, slowly moulding it to be his own. Gazing from the cab now, he felt as if he were peering into a mirror.

After paying the cab driver, he climbed the front steps. He thought of ringing the doorbell, decided against it, and awkwardly knocked on the front door. His hands tingled as he peered through the little front door window. Inside a shadow moved, then the door swung open and Adrian stood there in his pajamas.

"Daddy!" he yelled, jumping into Doug's arms. Doug held him as tightly as he could without crushing him.

"Adrian!" Diane's voice rang out as she came quickly down the hall. "I've told you never to answer the door at night. You never know who it might be."

"But it's Daddy, Mom," Adrian said, his head still buried in Doug's shoulder.

Diane smiled momentarily at Doug before continuing to scold Adrian. "I can see that, but..."

Another voice came from down the hall. Matthew, slightly more circumspect than his brother, walked to the front entrance. "Hi, Dad," he said. Doug put Adrian down and leaned forward to give his older son a hug. Matthew did not share Adrian's enthusiasm. "Are you staying?" he challenged as Doug released him.

Doug looked from Matthew to Diane; he hesitated, before ad libbing pathetically, "Well, I guess you know that the trial is still going on, so it may be awhile before I'm back for good."

"Thought so," Matthew huffed before retreating into the house.

Doug started to go after Matthew but Diane spoke up. "Leave him," she cautioned. "Nothing you can say right now is going to help."

He stood paralyzed at the door, his heart caught in his throat as he watched Matthew disappear into the house. Even after Matthew had gone he continued to stare down the front hallway, unaware of Adrian pulling at his coat until the little voice broke the melancholy spell. "It's okay, Dad. Matthew's just a big jerk."

Doug picked up Adrian to give him another hug. While he cuddled the boy against his chest, Diane leaned over and gave Adrian a kiss on the cheek. It was the closest she had been to Doug for some time. The scent of her skin mixed with the subtle fragrance of the perfume she liked to wear filled his nostrils. It was all so familiar.

"Your dad and I have to go now, sweetheart," Diane said. "Remember. Matthew is in charge. You go to bed when he says."

Adrian slowly slid out of Doug's arms and wandered back into the house. "See ya, Dad," he offered without turning to look.

Diane followed Adrian inside to get her coat, leaving Doug alone at the threshold, reluctant to enter his own house without an invitation. She reappeared shortly, wearing a long tailored overcoat and a purse over her shoulder. Doug admired her elegance, at the same time feeling a twinge of shame for having abandoned her in order to pursue women like Jenna and Cathy. He walked by her side to the garage and the car that once was his. When she handed him the keys, he opened the passenger door to let her in.

For a while they drove in silence, Doug still reeling from the experience of being a visitor at his home, like the neighbourhood canvasser or the newspaper boy. He was working up the courage to approach the subject when Diane spoke.

"So, how's the case going? Any new developments?" she asked in a voice that said *I don't really give a shit, I'm just trying to make conversation.*

It was a fair question, though. The case was the topic they had come to rely upon in order to avoid awkward silences. But for Doug, tonight had to be different. "I'm sorry, Diane," he said. "I really don't want to talk about the case tonight. Do you mind?"

"Of course not," she said with obvious relief.

He took a deep breath, and while he gazed through the rain-spattered windshield at the traffic before them, he blurted out, "What I really want to talk about is you and me."

Hunching down in the passenger seat, she turned and stared out the side window. "Oh, shit," she said.

"I know that it's uncomfortable to talk about, but I think we have to decide what we're doing."

Diane kept gazing out the window.

"You know what? I made a terrible mistake," he announced. "I made a mistake that I will regret the rest of my life. But I was consumed by this fear that life was passing me by. I felt that I was a spectator. Everyone else was living and I was watching. I felt that way the most when I was with Henderson. But I realize now that I had it all backwards. All those other people were the spectators; Henderson was the spectator, and I was the one with a life."

Diane remained silent, so he soldiered on. "I look at you and the kids and the house, all we've worked for, all those memories, and I think I must have been crazy. How could I risk that?"

Slowly, she turned to look at Doug, her eyes glistening in the streetlights like the rain-soaked windshield. "You've got on those rose-coloured glasses again, Douglas. It wasn't all wonderful. We were having real communication problems. We lived our separate lives, did our own thing. We haven't been the close family that you're imagining for some time." Then with a little more aggression in her voice she added, "What you're talking about is *your* problem. What you *don't* have always looks better. When you were home, single life looked better. Now you're on your own and married life looks better." She choked out the last words through sobs.

"I think I'm over that, Diane," Doug said with conviction. "But what about you?" He glanced at her but she had turned her head away towards the side window again. "My recollection is that you were all for separation as well. It wasn't just me wanting out. You wanted out too."

Diane was weeping openly now. "Do we have to talk about this?" she sobbed.

He wheeled the car into the parking lot of the restaurant where he found a space, turned off the engine and leaned over to Diane. For the first time in a very long while, he took her in his arms. She did not resist his embrace, nor did she welcome it.

"Diane," he whispered into her ear. "I want to try again. I want to come home. Will you let me?"

She breathed heavily against his shoulder. "Oh, Douglas. I need someone who cares for me. Thinks about me. Someone who notices how I look, who compliments me, gives me affection. You're not like that. You're independent, doing your own thing, leaving me to do mine. I don't want that, Doug. I've had that."

"I think I can change. Will you give me the chance?"

Diane gulped, then looked up into Doug's eyes. "I need time to think about it, okay?" She lifted her head off his shoulder and gave him a tear-soaked kiss on the cheek.

He hugged her. "I guess that's the best I can hope for," he said. "Come on, let's have some dinner. I've never been here before but it's supposed to be the hottest place in town. Apparently, the lamb is fantastic." He jumped out of the car and ran to open the passenger door for her.

The restaurant consisted of two large rooms divided by an extravagant bar of glistening dark wood panels. Glasses and bottles sparkled in its gigantic mirrors while bartenders and waiters busied around it. Each room held several elegantly adorned tables separated from one another by large, strategically-placed vases filled with dried flowers. On the walls, mirrors created a sense of space without compromising a certain intimate, romantic feeling.

The maitre d', dressed in a wing-collared shirt, black bow tie and suspenders, like a card dealer from an old Mississippi paddle wheeler, met Doug and Diane as they entered the restaurant. He graciously took their coats which he handed to the busboy hovering just behind him, then turned to scan the reservation list. Upon finding Doug's name, he raised one arm, ostentatiously summoning them to follow him to a table on the far side of one of the rooms.

Once seated, Doug ordered a bottle of Chardonnay while he and Diane contemplated the menus. He tasted and approved the wine when it arrived. Once it was poured, Diane lifted her glass and reached across the table to rest her free hand on his. "Here's to success in all we do," she proposed, and took a sip. Doug sipped too, while staring into Diane's smoky green eyes. In there somewhere he was sure he saw a flicker of hope for him, if he just played his cards right.

They spent the evening in gentle, nostalgic conversation. They ate salads of exotic greens dressed with warm shrimp and scallops, tender rack of lamb in a crisp coating of herbs and spices with tiny roast potatoes and zucchini boats filled with diced vegetables. For dessert they shared puffy profiteroles that languished in a thick, dark chocolate sauce. The meal was perfect in taste and presentation, and the atmosphere was thickly laden with sweet romance. Doug detected a slow softening of Diane's gaze upon him. The food and the wine were mellowing her, weakening her defences. But he decided against applying any more pressure. If they were to get back together, it had to happen naturally.

They talked about the kids, what they were doing, their school and their sports. They talked about how Matthew was reacting to Doug not being at home. He did not sleep well, she said; half the time she would be wakened in the middle of the night by Matthew wanting to climb into her bed. She smiled at Doug sympathetically, and explained that the only reason Matthew acted that way was because he loved his dad so much and wished that he were home.

Doug's heart ached. Children were so innocent, so susceptible to the selfish actions of grownups. His little walk on the wild side may have caused irreparable psychological damage to Matthew, and who knows what hidden effects it had had on Adrian. Was it worth it? Of course not. But what could he do about it now? Only try to limit the damage as much as possible. In that regard, he was trying his hardest.

While sipping a cappuccino after the meal, Diane peeked at her watch, then announced with real reluctance in her voice and a momentary scowl that she had to get home. Matthew was still a little young to be babysitting and he was sure to stay up until she returned.

He was about to summon the waiter for the bill when a familiar face by the entrance caught his eye. It was Marie, and she was just about to leave with none other than Tony Capetti.

"Jesus," Doug mumbled to Diane. "Don't look now but Marie's over there at the entrance and I'll tell you later who she's with."

Diane's back was to the entrance, but she was able to see its reflection in the mirror before her. "Oh, my god," she groaned and jumped up. "Suddenly, I don't feel very well. Please excuse me," she said as she raced to the restroom at the back of the restaurant.

"Doug!" Marie called. She and Tony navigated their way through the tables to where Doug was sitting. "I thought that was you." She leaned over to give Doug a peck on the cheek. "Didn't I just see Diane? Where did she go?" Marie looked around with a baffled expression on her face.

"To the restroom, I guess. All of sudden she felt sick." Doug shrugged.

"I was sorry to hear you two had separated. You make such a wonderful couple." She winked. "I hope things work out." Then turning to Tony she said, "Doug, you remember—"

"Hello, Tony." They shook hands. "I thought you would have left town by now," Doug said without hiding his acrimony.

"I'm going to the airport right now actually," Tony replied. "That's why we've got to leave here so early. Marie's going to run me back to the hotel for my things. Then, I'm gone." He smiled at Doug who stared back poker-faced.

Marie grabbed Tony's arm and hauled him towards the entrance. "Well, we really must go. You've got a plane to catch, Tony."

"See you again, Doug." He extended his hand for a farewell handshake. Doug ignored it. "I'm sorry I didn't meet...uh, Diane, is it?" Tony added. "From across the room she looked very nice." He turned to leave.

The waiter came by and asked if Doug wanted anything else, but Doug's mind was elsewhere, reflecting on the message from Detective Campbell: his office was working with the Ontario police in an effort to track down Tony Capetti. If Doug was able to advise Campbell that he had just seen

Capetti heading towards the airport, it might save a lot of police time. Ignoring the waiter's question, he asked if he could use the phone.

"By the side of the bar," the waiter advised.

As Doug strode to the bar he reached into the breast pocket of his suit, pulled out his wallet and rifled through the stash of business cards he had collected over the years. When he eventually found Detective Campbell's card he dialed the number indicated for night calls. A receptionist answered and promptly passed him on to a dispatcher, who eventually patched him through to Detective Campbell's cellular phone.

Doug advised Campbell that Capetti had just left the Yaletown restaurant and was on his way to the airport for the late night flight to Toronto. Campbell confirmed that they already had someone watching for Capetti at both airports because of the Marron investigation.

Confusion, anger and excitement all tugged at Doug's thoughts as he hung up the phone. If the anonymous letter was correct, he had just been face to face with Henderson's murderer. But why did Tony remain so close to Marie? Was Doug off base in thinking that Henderson's murder was connected with Mario's drug operation? Maybe Marie had contracted Tony to hit Henderson? But would she continue to hang out with Tony— almost daring Doug to figure it out? Or did that pony-tailed bastard have the amazing gall to insinuate himself into the trust and confidence of Henderson's mourning girlfriend and friends after killing him? Whatever, he apparently felt comfortable enough to make complimentary remarks about Diane. It made Doug's blood boil. But they were on to Tony now. Could it be very long before all the pieces of the puzzle fell into place, forming a clear picture of how and why Tony had killed Henderson?

Doug checked his watch. Fifteen minutes must have passed since Diane had run from the table. He stepped over to a waitress who was placing an order for drinks with the bartender. "Excuse me," he said. "My wife disappeared into the restroom about fifteen minutes ago and has yet to reappear. Would you mind checking to see if she's alright in there?"

"Sure." The waitress gave Doug a knowing smile as if to say *I understand. Family squabbles in public places are always embarrassing.*

A few moments later, the waitress and Diane came out of the washroom, Diane appearing shy and a little sheepish.

"Everything okay?" Doug asked placing a protective arm around her.

"Take me home, Doug," she whispered.

With growing concern, he nodded and directed her towards the main door. "What's happened, dear? What's the matter?"

She sighed. "Oh Doug. I need time to explain," she quavered.

The maitre d' retrieved their coats. Doug held Diane's for her; then, while standing behind her, he rested his hands on her shoulders, his face close to her flowing copper hair, and inhaled her fragrance. A rush of desire washed over him inducing him to lean forward ever so subtly and give her a tender kiss on her cheek. He thanked the maitre d' before walking Diane out to the parking lot. His arm loosely around her shoulder seemed protective, comforable. And she tucked herself closely into his embrace.

When they reached the car, Doug moved to open the passenger door for her. As he put the key in the lock, he was reminded of Henderson. Everyone has a favourite situation in which they feel they can best seduce their companion. For Doug it was on the dance floor, as he had re-established with Jenna. For Henderson it was when he was opening his date's car door. "You open the door for her," he used to say, "and as she slides past you into the car, you take her in your arms." Doug tried it now, as a small tribute to Henderson. He opened the door, and with his left arm around Diane's waist, he delicately directed her into the car. When she was about to enter, he reached around her with his right arm and held her against him. She looked up at him, a mysterious sadness in her eyes, as he bent and kissed her on the lips. They fitted together easily, naturally. For Doug, it was like coming home.

After they released each other, Diane lowered her gaze with a hint of embarrassment and curled into the passenger's seat. Doug closed the door for her, then walked around to the driver's side.

"Oh, Doug," came a familiar voice from behind him.

He looked around to see Tony Capetti walking towards him from out of the shadows behind the parked cars.

"Tony?" Doug said startled. "What the hell are you doing here? I thought you'd be on your way to Toronto by now." A creeping sense of foreboding rose up from Doug's stomach putting every nerve in his body on red alert.

Tony was beside him now. "I have a little unfinished business, Doug." He reached inside the breast of his black sports jacket and pulled out a large black pistol. "We have to go for a ride. So I want you to open the back door for me and then get into the driver's seat—really slowly."

Doug did as instructed and Tony climbed into the back seat. When Diane saw Tony and his gun she stifled a gasp, covering her mouth with her hand.

"Hello, Diane. I'm Tony. I'm sorry we didn't get a chance to meet formally in the restaurant earlier tonight. But, of course, we already sort of know each other, don't we?"

Diane's hand still covered her mouth as she looked at Tony with wild eyes. Either she would not, or could not, speak.

"What's this all about, Tony?" Doug demanded weakly. "For Chrissake, you're scaring the shit out of us."

"Not to worry, Doug. All will come clear in time. Now I need you to drive us to Stanley Park." Doug did nothing, so Tony put the gun against the back of Doug's head. "Start the engine, Doug," he said in a controlled voice.

Doug turned on the ignition, put the car into gear and steered out onto the street, turning north towards Stanley Park.

"I watched that move by the passenger door, Doug," Tony commented. "The old Henderson Hustle, eh? He always said it worked without fail. But, of course, you'd know all about that, wouldn't you, Diane?"

Diane was mute. She looked at Doug, then turned away, shaking her head slowly.

"Tony? What are you talking about?" Doug asked.

Tony leaned over towards Diane so that his mouth was close to her ear. "I guess he doesn't know, does he?"

"What? Doesn't know what?" Doug demanded.

Diane said nothing, although now Doug noticed tears rolling freely down her face as she looked straight ahead into the night.

"I guess cat's got her tongue, Doug," Tony chuckled. "Why don't I tell him, then? Would that be okay, Diane?" He scratched the side of his head with the barrel of the gun. "Some of this I'm piecing together, so you jump in anytime, Diane, if I get the facts wrong. Okay?"

Tony glanced up and met Doug's bulging, frightened eyes in the rear-view mirror. He smiled, then nodded while he confessed, "I killed Henderson, Doug. It was perfect. At least I thought it was." He shot a glance at Diane before returning his stare to the rear-view mirror. "You see, I'm waiting for him in the hallway by his apartment when I hear this argument going on downstairs in the lobby. I'm sure I hear Henderson's voice, so I go to the staircase for a peek. And there they are, Henderson and that little girl he was doing—by the way, I think he was a fucking pervert the way he went after her. The poor broad. He deserved to get it for that alone." Tony turned again to Diane. "Don't you agree?"

There was no answer.

"Well, as it turns out, they're standing in the perfect position. She's at the foot of the stairs with her back to me, and he's facing her about three feet away. You know, Doug, she's got this huge leather purse over her shoulder. Who the fuck knows what they carry in there? What do you figure, Diane? Christ, you could get a whole change of clothes and a sleeping bag in there." He grinned while he looked out the window at the rain and the streetlights. "Doug, don't think that I'm some stupid foreigner and don't know how the fuck to get to the park. I'm watching where you're going, so don't screw it up."

He paused for a moment. "Where was I? Oh yeah. So there they are and she's got this huge purse that's wide open. I can't pass up the opportunity. I take my gun out and flash down the stairs. I grab her around the throat and jam my gun into the purse and pull the trigger. Before you can say 'wham-bam and thank you ma'am' Henderson's sucking his last breaths. Now all I got to do is set up the little broad. So I give her a pop and she falls obediently to the floor."

Tony sat with his outstretched arms resting on the seat back, a self-satisfied smile on his face. "I'm telling you, Doug, it was the perfect crime." He nodded to Doug's saucer eyes staring in the rear-view mirror. "So now you're wondering, if it was so perfect a crime why is this dumb fuck confessing it all to me? Aren't you? That's what you're thinking," he chuckled and pointed at the rear-view mirror. Doug's eyes jumped back and forth, like a nervous twitch, from the mirror to the street ahead.

This time, Tony leaned forward so that his mouth was right at Doug's ear. "Because you see, my friend," he purred, "your wife saw me." He gave a big toothy smile to the reflection of Doug's uncomprehending eyes. "That's right. There I am stooped over this unconscious broad and I'm putting the gun in her hand, when I hear Henderson mumble something—who knows what. But I see he's staring past me with those half-dead eyes. So I look into that wall mirror like I'm looking at you now." He stared at Doug's reflection before continuing. "And who do I see looking back at me from the shadows by the entrance? Why, it's Diane." He reached over and stroked Diane's hair.

"Man," he sighed, "I was really worried because I didn't know who the fuck she was, and she was all hidden in that long overcoat and scarf. But you took your shades off to get a good look, didn't you, Diane? And we eyeballed each other for a split fucking second. Even so, I figured, shit, I'll never find you.

"'What'd you say?' I ask Henderson. 'What's her name?' But he's a corpse by now. All I can figure is she's somehow connected with him— which you confirmed, Doug, when we had lunch that day—but no one knew who the fuck she was. Marie didn't know. Mario didn't know. I even phoned the fucking apartment manager. Carmen, she called her, but knew fuck all of who she really was.

"Then, I'm in the restaurant tonight and I see her in the mirror. Our eyes met—didn't they, Diane—just like they did that night. And it was like déjà-fucking-vu. We both knew. You're fucking right we did. Then you hightailed it to the ladies' room." He sat back in his seat again, raising his arms in triumph. "Could there be any doubt? I said to myself, 'Thank you, Lord.'"

As he looked out the window he scratched his head again with the barrel of the gun. Suddenly the smile left his face, and in a menacing voice he warned, "I hope you plan on turning left up here, Doug. I'm telling you, don't fuck me around."

Doug swallowed involuntarily, almost choking as he stuttered, "I...I...am, Tony. No...no problem."

"Good." He thought for a moment. "Now let's see. Oh yeah. I have to piece this part together a little, so correct me where I go wrong, Diane. Okay? So when Henderson and the little broad are arguing I hear him say that she's got to leave because he's meeting someone else. And then I see this one all bundled up incognito-like, skulking in the shadows. She's obviously the broad Henderson's going to meet." He laughed. "Then I find out tonight that it's your wife. Now, I put two and two together and you know what I get? Henderson—your good buddy, Doug—was meeting your wife. And I'm sure it wasn't to exchange recipes."

Doug's eyes involuntarily slammed closed as if he had just seen a car crash. When he opened them again, he looked over at Diane. She slowly turned to him, her face wet with tears, her eyelids half-closed in defeat.

"Am I wrong, Diane?" Tony asked in mock bewilderment.

She did not answer, there was no need. Her sorrowful eyes pleaded for Doug's forgiveness. The tension he had felt from Tony's intimidation evaporated, leaving a numbing emptiness. He continued to stare at Diane without knowing what to say. She gazed back tenderly, sadly, repentantly.

"Oh, Diane," Doug moaned.

"Look out!" Tony yelled.

Doug looked back to the street, saw that the car had strayed over the centre line and instantly corrected his steering to avoid an oncoming car; a horn blared as the other car sped by within inches.

"Don't kill us before we get to the park, Doug," Tony joked. Then he continued. "I guess you see my predicament, eh? I can't have this witness sitting out there ready to say at any moment that the little broad didn't do it and I did. Until tonight, though, I didn't know who she was. And now it turns out that it's you, Diane. I just can't believe my fucking luck."

Doug continued to stare at the shiny black street in front of him as he steered the car toward Stanley Park. His mind desperately searched for some understanding of what had just happened. Ten minutes ago his life was coming together, now it was unravelling at light speed. Diane had been having an affair with his best friend. What's more, she had been outside his little West End love nest the night he was murdered. That was the same night Doug had announced with trepidation that they should sepa-rate. She had left him then. Not to exercise, as she had said. No. She had run to her lover. He turned again to her and studied her face in the flick-ering glow of the passing streetlights. "Jesus," he mumbled in defeat. "You're Carmen. You wrote the letter."

Diane spoke for the first time since Tony had entered the car. Falteringly, she stammered, "I'm so sorry, Doug."

Tony interrupted their anguished exchange. "Of course she's sorry. Just like you're sorry for fucking that slut, Jenna. Right Doug?" He laughed again and looked out the window. "Okay. We're coming to the park entrance. Take the scenic drive and I'll tell you where to stop."

Doug checked the rear-view mirror. "What's going to happen, Tony? You going to kill us just like you killed Henderson?"

"No," he smiled at Doug's reflection. "It'll be a little different than that. I figure a murder/suicide scenario. You know, you find out your love-ly wife was humping your good friend. You can't take it, so you kill her and then yourself." He sighed contentedly. "All very neat and tidy."

"But the police don't know about Diane and Henderson."

"Oh they will, they will. Just leave that to me." He checked out the window. "Pull into this parking space, here."

Doug steered the car into one of the angled spaces that shouldered the scenic drive of the park. During the day they were filled with cars of tourists and families coming to enjoy nature at the edge of the city. At night, however, they were empty, except for the odd pair of lovers attract-ed by the lack of street lights and the sparse traffic. The natural forest of the park created a secluded, peaceful, romantic setting like somewhere in the country.

"Now shift the car into Park, Doug, but leave the engine running," Tony directed. He sat forward, close to Diane, grabbed the back of her hair with his right hand and pulled her head against the headrest. "Don't move," he said. "I'm not as accurate with my left hand. And we want the first one to do the job, don't we?" He raised the gun to her temple.

Doug shifted into Reverse and jammed his foot down on the accelera-tor. The car shot backwards across the road, bumped up over the curb and slammed into a tree. The gun went off—the bullet missing Diane and passing harmlessly through the side window—as Tony, the only one in the car not harnessed by a seat-belt, catapulted forward over the front seat cracking his head on the dashboard. Doug pummeled him in the head with both fists, hard, while screaming at Diane "*Run!*"

Without a moment's hesitation Diane ripped off her seat-belt, jumped out of the car and ran blindly into the forest. Doug was close behind her, but in the dark he lost her. He crashed through the underbrush, bumping against tree trunks and tripping on roots, charging into the pitch blackness like a stampeding bull, without any sense of where he was going. Within fifty yards of entering the forest he ran into a tree that knocked him completely off his feet. Stunned, he lay motionless on his back in a thicket, feeling wet and cold; blood crept down from his forehead into his eyes; he wiped it away while the relentless rain washed his face. There were no stars, no moon; the only light was a distant glow from the city reflected off the clouds.

Tony's voice, close by, brought him back to his senses. "Doug!" Tony yelled.

Doug rolled over onto his stomach and looked back towards the car. He saw the silhouette of Tony standing on the road, the gun in his right hand, his left hand holding his forehead. Doug lay still, watching as Tony slowly walked to the threshold of the forest.

"Doug!" Tony yelled again. "I know you can hear me. Listen. I know exactly where Diane went. I'm going to take her out now unless you show yourself."

Doug remained silent. Tony waited. There was no sound other than the steady fall of rain.

"Okay, Doug!" Tony yelled finally. "If that's the way you want it."

He started forward into the forest. Doug lost sight of him in the darkness; the sound of crunching brush underfoot was the only indication of his movement. After a few moments, it stopped. Then, suddenly, the noise of frantic movement shattered the silence: breaking twigs, slapping leaves, creaking and swaying branches, as if a struggle was taking place. There were muffled voices but Doug could make out nothing over the constant patter of the rain. Then there was silence again. He waited.

"I've got her, Doug. Bet you can't save her," Tony challenged.

CHAPTER 19

Detective Campbell answered his cellular phone after the second ring. It was one of his field men, Corporal Richards. "Well, we're here and he ain't," Richards advised.

"What do you mean?"

"He didn't check in for the Toronto flight and he's nowhere to be seen at the airport."

Campbell was sitting in his overstuffed leather lounge chair in front of the blazing fire he had just lit. Around him were gathered the tools he needed and he was settling into one of his favourite pastimes—painting Scottish tin soldiers in official clan tartans. Unfortunately, his days of enjoying a single malt whiskey while dabbing the paint were gone. The liquor exacerbated his migraine headaches which tended to come on whenever he was forced to rethink a murder investigation.

The Henderson murder had been one of the easy ones to solve. From the very beginning all the evidence pointed to Laura Holden—so much so that Campbell had strongly opposed Christopher's offer to charge her with manslaughter in return for a guilty plea. Then the anonymous letter came. Its description of the murderer apparently fit one of Mario Bartelli's henchmen, Tony Capetti. What's more, the money-laundering scheme that Holden had explained linked Capetti to Henderson. Maybe Holden had written the anonymous letter; maybe he had lied about not knowing Capetti. But his eyes had said otherwise, and now the conviction that Campbell held of Laura Holden's guilt was beginning to erode.

He thought about what Richards had told him. Why would Capetti not have checked in for the flight? Two possible reasons. Either he never booked it, or he changed his mind about taking it. "Did you check if he was booked on the flight?" he asked.

"Yeah. Yeah. They had him booked but he never showed."

Then he must have changed his mind about taking the flight. And he likely would have made that decision after he saw Doug at the restaurant, because he and Marie were leaving the restaurant early so that he could catch the flight. Two questions: Why would he change his plans? And would Marie have known that he had changed them? Campbell sighed; he would have to put the paint away so it didn't dry out.

To Richards, he said, "It's likely that he never went to the airport, in which case he was either driven somewhere by the woman he was with, or he had her drop him at his hotel and who knows where he's ended up. I'm going to check out the woman. We have him staying at the Georgian Court Hotel. Check it out. See if he's there. If not, check with all the taxi fleets that service the hotel and find out if anyone has driven a guy that matches Capetti's description in the last couple of hours."

Richards confirmed the instructions and agreed to get back to Campbell on his cellular phone as soon as he had any information. Once they hung up, Campbell quickly put the lids on the paints. He dropped his brushes into a glass of paint thinner, raised himself out of his comfy chair with a groan, grabbed his shoulder holster, slid on his sports jacket and raincoat and headed out to his car. After starting the engine, he checked in with headquarters for the address of the apartment where Marie lived. He had been there once before when he had initially interviewed her after Henderson's death, but was unable to recall exactly where it was.

Upon arrival at the apartment building, Campbell pulled his car up to the curb on the opposite side of the street. It was an old colonial-style building, three floors without an elevator. Marie had the corner apartment on the top floor. From his parking spot Campbell surveyed the street and the outside of Marie's apartment. Nothing gained his particular attention except the fact that the apartment appeared to be in total darkness.

He pulled the car away from the curb and drove around to the alley in order to investigate the rear of the building. Again, nothing struck him as odd although he noticed there was no underground parking. Residents had to park on the street; typical in this part of town. Signs on the boulevard outside each apartment building advised that curb parking was restricted to residents only.

While he contacted headquarters to obtain a description of Marie's car, he returned to the front of the building and parked his car by the opposite curb once again. In a few moments he had the description—a 1995 silver BMW 325i, license number RJK 729—then peered up and down the street but found no match, even though there was plenty of parking space along the curb out front. The likelihood of Marie having parked in another block was slim, so it appeared that the lady was not at home. However, just to reinforce his suspicion, he picked up his cellular and dialed her phone number. No answer.

Campbell sat back in his seat with his arms folded across his chest, contemplating his next move. Capetti may or may not be with Marie; that should become apparent soon enough. The real question was: why did he change his mind about the flight? What happened at the restaurant, or after, that convinced him to stay in town? Maybe he was hitting it off with Marie so he decided he should stay awhile, or maybe he got last minute instructions from Mario—or someone—to take care of more business before he left. Or maybe something was said or happened between him and Branston to make him decide he better not leave just yet. At this point it was anybody's guess. Campbell concluded that there was nothing he could do other than wait for Richards to get back to him, and, hopefully, for Marie to show up.

His patience paid off. After sitting tight for about fifteen minutes he noticed a light coloured BMW coming towards him. He slid down into the shadows of his car interior while Marie parked by the curb alongside the apartment building. She was alone. Campbell waited for her to get out of her car and lock it before he jumped out of his and strode across the street to meet her.

"Marie," he called, preparing himself to give chase if necessary.

She turned towards him with a look of trepidation. Automatically her right forearm shot up to guard her chest, but she stood firm.

"Marie. Please don't be alarmed. It's me, Detective Campbell. You remember? I'm investigating the death of Mark Henderson." He pulled out his badge and showed it to her as he had done at their previous meeting. "I was hoping you could answer a few more questions for me."

She dropped her arm to her side. "Of course, Detective." She smiled. "Would you like to come in?"

"I'd love to."

Marie went to open the trunk of her car. "Good," she laughed. "You can help me take in these groceries."

"Certainly."

She piled his arms high with paper bags full of groceries, then led him into the building and up the stairs to her apartment. As he helped her unpack the groceries, he asked her his questions.

"Marie, we're trying to locate a fellow named Tony Capetti and I understand that you were with him tonight," he started, while passing her cans of fruit which she stored in one of the pantry cupboards.

She looked genuinely surprised. "Why? What happened with Tony?" she asked.

"No. There's nothing," Campbell stumbled. "We just want to talk to him now. He might have some information that could help us."

He held out a box of pasta to her, but she hesitated in taking it. For a long moment, she studied his face quizzically. "To do with Mark's death?" she asked finally.

He recognized that he was going to have a hard time hiding the reasons for his questions; Marie was too perceptive. Nodding guiltily, he said, "Possibly".

"I can't believe he knows anything. He's been so good to me since Mark died. He would have said something."

Campbell wanted to avoid a debate on this point. "Did he go to the airport tonight?" he asked.

"Yes."

"Did you take him there?"

She moved to the refrigerator, opened it and started loading in the dairy products that Campbell handed to her. "Well, no. I dropped him at his hotel. But he was in a hurry to catch his flight."

"The fact is that he never did check in and he never got on the plane. Were you aware of that?"

The surprise returned to Marie's face. "No. Why would he do that?"

"That's what we want to know."

They looked at each other for a long while, Marie's mind analyzing this new information. Campbell reached for a package of meat and handed it to her. "What did you talk about on the drive to the hotel?" he asked.

"Let's see. I guess Doug Branston and his wife mostly. We had seen them at the restaurant in Yaletown where we had dinner." She paused. "Well, we only really talked to Doug; Diane had ducked into the ladies' room before we got a chance to say hi." Marie accepted another package of meat from Campbell and stored it away in the refrigerator. "I don't know if you're aware, but Doug and his wife separated right around the time that Mark was killed. I was very sorry because I thought they had a good marriage. Anyway, I was pleased to see them together tonight."

"Do they know Tony Capetti?"

"Doug does. But I'm sure Tony hasn't met Diane because he was asking a bunch of questions about her when we drove to the hotel. You know, what she was like? What I thought the problem was with their relationship and everything. As I say, they were sort of the topic of our conversation."

Campbell checked the paper bags on the kitchen counter. They were all empty. "I think that's it."

Marie double checked before starting to fold up the bags. "Great. Thanks for your help. Would you like a coffee?"

"No, thank you, I've got to get going. But tell me, were there any other questions that Tony asked about Doug and Diane?"

Marie made a face as she tried to recollect the conversation in the car. "Oh, you know, who did I think had made the decision to separate? Were either of them having an affair? That sort of thing."

Campbell raised his eyebrows in forewarning of another question. "Were either of them?"

"Having an affair, you mean?" Marie looked at Campbell curiously. "I don't know."

Their eyes held each other's for a long moment. Campbell was about to thank Marie for her time when his cellular phone rang. Excusing himself, he wandered into the living room while he answered the phone. It was Richards. Apparently a driver for City Cabs remembered taking a guy that matched Capetti's description from the hotel to a restaurant in Yaletown.

"Okay. I want you to have someone drive by to see if he's there and get right back to me. But be subtle. I don't want him to know we're looking for him."

Campbell hung up the cellular phone. Returning to the kitchen, he found Marie at the window with her back to him. "He took a cab back to the restaurant. Why would he do that?" he asked.

Marie shrugged.

"When you had dinner was there anyone else at the restaurant that Tony knew? Anyone he talked to or even acknowledged?"

Marie turned to face him shaking her head.

"Anyone else you knew?"

"No."

Campbell checked his watch; it was just before eleven. Maybe Doug was still at the restaurant. He asked Marie for a phone book. In a couple of minutes he was talking to the maitre d' who told him that the "Brandons" had left about fifteen minutes earlier.

Campbell calculated roughly the time needed to drive from the restaurant to the area of Doug's house. Twenty to twenty-five minutes, he figured, depending on the route. Marie's apartment was closer to Doug's house than the restaurant was. If he hurried he should get to the house at about the same time as Doug and Diane. He thanked Marie for her help then left the apartment.

Just a few minutes before Campbell arrived at Doug's house his cellular phone rang. It was Richards again, advising that there was no sign of Capetti at the restaurant. Campbell told him to sit tight until further notice. He disconnected at the same moment that he pulled up outside the house.

The front entrance was in darkness. Campbell got out of his car and walked over to check the garage. Empty. He went to the front door and knocked. While he waited he noticed through the little window in the door the unmistakable metallic blue glow of a television from a room at the back of the house. Someone must be home. He knocked again and, this time, rang the doorbell. Soon, a shadow moved across the television light. Campbell waited but the door remained unanswered. He knocked a third time and rang the bell again. Then, from the corner of his eye, he spied a small face peeking out from behind the curtains of the large picture window to his left. A youngster was watching him like a stage-frightened understudy before the opening overture. Campbell guessed the child must be alone in the house.

He pulled out his badge and held it up. "Son," he called. "I'm a police officer. My name is Detective Campbell. May I speak to you for a moment?"

Matthew remained still, unsure of what to do. His mother's instructions were never to open the door to a stranger, especially when alone in the house at night. If the stranger persisted, Matthew was to phone a neighbour, or the police, and then his mom wherever she might be. But this man said he was the police; besides, Matthew had already checked with the restaurant and his mom and dad had left.

Campbell sensed the boy's dilemma. "Son," he called again, "is there a neighbour I can talk to?"

Matthew's face softened; he nodded and pointed to his left. "Next door. The Finnegans," he hollered.

Campbell gave him a mock salute before jogging over to the next door neighbours' house. In a few minutes he returned with Mr. Finnegan alongside. After receiving Mr. Finnegan's assurance, Matthew opened the front door and let the two men in.

They all went into the living room where Campbell explained that he needed to talk to Matthew's dad quite urgently. Matthew confirmed that his mom and dad had gone out to dinner together in the family car; he had phoned the restaurant about fifteen minutes ago; apparently they had already left, so he expected them home any minute. In answer to Campbell's question, Matthew conceded that his mother never left him to babysit his brother after eleven at night. If she were running late she always phoned, although she must have forgotten to phone this evening.

Campbell's watch read just after eleven fifteen. A bad feeling was seeping into his guts like water into a sinking ship. His conversation with the maitre d' had indicated that Doug and Diane actually left the restaurant about half an hour ago. They were still not home and they had not phoned.

A thought occurred to him. "Son, does your mom have a cellular phone?"

"Yeah. She has a car phone. But I'm only supposed to use it in emergencies."

Campbell took out his own cellular phone. "Well, let's give them a call and see what they're up to, shall we?"

He punched in the numbers Matthew gave him from memory. After a couple of rings a recorded message indicated that the receiving cellular phone was presently disengaged. He hung up and immediately dialed headquarters. While waiting for the call to be answered he asked Matthew to describe the car his mom and dad were driving. The receptionist at headquarters soon came on the line and Campbell asked to be connected with the motor vehicle division.

After obtaining the license plate number for a car matching the description Matthew had provided, Campbell called Corporal Richards. "I want an APB on the Branston white Taurus, 1992, license number KL5 78W," he instructed. "I don't want the car stopped. Just keep an eye on it. Get back to me as soon as you've got anything." He hung up.

Only then did Campbell notice Matthew's eyes staring at him like a frightened kitten's. The boy's face was pale and limp. "What's wrong?" he stammered. "Has something happened to Mom and Dad?"

Campbell's eyes jumped from Matthew to Mr. Finnegan and back while he madly sifted through his memory for an appropriate response to reassure the boy. "No, son," he smiled. "By the way, what's your name? I always like to know the name of the man I'm talking to."

Matthew strengthened slightly and told Campbell his name.

"To answer your question, Matthew, no. Nothing has happened to your parents. They have probably just had some engine trouble."

"Or maybe they've gone somewhere and lost track of the time," Mr. Finnegan suggested with a sympathetic grin towards Matthew. "That's certainly happened to me."

"That's right," Campbell agreed. "Anyway, I have to go, but I don't want you to stay here alone at this hour. Mr. Finnegan, would you be able to stay until Matthew's parents get home?"

Finnegan expressed his pleasure in helping out. But when Campbell left, Finnegan walked him to his car. "What's really going on, Detective?" Finnegan asked when they were out of earshot of the front porch where Matthew stood.

"I honestly don't know at this point. But there have been a few coincidences tonight that worry me. That's why I want to find the boy's parents and make sure that they're safe." Campbell opened the door of the car and got in. "Thanks for staying with the lad. I'll let you know what's happening as soon as I can. And if you hear from either of them, please call me immediately on my cellular."

Campbell handed Finnegan his card, then started the car and drove away. He wanted to be on the road when they pinpointed the location of the Taurus.

Around the corner from Doug's house, Campbell found a 7-Eleven. Many times he had sworn off junk food, but there was something about his job that lent itself to the occasional burnt coffee and doughnut.

He was strolling back to his car with his refillable coffee cup, full and steaming hot, in one hand and a gooey pastry in the other, when his cellular phone rang. He set the coffee and pastry onto of the roof of the car and answered the phone.

"Well, we got the car," Richards said. "It was spotted during a routine pass through Stanley Park. Apparently it's abandoned and there's a bullet hole in the windshield. Officers are at the scene now if you want to speak to them."

"Okay. Stay on the line," Campbell ordered. He opened the car door, slid in behind the wheel and picked up the microphone to contact the police in the park. "What do you have?" he asked after Constable Terry's voice crackled over the radio.

"I got a white '92 Taurus with license plate KL5 78W. That the one you're looking for?"

Campbell confirmed that it was and asked for details.

"Its back end is slammed up against a tree. I think whoever left it here was in a hurry. The engine's running and both the passenger and driver's doors are open. There's a single bullet hole in the passenger side window." He paused. "Just a second," he said. A few moments of static echoed over the radio before Terry came back on. "Yeah. My partner says that it looks like there may be a little blood in the middle of the front dash. Hard to tell though."

"Any idea of where the occupants might have gone?" Campbell asked.

"It's pretty dark out here even with our headlights on. I don't know. There may be some footprints in the mud leading into the woods. But it's really hard to tell."

"Okay. Stay put. I'm on my way and I'm going to get the dog squad out there as well."

As Campbell started the engine, Terry advised him of their location in the park.

Campbell signed off with Terry and got back on the line with Richards. "Did you hear any of that?" he asked.

Richards had heard only bits and pieces.

"I'm going to the park right now. I want you to get the dog squad out there to meet me. And then make your way down there as well."

He hung up the cellular phone, put the car into reverse, and stepped on the gas. The tires squealed, the car shot backwards and the coffee on the roof flew forward dumping its contents all over the windshield; the pastry leapt onto the car hood, landing in a sloppy, sugary splat.

"Shit," Campbell grumbled as he stopped the car, "that never happens in the movies." He got out, gingerly picked the pastry off the car hood and threw it in the garbage. Back in the car he turned the wipers up to high to clear the coffee off the windshield. *At least the rain will help clean up this mess*, he thought.

He arrived at the location of the Taurus before the dog squad and quickly inspected the car to confirm Constable Terry's information. Then with a flashlight he went to the edge of the forest and peered around. Thick underbrush covered the ground; even with the flashlight he could see only twenty or thirty yards into the woods. He walked back and forth at the threshold of the forest shining his flashlight, hoping to glimpse something that might indicate where the occupants of the car had gone. But with the darkness and the constant rain, it was impossible.

Opposite the forest, beyond the parking shoulder on the far side of the drive, there was a green boulevard sloping gently down to a seawall which outlined the perimeter of the park and divided it from the bay. It was a beautiful seaside walk but lacked hiding places, a consideration which Campbell suspected was foremost in the mind of at least one of the occupants of the Taurus. No. He guessed that they were in the forest. The dog squad would be able to confirm it.

As Campbell returned to the area of the Taurus, Richards' police cruiser pulled into view with three dog squad wagons behind it; one dog and one cop were in each. They parked, jumped out of their vehicles and gathered by the Taurus, the dogs whooping and wailing and straining at their collars in frenzied anticipation of a hunt.

Campbell briefed everyone, then opened the doors of the Taurus for the dogs to investigate the scent of its occupants. They bounded through the car, sniffing and snorting; finally, with blood-curdling yelps, they charged to the edge of the forest, their handlers fighting to restrain them while Detective Campbell gave further orders.

"Okay, everyone," he yelled over the howls, "I want you to put on your bullet-proof vests. Terry, you and your partner go with the dogs. Richards, you go with them as well. Remember, there's at least one person who's armed in there. So take it easy. I'm going to have road blocks set up at all exits from the park and then I'll follow you in."

CHAPTER 20

Doug lay silently in the thicket wondering what he was going to do next.

Tony taunted him again. "Come on, Doug. She's pretty cute. Maybe I'll take a run at her before I shoot her. You want that?"

From some distance beyond Tony, a voice called out. "Don't believe him. He—"

Immediately, Doug heard the repeated report of a gun—*crack, crack, crack, crack!* Sharp flashes of light cut the darkness, followed by a short choking scream.

"Too late," Tony yelled. "I guess I won't be jumping her after all. Looks like it's just you and me now."

Doug stayed still in his hiding place. The rain provided a constant drum roll for his racing mind. Did Tony actually shoot Diane or was he firing blindly into the woods? Diane's voice seemed to have been some distance away from Tony when she had called out. Maybe he had just shot in that direction hoping he might hit her. Even if he had missed her, she would surely remain silent now.

There was movement in the woods, sounds of slow careful steps crushing and snapping the underbrush. Probably Tony. But where was he going? If he had missed Diane and was searching for her Doug needed a diversion quickly. His eyes had adjusted to the dark; looking around he was able to make out the black vertical shapes of trees against their shadowy backdrop. It was dank and eerie, silhouette overlapping silhouette, but he thought he could distinguish enough to find his way further into the forest and, in the process, hopefully draw Tony after him.

Suddenly Doug leapt up. "Come and get me, asshole," he yelled, then turned and plunged deeper into the wood.

Again, there was the quick report of a gun; this time Doug missed the barrel fire because his back was turned and he was running like a maniac, zigzagging around trees, crashing over bushes and fallen branches. He thought he heard two shots, but couldn't be sure. One shot must have come close because he heard a sharp thud on a tree trunk just behind him. He kept running. The ground was soaked and muddy; at times his leather slip-ons were sucked off his heels. He tried to keep them on by curling his toes in his shoes, but soon one shoe stuck to the bottom of a muddy pool of rain water. After that, he tried skipping to save his socked foot from the sharp stems of the underbrush. All the time, from behind, he heard over the clatter of rain the steady pace of Tony smashing through the bush.

After scrambling over an enormous log, Doug landed on bare, flat ground. He stood for a second, straining his eyes to see what was around him. It appeared that he had stumbled onto a trail. Behind him the sounds of Tony bulldozing through the undergrowth were getting louder. Doug assessed both directions along the trail, chose one and broke into a kind of hopping sprint. The path was clear of brush and quite dry, having been built with a base of drain rock.

Doug counted his strides while listening hard for a change in the sound of Tony's pursuit. When he had run about sixty paces, the crash of Tony's heavy feet on the underbrush stopped. Tony had now reached the trail and was about sixty yards behind. Soon he was going to catch up. Doug desperately needed a plan.

"I'm gaining on you, Doug," Tony yelled.

The gun fired again. Doug heard the zing of the bullet over his head. Then, just as he was thinking that he might be better off diving back into the bush, the path began to curve to the left. A short distance further on Doug reached a cross trail. He reckoned Tony was about ten seconds behind and momentarily out of sight due to the curve of the trail. Without hesitation Doug veered down the path to the right and continued running for about five seconds before he slipped off the trail into the brush. Standing silently in the camouflage at the side of the trail, like an Indian scout, he listened for Tony's footsteps. They came pounding nearer and nearer; then they stopped. Tony was at the intersection of the trails trying to guess which way Doug had gone.

Doug prayed that Tony would take one of the other directions, either straight ahead or to the left, buying Doug some time to plan an ambush in the event that Tony returned. After a moment he was relieved to hear the sound of Tony's measured pace fading away. He stepped back onto the trail and continued quietly, straining his ears all the time for any sound of

Tony returning and constantly searching in the murky darkness for something that might help him stop Tony if he did.

A short distance further on Doug noticed a large tree limb down beside the trail. It appeared to belong to the great old maple that overhung the path just before it and must have come down due to age and the weight of the ceaseless rain. It was a rat's nest of boughs, broken branches and twigs. Doug examined the limb for a moment, then, grabbing two sturdy boughs, hauled it in jerks and strains across the trail so that it provided an effective barricade to the trail beyond. He then searched around in the bush for something to use as a club, eventually discovering an oval-shaped rock about the size of a football which he was able to hold comfortably between his two hands. With the rock held under his chin like a weight lifter's barbell, he stepped behind the trunk of the old maple to wait.

The rain fell in a continuous wet curtain; the maple, without its leaves, provided little shelter. Doug soon began to wonder if he would be better off just to run. Maybe Tony would continue down the wrong trail and never come back this way. Even if he did come back, the tree limb would slow him down a little bit. Doug might have time to get out of the forest and find some help.

No. It was too personal with Tony just to run for help. This was the guy that had killed Henderson and maybe Diane. His best friend and his wife. But that thought immediately brought back to mind Tony's story in the car; and Doug's momentary conviction began to dissipate. Why should he even care? They had been fucking behind his back.

He leaned back against the trunk of the tree and slid slowly down so that he was sitting on his heels with the rock in his lap. Lifting his head to the sky, he felt the rain wash over his face. His best friend and his wife. Could he ever forgive them?

Exhaustion and self pity were near to overwhelming Doug's fortitude when he was suddenly aware of the regular sound of footsteps on the trail. Adrenaline burst into his system as if a dam had broken, washing aside all reflection in its wake. Tony's steady stalking pace, relentless and indefatigable, grew louder. Doug recoiled behind the tree and stood up. Tony had made the decision for him. It was too late to run. He had to take out Tony now, or be taken out himself. This was as personal as it got.

Doug remained motionless as Tony approached the tree limb lying across the trail. Even in the gloomy depths of the forest the contrast between the trail and the limb was enough for Tony to see the obstruction before he ran into it. He jogged up to the limb and stopped to inspect it for a moment.

Doug heard him laugh to himself, then mumble "Good work, Doug. At least I know I'm headed in the right direction. You're an idiot if you think this will slow me down."

Tony put his gun in his waist belt; then using both hands he spread the branches of the limb in order to climb over it. At the same time, Doug eased himself around the side of the maple so that he was watching Tony from behind. The distance between them was less than ten feet.

Suddenly, Tony turned as if jolted by a noise behind him. Doug quickly twisted back behind the tree while Tony's eyes scanned the forest and trail like searchlights. Doug's body shrank silently against the trunk, his ears perked for any indication that Tony was moving toward him. He waited, his heart pounding and his stomach churning. Seconds passed like minutes with only the steady sound of the rain muffling the silence. Had Tony seen him? Was he coming after him? Doug tried to work out a plan of action in case Tony leapt in front of him, but fear had numbed his brain. He fought hard to hold on against the exploding sense of helplessness.

A branch snapped, apparently where the limb crossed the trail. Doug tentatively peeked around the tree trunk. Tony was straddling the fallen limb with both hands occupied in separating the branches. Taking a deep breath Doug charged with the rock held high over his head.

Initially, the rain muffled his approach. Only when he was within five feet did Tony, sensing a threat, look back towards Doug while instinctively grabbing for his gun. But his balance was precarious and he faltered. Another moment and Doug's advantage would be lost. Adrenaline again shot through him like a bolt of lightning. He screamed and lunged at Tony, bringing the rock down with all his strength. Tony was able to get his right shoulder up only slightly to deflect part of the crushing power of the rock. It glanced off the side of his head, knocking him to the ground on the far side of the limb. The force of Doug's lunge caused him to topple over the limb as well. He landed face-down on the ground by Tony's feet, dropping the rock in the process.

In a daze, Tony slowly struggled onto his hands and knees. Meanwhile, Doug raised his head and spat the earth and gravel out of his mouth. His left hand reached to clear away the grit that was stinging his eyes while his right desperately searched for the rock. Tony shook his head to clear the blow. "You're a dead man," he growled, just as Doug's hand found the rock.

Instantly Doug grabbed the rock with both hands and scrambled to his feet. When Tony saw Doug rearing up with the rock over his head, he rolled onto his back and reached desperately for his gun. "Fuck you!" Doug yelled and slammed the rock down on Tony's face. The sound on impact was like a clay pot shattering. Warm blood mixed with shards of bone spattered Doug's face and arms. He stood motionless over Tony and watched in frozen dread as Tony's hand shook over the handle of the gun.

Only when Tony's hand dropped limply to the ground did Doug fall to his knees and release the rock. It sat momentarily in the concave mush of Tony's face before rolling awkwardly off onto the ground. Doug quickly grabbed the gun from Tony's waist belt then sat back on the trail, staring without emotion at the crumpled, lifeless shadow in front of him.

The sound of distant yelps began to stir Doug's consciousness. He raised his head to concentrate. Yes, the sound of barking dogs was getting nearer. As he stood up, for the first time he felt the pain in his shoeless foot from the sharp ends of the underbrush. The bitter cold that had seeped into his bones through his rain-saturated clothing caused him to shiver as he pulled his sopping coat around him.

Soon, the rays of flashlights bounced in the bush behind him. They danced with the baying of the dogs, light and sound piercing the stillness of the forest. He waited in fascination as they came nearer and nearer. Then, he heard the voices: "Good boy. You get him. Come on Rex. Good dog." The lights jousted down the trail towards him stabbing into the darkness of the surrounding forest and the path ahead. The barking grew in pitch and intensity as the animals sensed they were closing in on their quarry.

Finally light flickered over Doug's face. Holding up his hands, he yelled "Here! I'm here!"

Several flashlights settled on him, their brilliance blinding him. Over the growl of the dogs he heard exaggerated praise for a hunt well done, and he prayed that their handlers had them under control.

"Drop the gun!" ordered a voice from behind the wall of light. Doug had forgotten that he held Tony's gun in his left hand. He let it fall to the ground while leaving his hands in the air.

"Now step slowly to this side of the limb."

Doug separated the branches as Tony had done shortly before, then stepped gingerly over the limb. Raising his hands once more he said, "My name is Doug Branston. There's a man here named Tony Capetti. He's in serious need of medical attention."

Mumbling came from behind the light; eventually an officer stepped forward, his gun in one hand and his flashlight in the other. He walked up to Doug, frisked him then asked for the location of the injured man. When Doug pointed to the far side of the tree limb, the officer turned his flashlight onto Tony's body. It was the first good glimpse Doug had had of the damage caused by the rock. Between Tony's forehead and his mouth, a pool of blood and bone fragments had gathered. His nose no longer existed and his eyes were hidden under the crimson ooze.

"Jesus," the officer exhaled. "Did you do that?"

"He was trying to kill me," Doug replied without emotion.

The officer fought his way over the limb. Kneeling down beside Tony's body, he checked for breathing and took a pulse. In a moment he stood up. "Nothing we can do for him now," he said. "This guy is dead." He called back to the faceless men behind the wall of light. "We got a dead one here. Better radio in another ambulance."

The light gradually fragmented as officers began to move. The dog squad backed off, sensing that their job was now over, while others came forward to see what had happened.

Doug's mind was paralyzed with fatigue but something struck him about what the officer had just said. "Another ambulance? Have you already radioed for one?"

"Yeah. I'm afraid there's a lady back there with a serious bullet wound."

Immediately, Doug started to limp down the trail toward where the police had come, but his foot screamed with pain. As he stumbled the officer grabbed his right arm. "I can't let you go just yet, Mr. Branston. I'm sorry but I'm going to have to arrest you for the death of Capetti here. It's just a formality and I'm sure the prosecutor will sort it out. I'll need you to put your hands behind your back."

"Look," Doug said desperately, "It's my wife that's been shot. I've got to see her." He tried weakly to pull away.

"I am sorry, Mr. Branston, but there is nothing you can do for her right now. The paramedics are looking after her. Please let me put these cuffs on you."

With the condition of his foot, Doug could hardly move anyway. He was shaking uncontrollably from the cold and felt emotionally drained. What he really wanted to do was sit down and cry. Instead, he placed his hands behind his back in surrender.

The officer cuffed him while advising him of his rights, then placed a hand under his arm to lead him down the trail. But Doug's foot resisted. The officer shone his flashlight down, revealing the sock torn to shreds and saturated with mud and blood. He bent and picked the remains of the sock off to expose the damage. Shredded with lacerations and punctures, Doug's foot hung limply from an extremely bruised ankle.

A voice came from the shadows. "Take off those bloody handcuffs," demanded Detective Campbell as he approached. The officer with Doug immediately obliged. "A little overzealous, but he's still young," Campbell commented to Doug in apology. "How are you, Branston? You look a little the worse for wear."

"What's happened to Diane?" Doug whispered.

Campbell was glad for the darkness to hide the concern on his face while he answered. Unfortunately, it could not mask the pain of his words. "She's in good care, Doug," he sympathized.

"What happened?"

Sighing, he explained. "She took a bullet in her left leg above the knee. She's lost a lot of blood, but she's going to make it."

"What do you mean, 'make it'? Could she die?"

"No! No! I'm sure she's going to be fine." Campbell hesitated before deciding to explain what he knew of Diane's injury. "Look. The bullet hit an artery in her upper left leg. Those are major blood suppliers up there, so she bled badly. Had we not arrived when we did, there was a possibility she could have...uh..."

"Bled to death?" Doug cried. "Oh, my God. I have to see her." He started hopping along the trail on his good leg.

Campbell ordered another officer over to assist Doug out of the forest. As Doug worked his way down the trail, an arm over each officer's shoulder, Campbell called after him. "Make sure you get that foot looked at by one of the paramedics."

Doug had suddenly lost interest in his own pain. All he could think of now was Diane and the fact that he might have lost her—might still lose her. His exhausted mind could not compute all the convoluted information acquired in the last few hours and how he was supposed to react to it. Instinct alone drove him on, assuring him that his future depended upon Diane surviving this. All he knew was that he had to be there to assist her recovery.

As he struggled down the trail, he tried to think of what to say to Diane, but his mind refused to function. There was no energy left to make a plan. Where the trail ended, about 100 yards away from where Doug had crashed the Taurus, he stopped for a moment to take in all the activity. The dog squad was there, packing up to leave; a tow truck, its yellow light flashing, was backed up to the Taurus and a big-bellied hippie with a chain in one hand was peering under the car's bumper. An ambulance was parked, its red emergency lights flashing, while two paramedics, a stretcher between them, jogged towards Doug; a policeman ran alongside. Doug thought that the stretcher might be for him, but the three ran past him and down the trail.

"I thought there were two ambulances," he said to the officers assisting him.

"There were," said one of the officers. "I guess one has already left for the hospital."

With the help of the officers Doug hobbled over to the remaining ambulance. Through the open rear doors he saw a paramedic putting instruments and medication in place for the next patient.

"Where's the other ambulance?" Doug blurted out.

The paramedic had not seen Doug approach and was startled. She turned abruptly. "I'm sorry?"

One of the officers said, "There was another ambulance here. Has it returned to the hospital?"

"Oh, yes—just a few minutes ago. They needed to get their patient to O.R. in a hurry."

"My wife—" Doug choked.

"Oh, I'm sorry, sir. I'm sure she'll be fine. Apparently, the bullet severed an artery. They'll need to sew it up."

"I have to see her," Doug announced as he looked around desperately for transportation to the hospital.

Just then, Detective Campbell appeared at his side. "You need to have that foot looked after first, Doug, and I need to talk to you as well. After, we'll have a cruiser take you to the hospital, if you like."

As both officers helped Doug into the back of the ambulance, the paramedic offered, "I doubt she'll be seeing anyone tonight if she's in O.R."

Doug sat forlornly while the paramedic inspected his damaged foot. She rocked the ankle each way to assess its mobility while Doug gritted his teeth against the flaring pain. Then, she reached into a nearby drawer, brought out a brown bottle and poured a little of the contents onto some gauze.

"This may sting," she cautioned. Without a moment's hesitation, she began mopping up the dried blood and muck that hid the lacerations on Doug's foot. When the disinfectant eventually cut through the crusted layers and reached the shredded skin, Doug screeched, then growled steadily until the cleansing was finished.

Detective Campbell appeared at the rear door of the ambulance as the paramedic finished wrapping the elastic bandage onto Doug's foot. "You ready?" he asked.

Doug nodded. After easing himself out of the ambulance, he limped across to Detective Campbell's car, like a soldier returning from battle. Campbell guided him into the back seat, then jumped into the front passenger seat, started the engine and turned the heat onto high. He waited until the air had warmed, then asked Doug to tell him what had happened.

Doug cleared his throat before he began. In that moment, he decided to start at the restaurant. And, in the course of recounting events, he chose, as well, to leave out the part about Diane being the witness to

Henderson's murder, advising simply that Tony had returned to the restaurant, apparently to kill him. Because Diane happened to be there, he explained, she had to die as well. He went on to describe the chase in the woods, and finally, how he managed to ambush Tony on the trail.

Campbell considered this explanation for a moment. "There's something that I just don't understand about that though, Doug," he mused. Doug turned his head away from Campbell's probing eyes. "Why would Capetti want to kill you?"

"I don't know. Maybe he thought I'd figured him out."

Campbell frowned as he thought about this. "Maybe," he said unconvinced. For a long moment he stared at Doug as if searching for something in Doug's countenance that would clarify Capetti's actions. Finally, he put his note pad and pen down. "Okay, I'll get someone to run you down to the hospital. But, I'll need to get more details from you later."

"Great," Doug sighed with relief just before remembering his children at home. "Jesus. The kids..."

"No worries. Your neighbour—ah, Mr. Finnegan?—is staying with them. But you should probably call and tell him you're going to be awhile." He handed Doug his cell phone.

Finnegan was pleased to help and expressed relief that Doug and Diane's ordeal—whatever it may have been—was over. Before Doug handed the cell phone back to Campbell, he made one more call.

"Elvis. It's Branston. Listen, I don't have time to explain, but the charges against Laura are going to be dropped. I'm not going to make it back to the apartment tonight, so I'll explain it all to you tomorrow."

With a sense of déjà vu, Doug entered the same hospital where Laura had convalesced following Henderson's murder. This time, it was Diane who had fallen victim to Tony Capetti. And, this time, Doug was passing through the macabre world of the hospital's Emergency rather than the serenity of the front lobby. Around him sat those unfortunate enough to be suffering from only minor ailments and, therefore, able to wait until one of the emergency doctors could find nothing better to do than attend to their complaints. These were the reluctant spectators, the captive audience for the doctors and nurses who moved about them with aloof boredom, like actors who had played the same role a million times before.

"Excuse me," a nurse ordered as she pushed a gurney passed Doug. A body lay on the mattress, its face wrapped in bandages like a mummy and a hose running from its arm to a plastic bag, filled with clear liquid that bobbed on a hanger overhead.

Doug waited for the gurney to pass, then shuffled over to the reception desk.

"Stub your toe?" the receptionist asked with affected derision.

Her manners improved only after Doug explained that he was not there for himself, but for the woman, Diane Branston, who had come in with a bullet wound to her left leg. "I'm her husband, " he said. "Please, I need to see her."

The receptionist typed something into her computer, then scanned the screen for a moment. "I'm sorry, sir," she said, still peering at the monitor. "It seems she was taken straight into O.R. on her arrival."

"When will she be out?"

"Hard to say." She continued to study the monitor as if the answer lay somewhere in the abbreviations on the screen. Finally, she turned to face Doug. "Perhaps, if you could take a seat, Mr., uh, Branston, is it?"

Doug nodded.

"Please take a seat, Mr. Branston. I'll have one of the doctors or nurses come to speak to you as soon as possible." She gave an encouraging nod towards the waiting area.

Amongst the all-but-forgotten, Doug found a seat and began the interminable wait for news on Diane. As calamity whirled about him, his mind retraced the events over the last few weeks that had landed him there. He knew he had been drawn to Henderson's lifestyle because it was exciting and reckless; Henderson had always taken what he wanted without apology. Now, Doug realized that that lifestyle was shallow and unreal, and he felt ashamed for having given up his family to pursue it.

But what about Diane's affair with Henderson? How was he supposed to feel about that? He tried to peer into that Pandora's box of emotions, but each time he was met by an overpowering sense of guilt. Guilt for what, though? Sure, he had abandoned his family, but he was making amends. Hadn't Diane cheated on him? And with his best friend? Shouldn't he be outraged? He had felt that outrage in the forest while he waited for Capetti. Why didn't he feel it now? Why did he only feel that, somehow, everything was his fault?

His foot ached. Fatigue was confounding his thoughts like a drug. He tried to concentrate, tried to analyze his reaction—it was important to come to grips with his feelings—but his neck was jelly, unable to support his drooping head. It was all too difficult, too complicated.

"Mr. Branston, I'm Dr. Goldman."

Doug opened his eyes to see a tall husky man in green pajamas and a green brimless cap standing before him. Recognizing that this was not part of his dream, he moved to stand.

"Please sit," Goldman mildly instructed.

Doug resumed his seat without protest.

"Mr. Branston," the doctor started, "Your wife has suffered a serious wound to her upper left leg. She lost a lot of blood due to the bullet severing an artery. We have managed to repair that, so she is out of any serious danger."

Doug relaxed momentarily.

"However," Goldman continued, his heavy eyebrows forming a shadow of concern over his eyes, "she will need time to regain her strength. We'll need to keep her in Intensive Care for twenty-four to forty-eight hours. And"—his hand rose to stop Doug from interrupting him—"You should be prepared for the fact that she will be left with a permanent disability. You see, the bullet passed through the hamstring muscle and caused some nerve damage. As a result, she will be forced to favour her left leg to a significant extent when she walks."

"You mean she will walk with a limp for awhile?"

"Always," Goldman emphasized.

Given what could have happened this was not a terrible disability, but Doug recognized immediately the devastating impact it was going to have on Diane. Doug gazed at Goldman, who confirmed what he had already recognized. "She will need all your support and encouragement," the doctor said. Then he nodded toward the large glass entrance doors to the Emergency Room. "You should go home and get some rest. You're going to need it."

Doug's eyes followed the doctor's and noticed for the first time that it was brightening outside. "My God. What time is it?" he asked.

Goldman pointed to the clock on the nearby wall. "6:30."

"I must have dozed off," Doug mumbled to himself as he readjusted his mind to the fact it was early Saturday morning. He looked back to the doctor. "Can I see her?"

Goldman shook his head slowly. "No. She's still coming out of the anesthesia. Give her twenty-four hours."

Doug's head was pounding, his foot throbbed, and his eyelids weighed a ton—so he didn't protest. Instead, he thanked the doctor and shook his hand. It occurred to him, as he shuffled over to the bank of payphones to call a cab, that Laura Holden didn't know she was about to be cleared of killing Henderson. After recovering a quarter from his pocket, Doug lifted the receiver on one of the phones, dropped the quarter in the slot and dialed Tom's number.

The phone rang and rang before a hoarse voice finally answered, "Yeah?"

"Elvis. You awake?"

"No."

"It's Branston."

A grunting sound over the phone line suggested that Tom was trying to raise himself into a sitting position. "Branston," he coughed. "It's Saturday morning. Why are you calling so early? Didn't you say this thing is over?"

"That's right," Doug sighed. "But no one has told Laura. We need to see her and tell her."

There was a pause before Tom ventured, "Now?"

"The sooner the better. She needs to know."

Another pause. "You're right. I'm getting up," Tom groaned. "I'm getting up."

"Listen. I need you to pick me up at the hospital."

"The hospital? You okay?" Tom was awake now.

"Yeah Elvis. Everything is fine. I'll tell you the whole story when you get here." He dug into his pocket and retrieved another quarter. "I'm going to call Holden and tell him we're on our way."

"I'll be there in a few minutes," Tom said.

Doug dialed the Holden number. When Frank Holden eventually answered, Doug told him that he and Tom were on their way over with some very good news.

"Is it over?" Holden asked, hope clearing the sleep from his throat.

"It is. Now make sure Laura's up when we get there. I want to see her face."

A moment passed before Holden exhaled, "Jesus. So do I."

The roguesmobile chugged over to the Holden residence while Doug recounted to Tom the events of the previous night. Just as he had when speaking to Detective Campbell, he chose to leave out the fact that Diane had witnessed the murder.

Tom frowned and shook his head when Doug was finished. "I don't get it. Why did Tony want to kill you? You had nothing on him except some anonymous letter." He looked over at Doug. "Right?"

Doug turned away from Tom and stared out the passenger window at the buildings passing by. He wondered if he should tell Tom about Henderson and Diane, then decided against it—at least until he understood where his relationship with Diane was headed. "Beats me," he shrugged. "Maybe he got a little paranoid. I don't know." He slid down in his seat and closed his eyes.

They drove in silence for a time. Doug felt an unusual warmth on his face from the rising sun shining through the windshield. The AM radio was buzzing in the background—an investment talk show. The steady throb of the Montego's big V8 engine was subtly rocking Doug to sleep.

"Here we are," Tom announced as he pulled the roguesmobile up to the curb in front of the Holden residence.

Doug worked his way out of the car and then limped up the walkway beside Tom. Before they reached it, the huge oak entrance door swung open and a jubilant Frank Holden stood in the doorway wearing a silk bathrobe. His smile quickly faded when he saw Doug struggling toward him. "What the hell happened to you?" he said while stepping forward to help Doug into the house.

"Nothing a cup of coffee can't cure." Doug smiled.

"I'm on it," Holden said as he ushered Doug and Tom into the sunken living room, the same room where Doug had first met Laura at the Holden party that seemed so long ago. Now Laura sat alone at the edge of a sofa in a heavy cotton housecoat over a long white nightgown. Doug and Tom walked over to her while Holden disappeared into the kitchen to get the coffee. As they approached her, a look of nervous expectation came to her face.

"Is it really true?" she asked. "They don't think I killed Mark anymore?"

"It's true, Laura," Doug said. "It turns out a man named Tony Capetti killed Mark and tried to frame you."

"Oh my god." She burst into tears. Slowly she rose from the sofa and gave Doug and Tom a hug. "Thank you so much," she mumbled.

Doug held Laura back at arms length and looked at her. A smile of genuine relief worked its way across her face even while the tears continued to slide down her cheeks.

"There it is," Doug said to Tom. "That smile is what I've been wanting to see."

"Isn't that beautiful?" Holden asked as he entered the room carrying a tray filled with cups, cream and sugar and a coffee thermos. He placed the tray on the coffee table. "Sit down. Sit down," he said. "Tell us what happened." Laura sat back down on the sofa. Her father sat beside her and gave her a tender hug. "Help yourself to the coffee," he added with the sweep of his hand.

Doug reached for a cup as he and Tom sat down on the opposite sofa. While he poured the coffee, he reminded everyone that he had been convinced from the description in the anonymous letter that the murderer was Tony Capetti. Then he described the meeting in the parking lot outside the restaurant, the drive to Stanley Park when Capetti confessed to murdering Henderson, and finally the chase through the park and Capetti's ultimate demise.

The story captivated Holden and Laura. They sat stunned for a time after Doug had finished, apparently picturing the chase through the woods in their minds. Finally, Holden shook his head. "Wow," he said and sat forward on the sofa. He reached for a coffee cup. "And how is Diane faring?" he asked.

"I think she'll be just fine, thanks." Doug offered.

A few more moments passed while they all contemplated Diane's fate. Eventually, Laura asked, "Why did this Tony guy want to kill Mark?"

Tom spoke up. "Well, we think it might have been related to some business deal that Mark was involved in."

"Drugs?"

Tom and Doug looked at each other, then at Holden who returned their gaze pleadingly. "We're not sure, Laura. The police are still investigating that," Doug answered vaguely.

"What about the letter?" Laura continued. "Did they ever find out who wrote it?"

Doug hesitated. "No," he said finally.

"Well I guess I owe her, whoever she is. If it hadn't been for that letter nobody would have known about that other guy, Tony, right?" She looked at her father who nodded contemplatively. "Funny, isn't it," she added. "I guess in a way Mark actually saved me by having an affair with that woman."

Doug wasn't going to debate this rationalization, particularly if it gave Laura some peace. Instead he smiled and said, "I think in his strange way Mark helped all of us resolve our problems." He looked over at Holden. "Anyway, we've got to go." Doug and Tom stood to leave. "Thanks for the coffee. I'm going home to bed. We'll let you know how things progress from here."

Laura and her father walked them to the front door. Doug and Tom shook hands with Holden and hugged Laura once more before leaving.

After they slid into the roguesmobile, Doug ordered, "Take me home, Elvis."

"Not a problem, boss." Tom started the engine. "You know," he added while pushing the handle into first gear, "the way you got Laura off that charge was a little unorthodox, to say the least. But you did a good job."

Doug chuckled. "So did you, buddy," he said and closed his eyes.

CHAPTER 21

"**H**urry up, Dad. I'm hungry," Matthew demanded while shuffling his knife and fork impatiently around the kitchen table and waiting for his father to serve the scrambled eggs that were steaming on the stove.

Doug placed a plate of eggs on the table in front of Matthew. "Enjoy," he said. "The toast will be ready in a moment."

Matthew looked around the table. "Where's the ketchup?"

Doug sighed and retrieved the ketchup from the fridge. If the kid wanted to bury Doug's scrambled eggs in a landslide of ketchup, who could blame him? He looked at the clock over the stove. 8:00 a.m. Still hours before his second son, Rip Van Winkle, would rise.

Doug had only been back home for twenty-four hours, but he was already enjoying feeling the soft peaceful quilt of the family wrap itself gently around him. Diane was still in hospital and he would visit her as soon as Matthew finished breakfast. He knew they had issues to discuss and work out, but that all seemed distant now. Like a bad dream, it had been so real at the time, but now it was over; and any attempt to understand it or derive meaning from it was ultimately futile. Still, he wondered what had allowed him to let it go. Two nights earlier he had sat in the forest of Stanley Park, in the rain, with a boulder in his lap, waiting for Capetti and obsessing on Diane's and Henderson's betrayal. Now the thought of Diane with Henderson dredged up no emotional response, even though his own desire for Diane was rejuvenated. Why was that? What had happened?

Perhaps it was the fact that Henderson and Capetti—the betrayer and the messenger—were both dead, burying with them the entire sordid affair. But it was more than that. Deep down, Doug knew that, for some reason, Diane's wounding by Capetti played a significant role in his ability to put the whole mess behind him. Maybe it proved her vulnerability. Maybe it illustrated how Diane was just as confused and susceptible as he was and that her affair with Henderson was no different than his own recent journey. In that case, the bullet in her leg served as a wake up call, a bolt of lightning, shaking him from his petty jealousies and allowing him to see how much he needed her. Or maybe—and Doug banished this thought from his mind the moment it stole its way in—Diane's wounding and resulting disability satisfied a subconscious desire for retribution.

When he arrived at the hospital he noticed Detective Campbell in the waiting area across from Diane's room. Campbell stepped over to meet him before he went in to see Diane.

"I thought you'd be along," Campbell said. He shook Doug's hand, then pointed to the door. "She's doing very well. Nasty, nasty wound." There was a moment's silence as both men contemplated Diane's injury. Finally, Campbell cleared his throat and said, "You should know that we've taken a statement from Diane about the events of the other night. Frankly, what she tells us does not entirely jibe with the story you gave me at the scene." He put a hand on Doug's shoulder and lowered his voice. "Now, what I'd like you to do is visit with Diane alone for awhile and take some time to remember what really happened. Then, when you've finished, I'd like to take a formal statement from you." In the waiting room, where he gestured, sat primly a young court reporter reading a *Cosmopolitan* magazine.

Doug's eyes met Campbell's; the message was clear and Doug nodded his understanding. Pushing open the door, he found a room almost identical to the one Laura had been in some time ago. Diane was sitting up in her bed reading a paperback. Although he closed the door quietly behind him not to disturb her, he noticed her smile as she continued to read.

"It's about time you got here," she said without lifting her eyes from her book. "I've missed you."

Doug stepped swiftly across the room and took Diane in an embrace. "How's the leg?" he asked after a moment.

She pulled back the sheets of the bed to reveal her left thigh wrapped in gauze. "This is all you get to see. If you get a peek at the carnage under this bandage you'll leave me for good." A smile crossed her lips, but it failed to hide the question in her eyes: *Does this scare you? Does my affair with Henderson haunt you? Are you going to run again?*

Doug drew his hand over the bandage—softly and sensually—then continued down over her knee and calf to her foot. His fingers intertwined with her toes, lightly caressing each one in the process. "I've finally got you where I want you," he whispered, "and you can't escape." Playfully, he grabbed her ankle as if in a shackle, and shook it.

She stared at him for a moment. "I told the Detective about Mark and me," she confessed.

"I know."

"I need to tell you what happened."

"No you don't." He shook his head and touched her cheek tenderly. "I don't want to dwell on what happened. It's over. We both made mistakes. Let's move on."

"Doug, I've got to get this off my chest," she said, then held her hand to his lips before he could protest. "Mark charmed me, at a time when I was very lonely." Sheepish guilt flooded through Doug's body because he understood the cause of her loneliness. "I knew there was no fuss with Mark, no risk of long term attachment, no feelings hurt." She paused before saying, "you won't believe this, but Mark actually helped me understand the significance of what I had with you."

Doug smiled with realization. "I never thought about it, but maybe that's what he did for me too. For me, Henderson wasn't just a friend; he was everything I wasn't but always wanted to be: bright, charming, wild, loved by women, always moving in the fast lane. Like a real-life James Bond." He chuckled, "every guy wants to be James Bond, but he isn't real. And the fantasy life I had built for Henderson wasn't real either."

"We were both attracted to the same thing, Doug, something shining and brilliant. The only difference is that I recognized it for the illusion it really was, so it provided me with an escape. But you saw it as real. And maybe, maybe from all of it, we learned something about each other. Maybe," she looked at Doug with mock surprise, "maybe Mark taught us something."

Doug laughed at the irony, that they could learn something about themselves and the good things in their marriage from his best friend, a wretched scoundrel. He lay down gently on the edge of the bed by Diane. "I guess we're human."

"That's what's lovable about people, their imperfections, not their perfections. God knows that's what I love about you." She ran her fingers through his hair.

He closed his eyes contentedly. "I guess so. As long as we can learn from our mistakes."

After leaving Diane to rest, Doug met with Detective Campbell and the court reporter to give a sworn statement about the events that led to the death of Tony Capetti. In the course of doing so, he confirmed what Campbell already knew, that Capetti's target was really Diane because she had witnessed Henderson's murder from the shadows outside the Barclay. He straightened his shoulders when he had finished, as if finally shrugging off a heavy burden. "Can I go now?" he asked, about to stand.

"I'd like to show you something first, if you don't mind," Campbell said. He pulled a file folder out of his briefcase and handed it to Doug. "Based on Holden's evidence we were able to obtain a warrant to search Bartelli's residence and nightclub. That produced enough documentation verifying the whole drug operation to put him and his colleagues away for a very long time." Turning to the file, he said, "In the process we uncovered a company that was formed by Bartelli's group. Buenavista Holdings. Ever heard of it?"

Doug shook his head while he opened the file folder. On top of the loose handful of documents was a list of shareholders including the same familiar names that were shareholders of companies involved in the money laundering scheme. One shareholder was Mark Henderson. Doug flipped through the documents briefly before raising his inquiring eyes to Campbell.

"This company is somewhat unique," Campbell explained. "Although it was capitalized, it never acquired any property. Initially, we assumed this was simply because there was no suitable property available. But, when I took a little closer look at the accounting documents—" he reached over to the file, now in Doug's lap, and flipped through the documents until he reached one containing a breakdown of shareholder loans, "I noticed that all the shareholders had contributed loans to the company of $50,000 each, except Henderson. You see these lists of numbers by each shareholder's name? These are the bank accounts that each of the shareholders drew money from. We traced these accounts and, as with the other companies, each account had received a deposit of just under $10,000. Presumably, this was because the banks require a report on the source of the funds for deposits over $10,000. What's interesting is that all of Henderson's accounts indicate that the funds were withdrawn, but the money never made it into Buenavista Holdings."

Doug glanced over the document before him. "So what you're saying is that Henderson ripped off Mario for fifty grand."

"I think so…"

"Which is why Capetti killed him?"

"It makes sense," Campbell nodded. "I'm going to meet Marie now, to review Henderson's personal banking and investment records. Maybe we can figure out where the funds from these accounts went."

"Can I join you?" Doug asked.

"I was hoping you would, actually."

The meeting with Marie uncovered more pieces of the puzzle. Henderson's personal and investment records indicated that he had purchased approximately $50,000 worth of shares in a biotech company shortly after the funds had been withdrawn from the bank accounts. Unfortunately, the company's stock value plummeted and the money was soon lost. Yet another of Henderson's crazy investments. But this time he had gambled a crime boss's money rather than his own, and, in doing so, had apparently sealed his fate.

For Detective Campbell the investigation of Henderson's death was now complete. Doug, too, recognized that all the pieces of evidence fit nicely into an explanation of why Tony had killed Henderson. It occurred to him, however, that one piece was still missing from the story. Henderson's business deal with Joey Marron. What had Henderson been planning with Mario's mule? Doug pondered this question for an instant before realizing that he didn't really care anymore.